Meet Me on
the Beach

Also by Hilary Boyd

Thursdays in the Park
Tangled Lives
When You Walked Back into My Life
A Most Desirable Marriage

Hilary Boyd is a former health journalist. She has
published six non-fiction books on health-related subjects
such as step-parenting, depression and pregnancy.
This is her fifth novel. She lives in West Sussex.
www.hilaryboyd.com

Hilary
BOYD

Meet Me on the Beach

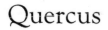
Quercus

First published in Great Britain in 2015 by

Quercus Publishing Ltd
Carmelite House
50 Victoria Embankment
London EC4Y 0DZ

An Hachette UK Company

A CIP catalogue record for this book is available
from the British Library

HB ISBN 978 1 78429 357 4
EBOOK ISBN 978 1 78429 403 8

10 9 8 7 6 5 4 3 2 1

Printed and bound in Great Britain by Clays Ltd, St Ives plc
Typeset by Jouve (UK), Milton Keynes

To Clare and Kate, with love and thanks for all your incredible support.

PART ONE

CHAPTER ONE

Karen watched her husband. He sat at the end of the kitchen table, leaning back against the paisley cushion which padded the wheel-back chair – his chair – a glass tumbler of whisky cradled in both hands, eyes half shut, his face sweating and suffused with red.

Normally Harry would carve the chicken. Karen was quite capable of doing so, of course – in fact considered herself better at it than her husband, who hacked away at the bird, dumping heavy slabs of meat on to everyone's plate as if they were cavemen – but Harry was a stickler for tradition. Tonight's roast sat waiting on the worktop beside the range, but Karen knew it was pointless to ask him. He had been boozing all day, as usual, and was past nego-tiating anything but another drink.

'What are you staring at?'

His voice, suddenly sharp despite the whisky, interrupted her thoughts.

Karen sighed. 'Nothing.'

'Nothing?' Harry raised his tone an octave, meanly mimicking her. 'Nothing, nothing . . .' his voice trailed off.

She turned away. 'No point talking to you when you're like this.'

'Like what? What am I like?'

'You know perfectly well. You're drunk, Harry. You have been all day . . . all year, in fact.'

Her husband just shook his head, his eyes closed. 'Here we go. Here we bloody go again. Nag, nag, nag. Get the lecture over with then, woman. Tell me I'm a drunk, tell me the booze'll kill me, tell me you can't stand the sight of me any more.' His eyes snapped open: blue eyes, now faded with age, but nonetheless focused and full of annoyance.

Karen felt tears gathering behind her eyelids. She thought of all the countless times she had attempted to stop him drinking. Cajoling, entreating, threatening, appealing to his ego by telling him how much his extraordinary character was demeaned by drunkenness – which it was. And so on . . . and so on. All to no avail. She no longer had the will to try again.

'You're the only one who has a problem,' he was saying as he heaved his bulk out of the chair. For a moment he stood swaying in his brown cords, striped shirt and loafers, before beginning an unsteady potter across the worn terracotta kitchen tiles to the bottle awaiting him by the sink. Largo, the Labrador, started awake in his basket at the screech of the chair legs, then almost immediately fell back asleep. He was used to his master's ways.

'Sophie was here for what? A week? Ten days? She would have noticed if I was as drunk as you make out. She would have said something.'

Karen watched him lay his glass down on the stainless-steel draining board with the slow deliberation of a person who realizes they aren't quite in control of their faculties. He reached for the bottle, the top already off, and slopped a large measure into the glass. The ice tray, also to hand, still contained a few half-melted cubes, which he tipped out on to the draining board and then scooped into his drink. Turning, wiping his wet fingers down his trousers and leaning against the side for support, he raised his glass to her.

'True, no? Admit it, Sophie has no problem . . . at all . . . with my alcohol intake.'

Karen didn't argue because Harry was right. Her stepdaughter had no problem with anything her father said or did, just so long as the cheques kept on coming.

Harry was eyeing the chicken. 'Is that bloody bird going to sit there all night?' His words were beginning to slur slightly now – Karen marvelled at the amount of alcohol her husband, nearly seventy-five, could consume and still be coherent. He pulled himself away from the worktop and weaved his way back to the table, grabbed his chair and slumped back down. 'Bring it here. I'll carve the damn thing before it gets stone cold.'

She did as he asked, her gut dull with resentment. But she knew there was absolutely no point in tackling him when he was this far gone. She knew all too well where that could lead.

They sat in silence, their plates of food in front of them. The kitchen seemed suddenly hot and airless to Karen as she observed Harry attacking his meat and potatoes with gusto, piling, cramming the food into his mouth as if he hadn't eaten in a week, gravy smearing his chin. He always ate like this, as if his life depended on it, as if he were trying to fill a bottomless pit. But in years past she had enjoyed his appreciation of her cooking. Now she just saw it as greedy. Karen had no appetite. All she wanted to do was escape that airless room, step outside into the garden – even though it was early January, pitch dark and icy cold – and fill her lungs with fresh air. Most of all she wanted to stop witnessing the sad degeneration of a man she had once worshipped. And to forget what he had done to her last night.

It was Sophie's final day with them, the end of her stepdaughter's long and fraught Christmas visit. Sophie had never cut Karen any slack. She was ten when her parents had split up – two years before Karen even knew Harry – but in those two years, Sophie had had her father all to herself, and had been spoilt to princess level, led to believe she was, and always would be, the only love of Harry Stewart's life.

So Karen understood that it would be an uphill battle, that she could expect a certain amount of animosity from the girl at first. But she had hoped – foolishly as it turned out – that they could mend their bridges over time. Eighteen years later, however, that was very far from the case. If anything, as her father approached seventy-five, Sophie's attitude to Karen appeared to harden, the girl's determination to belittle her in front of Harry, point out all of Karen's faults, perhaps having something to do with the unknown details of her father's will.

Last night the three of them had been due at a local dinner party. Harry was hugely popular in the village and the surrounding area, a larger-than-life character whom everyone adored, told stories about, welcomed at any event. They were always in high demand as a couple.

'Is that girl coming down this century?' Harry had groused as they waited in the kitchen for Sophie – who didn't seem to understand time in the way most people did – to finish dressing. As usual, his mind permanently trained on the next source of his addiction, he reached for a glass from the cabinet and dragged the bottle off the tray in the corner.

'Don't, Harry, please,' Karen had said. 'You've already had a

6

couple and you can't arrive at the Standings drunk . . . think how embarrassing Sophie would find that.' She'd known she was manipulating him, using his daughter as backup, but she didn't care.

At first he had just shaken his head, tutted, and put the bottle down. Karen had sighed with relief. He would be drunk by the end of the night, but then so would half the dinner party. But as Sophie still failed to appear, he began pacing the room, clearly on edge.

'Sod it, one won't hurt. Who cares what the Standings think? Don't think I've ever seen Roger sober, anyway.' Which was a gross exaggeration, but she didn't challenge it.

'Please, just this once—' Karen started, and she could hear the unattractive pleading in her voice.

But before the rest of the sentence was out of her mouth he had turned on her, his eyes blazing. She didn't have time to back away before his large hand swung at her, his open palm catching her square on the cheek, her head snapping to the right with the sheer force of it.

'Shut up! Just shut up, woman. If you'd stop whining for one bloody second . . .'

He turned away, but not before Karen, standing stock-still with shock, had seen the panic in her husband's eyes. Harry was not a bad man. He was just a bad drunk.

She lifted her hand to her burning cheek, tears springing to her eyes. Without a word she began walking to the door, but Harry was fast behind her. His hand gripping her arm, he swung her round to face him.

'Karen, listen . . . sorry, sorry, I shouldn't have done that. I've . . . I've never, *ever* hit a woman before . . .' He paused, clearly bewildered by what he'd done. 'It's just when you nag like that . . . I saw red.'

She had looked blankly at him.

'Please,' he'd lowered his voice, 'please don't tell Sophie . . .'

And when she'd still said nothing, he'd gone on, more urgently, 'You won't, will you? Please, Karen, don't. She'd be absolutely horrified.'

Karen hadn't told Sophie. She did the same thing as she'd done in the face of all the bullying and belittling, all the cruel taunting, all the foul breath and stinking alcohol sweat, all the mindless, repetitive whisky-induced drivel that had gone on over the last few years. Nothing.

'I can't go to dinner with this,' she told Harry, holding her hand to her cheek as he stood in front of her, momentarily cowed, waiting for her forgiveness. Even this minor rebellion felt like a victory.

'You've got to come. What'll I say to the Standings?'

'Say what you like. I don't care, I'm not coming.' She couldn't look at him any more. Him in his pristine blue shirt and maroon tie, his tailored suit and polished brogues, his short, grey hair, still plentiful, brushed neatly back from his brow, his handsome face tanned from hours on the golf course. The picture of a smart, successful man, despite his advancing years. He was looming over her, standing close, blocking her way, not really threatening, just a solid barrier. But she pushed past him and hurried upstairs, shutting herself in their bedroom before Sophie had a chance to see the hot red welt spreading across her cheek.

When she'd checked in the mirror for damage, she saw a stranger. Her blonde crop – not dyed, she and her brother, Johnny, had been white-blond since they were children – was uncharacteristically dishevelled, her hazel eyes huge and shocked in her heart-shaped face, the redness on her left cheek like some childish attempt at make-up.

Now, as she rinsed the plates, filled the dishwasher, wrapped the remains of the chicken in foil, wiped splashes of gravy from the table, swept up the bits from the floor that Largo had disdained, her thoughts returned to her predicament. *He's an old man, a sick old man. How can I leave him?* It was a chant almost, that ran around her head on an hourly basis, had done for at least a year now. She understood that no one grew up wanting to be an alcoholic. It was addiction, pure and simple. But did that mean she had to stay and put up with this abuse for the rest of her life? He was tough, he could live another ten years at this rate. Maybe, she thought, Sophie could do what she was always threatening to do. Move in and look after her father, make sure she copped his millions when he died. Maybe he would clean up his act for her.

But each time she reached this point, where she, Karen, was free, her stomach knotted with anxiety. Freedom felt more like being adrift in a vast, empty ocean. No house, no beloved Largo, no husband, no community. And she loved Harry, or at least loved the man that Harry used to be.

The very first day she met him, at the interview for a job as his PA, she had been struck by his charisma. Despite being in his later fifties, he was so full of life, so funny, so handsome, so sure of himself.

'You can type, I presume?' He'd asked, eyebrows arched, eyes full of laughter as he gave her an almost insultingly bold stare. He was standing in his shirtsleeves by the window of his modern, fea- tureless office on the outskirts of Portsmouth, looking out on to a well-laid lawn and a plinth holding the shiny metal company logo of Stewart Engineering, cars parked off to the right. Harry had built his company from scratch, specializing in fencing – such as pedestrian barriers, railings, gates, security and electric fencing, anti-climb panels – and it was a success.

'Just about,' Karen had said, more cheekily than she intended, but unable to ignore his teasing look.

'Well, Mrs Rawlings seems to like you. Which is unusual, to say the least. ' He waved at her to sit down in the chair opposite his wide teak desk – piled high from end to end with papers interspersed with an odd assortment of keypads, fobs, cable loops and other unidentifiable widgets.

Karen had said nothing. Mrs Rawlings was an office manager of the old school: grey hair in a severe French pleat, black pencil skirt, plain white blouse, black court shoes, a single string of pearls at her neck, immaculate nails polished with a fearsome cranberry. Initially she had peered over her glasses at Karen as if she were something the cat dragged in. But for some reason she'd softened when Karen had been honest and told her she knew absolutely nothing about engineering and was probably most unsuitable for the job.

'Don't worry about that,' she'd said briskly. 'You might be just what Mr Stewart needs.' A comment Karen could not fathom, but chose to ignore.

Her previous job as PA to the boss of a recruitment agency in Southampton was so dire, her boss so sleazy, that she would happily settle for almost anything, even if it meant a half-hour commute. And although she'd been hoping for a job in the travel industry, where her almost fluent French – learnt during a two-year stint as a chalet girl in Courchevel when she was nineteen – would be an asset, nothing had come up in the months she'd been looking.

'It's a boring bloody job,' Harry declared with a curious satisfaction when they were both seated on either side of his desk. 'You'll have to deal with me, for a start, and I'm tricky at the best of times. Then there's Mrs Rawlings to sweet-talk. And the men will ogle you every time you set foot out of the office.' He'd smiled his most winning smile. 'In fact, you should probably run a mile.'

And she'd replied, 'I'll risk it, if you will.'

So the flirtation began from day one. Karen herself, when she started working for Harry, was in a sort of relationship, with Russ. On off, on off, neither could properly commit to moving in together, but they were close, real friends. As her mother, in her more sober moments, kept telling her, 'Many good marriages have flourished on less.'

But Harry was free, divorced from his wife, Theresa, for two years by then. Office gossip went that the marriage had fallen apart after he'd been spotted by a friend of Theresa's in a hotel in Paris, holding hands with a tasty French sales rep, when he'd told his wife he was in Newcastle. And the friend had dobbed him in. Theresa, a feisty Greek with a Mediterranean temper, had not only taken a very dim view of his behaviour – reasonably enough – but had seen it as a complete deal-breaker. The marriage, as far as she was concerned, was over from that moment. 'She didn't understand about my work,' was Harry's excuse when Karen asked what had gone wrong.

It was a few months before anything beyond flirtation happened. That Tuesday, snow threatened, a lot of snow according to the forecast, and Mrs Rawlings had closed the office at lunchtime to prevent the workers from having trouble getting home. But Harry had asked Karen to stay a little longer.

'Load of nonsense, these forecasts. Putting the wind up us to cover their arses. Not frightened of a little snow, are you?' he'd teased.

'Of course not,' she'd replied, marvelling at the way Harry Stewart thought even the elements were at his command.

And it did snow. By the time they looked up from their work, vast amounts had dumped out of the sky in a matter of hours. There was no way Harry's sleek silver Jaguar was going to make it past the end of the drive. They were trapped.

Luckily, the prudent Mrs Rawlings kept the office fridge stocked with her boss's favourites: sausage rolls, corned beef, Brie, orange juice, beef tomatoes, pickle. And Harry's desk drawer yielded an almost full bottle of finest malt. As evening set in, the world outside a flawless, silent white, the office became cosy, womb-like, in the single light from the desk lamp. Karen and Harry seemed to adopt a siege mentality as they picnicked on a cleared patch of desk, munching hungrily on the sausage rolls, with the whisky – not something Karen was used to – gradually loosening the boss-PA boundaries.

'What will we do?' she'd asked him.

'Do? Nothing we can do.'

'But supposing it keeps on snowing?'

Harry had laughed. 'Well, then, we'll be found in twenty years time, like Scott of the Antarctic, curled around each other for warmth, clutching our diaries, which'll contain something brave and heroic they'll turn into a book . . . which will make millions for our descendants.'

And while Karen was laughing at the ridiculous scenario, Harry was putting his glass down and coming round the desk and grabbing her out of her chair with such passion she was not given time even to think, let alone protest.

The night they spent on the office floor, wedged on cushions from the leather sofa and covered with the tartan car rug from Harry's Jag, was unique. With all the time in the world, no chance of intrusion, they were free of restraint. And Harry was expert, a sensualist, hedonistic by nature and keen to milk every ounce of pleasure from their entwined bodies. Russ's dogged drive to his own orgasm – usually less than ten minutes, tops – was hardly in the same ballpark.

'I hope they don't rescue us too soon,' Karen had whispered into his neck in the small hours of the night. 'The food should last us at least another couple of days.'

And Harry had just chuckled and pulled her closer against his body.

Even in those days, Harry had been a heavy drinker. But his drinking was part of his zest for life. A zest which seemed to drain clean away as soon as he sold his company – his beloved baby – on the eve of his seventy-second birthday. Such plans they had! Harry, a workaholic, was determined to catch up on all the things he'd missed, such as seats at the Masters golf tournament, taking a yacht round the Med, African game parks, Las Vegas . . . the list was endless. And now they had the money . . .

But her husband, from day one of retirement, seemed not to want to travel even thirty miles, let alone three thousand. Karen watched in dismay as he fell in on himself, lost all of his joie de vivre. Instead of travelling the world, he played golf and drank, drank and played golf. Then, increasingly, as his right hip became more and more painful with arthritis, he mostly just drank, albeit at the golf club. 'We'll go next year,' was his monotonous response to Karen's tentative plans.

She hadn't given up hope that things would improve, however.

Not even now. Her husband might still see the light, get help, stop drinking. Then he'd revert to his old self. And love her again.

On her way up to bed, after she'd let the dog out and spent a few minutes gazing up at the stars, she made her nightly detour to the den, where Harry had set up his vast flat-screen television, his red leather recliner, his fifties drinks cabinet. He was asleep, of course, the remote clutched in his left hand, a nearly empty glass nestling in his lap as he snored for Britain in front of one of the endless golf replays that blared out into the stuffy, wood-panelled sitting room.

'Come on, Harry . . . wake up . . . it's late.' She gently prised the glass from his hand and put it on the side table.

He harrumphed, half opened his bloodshot eyes without registering her presence, then closed them again.

'Harry . . . come on, get up. Time for bed.'

This process could go on for a while. And he was such a heavy man – tall and a dead weight – that Karen's small frame stood no chance of lifting him unless he helped her.

Once she'd dragged him upstairs, undressed him, left him flat on his back under the duvet, she went to one of the spare rooms to sleep. She hadn't felt comfortable doing so when Sophie was there – not wanting to give any ammunition to her stepdaughter that she might use to drive a bigger wedge between Karen and Harry. But now it was a blessed relief to sleep alone between the chilly sheets and not have to endure the stale whisky fumes or listen to the tractor snores all night.

The next morning was a perfect winter day, cold, but with a bright-blue, cloudless sky, the sun pouring in the kitchen window. Karen made herself toast and marmalade – her own home-made preserve, which she'd boiled down and potted into twelve sterilized glass jars of assorted sizes only the previous week – and a mug of filter coffee. She ate quickly, impatient to be outside, to escape with the dog on to the Sussex downs behind the house. Because if Harry woke up he'd expect her to stay and make his breakfast, which always involved a tedious round of orange juice, eggs, bacon, tomato, toast, tea and the *Telegraph*.

The ground was frosty and crackling under her boots as she strode up the path on to the hill. Largo was delirious, charging over the rough ground, snorting and snuffling and wagging his tail as he stuck his nose down rabbit holes and inhaled all the scents brought out by the sunshine. Karen sucked in the fresh air, lightheaded with the sense of release from the confines of the house. She loved being outdoors – even as a child, she was always badgering her mother to let her play out, never happier than when she was allowed to take Johnny, her brother, into the Devon hills with their collie dog and sandwiches in her backpack.

She saw someone up ahead. The new vicar. He looked lost, just standing on the brow of the hill as if he were trying to get his bearings. She groaned silently. Reverend Haskell had only arrived last November after the parish's previous incumbent, Bob Parkin, had been finally diagnosed with Alzheimer's.

Largo, racing up to him, obviously startled the man out of his reverie because he jumped and looked around.

'Oh . . . Mrs Stewart,' he said.

'Reverend,' she replied.

'Please . . . call me William, everyone else does.'

'Only if you call me Karen.'

They both smiled.

'Deal,' he said.

There was an awkward silence, made more uncomfortable on Karen's part because ever since William Haskell's arrival in the village, she had felt a subtle pressure from him to become part of the congregation. He had asked her three times now – no doubt prompted by her husband – if she would like to meet him to 'discuss things over coffee'. But Karen was not a churchgoer, did not believe in God – or at least not the organized-religion version. She had managed to resist all Harry's blandishments over the years to come to services with him, and she was not about to give in to this new attack on her faithlessness.

'Isn't it just the most stunning day?' he said, gazing out over the hills. He was in his mid-fifties, Karen reckoned, maybe a bit younger, slim but with broad shoulders and an upright posture that made him look taller than he was. His colouring reminded her of an Irish boyfriend she had once had with his dark hair – the thickness making the short cut unruly – fair skin and very light-blue Celtic eyes surrounded by dark lashes. She wouldn't have called him good looking exactly, but his face was strong, lived in, with a deep furrow between his eyebrows as if he were permanently worried. He was certainly a breath of fresh air in the village after decades of Bob's plodding, unimaginative ministry. Haskell was charismatic, energetic and intent on shaking the parish up, raising money for just causes, involving everyone in 'community' – his favourite buzzword.

'We need it after all that rain,' she said, dying to get on with her walk.

They both stood, hands in the pockets of their jackets, breath steaming in the cold, looking at the view rather than at each other. Where they were standing gave a toytown impression of the village below, so neat and pretty and tranquil, the square tower of the

Norman church majestic in the shaft of sunlight coming over the hill. Her house, the Old Rectory – large and elegant, early Victorian brick – sitting contentedly beside the church. The vicar's, by contrast, a dull, boxy, seventies build further down the lane where he lived with his wife, Janey, and seventeen-year-old daughter, Rachel.

'Is Harry OK?' William asked. 'I didn't see him in church yesterday.'

Her husband was a church warden, a pillar of the parish council, frequent benefactor to the church bell-tower fund, and allowed the church fête to be held in their garden every summer. In the past he would rarely miss a service, sometimes going to evensong as well as to matins. But the drinking had made his attendance erratic.

'He wasn't feeling well,' she said, entirely truthfully as Harry had barely been able to stand with his crippling hangover on Sunday morning.

'Nothing serious, I hope?'

'I don't think so.'

'Give him my best, will you?' The reverend seemed to stir himself. 'Right, better get on. So many things to do . . .' He paused, taking a long, slow breath. 'This is such a lovely part of the world. What luck to be able to work here.'

Karen nodded, but although his words were delivered with his usual enthusiasm, they fell strangely flat in the still morning air, as if he were trying to convince himself that he was happy to be there by virtue of saying so.

'Is it time for that coffee yet?' was his parting shot as he waved, grinned and strode off towards the village.

Is he not quite as happy as he seems? she wondered, as she walked on up the path. She'd detected a pensive, almost disconsolate look in his light eyes, quite out of sync with his determinedly cheery vicar persona. *Still, it can't be that easy being a religious man in today's secular world.*

'Where have you been?'

The kitchen was dim with smoke and rank with the smell of burning fat. On the stove was a frying pan containing a scorched rasher of bacon, now cold and congealed. The table was a litter of crumbs and burnt toast, the lid off the marmalade, a greasy knife resting on the open butter packet, the filter machine still on despite the glass carafe being empty, adding the aroma of singed coffee to the mix. Harry was sitting with the newspaper spread out in front of him, his reading glasses balanced on the end of his nose, his colour high, a light sheen of sweat on his forehead.

'A walk, it's such a beautiful day,' she replied. 'I met the vicar on the hill.'

Her husband gave a low growl. 'Preposterous man. All that hail-fellow-well-met rubbish. He's a Happy Clappy, no question. Mark my words, he'll have us singing "Kumbaya" next. Bob may have been dotty, but at least he knew tradition when he saw it.'

This seemed a bit unfair to Karen, but she knew better than to challenge her husband over religion.

'How are you feeling? You look a bit rough.' She rinsed out the coffee jug and filled the filter paper with fresh grounds.

Harry turned back to his paper. 'What's that supposed to mean?'

'It means you look ill, Harry. You're bright red in the face and sweating.'

'I just drank four cups of coffee and ate a massive fry-up, that's why I'm sweating.' He shot her a warning look, obviously hoping to silence her on the subject of his hangover.

'The vicar wondered why you weren't at church yesterday. I said you were ill.'

'It's none of his bloody business. He should spend more time preaching and less time poking his nose into my affairs. He was banging on about "syncretism" last week. What the hell's that supposed to mean? The man's an idiot.'

Karen had no idea what it meant. She did know, however, that Harry's absence from church had nothing whatever to do with Reverend Haskell's preaching, but she was not going to have that argument right now. 'He seems like a good man, though, don't you think? He's already started a lunch club for the old people, Sheila said. At least he's enthusiastic.'

Harry gave her a pitying look. 'Ha! "Enthusiastic". Just what we need in a man of the cloth. Although I'm not sure what qualifies you to judge, seeing as you never set foot in church.'

'He's not in church all the time, Harry. I've met him out and about, I hear people talk, I'm perfectly entitled to say whether he seems like a good person or not.'

'I'd rather assumed it was part of a vicar's job description to be good,' Harry retorted. 'Or have I missed something?'

She didn't respond to his sarcasm, just began to clear away the mess in silence.

CHAPTER TWO

Later that afternoon Karen phoned her brother, Johnny. He was the only person she felt she could confide in on the subject of her marriage. She couldn't talk to her friends in the village because the community was so tight-knit, so gossipy, that everyone knew everyone else's business almost before they knew it themselves. And worse, few had seen the rough side of Harry Stewart. He was always so charming, so polite, so outwardly concerned with his neighbours and the wider community. And in the past he had truly meant it. No one would believe her if she told them what he was really like now.

'Yeah, not so good,' Karen responded to her brother's question.

'Still boozing?'

'Ooh, yes.' She told him about the vicious slap.

'What? Christ!' Johnny exploded. 'Honestly, you can't go on like this, Karen. You've got to get out of there.'

'I don't think he meant it . . . well, he meant it at the time, but you could see he was shocked at himself.'

'And that makes it OK? Listen to yourself! A slap this week, a beating the next, killing you the week after. Are you genuinely just going to sit there and wait for that?'

Karen laughed. 'Don't be so melodramatic, J. You spend too much time with downtrodden women. Harry's not going to kill me. I wish I hadn't told you now. Part of me'd love to leave, you know I would, but he's sick. And old. It's the drink talking. He never used to be like this. We had fun.'

'He always treats you like a "little woman". I hate that.'

'I know, but that's my fault as much as his for allowing it.'

'Whatever. But honestly, you can't just ignore the signs. You hear about it every day, women dying from domestic abuse.'

'It's really not that bad,' she said firmly, wanting to stop her brother winding her up, sensationalizing what had just been a one-off, however horrible at the time. 'And anyway, I don't know where to go, what to do. I hardly have any money of my own. And there's the dog. I can't leave Largo.' She felt so helpless and pathetic but she didn't want to cry again, she'd done that so often while on the phone to Johnny this last year. And he was three thousand miles away in Toronto, how could he help?

There was a long silence. Her brother clearly didn't know what she should do either.

'You must have enough money to leave and rent somewhere for a while. Maybe if you make a stand it'll shock Harry so much he'll shape up, stop drinking.'

'Maybe.' She'd thought of that too.

'Could you at least look into it? Promise me? I'm worried about you, have been for months. Even if he doesn't attack you again, you sound so utterly miserable. It's not worth it, Karen.'

'I know . . .'

'Get out while you're still young enough to make a life. If you sit there another ten years you'll be past it.'

'Great, just what I need to hear.'

'Well, it's true. You're fifty-seven. Think about it.'

Johnny, three years younger than Karen, had always behaved like the elder sibling. Bossy and practical, a solicitor, husband, father of three and passionate campaigner for human rights, he wasted no time on self-doubt. Karen knew that her own inaction must be a constant source of frustration to him.

'Harry's drinking is *his* responsibility, not yours. You know quite well he could do something about it if he chose.' His tone had softened.

'Could he? It wouldn't be that easy.'

'You're too bloody sympathetic. And I know why. But Harry isn't Mum, Karen. Of course he could stop. She did. And no, it can't have been easy but she still went ahead and did it.'

'Spurred on by acute pancreatitis and the doctors telling her she would die if she didn't.'

'True, but that doesn't always act as an incentive. Look at George Best.'

Their mother, Gloria, had not been a nasty drunk like Harry, more of a helpless, hopeless drinker. She'd got through the day, walked them home from school, cooked them all supper, functioned on the surface pretty well in the early days – perhaps on autopilot much of the time. But they heard the arguments with their father at night and, as Karen and Johnny got older, she let things slide more and more. It got to the stage where both children dreaded coming home to the stale, airless house and Gloria slumped in the armchair in her house-coat, slurring her words and waving her cigarette over the bulging ashtray, pink lipstick smudged, a glass of cheap sherry on the table beside her. Neither of them ever dared bring friends home.

'Don't know how Dad stood it so long,' she heard herself say, realizing the irony of her words.

'He probably thought he couldn't leave us with Mum in that state. He was OK, Dad, he did his best.'

'Yeah . . . have you heard from Joan recently?'

Joan was the girl in the tea shop their father ran off with as soon as Gloria was sober. Apparently he'd dropped in there most days on the way home from his job at Exeter town planning office – delaying his return to his wife, no doubt. He admitted later that it was a long-standing affair, but neither of them chose to blame him.

'Christmas card, that's all. I should ring, but the time difference makes it tricky . . . at least, that's my excuse. Anyway, I'd better go, sis, I'm at the beginning of my day here. Please tell me you'll do something this time, not just wait around till he comes at you with a kitchen knife.'

Karen couldn't help smiling at this. 'No worries there. Harry doesn't have the first idea where the knives are kept!'

'Seriously, though . . .' He paused. 'And if you need money . . .'

'Thanks, but I don't. I'm using the money thing as an excuse, I suppose. For not going.'

'I told Johnny you hit me,' Karen said, as she and Harry drove through the gates of the golf club the following day. She wasn't telling him in order to score points, but in the hope it might bring him up short, make him think about what he'd done . . . persuade him to take action.

'And?' Harry waved at another golfer.

'He's worried things'll escalate and you'll kill me.' She spoke with deliberate nonchalance as she pulled into one of the parking bays. There were few people about on a Tuesday morning at the club.

Harry let out a harsh laugh. 'Wouldn't dare. Don't want that pious numpty camping on my doorstep waving a banner for women's rights.' He sighed, turned to her. 'Listen . . . I didn't mean that. I'm ashamed of what I did. Of course I am. It was unforgivable.' He picked up her hand from where it lay on the steering wheel, gave it a kiss. 'I'm sorry, really I am.'

Karen, for the first time in months, heard the voice of the man she had fallen in love with, saw the softness in his eyes that told her he still loved her. She said nothing, just held tight to his fingers.

'I know I can be a bit of a brute when I'm drinking . . . I'm not entirely stupid.' There was another sigh, this one deeper and more emphatic. His weather-beaten face went very still. 'I promise it won't happen again, Karen . . . not ever, not as long as I live. And you're right, I should cut down on the old booze . . . it's not doing either of us any good.'

It wasn't quite what Karen had longed to hear, but maybe it was a start. It was certainly the first time her husband had even vaguely intimated that he might have a problem.

'We used to have such fun,' she said softly.

He looked surprised. 'We still do, don't we?'

'Ring me when you want me to pick you up,' she said as he clambered out of the car, her heart a small bit lighter than it had been in weeks.

But when she finally got a response to her texts and drove up to fetch Harry at the club, he was in a terrible state, sprawling in one of the bar chairs, the inevitable glass in his hand, eyes closed despite the group of friends sitting in the circle around the low table.

His friend Dennis pulled a face when he saw her, nodded towards Harry's slouched figure. 'I thought I'd text you . . . Harry wasn't about to. He's not in a good way, I'm afraid, Karen.'

For a moment they all looked up at her, sheepish, waiting to see what she would do.

'Do you want a hand getting him to the car?' another friend, George, said.

Karen stared at them. 'Please, yes.' She paused. 'But the best help I could get is if you guys wouldn't let him get so wasted every time. You could have called me earlier. You're supposed to be his friends.'

The four men continued to look shifty, they seemed to be waiting for someone else to reply.

'It's not easy,' Dennis volunteered eventually. 'Harry's a force of nature, especially when he's had a few.'

'We do say, sometimes. But short of banning him, there's not a lot any of us can do,' George added.

'Yeah . . .' Karen forced a smile. 'Sorry . . . it's not your responsibility, I know that.'

Dennis and George both got up and began heaving their friend upright. It took them almost twenty minutes to get him strapped into the car because each time they tried to make him walk or bend or sit, Harry would struggle and fight them off.

'I'll come back with you. You won't get him inside on your own,' George offered, and Karen reluctantly agreed.

On the way home, George was silent.

'It's got really bad,' she said, 'the drinking. I don't know what to do.' She felt like crying with humiliation at seeing her husband in such a state in front of his peers.

George glanced over at her. 'Lucky he's got you.'

She didn't bother to reply. It was impossible to break through the male-dominated world of the golf club, where drinking was a badge of belonging and excess just laughed off as a personality quirk. She wasn't blaming the club for Harry's problem – he managed to consume the same amount at home without any help from his mates — but she certainly felt that their continued approbation only served to cement his denial.

Harry slept off the lunchtime binge, and by supper seemed in an unusually mellow frame of mind.

'You know what?' he said, as they sat in front of the television with a ham and baked potato supper on trays. It was during one of the ad breaks in an old episode of *Morse*. 'We should get away, take one of our weekend trips to Paris. We haven't done that in a long time.'

Karen smiled. 'That would be nice.' But she knew they would never actually go, because she was the one who did all the travel arrangements and she could never risk taking Harry abroad while he was drinking like this.

'You'll sort something, will you?' he said, as the programme resumed, and she nodded.

Harry fell asleep after supper, propped in his chair, head lolling back, his gentle snoring a backdrop to the television.

She tidied up the supper and got ready to get him upstairs to bed. It had been a better evening, as evenings go, and she was hopeful again that things might change between them.

'Come on . . . up you get, it's bedtime.' She delivered her usual speech.

'Get off . . . leave me alone,' he said, pushing her hand away roughly.

'Harry, it's after ten. Please . . . get up.'

He opened his eyes, but whereas normally when she woke him like this his expression would be unfocused, this time he didn't seem at all disorientated.

'I was just having a nap, I don't want to go to bed yet. I'm watching this,' he said, waving at the screen, which she'd turned off some time ago.

'OK, up to you.' She turned to go. 'But don't fall asleep again, or you'll be there all night.'

Harry pulled himself up in the chair. 'No harm sleeping in the chair if I want to.'

He didn't speak with any force, it was more a mild grumble, but Karen felt something shift in her brain, the wall of tolerance finally breached. She sat down heavily on the sofa.

'This can't go on, Harry.'

He blinked. 'What can't?'

'Us.'

'What do you mean?' He looked befuddled.

'Do I really have to spell it out? I mean if you don't stop drinking, I'm going to leave you. I've had enough.'

Her husband shook his head in disbelief. 'Leave me? You can't leave me. Don't be ridiculous, woman. Where would you go?'

'I'll find somewhere . . . but I can't do this any more. Day in, day out, watching you drink yourself to death, dragging you to bed, putting up with your nastiness.' She spoke softly. 'Well, I *could* put up with it, of course . . . I just don't want to.' She paused again. 'Why should I?'

Harry had gone very still. He was not looking at her, but off towards the window and the heavy magenta and cream striped curtains. When he finally turned his gaze towards her, she could see the cold resentment lighting up his faded eyes.

'Don't threaten me, Karen, if you don't mean it. And don't tell me how to live my life.' He pulled himself slowly to his feet.

'I'm not telling you how to live your life, I'm telling you how I want to live mine,' she said. She didn't even feel angry any more, just very tired. She got up too, laid a hand on his shirtsleeve. 'Harry, please. Can't you see what it's doing to you . . . to us?' He jerked his arm away but she went on, anyway. 'This isn't you.'

He seemed at a loss for words, standing there swaying in front of her.

'You could get help . . . to stop.'

'You honestly want to leave me?' he asked, clearly baffled. 'Is it that bad? Is it really, honestly that bad?'

She just nodded. Was she finally getting through to him?

But he turned away abruptly, sat down again in his chair and began fiddling with the remote until he'd found a golf game to watch.

'Harry?'

He looked up at her as if she were an annoying interruption, a buzzing fly. 'What?'

'Have you heard a word I just said?'

Harry raised his eyebrows at her, his expression not far off patronizing. 'Loud and clear, loud and clear, my dear. You said you're going to leave me because I'm a tiresome old drunk.' He turned the volume up and the soft thock of a golf ball and polite spectator clapping filled the room as he reached for the whisky glass on the side table, settling back comfortably in his recliner. 'Well, go if you want to. I just don't believe for a single second you will.'

She stood for a moment, stunned, then walked slowly out of the room.

Does he not believe me because I don't believe myself? she wondered as she sat at the kitchen table, a mug of tea in front of her, barely touched because her stomach was churning with anxiety. She'd never threatened to leave before, but if he was shocked, he certainly hadn't shown it.

Sitting there, Karen felt completely deflated. Here it was, the moment she'd been dreading for months, the scenario picking away at her thoughts whenever she let it and turning her guts to water. And now, when she'd finally plucked up enough courage – or been driven to it, more like – and told him that it was over, he had virtually ignored what she said.

The silence in the kitchen was only broken by Largo's soft snores in the corner. For a long while she just sat, barely thinking. But as she sat, her will gradually hardened. Gone was the 'he's old, he can't help it' excuse, gone was the hope that he might change, and gone, finally, was the fear of leaving her home and the current rhythms of her life. She would find a flat where they allowed pets, she would get a job, she would sleep alone at night without the constant toxic presence of her drunken husband.

'Karen! Karen . . . are you there . . . *Karen?*'

She heard his voice coming from the den as if from a thousand miles away. She didn't answer. *If he wants to speak to me, he's quite capable of getting up and coming to find me.* She wouldn't pander to him even one more time. He would be beyond rational debate by now, anyway. It was at least an hour since she left him with his golf tournament, and there had been nearly a full bottle of whisky to plunder.

'*Karen* . . . come here,' she heard him bellow again. But she got up, put her mug in the dishwasher, stroked the dog, turned off the lights and walked slowly upstairs. She could hear the television, but Harry had gone quiet. *Let him sleep in his bloody chair all night and see how rubbish he feels in the morning.*

As she brushed her teeth she thought she heard him shout another time, but the en suite had an extractor fan linked to the light which blocked out most other sounds. *Probably wants me to help him up to bed, stupid sod,* she said to herself as she got into bed. *Well, he's had his chance.*

The digital clock read three seventeen when she woke up, wandered to the loo, and realized Harry was still downstairs. The anger from the night before had dissipated and she took pity on him, knowing how cold and stiff he would be if he didn't get to bed. She put on her navy, striped jersey dressing gown and sheepskin slippers and padded downstairs, sighing in preparation for the struggle she faced in lugging her husband upstairs. The house was chilly and very quiet although, as she approached the den, she realized the television was still on.

Harry was asleep in his chair, his head lolling against the wing of the recliner, his legs stretched out in front of him, his left hand dangling off the chair arm, his right clutching his mobile cradled in his lap, exactly as predicted. He'd dropped the remote and she picked it up and switched off the TV.

'Come on . . . wake up, Harry, it's three o'clock in the morning—' she began, hearing the rote delivery with a heavy heart. But as soon as she peered into his face, touched his hand, she absolutely knew.

Harry Stewart wasn't asleep. He was stone cold dead.

She held her breath, her heart skittering into a syncopated beat, all the blood seemingly drained from her body. For a moment she just stood there like a statue, looking down on her husband's lifeless form, waiting for him to wake up, to show some sign that she was mistaken. But she knew she was not. She bent and pressed her fingers to the spot on his neck, under his jaw, that she had seen people do in such circumstances on television, feeling for a pulse. But she couldn't find one, wasn't even sure if she was doing it right, and anyway, his skin was clammy to the touch. Then she held her palm close to his nose and mouth.

No breath of life, no sound, absolutely nothing emanated from the pale figure nestled so convincingly asleep in the recliner.

Karen, shaking, reached for the landline phone on the table beside Harry's chair and dialled 999.

CHAPTER THREE

Her friend Maggie, who lived just across the village pond from Karen, sat next to her on the sofa in the sitting room, holding her hand. It was still very early, not yet dawn, and the curtains remained drawn against the night, one lamp shedding a small pool of light on the two silent women. Karen was fully dressed — jeans, a white cotton vest, dark green sweater, red socks, her sheepskin slippers — it had seemed important to get out of her night clothes. But Maggie was still in the T-shirt and tracksuit bottoms she wore to bed. She had simply put on her parka and wellington boots and run across the green to the Old Rectory. Younger than Karen, not yet fifty, she was a physiotherapist — small, strong, fit, with short blonde hair like Karen, earning them the nickname 'the twins' in the village. She was married to an eminent eye surgeon, Rakesh, who travelled the world setting up cataract surgery camps in India for an NGO. He was hardly ever home.

'God, Karen, I can hardly believe it,' she said for at least the tenth time.

Karen couldn't either. She was waiting for his tread on the stair, the predictable groaning about his aching head, the demand for coffee and orange juice, the grumbling that accompanied his search for the newspaper outside the front door – the paper boy was notoriously inaccurate in his aim. That this daily sequence would never happen again was simply unbelievable.

When Tom, their GP, had answered her call, his voice immediately alert as someone practised in being woken in the middle of the night, she had heard herself speak with almost measured calm.

'I think Harry's dead,' she'd told him. 'I've called the ambulance.' In fact, Karen didn't 'think' her husband was dead, she knew it for certain, but somehow couldn't say so.

The doctor hadn't asked questions. 'I'll be right there,' was all he said. The ambulance had arrived before Tom, the men bending over Harry, conferring quietly with each other, then with the doctor when he came through the open front door. Tom had sat Karen down in the kitchen and offered her some tea, which she had accepted, then not drunk. She remembered the kitchen being very cold. Eventually the men had taken Harry away, strapped to the stretcher, his face covered – grim confirmation that oxygen, a requirement above all others for every living creature, was no longer necessary.

'And so sudden,' Maggie was saying. 'He wasn't even ill . . . was he?'

'No . . .' Karen hesitated. 'But he drank way too much,' she added.

'Yeah, but we all do. Except Raki, of course.'

Karen didn't reply. Was there any use in bringing up the nightmare of Harry's drinking, now that he was dead? Those who knew had kept quiet about it – including herself – when he was alive, when it might have helped to speak out, to call him on it. What would be served by sullying his name now, even to her best friend? And Maggie knew, anyway. She'd been round and seen Harry in his cups on more than one occasion, and listened to Karen worrying about it. But on the whole she had avoided the issue because Karen did. Such was the etiquette of an English country village.

'I should ring Sophie,' Karen said, as if she had only just thought of it. In fact, she had been just putting off the dreadful moment. But she still continued to sit there, clutching her friend's hand, until Maggie got up.

'You call her, I'll make some coffee.'

Without her, Karen felt oddly frightened and vulnerable, as if she weren't safe in her own home. The room seemed so dark, the large, creaking house so empty. She reached for her mobile.

Sophie's message service kicked in.

'Sophie, it's me, Karen. Please can you call me as soon as you get this.'

Karen wasn't surprised that she didn't answer. It was not yet seven, and her stepdaughter wasn't the earliest of risers. Not to mention the fact that she never picked up for Karen, only her father. It occurred to Karen to ring from her husband's mobile, but that seemed too creepy. She would wait. There was nothing anyone could do now, except weep for Harry Stewart, and she couldn't even do that. Karen tried not to dwell on the possibility that she might be relieved. She certainly didn't feel relief right now, just emptiness, disbelief.

An hour later, Maggie had gone home to get dressed, urged on by Karen, who wanted to be on her own. But as soon as she was alone, the echoes of the empty house began to clamour, pressing close, specifically Harry's voice, shouting for her as if he were still in the den, still watching golf replays, still drinking, still very much alive.

She was drawn back to the scene. The curtains were closed,

the lights on, the furniture shifted about to clear the way for the stretcher. Karen bent to pull back the Turkish rug which overlaid the polished parquet floor. As she did so a mobile rang close by. Harry's. She froze, a shudder passing through her body as she remembered it had been lying in his lap when she found him. Following the sound, she located it on the table by the window. The lighted display read: Sophie.

'Sophie? Hi, it's Karen.'

'Oh, hi. Where's Dad?' Her tone held the usual lack of enthusiasm she adopted – almost on principle, Karen thought – when talking to her stepmother.

'Umm . . . Sophie, I've got some very bad news.' She took a deep breath. 'Your dad . . . he had a heart attack last night . . .' She paused again, but Sophie said nothing. 'He died in the night . . . I'm so sorry . . .'

There was what seemed like an interminable silence at the other end of the phone.

'Sophie?'

'Dead? He can't be. He phoned me.' She sounded relieved, as if this proved Karen was mistaken.

'Phoned you? When?'

'Not sure . . . I was out and didn't see the missed call till it was too late to ring back. He didn't leave a message.'

'Oh.' Karen felt almost sick. Harry, possibly in pain and desperately needing help, had obviously tried to contact his daughter when she herself had ignored his shouts and callously gone to bed.

'Did he die in his sleep, then?' Sophie's question was so matter-of-fact, as if she hadn't grasped the fact that this was her father they were talking about.

'I think so.' She hesitated, her whole body shaking with the lie, yet at the same time fervently persuading herself that it could be true. Harry might have just been shouting at her in the way he often did recently, merely wanting her attention. Then dozed off from all that booze and had the heart attack later in the night – when he was, in fact, asleep. She told herself that it might not have made any difference if she'd gone to him when he called, dragged him upstairs, tucked him in. Then he might, she told herself, have had the heart attack right there, next to her in bed. 'I left him watching golf and went to bed. I tried to get him to come up with me, but he didn't want to. You know what he's like when he's had a few. When I woke up around three, he wasn't in bed. I went to look for him and he . . . well, he was already dead.'

Silence.

'Sophie?'

'He can't be dead.' Karen heard a wrenching sob. 'Daddy can't be dead . . .'

'Oh, Sophie . . . I'm so sorry . . .' she felt helpless at the other end of the phone and, for the first time in her life, truly sorry for the girl. 'Are you alone? Is there someone you can call to come and be with you?'

'Umm . . . no, Daisy's here . . . she's asleep.'

For a while Karen just listened in silence to the tearing sobs. She wanted to cry herself, to let go, join her stepdaughter in her grief, but her eyes were dry as a bone. True, her heart was palpitating like a wild thing banging against her chest wall, as if desperate to get free. But it was guilt that had set it off, not sorrow and the pain of loss. Had she been the cause of Harry Stewart's death? This was the question that refused to go away.

'What shall I do?' Sophie wailed. 'I don't know what to dooo . . .'

'Maybe you should wake Daisy?'

There was silence, then a long sniff. 'Yeah . . .'

'Shall I ring you later?' Karen was hoping that at least Harry's death might foster some sort of rapprochement between her and his daughter. Sophie could be both funny and clever when she chose, and had inherited a lot of her Greek mother's feisty Mediterranean temperament, which meant she would suddenly explode, ranting on for hours about something that annoyed her. Karen admired that side of her. What she didn't appreciate was the hostile brat act – a role ill-suited to a woman just turned thirty. But Harry's lifelong indulgence of his daughter had taken its toll. With the result that Sophie was still mooching about, toying with various career paths, from dress designing to jewellery making to running a stall on the Portobello Road selling second-hand clothes. None of which lasted for more than a year and all of which *cost* money, rather than making it. Daddy's money, of course.

'I'll come down. I should be there,' the girl said.

'OK . . . although there isn't anything to do, really.' There was masses to do, of course. A funeral to arrange, people to inform, solicitors to consult, bank accounts to close, utilities to transfer into her name – Harry had taken care of everything to do with money – the list was endless, but the thought of having to cope with an hysterical stepdaughter on top of everything else was more than Karen could bear.

'I want to be there. I want to see Daddy one last time. You can't stop me doing that.' Her voice took on a childish and familiarly belligerent tone.

'I'm not trying to stop you, Sophie. Of course you can come. I was just saying—' Karen sighed. There was no point in continuing, it would only escalate into a row.

★

Sophie, with her usual penchant for drama, took on the role of Chief Mourner with much more zeal than Karen had the energy to muster. She didn't doubt Sophie's genuine sadness at the loss of her father, but the way she languished, damp-eyed and sighing, on the sofa for most of the day like *La Dame aux Camélias*, while Karen rushed madly about trying to choose a coffin, put an announcement in the paper, organize sandwiches, select hymns for the service sheet, order flowers, ring round Harry's hundreds of friends and previous work colleagues, etc., etc., was irritating, to say the least.

And Sophie's funeral hat could not have been larger without lifting her bodily off the ground, her heels higher without toppling her into the grave on top of her father, the bags under her eyes blacker without making a case for hospitalization. Karen knew she was being mean, thinking these things, but Sophie seemed to assume she was the only one grieving. She barely gave a nod to Karen's very real distress.

It didn't matter that Karen had been on the point of leaving Harry – which Sophie obviously didn't know – she was mourning for the only man she had ever truly loved.

'How are you coping?'

It was two days after the funeral and Reverend Haskell was seated beside her on the sofa in the sitting room. Karen had avoided being alone with the vicar since her husband's death, but this morning he had just dropped by unannounced and she'd had no choice but to ask him in.

'I'm OK,' she said.

A strained silence followed, where William looked at her intently – waiting for the dam to burst on Karen's grief perhaps – and Karen studiously avoided his gaze.

'Such a fantastic turnout at the service, he was obviously a very special man . . . and much loved.'

'He was.'

The reverend shifted about on the cushions. She detected a strange contradiction in the man. He was able to focus and be very still, very intent when people were talking, almost as if he'd stopped breathing. But alongside this she also sensed a powerful physicality, a sort of impatience at being contained.

Just go away, she pleaded silently, twisting her fingers together in her lap, waiting for him to get up. *Leave me alone.* But that was obviously not the plan.

'I know you must be in shock, Karen. It was so sudden . . .' He paused. 'And Harry was such a life force. You're going to miss him terribly.'

She didn't reply. *Why should I? I didn't ask him to come round.* And although she was being truculent, knowing he meant well and was only doing his job, she couldn't help resenting the intrusion. Life was tricky enough, with Sophie still showing no signs of going back to London. And worse, she was beginning to take over in the house. Small things, like buying a new machine for the coffee – one of those super-trendy, press-button pod things – which produced lukewarm, tasteless coffee in mug-sized portions, but did it instantly.

'Thought we needed an update,' Sophie had said, proudly, the machine already unpacked and installed when Karen got back from the solicitors. Maybe, Karen thought, she'd been waiting, dying to prod them into modern life, but hadn't dared when her father was around. She obviously thought her stepmother was fair game.

'How does it work?' Karen had asked, looking around for the old filter machine, but seeing no sign of it. She was trying to be kind to her, keep antagonism to the minimum, but she had assumed Sophie would go home after the funeral.

'Karen . . .' She heard the vicar clear his throat. 'I know you think I'm trying to drag you into the church. And it's true, Harry was very keen for me to reach out to you. But honestly, I understand if you aren't religious. I'm not here to put pressure on you. I just want to help.'

She looked up at him, finally, and saw the genuine kindness in his light-blue eyes, his eyebrows knitting together in a concerned frown. She felt her own eyes fill with tears, the first since Harry had died.

'He used to be a good man . . .'

William nodded, but he said nothing.

Karen took a deep breath. The need to talk to someone, even if it was the vicar of a church with which she had no affinity, suddenly seemed overwhelming. All the prevarication she had gone through this last week, in the face of so many kind condolences – yes, what a wonderful man; yes, he was such a character; yes, so funny, so kind, a one-off; yes, he will be sorely missed; yes, yes, yes – had become such a terrible strain that she had begun to feel as if she were frozen in the lie. And if she didn't spit it out soon, it might be too late, and the truth would be submerged forever in everyone else's construct of her husband.

'He drank,' she said bluntly.

'I know,' was Reverend Haskell's equally blunt reply.

She stared at him. 'You did?'

He nodded. 'Of course. People talk. That must have been really hard for you.'

'It made him very—'

She heard Largo bark in the hall, then the sound of the front door opening. She quickly blinked the incipient tears away, taking a tissue out of the sleeve of her sweater and blowing her nose.

'That'll be Sophie,' she said, getting up from the sofa.

The vicar followed suit. 'Listen, if you ever want to talk . . .'

She gave him a quick smile as the door swung open and her step-daughter walked in.

'Oh . . . sorry. Hi, William.'

'Hi, Sophie. How are you?'

Sophie knew the vicar. She had always gone to church with her father whenever she visited. Karen had no idea if the girl was actually religious or not, but it had made Harry very happy.

'You know . . . not so good,' she replied, the smile she'd worn in greeting replaced by a sigh.

William gave her a sympathetic pat on the arm. 'At least you've got each other for support,' he said brightly, glancing between the two women. 'Well, better be off. Remember where I am, both of you.'

'Why was he here?' Sophie asked.

'He came to see if I was alright.'

'Kind of him, considering you aren't one of his flock.'

'He is kind,' Karen said, remembering the argument she'd had with her husband about the vicar's goodness.

Sophie threw herself on to the sofa with an exhausted sigh. 'When's Barry arriving?'

'Two thirty.'

Sophie looked pleased. But Karen didn't tell her she already knew the contents of Harry's will – Barry Rivers had given her the headlines when she'd visited his Portsmouth office the day before. She, Karen, kept the house for her lifetime, unless she married again. It would be managed by a trust, then eventually go to

Sophie. But Harry had left most of his money to charity – the Church and the Institute of Mechanical Engineers both major beneficiaries. Karen would also receive a small annual amount from the trust, but Sophie had been left only a token sum of £10,000. Large by many people's standards, but probably barely enough to pay off the girl's credit cards. Maybe he thought he'd shelled out enough in that direction already – which was certainly true – or perhaps he was more astute about his daughter than Karen gave him credit for, realizing that a substantial legacy would only stop Sophie from ever getting her life together.

Whatever Harry Stewart's reasoning, and however annoying she found the girl, Karen was dreading her stepdaughter finding out the details, knowing she would be relying on a massive payout. And she was sure Sophie would blame her, even though Harry had never, ever discussed a word about his affairs with her.

'How long does it take to sort all the money out, when someone dies?' Sophie was asking, pulling her long dark hair out of the ponytail and shaking it loose around her broad shoulders. The girl was tall – she had at least four inches on Karen – her figure a combination of Harry's big bones and her mother's Mediterranean curves. And although she was pretty with her dark eyes and thick, luxuriant curls, her face was not open or smiling, but rather held a wariness that verged on the sullen.

'Not sure. Usually about six months . . . depending if it's all straightforward.'

'*Six months*?' Sophie looked horrified. 'Why so long?'

'Well, I suppose there's death duties and investments to sell, the bank, endless legal documents . . . stuff like that.'

Her stepdaughter, picking absent-mindedly at a stray thread

from the arm of the sofa – Karen had recently had the armchairs and sofa re-covered in a pretty cornflower linen – suddenly eyed Karen suspiciously. 'You know, don't you? You know what's in Daddy's will. He must have told you.'

'He didn't, Sophie,' she replied, truthfully. 'Your dad wasn't one to discuss anything related to money with a mere woman. He never said a word about it, and I didn't ask.'

Sophie's face relaxed. 'Yeah, he was a bit crap about trusting anyone female with finance.' She gave a heavy sigh. 'Oh, well. Just have to wait to find out my fate.'

Barry Rivers did not conform to expectations. With his grey ponytail and gaunt, tanned frame, black Nike trainers with his dark suit, he looked more like the manager of a rock band than a country solicitor. Apparently every spare moment of his time was spent on his boat, moored in Gosport marina. Harry had always joked that he felt bad asking Barry to do anything because it dragged the man away from his obsession.

Karen had taken him through to the kitchen, and now the three of them sat around the table, mugs of tea already poured, ginger biscuits on a plate in the centre, a copy of Harry's will – bound neatly in a clear folder with a black plastic spine, the document itself typed on cream paper – in front of each of them. Barry gave Karen and Sophie a sympathetic smile.

'First I'd like to say how sorry I am about Harry. You must both be heartbroken . . .' He paused as if searching for the right word. 'I represented him for over thirty years, and he was tough alright, but such a gentleman, a real pleasure to work with. And a friend.'

Karen nodded in acknowledgement, but she could feel the tension in the room as Sophie stroked the smooth surface of the folder

43

with the flat of her hand – her nails painted a funereal purple, almost black.

'So . . . down to business. I'm not going to read all the waffle now, all the clauses, etc. We can go through the whole thing in more detail at a later date, when things have settled down. I'll just give you the gist.'

Barry worked his way through the will slowly, looking up every now and then, his eyebrows raised, checking that the two women understood what he was saying. He explained about the trust which would manage the house, he told Karen how much she could expect per annum, he informed Sophie of the £10,000 legacy. He conveyed the amount of all the various charitable donations. He finished reading and closed the document. Sophie seemed quite calm, she had made no comment when she found out how much she would get.

'So, that's it, ladies.' Barry sat back in his chair and reached for his now cold tea, drinking it thirstily to the dregs.

'That's it?' Sophie was frowning, first at the solicitor, then at Karen. 'I don't understand.'

Karen said nothing.

'Which bit don't you understand?' Barry asked. 'I can read it again.'

'You said that Daddy's left me ten grand . . . that's great, but it can't be all, obviously.'

'Umm, yes . . .' Barry opened the document again and thumbed through till he got to the bit about Sophie's legacy, turning his own copy round for the girl on the other side of the table and pointing to the paragraph. 'And the house, of course, which becomes yours on Karen's death or in the event she remarries.'

Sophie stared at the page. Tears filled her eyes. 'You're honestly telling me that Daddy has only left me ten thousand pounds? *Ten thousand pounds*? That there's nothing else?'

Barry nodded, his expression cautious.

'He can't have . . .' her voice trailed off.

Karen didn't know what to say. She reached across the corner of the table and put her hand on Sophie's arm, but the girl shook her off, turning the full force of her distress on her stepmother.

'This is your doing, isn't it? You turned him against me. He'd never have thought of this on his own . . . he loved me. He really, really loved me.' She began to cry – loud, dramatic sobs, her head bent on her folded arms.

Barry shot Karen a worried look. 'I assure you, Sophie, Karen had nothing whatever to do with your father's decision.'

Sophie raised her head, glared at him. 'What do you know? She wouldn't have discussed it in front of you. She's been pouring poison in Daddy's ear for years now, making damn sure she keeps everything for herself.'

'No,' Barry said firmly. 'No, it wasn't like that. This really has nothing whatsoever to do with your stepmother. We talked about it at some length, me and your Dad. And he told me he thought he'd given you too much money already, and that it hadn't helped you get on your feet and make a proper go of your life. In fact, it had done quite the reverse, in his opinion. He blamed himself for indulging you.' Barry hesitated, obviously torn between telling Sophie the truth and upsetting her further. 'He wanted the best for you, trust me. He just thought that giving you more money would basically ruin your life.' For a moment the only sound in the room was angry sniffling from the bowed head. 'He believed in you, Sophie. He loved you so much. He was sure you'd find something that you'd be brilliant at . . . just not if you were too cosy with his money.'

'I don't believe he would do that to me.'

The solicitor shrugged. 'He said it was very hard to refuse you, when you asked him for funds. This was the only way he felt he could do it.'

'I didn't ask him *that* often. You're making me out to be a bloody sponger. I've just been through a bad patch these last few years and I didn't know who else to turn to.'

'No, I'm sure. And I didn't mean to imply anything, I was just trying to explain the circumstances of your father's decision.'

'What am I going to doooo?' Sophie wailed, clutching her head. 'Ten grand won't even begin to get me out of the hole I'm in. Isn't there something you can do?'

Barry shook his head. 'Not really . . . sorry.'

Sophie turned to Karen, her eyes narrowing. 'You're enjoying this, aren't you?'

'Of course I'm not. I hate seeing you so upset.'

'Ha. Right. But you're not going to do anything about it, are you?'

'There isn't anything I can do about it,' Karen replied. 'Your father hasn't left me much money either.'

There was another tense silence in the quiet kitchen.

'It's your fault he's dead, anyway.' Sophie had dropped her voice to a whisper.

The girl's words felt to Karen like a stab at an already painful wound. She had tried, in the intervening weeks, not to dwell on the circumstances of her husband's last moments. But the image she could not delete was of herself climbing into bed that night, full of righteous anger at Harry, while he, alone and terrified, called desperately for her to save him.

46

'I know you're upset,' Barry Rivers was saying, his tone reproachful. 'But you shouldn't say things you'll regret. Karen is grieving too.'

'He drank because you made him so unhappy,' Sophie continued as if he hadn't spoken, her voice sullen. Brushing her thick hair back from her face, she got up and yanked a piece of kitchen towel from the roll hanging from a holder on the wall, blew her nose noisily, her back to the room.

Karen had had enough.

'Thanks, Barry,' she said, briskly. 'I'll give you a ring in a week or so.'

She got up and so did the solicitor. He gathered together the documents he'd brought and stuffed them into his old leather briefcase.

'Sure. And if either of you have any questions, please don't hesitate to get in touch.'

He kissed Karen lightly on both cheeks, then moved towards Sophie, who held her hand out stiffly to be shaken.

When Karen came back into the kitchen, having seen Barry out, Sophie was gone.

CHAPTER FOUR

'Poor Sophie. It does seem a bit brutal,' Maggie said, as they walked up the hill. The late January day was cloudy and cold, a light drizzle being driven towards them by the cruel east wind. But Karen needed to be away from the house. It was the morning after the reading of the will and Sophie hadn't emerged from her room until Karen had gone to bed, when she'd heard the girl in the kitchen, banging about.

'I know. She's a pain, but it must have been a shock. Although ten thousand is hardly nothing.'

'He'd already given her loads of money, I suppose.'

'Thousands and thousands over the years, yes.'

'So it's not as if he cut her off without a penny.'

'Far from it. But it does seem a bit weak of Harry not to have warned her.'

They walked in silence for a while, the only sound their panting breaths as they climbed the steep path.

'Maybe he meant to . . . he just didn't think he'd die so soon. And he was right not to leave her any more if the money wasn't doing her any good.'

Karen sighed. 'Yeah, but how do I get her to understand that and stop blaming me? I'm sure she expects *me* to bail her out now Daddy's gone.'

Maggie turned to face her friend. 'You're not to, Karen. Promise? That's your money to live on, you can't go giving it away to Sophie. Anyway, it's not what Harry wanted.'

'I know, but believe me, my dear stepdaughter is very persuasive when she's broke.' She looked around. 'Where's Largo?'

They both stopped. 'Largo . . . *Largo.*'

The dog came bounding over the crest of the hill, tail wagging, lurching his big bulk to a halt against Karen's leg. She bent to stroke his damp fur.

'I wish she'd just go home,' she said.

Maggie was peering at her. 'Apart from Sophie, how are you coping?'

'Not great.'

'You miss him.'

'No . . . well, yes, of course I do. But . . . it's . . .' She stopped. She couldn't say the words, couldn't explain the misery that it had been, living with Harry, or the guilt that tormented her now. But almost worse was the feeling of discombobulation. The rug had been pulled so dramatically from under her feet that she simply couldn't understand what was going on half the time. Nothing seemed entirely real.

'I just don't know what's going to happen,' she finished lamely.

Maggie grabbed her and gave her a tight hug. 'Poor you, it must be so hard. I don't know what I'd do if Raki died. But you should try not to think about the future right now. It'll take time to work things out and you're not in a fit state to do that yet.'

Her friend's words slid emptily across Karen's consciousness. She appreciated Maggie's attempts, but without Karen telling her the truth, no comfort was available.

The view from the top of the hill was spectacular, even on such a dull day. As they stood in silence for a moment, taking in the panorama, Largo began to bark, his tail wagging furiously. Karen, turning, saw the lone figure of William Haskell, hands deep in the pockets of his donkey jacket, making his way up the steep path.

'Oh, God, it's the bloody vicar again,' she muttered. 'Seems like everywhere I go, he pitches up too. I think he's stalking me.'

Maggie turned too. 'Ah, he's lovely, William. Why don't you like him?'

'I *do* like him. But he looks at me with those zealous eyes of his, all Christian-like, and I just know all he wants is to drag me into church, despite what he says to the contrary.'

'You make it sound like he's trying to seduce you!'

'I said "church", not bed.'

Her friend laughed. 'Well, if he's trying to turn *you* into a believer, he's picked a tough nut to crack.'

They watched as the reverend sprinted up the last steep incline.

'You know he's an archer?'

'An archer? The vicar?'

'I know, it's bizarre. Although I'm not sure why it's bizarre.'

'I suppose archers are sort of strong and heroic. And there's nothing very heroic about being a vicar these days.'

'Perhaps not, but he's only shooting at a target, not slaying mountain lions or the Normans. He's pretty good, Jennifer was telling me. County standard in the past. He teaches disabled kids at the local club in his spare time, apparently.'

Haskell arrived beside them at the top of the path, not even short of breath, and smiling.

'Hi there, ladies.' He took a long, steadying breath. 'Good workout, this hill.'

'Yes, and worth it when you get here,' Maggie replied, sweeping her arm around to show off the view as if it were her own.

'Oh, certainly.' He gazed at the distant hills, his breath smoking in the chilly air, then switched his focus to Karen. 'So, how's it all going?'

'Fine, thank you,' she said, unable to keep the wariness out of her tone. She saw his eyebrows go up, as if he knew what she was thinking, but he didn't say anything.

'I saw Janey yesterday,' Maggie was saying. 'She mentioned you were thinking of starting a women's group.'

He nodded. 'Yes, my wife's very passionate about the idea. What do you think? Would there be any take-up in the village?'

'Depends what it's for,' Karen said, suspecting it would be just another recruitment drive.

'Well . . . I thought it would be good to have a forum to discuss things that mainly concern women. It could be anything from baking cupcakes to the meaning of life.'

'Aren't they one and the same thing?' Karen asked, slightly waspishly, annoyed by what she took to be a patronizing tone.

But William just laughed, his eyes lighting up in genuine amusement. 'Could be. A good cupcake certainly lifts the soul.'

'Blood sugar, more like,' Karen said.

'That too.' William wasn't rising to any of her jibes.

'I think it's a great idea,' Maggie said, shooting a small frown at Karen.

'Would you be interested?' His question was addressed to Maggie, but he included Karen in his encouraging, very charming smile.

'Probably. Might do us all good.'

Karen didn't say anything, just bent to stroke Largo, who was fussing at her feet to get on with the walk.

'It's never easy to open up if you've got a problem, especially in a small village. I just thought it might be helpful . . .'

Karen felt herself tensing with irritation, knowing that his remark was directed straight at her.

'We should get going,' she said, looking pointedly at Maggie.

As they began to descend the hill, William went striding off the other way, up the path which led further into the hills. Maggie dug her friend in the side.

'Did you have to be so rude?'

'I wasn't rude.'

'Yes, you were. Everything the poor man said, you jumped on. It's not like you.'

'Well, he's so annoying. All that fake concern for everyone.'

Maggie looked shocked. 'That's really unfair. He obviously cares deeply. I don't understand why you're being so mean about him. Would you rather we had creepy Bob Parkin back, with all that pious droning and those leery smiles?'

'I just wish William'd leave me alone.'

'Well, tell him, then. Tell him you don't need his help. He's got a broad back.'

'I have. But he doesn't seem to hear me.'

Maggie didn't reply, but Karen could tell from her stiff back and the increased pace with which she stamped down the path in her red anorak that she was irritated with her.

'OK, OK. I'll be nice to him. I just . . . I don't feel myself at the moment.'

Maggie turned at her words, her face full of sympathy again.

As Karen drew level with her, she said, 'People don't know what to say when someone dies. They don't know what to do for the best.'

Karen didn't think this was the vicar's problem, and knew Maggie was speaking more about herself.

'I know. And I'm sorry I'm being such a curmudgeon. I have no idea even how I want anyone to behave. All of it seems wrong.'

Maggie linked her arm with Karen's. 'I'm sure it does. It will for a while, I expect.'

Sophie was waiting for Karen when she got back from her walk, sitting at the kitchen table, clutching her phone tight in her right hand, obviously tense. Karen took a deep breath, waiting for the onslaught.

'Hi.'

'Hello, Sophie.'

'We've got to talk,' she said.

Karen nodded and sat down opposite her stepdaughter.

'This money thing . . . I've decided . . . I'm going to have to let out my flat for the time being. It's the only way I can pay the mortgage.' Her tone of voice, surprisingly, was not hostile, just weary. 'I've talked to Mum and she thinks it's a good idea.'

'Right, well, that sounds like a plan,' she said, not really listening, feeling detached, uninvolved in Sophie's problems.

But the girl looked puzzled by her reply and Karen wondered what she was missing.

'Obviously, if I rent it out, I'll have to come and live here for a bit . . . until I'm straight. I can't go to Mum's.'

Karen assumed Sophie was referring to the fact that her mother lived in the Lake District.

'Here?' Karen could hear that the word sounded almost stupid, and she tried to lift herself from the lethargy that had overtaken her.

Sophie nodded.

Living here. Sophie, living here. Karen took a deep breath as the reality of what the girl was saying began to sink in.

'How will that work?' she asked. 'We don't get on.' She had never said it in so many words, but there was no point in beating about the bush, now that the catalyst for them being polite to each other was no longer around.

The dismissive shrug that Sophie gave implied that it was immaterial to her if they liked each other or not.

'I don't have much choice, do I? I'm like totally broke. Anyway, it's a big house, we won't have to see each other if we don't want to. It'll only be till I get straight.'

She was eyeing Karen as if daring her to refuse, her stare both pleading and hostile at the same time. *Is she testing me, seeing if I'll pay her off like Harry did, just to keep her out of the house?* Karen wondered.

'Fine,' Karen said eventually. She could hardly say no, but she was surprised to find that, in fact, she was strangely relieved the girl would be staying. The house felt echoey, spookily quiet, the winter nights very long and dark since the bluster and drunken boisterousness of her husband – accompanied by the relentless background noise of golf replays – had been removed.

'So it's OK?'

'Yes. If that's what you want.'

Sophie looked amazed, almost deflated, as if she had been busting for a fight. She got up, muttering a grudging thanks.

'I've got a friend I know will take my flat for a while.' She hovered, as if there were something else on her mind. Then her face cleared. 'I'll get off then, go home and start sorting things out. It'll probably take a few days.'

'Just let me know when you're coming down.'

Her stepdaughter was walking towards the door when she hesitated. 'Thanks,' she repeated, her expression softening for a second from its habitual wariness.

Karen smiled. 'Just one thing. We're going to have to try and get along. It'll be hell otherwise . . . for both of us.'

The shutters were down again as the girl replied, 'It's not my fault we don't.'

Karen had to bite her tongue.

Almost as soon as her stepdaughter had driven off, Karen went up to bed – despite it being only three o'clock in the afternoon – dragging one foot in front of the other, she was suddenly so tired. For nights now, she had barely slept, waking multiple times in the darkness, thinking she heard Harry calling her. Often she would forget for a moment that he was dead, and found herself leaping up and grabbing her dressing gown in order to go and help him upstairs. And with each wakening, with each realization that he was beyond her help, would come the guilt, descending on her like a pall that was impossible to shake off.

When she woke it was gone eight in the evening. Her body felt heavy and lethargic still, as if the sleep had only intensified her tiredness rather than alleviated it.

She dragged herself out of bed and went downstairs to make some tea, which she took into the sitting room. But the room seemed full of shadows and she hurried back to the kitchen. She rang Maggie, but her friend's phone went to voicemail, then tried her brother in Canada, but his mobile also just asked her to leave a message. She had never felt so uneasy, sitting there in her own home – which she'd always considered so cosy and safe – with nobody for company but her husband's reproachful ghost.

Even the presence of her spiky stepdaughter would have been preferable.

The following morning, after another sleepless night, during which she'd read an entire Michael Connelly novel cover-to-cover and only shut her eyes around six a.m., Karen knew she had to focus. She had always been a very organized person, a list person. Someone, what's more, who actually consulted her lists, didn't just write them and forget them. She liked to have a plan. It came from living with a mother whose ability to organize was perpetually fuddled by sherry – Karen had been in charge of the household much of the time. But currently there was no plan. Yes, she had the house. Yes, she had enough money to live on, if she continued to live in the rectory. But what would she do with her time, now there was no husband to focus on, to look after and worry about?

Back when they'd first married, Harry had been adamant that no wife of his would need a job, and she hadn't argued at the time, not after twenty years of being at her various bosses' beck and call, her support often going unappreciated. But she'd also known that if she sat at home while Harry worked, she would not only go stark staring mad, but she would barely set eyes on her workaholic husband from Monday to Friday. He had hired another PA when they got married, so Karen had gradually begun to take on the promotion of foreign trade – which had been largely neglected till then – liaising with companies and accompanying her husband on the trips abroad to visit them. It was work she loved, not least because she and Harry were together and made such an impressive team: he the charismatic front man, bombastic, who saw the bigger picture; Karen the finisher, the details person, who smoothed the path to contract signing and ensured the participants were satisfied. And so the company had happily absorbed most of their waking hours for nearly fifteen years. Even at home they talked about little else. Perhaps it wasn't surprising, therefore, that things had imploded after Harry sold up three years ago.

Since then, she realized, the two of them had sunk into a mire. Harry had turned to alcohol and needed his wife to prop him up in his addiction; Karen took on the role of worried observer, monitoring each and every drink and witnessing her husband's decline into drunkenness whilst at the same time being helpless to change things. There was no other focus for either of them, their world had shrunk almost to nothing. It seemed hard to believe, when she thought about it now, that their previously lively, enjoyable partnership had been reduced to nothing more than resentment and bickering.

What happens now? she asked herself as she rinsed Largo's water bowl out and filled it with fresh water. *What on earth do I do?* She took a tin of dog food from the cupboard and spooned the meaty, gelatinous chunks out into the enamel dish, breaking them up then sprinkling a handful of kibble on top, taken from a large sack under the sink. Largo was watching intently, his mouth open, tongue out, tail whacking back and forth in his eagerness. *What will become of me without Harry?*

'Here you go, boy.' Karen put the dish down on the tiles and gave the dog a stroke, digging her fingers into his soft coat.

The farm shop was busy. Karen wandered down the vegetable aisle, scanning the boxes of fat, shiny leeks and carrots with their green, feathery tops still attached. She had no appetite, and had been surviving for the past few weeks on scrambled eggs and tomato soup, those being the easiest and quickest things to prepare. But now she had run out of even these, and Sophie would be arriving the following day. *Not merely 'arriving'*, Karen thought gloomily, as she pulled a brown paper bag from the string hanging beside the potatoes and began to fill it with parsnips, *so much as 'moving in'*. Her previous notion that it would be good to have someone else in the house had quickly waned. It had been two weeks since her stepdaughter had left for London, and Karen still hadn't fully come to terms with the fact that from tomorrow she would have to live side by side with Harry's daughter, find some sort of harmony with the difficult girl.

Her basket now contained carrots and parsnips and a savoy cabbage, vegetables that she selected because they were virtually the only ones that Harry – not the most enthusiastic vegetable consumer – had tolerated. For years she had reached for them without thinking.

'Karen?' She looked round to see Janey Haskell smiling tentatively at her.

'Hi,' Karen said, thinking, not for the first time, that the vicar's wife was straight from Central Casting: neat, sweet, unassuming, yet with a steely determination that you ignored at your peril. Janey's success, for instance, at bludgeoning the village into handing over money for Children in Need was astonishing – twice as much as was raised in previous years. She was impossible to refuse.

'How are things?' Janey asked. She had an odd way of not moving about very much, as if she were trying to balance a book on her freshly washed dark hair, blunt cut to her shoulders.

'Umm, yeah . . . you know . . . getting there.'

The vicar's wife nodded sympathetically. 'It'll take time.'

Karen gritted her teeth. If one more person said that to her she would surely stab them. Did they think that she was a complete idiot? Did they think she expected the death of a husband could be overcome in an instant? Did they really think that?

'I suppose,' she replied, trying hard to smile.

Janey just looked at her, as if she were waiting for her to confess her innermost torment. *She must have learnt the technique from her husband.*

'Will was trying to get hold of you earlier. In fact, he tried yesterday too.'

'Really?' Karen's voice squeaked guiltily. She'd received three messages from Reverend Haskell on her mobile and had ignored them all.

'Yes, he wanted to talk to you about the headstone.'

Karen raised her eyebrows.

'You asked him for the name of a stonemason?' Janey was clearly beginning to feel a little uncomfortable with Karen's lack of responsiveness, because she was nervously nibbling her top lip with her small bottom teeth.

'I'll give him a call when I get home,' she said, unrepentant. *Just because my husband has died, doesn't make it open season on sharing*, she thought crossly.

Janey began to move off. 'If there's anything either of us can do, Karen,' she said, laying a gentle hand on Karen's arm, 'you know you can ring us . . . or come round . . . at any time.'

The words seemed sincere, and Karen felt mean.

'Thanks, Janey. That's good to know.'

And she was rewarded by a relieved smile from the vicar's wife.

★

Karen kept William in the kitchen this time. She didn't want him to get too cosy.

'You didn't have to come over,' she said, when she'd plonked a cup of tea down in front of him. 'I know you're busy, you could have told me over the phone.'

Will smiled. 'It can be an emotive subject, the headstone.'

'Right. Well, all I wanted was a name. I can deal with them myself.'

For a minute he didn't look at her, then he brought his gaze up to hers, his eyes suddenly very intense.

'I know you're avoiding me, Karen, and I'm not remotely offended. But I wish you'd just let me be your friend, without being so aware of this collar here.' He touched the white dog collar he wore, almost apologetically.

'It's not that I'm avoiding you . . .' She picked at a small splinter on the wooden table.

'Look, what you're going through must be hard. I have no idea how hard. But bottling it all up, in my experience, makes it harder.' His tone was tough, almost businesslike. 'I'm not trying to force you to tell me how you're feeling, but I hope there's someone you can talk to . . . Maggie, for instance?'

He burbled on, about death and bereavement, anger, regret . . . she wasn't really taking it in. But the sound was rhythmic and oddly soothing, like the beat of a distant drum. She was so tired. Continuing to avoid his gaze, both hands around her warm mug of tea, she felt her breathing gradually slow from the shallow, snatched breaths that had become normal over the past weeks. And in her chest there was a sensation like a trip switch going, as if something taut and strung out had finally snapped. Her cold body flushed with heat and for a moment she luxuriated in the feeling, which was like a warm, peaceful blanket being wrapped around her soul.

'Karen?'

She looked up and met his eyes, not sure what he was asking. 'Sorry . . .'

'Are you alright? You look quite . . . flushed.'

There was a heavy silence.

'Do I?' Then she felt her face crumple, her eyes flood with hot, stinging tears.

William, sitting opposite her, let her cry. He did nothing, made no attempt to reach over and touch her, and his inaction seemed to be giving her permission to weep, to take her time and let everything go.

After a while, she wanted badly to speak. 'I let him die,' she said. 'He called and called and I didn't go to him. If I had, he might still be alive today.'

The vicar just nodded.

'Did you hear what I said? I killed my husband. I left him there . . . the stupid drunken sod. *Come and get me if you want me*, I thought, and I went to bed. WENT TO BED when my husband was in pain and dying downstairs.' She stared at him through her tears. 'What sort of a person does that make me? Eh?'

'Human,' was his quiet reply.

'No, NO, that's *not* "human". Any normal human being would have gone to him, been there when he needed me.'

'Did you want him to die?'

The question shocked her. 'No, of course not.'

He met her gaze, waiting for her to go on.

'I wanted him to stop drinking,' she said, but the other words, the ones she knew she had to say, stuck in her throat. William wasn't helping her out. 'He was such a nightmare when he was drunk. Which was most of the time recently. I didn't know what to do, how to stop him. He even hit me a few weeks ago . . . I don't think he meant it, but still . . .'

'I'm so sorry. It must have been hell for you both.'

The word 'both' brought Karen up short. Was it hell for Harry too?

'If it was such hell for him, then why didn't he make even the tiniest effort to stop?'

William shrugged. 'I don't know.'

'And why didn't anyone say anything? You all knew, but you didn't do a blind thing. Those friends of his at the club, watching him drink himself unconscious week after week? Why didn't anyone help him . . . help me?' She was almost shouting now. 'Why didn't you?'

'I understand what you're saying, but I never really saw him drunk. I knew he drank — other people said it, and his flushed face and the smell of alcohol, even at the morning service, was a bit of a giveaway. But I didn't feel I knew him well enough to say anything yet.'

Karen slumped, her head bowed, her arms resting on the table. The anger had drained away. 'Sorry, I didn't mean to attack you. I feel so guilty . . . and I suppose I want to blame everyone else.'

Silence fell on the warm room. There was just the sound of the boiler chunnering away in the utility room next door.

'Did you know he was ill?'

She shook her head. 'His blood pressure was high, but he was on beta blockers, had been for years. He always said Tom had given him a clean bill of health whenever he went for a check-up. I don't know if that was true—'

'So you couldn't have known he was at risk.'

'Well, no. But anyone with half a brain knows that a seventy-five-year-old who puts away a bottle of whisky a day – minimum – is going to end up with health problems.'

'Was it a heart attack?'

'So the post mortem said.'

Another silence.

William's ability to be absolutely still and thereby make silence seem alright was almost as if he were stopping time. Maybe it was the archery discipline, she thought, the need to be completely focused in order to take aim. Whatever it was, she found it calming, not feeling the need to speak. She felt they could have sat there all night.

'I'm glad you were able to talk to me about it.'

'You won't tell anyone else about me leaving him and going to bed? Please. They'd be so shocked.'

'You haven't done anything wrong, Karen. How could you know that he was about to die? But no, of course I won't tell anyone.'

'Not even Janey?'

'Not even Janey.'

She sighed. 'Thanks.'

William got up, took his mug to the sink and tipped the dregs of his tea away, rinsed it out and placed the mug on the draining board.

Karen got up too. 'Listen . . . thanks . . . thanks for being so . . . for not judging me.'

He smiled. 'Nothing to judge. Why don't we meet again soon. I'm around.'

When he'd gone out into the cold February evening, Karen sat back down at the table. It had been such a relief to speak of her guilt to another human being. But although she felt calmer than she had in days, William's insistence that she had done nothing wrong did not ring true. Not that she didn't believe him to be sincere. She absolutely did. But he only knew what she'd chosen to tell him, he hadn't been there. Because she finally admitted to herself, as she trawled through the events yet again, minute by minute, of Harry Stewart's last night on earth, that part of her *had* known, right from the start, that there was something wrong. His cry was not that of someone just wanting attention, but a cry of real distress.

I didn't think he would die, she told herself now. *I honestly didn't.* But there had been times in the past, she knew, when the thought *had* crossed her mind that it would be easier if he did. Not in a serious way, she hadn't followed it through. It had been more of an exhausted, end-of-the-road, no-other-options-left-to-her sort of thought when he was being particularly difficult. And it was quickly dismissed and accompanied by immediate shame. Shame at the thought itself and also at her own cowardice in not being able to just pack a bag and leave him.

She hadn't told the vicar *that*, had she? Hadn't told him of the burning resentment she felt each time he threatened her, or belittled her, or ordered her about in his drunken state. Nor had she mentioned that she was on the brink of leaving Harry.

What would the Reverend Haskell have thought if he knew the unedited version of the truth? she wondered. *No doubt booked me a place in hell.*

CHAPTER FIVE

'Can you at least put your stuff in the dishwasher when you've finished eating? And the food back in the fridge.'

It was three weeks into Sophie's residency and Karen was sick to death of coming into the kitchen and finding the place covered with layers of her stepdaughter's mess.

Sophie looked up from her phone, raised her eyebrows in mock alarm. 'Oops, sorry. Didn't mean to contravene house rules.'

Karen felt the familiar, now almost permanent knot of tension in her stomach. It was like having a hostile teenager to stay; Sophie seemed so much younger than her years, almost as if she refused to grow up.

'I don't see why I should run around picking up after you,' Karen snapped.

With a theatrical sigh and a brief eye-roll, Sophie said, 'Yeah, well, you don't have to. I'll do it eventually.'

They seldom ate together. Sophie kept strange hours, often not emerging before the evening, then staying up till late, curled up in her father's red leather recliner in the den and watching film after film on the wide screen – horror her favoured genre, judging by the tinny screams that filtered through to Karen's bedroom.

She had also adopted a diet since Harry's death that seemed to consist only of great mounds of raw, indigestible vegetables. 'You should try it,' Sophie had said, having primly refused the offer of some parsnip soup that Karen had made, on the grounds that it was cooked. 'Raw food is pure energy,' she added, as if quoting from a book. 'And a total detox. You'd feel so much lighter if you stopped clogging up your system with all that bread and stuff.'

'So you can't eat chocolate. That's cooked, isn't it?' Karen was being provocative – she knew Sophie adored chocolate of any sort.

But Sophie just grinned triumphantly. 'Chocolate doesn't have to be cooked. Raw chocolate is a superfood, actually. It's higher in antioxidants than green tea and has over three hundred nutrients. So I can eat as much as I like.'

That had shut Karen up.

But the girl seemed worryingly over-zealous about her diet. OK, she had weight she could lose, but Karen hoped this wasn't some bizarre reaction to her father's death that would end up making her ill.

Johnny harrumphed at the other end of the phone. 'Why didn't you just tell her she couldn't move in? It's not your fault Harry finally saw sense and cut her off without a penny . . . or at least not enough pennies.'

'Maybe not, but she thinks it is. And this house is big, I don't see how I could have refused.'

'You don't? Well, it goes like this: "Sorry, Sophie, you're an annoying brat and I don't want you living in my house."'

Karen laughed. 'Sounds good when you say it. Could you pop over and do it for me?'

'You do take prizes.' Her brother's tone held a familiar frustration. 'You let Harry walk all over you, even hit you for fuck's sake, and you do nothing. Then no sooner are you shot of him – God rest his soul – than you let your bloody stepdaughter railroad you instead. I give up. I totally give up.'

'Yeah, well, things are never as black and white as you make out. She's not in a good way . . . she's eating a weird diet and not getting up till teatime. And however bratty she is, she did love her dad.'

'So you can be incredibly sympathetic. You just don't have to let her live with you, Karen. Really, you don't.'

'No, OK, OK, I hear you. It'll only be for a short time, I'm sure. She'll get bored to death down here, away from all her friends.'

'And where is she going to live, now she's rented out her flat?'

'Oh, I don't know. I'm sure she'll find someone to look after her, she usually does.' Now it was Karen's turn to be irritated with Johnny's relentless practicality. She didn't want to hear that she might be stuck with Sophie permanently.

Neither of them spoke for a moment.

'You know you'd be very welcome to come over and stay with us for a while. Have a bit of a breather. I'd love that and so would Briana.'

'Thanks . . . nice idea. I'll see how it goes.' She was grateful for the suggestion, but Johnny and Briana's household was frenetic, high-octane, run within an inch of its life. All three boys, in their teens now, played at least one musical instrument; Mason, their eldest, was an ice hockey star; Blake a potential Olympic swimmer; Jakey academically two years ahead at school. Added to which, the kids had to do an onerous amount of chores around the house – marked out on a strict weekly rota. Briana, who called herself a 'homemaker', also made it a matter of pride to schedule what she called 'Fun Time', which was as mandatory as the chores and the schoolwork and the various practice times. But the 'fun' was always improving in some way and never included chilling in front of the television. So the poor boys – as Karen saw them – barely had time to breathe, let alone slob about being grumpy teenagers or hanging out with their mates.

'Seriously, think about it . . .' He paused. 'But aside from the step-daughter issue, you're OK, are you? Not too depressed.'

'I'm not great, if I'm honest . . .' She hadn't told her brother about what had happened with Harry, and didn't intend to. She knew he'd be judgemental about her husband, as usual – and worse, he'd try to solve the problem. She didn't need a solution, she needed to stop feeling guilty, or at least come to terms with her guilt. That was why she had given in so easily to Sophie's black-mailing. Guilt. 'And please, don't tell me it'll "take time",' she added.

'I wasn't going to.' She heard him chuckle. 'Although I'm sure it will.'

'Shut up.'

'But hey, bright side, sis . . . you were going to leave him and now you don't have to. You've got money to live on and a house, once you've got rid of you-know-who. You can begin to have the life you want at last.'

'I know. It's good.'

'It *is* good,' he echoed, resolutely ignoring her gloomy tone.

'OK . . . well, I'd better go, I suppose. I'm meeting the vicar for a walk.'

'The *vicar*? Gracious, don't tell me Harry's death has brought about a miraculous conversion.'

'Ha. Definitely not. But he's been kind. We talk and it helps.'

They said goodbye, Johnny now fixated on Karen coming over to Toronto to stay with the family.

'Shall we sit for a minute?' William asked, indicating a bench along the path that offered a peaceful vista across the high downland, towards the distant hills. This was the fourth walk they'd had together since that talk at her kitchen table a few weeks ago, and Karen had really begun to look forward to seeing him. As they strode side by side through the Sussex countryside, they talked about Harry a lot, and Karen's guilt, but also about wider issues around relationships and addiction, about loneliness and loss. William seemed so easy to talk to, she felt she could tell him anything and not be judged.

The old, bleached wooden bench, greened in places with a patina of moss, was rickety and damp from the rain during the night. Karen pulled her brown parka under her bottom before they sat. She took a long breath. March had been warmer than usual and this morning the sun was almost hot on her face. It felt so good. Up here she could forget.

Neither of them said anything for a while. She knew she didn't have to speak, to make conversation with William.

'This is heaven,' Will said, unzipping his black North Face jacket.

Karen grinned. 'Odd use of the word from a man of the Church.'

'Heaven on earth,' he corrected. 'But I'm not *just* a "man of the Church" as you put it. I'm quite normal underneath.'

'Hmm . . . not sure being a vicar *is* very normal these days, when virtually no one under ninety goes to church. You're an endangered species.'

He laughed. 'Not quite true, but I wasn't always a vicar. I started out in advertising . . . a copywriter.'

'A *copywriter*?'

'Is that so odd?'

She thought about it. 'I suppose not . . . you sort of assume vicars start their life as vicars, dedicated to being good, not making up dodgy copy for toothpaste commercials and the like. But then you do archery, which seems incongruous too.'

'I think you've got a bit of a Jane Austen view of vicars, Karen. My grandmother taught me to shoot, which you'll probably find peculiar too.'

Karen laughed and nodded.

'My mother died when I was born and Dodie, my grandmother, brought me up. She was a keen archer, won tournaments and all sorts. We spent hours and hours in the orchard practising. I think she was worried I would be too namby-pamby, not having a father around very much.'

'Where was your father?'

'He was a biochemist, worked for ICI, and spent a lot of time travelling, mostly India. Dodie came to live with us after my mother died, and Dad used to come and go – more go than come.'

'That's really sad, not having a mother . . . or much of a father. So you have no memory at all of your mum?'

William's face went very still for a moment.

'Only photographs. But I thought of Dodie as both a mother and a father, I suppose. She was an incredible woman.' His expression softened as he remembered. 'So strong, a feminist before feminism really got started.'

Karen was silent as she imagined William as a small boy, bow in hand, alongside this Valkyrie-type grandmother, surrounded by apple trees. *What a strange upbringing*, she thought.

'And Janey married an advertising man . . .' the vicar was saying.

Karen wasn't sure what to make of this comment, and waited for him to go on, but he didn't.

'So why did you switch to the Church? I mean that's an enormous leap.'

For a moment William didn't answer. 'I just . . . I wanted something more.' His eyes lit up. 'This is such a shitty world, and most of us just accept it as shitty. Advertising seems to epitomize all that is wrong with it. I spent my days thinking up manipulative ways to make people buy things they didn't really need and might not be able to afford.' He laughed. 'Don't get me wrong, it was huge fun, but it left a bad taste in my mouth after a while.'

'Still, you could have just volunteered at weekends or something – you hear of bankers doing that to assuage their conscience.'

'I could have . . . it wasn't a moment of epiphany or anything, just a slow realization that became too painful to ignore. But in the end my work just felt wrong. And then I met this extraordinary man, the vicar at our church, and he seemed to have some answers.'

'So you were already religious.'

'I've always believed in God. Dodie insisted on it!'

'So has it ever wavered . . . your faith in God and heaven and all of it?'

He shot her a rueful grin. 'Only almost every week. But it's mostly the Church I question – its teachings, I mean – never God himself.'

'It must be wonderful to be so certain.'

'It is . . .' He glanced sideways at her.

'But?'

'But . . . there's also a responsibility. Trying all the time to live up to God's ideals.'

'I'm sure you do,' she said.

'Oh no. I definitely don't.'

She laughed. 'Well, if you don't, then what chance do the rest of us stand?'

He didn't respond for a minute and his face wore a fleeting frown. 'Yes, but that's the thing, Karen. I wear this collar and do good works and stand at the pulpit delivering sermons about how we should all behave . . . and everyone thinks that makes me a good man.' He sighed. 'Believe me, it doesn't.'

Surprised at the sudden gloom in his tone, she said, 'Come on, Will. You may not be perfect, but at least you try.'

The silence this time was not peaceful. The vicar's unease was almost palpable.

'This thing we do,' she said, 'where you talk to me about my problems . . . well, it cuts both ways. You can tell me stuff too, you know.'

'I . . . thanks . . . thanks for that, Karen. But I'm OK, nothing to discuss.

'That's what I said before and you told me it never worked, bottling up your feelings.' She thought of his solitary childhood, and understood why William might choose to keep things to himself.

He went silent and for a moment she thought he was going to confide in her.

'No, well . . .' he began, but then he gave her his cheery vicar smile and got up.

'Shall we get on?'

Karen nodded, looking around for Largo just as he bounded out of a clump of bushes. She was intrigued that the reverend might hold a secret too dark for normal disclosure. But over the past weeks she'd become used to that contradiction in William – the wholehearted enthusiast vying with the troubled alter ego always hovering behind his light eyes.

'So tell me, how's it going with Sophie?' As they set off along the path, William disappeared once more behind the safe shield of the counselling role.

'It's fine. Not *fine*. Awkward. Annoying. I don't know.'

He didn't reply.

'If one of us was actually doing something, instead of just hanging about all day, it might be easier.'

'Well, there's always plenty to do volunteering, if either of you fancy that.'

'Church things?'

'Don't worry, I'm not trying to drag you in by the back door.' He laughed. 'Although perhaps you're right not to trust me on this.'

'Oh, don't bring that up again! I was stupid to be paranoid about you before. It's just Harry went on and on for years about me "turning to God". Much good it did him.'

William turned to her. 'I wish I'd been able to help him.'

'Sorry, I really didn't mean to cast aspersions on your god. Or on you, for that matter. You've been my saviour these last few weeks. I don't know how I would have coped without you.'

For a moment they just stood still in the March sunshine, looking at each other. She wanted to smile, but a smile wouldn't come. She felt as she did when they sat in silence sometimes, a sort of odd absorption in William's presence. As if there were an open channel between them, connecting them, bringing calm to her scratchy, guilt-ridden soul. But this time, as her eyes met his, there was no calm, just a sudden fluttering around her heart. She saw him blink rapidly and take a short breath, turning quickly away.

They walked on, the vicar increasing the pace, Karen almost running to keep up as they descended the hill that led to the village in silence. It wasn't till they reached the drive of her house that either of them spoke, and then Will's voice had taken on a more formal note.

'I . . . let me know if you or Sophie are interested in voluntary work. There's so much – visiting people who can't get out, helping at the new lunch club or community centre, charity shops – the list is endless.'

'I'll suggest it to her.'

'Right, well, thanks for the walk.'

'Yes . . . thanks.'

'Talk soon.'

'Bye.'

She walked up to the house, the dog pottering along behind, lost in thought. *What just happened there?* she asked herself, feeling oddly confused.

'Karen.' A voice from the street brought her back to reality.

She turned to see Patrick Gascoigne, her next-door neighbour, making his way across the gravel drive. Although a weekender – his home was a flat in Covent Garden, which he shared with his Turkish partner, Volkan – his family had owned the cottage for generations, and he was more of a fixture in the village than most of the full-time residents.

'Patrick!' She was pleased to see him. A successful character actor, now in his sixties – his CV included everything from television to film to theatre – he had an ebullient spirit, a seemingly unquenchable 'can-do' approach to life.

As he reached her, he bent down and gave Largo a friendly pat, rubbing his ears with both his hands, sending the dog into a frenzy of welcome.

'Darling one.' He straightened up, focusing on Karen. 'How's it going?'

'Oh, you know.'

'Well, mercifully, I don't.' His round, always tanned face, framed by a greying tonsure on his balding head, held kind brown eyes that peered at her intently now. 'Is it hell, darling?'

She laughed, relieved by his direct approach.

'Not really "hell" exactly.'

'What, then? Tell me.'

'It's . . . sort of empty . . . sad more than hellish. I . . . I feel lost, I suppose.'

Tears sprang to Patrick's eyes. 'Oh, darling, that's so horrid. Come here for a hug.' He squeezed her in a long bear hug, his plump body enveloping her, so comforting. Karen didn't want it to stop.

'Now,' Patrick said, when he'd finally released her. 'You need some fun. Which was why I wanted to talk to you.' He pushed his hands into the jacket pockets of his antique green Barbour and gave her an eager grin. 'It's Volkan's fiftieth next week. We've got endless jamborees in town, but I thought I'd do a spontaneous little supper party at the cottage as well. He loves it here.' Volkan, who did something in IT that Karen had never properly fathomed, was as quiet as Patrick was boisterous, but they'd been together for nearly twenty-five years and seemed utterly devoted.

'That's a great idea.'

'Saturday week. Are you free?'

'Wouldn't miss it. Can I bring Sophie?'

'Of course you can, my dear. She's staying for a while?'

'Looks like it.' Karen glanced at the house, not knowing if her stepdaughter could hear them. Patrick, quick to notice her expression, raised his eyebrows and she gave a small frown to imply she couldn't say any more.

'Oops,' he winked. 'Another time,' he added in a whisper. 'I'm down from Thursday next week, organizing things, so pop over and we can have a chat then.'

'Will do. And if you want any help with the party . . .'

Patrick's parties were always riotous, drunken affairs, accompanied by mounds of delicious food cooked entirely by himself.

'That's so sweet. I may take you up on that.'

Karen's heart was lighter for seeing Patrick, and she unlocked the door with a smile on her face.

Sophie was lying on the sofa in the sitting room, gazing at her phone. As far as Karen could make out, she seldom did anything else. When her stepmother came in, she swung her feet off the sofa and sat up.

'Hi . . . where have you been?'

'I went for a walk on the Downs.'

'With Maggie?'

'No . . . with William Haskell.'

Sophie's face took on a sly expression. 'Ah, the sexy vicar again. I must say, he's very attentive. You'd think he'd be rushed off his feet with his real parishioners.' She threw her phone down on the blue cushion. 'God, I'm bored. Who were you talking to outside?'

'Patrick. He's having a party for Volkan's fiftieth, Saturday week. You're invited.'

Sophie groaned. 'Thrilling. I might invent a reason to go up to town that weekend.'

'Well, let me know so I can tell Patrick.' She turned to go. 'I'm making myself some lunch, do you want a drink or something?'

Sophie got to her feet. 'No, thanks.' But she followed Karen into the kitchen and sat at the table, watching Karen make toast, take the hummus out of the fridge, slice a tomato, lift the chamomile tea bag out of the cup, squeeze it over the sink and put it in the bin.

Karen took her plate and cup over to the table and sat opposite Sophie. As she ate she began to feel self-conscious. Her stepdaughter had an odd way of staring but not really focusing, so those dark eyes were upon her, but Karen wasn't sure if Sophie was actually watching.

'How are things?' she asked, to fill the silence.

Sophie shrugged. 'Pretty shit.'

'If you're bored, the vicar says there are lots of volunteering opportunities around. Maybe you should talk to him.'

'*Perleese.*' She rolled her eyes. 'I can't think of anything worse than hanging around a smelly charity shop or handing out soup to homeless people.'

'That's a bit mean of you.'

'Yeah, well . . . I don't see you lining up to do it either.'

Which was true, but Karen was at least considering it.

'Have you thought about what you might do . . . work-wise?'

Karen knew this was a dangerous subject and steeled herself for some invective. But Sophie just sighed.

'No one'll ever give me a job. I'm fit for nothing.'

'Oh, come on. That's ridiculous.'

'Really? Well, you tell me. What exactly am I qualified for?'

Karen did a quick mental trawl through her stepdaughter's CV and knew there was a problem. Her hesitation was noted.

'See? There isn't anything, is there?'

'Maybe you should train for something.'

'I can't *afford* to!' Sophie snapped.

'No, OK . . .' Karen didn't know what to say. No University degree, no consistency or focus on anything but random entrepreneurial ventures, which hadn't worked out. She felt a shard of panic in her gut. Would Sophie ever leave?

She looked up to see tears forming in the girl's eyes. Reaching over to lay a hand on Sophie's arm, she was surprised when she wasn't rebuffed.

'I miss Daddy so much,' Sophie said. 'I still can't believe he's gone and I'll never see him again.'

'I know . . .'

'Do you?' The girl wasn't being aggressive, her frown was simply questioning. 'You seem to be fine. I haven't seen you shed a single tear since he died.'

Sophie was right. Karen had barely cried, except in front of William. It was surprisingly easy to cry with him. She wasn't even sure if she was really grieving. Harry had left a very big void in her life, certainly. But was she really missing *him*, or the fact of him? She didn't know. Feeling so leadenly sad and lost seemed as much to do with an inability to decide what she should do next as a genuine bereavement.

'I have cried.'

'Not in front of me.'

Karen didn't answer, she could see Sophie was spoiling for a fight.

'Did you even love Daddy any more?' The girl suddenly leant forward across the table, her dark eyes boring into her stepmother.

Karen, who had never been a person who blushed, suddenly found her cheeks reddening.

Sophie's eyes widened with shock. 'Oh, my God, you didn't, did you? You didn't love him.'

Karen swallowed. Pretence no longer felt like an option. 'I did love your father, very much. But for the last few years he's been drunk most of the time . . . I mean really drunk. And nasty—'

' "Nasty"? What do you mean, "nasty"?'

'I mean cruel, Sophie. You didn't see it – and he would hate me saying this to you – but your dad could be very cruel when he was drunk. I don't think he meant it, but still, it was hard to cope with, day in, day out.'

Sophie was shaking her head in disbelief.

'That's crap and you know it. You're just making excuses. I saw the way he treated you. He totally adored you . . . although personally I never knew why.' She paused, still shaking her head. 'Was it just the money, then? Was that why you married him?'

'Don't be ridiculous. I adored him too. But since he sold the company it's been so different. All he did was booze. Ask his friends at the club. I literally had to pick him up and carry him to the car most days, he was so drunk. And when he'd had too much, he took it out on me.'

As she watched her stepdaughter's bewildered expression, Karen immediately regretted her words. She felt horribly disloyal to

Harry. *He was drunk for three years, loving for fifteen*, she told herself. *I'm not being fair.* And there was no need for Sophie to know the grim details of her father's behaviour, it could only cause the girl pain, and Karen had vowed to herself not to say anything. But she felt she'd been goaded.

'You're such a bitch,' Sophie said quietly, getting up and standing, arms crossed, staring defiantly at Karen. 'Unbelievable. You're totally unbelievable. How dare you slag Daddy off like this when he's barely dead and can't defend himself. I don't believe he was ever remotely cruel to you.' She turned to go, then clearly changed her mind. 'If anything, *you* were the one who was cruel to him. Daddy would never have drunk so much if he'd been happy. I said it before and I'll say it again: you killed him.'

It was on the tip of Karen's tongue to tell Sophie that Harry had hit her. But she restrained herself. Her stepdaughter wouldn't believe that either. She knew by telling her she would only be trying to justify what Sophie had managed to intuit, that she did no longer love Harry – not in the way she had. She felt sorry for the girl now, clearly lost in so many ways, but she didn't see how she could help her.

Nonetheless, as Sophie reached the kitchen door, Karen called out, 'Please, Sophie. Come back. We've got to talk about this . . .'

But her stepdaughter kept going and didn't bother to reply.

CHAPTER SIX

'If you could start laying the table for me, darling . . .' Patrick, swathed in a pristine red apron with a round, sweating face to match, wiped his forehead with the back of his hand and took a long breath as he surveyed the chaos around him. The small kitchen was almost buried in vegetable peelings, jam jars with herbs of every kind sprouting from the neck, bottles of oil, cut lemons, an opened packet of butter, chopping board and knife, rolling pin, cream-clogged balloon whisk and bowl, frying pan with sautéed mushrooms and onions, roasting tin holding a large fillet of beef covered in a tea towel, two round, cling-filmed lumps of pastry, watercress soup in a Pyrex bowl waiting to be liquidized, a tray cooling with sweet, peaked, coffee-coloured meringues next to stacked punnets of strawberries and blueberries. And everywhere were dabs and spills and smears and dollops. Patrick was not the sort of cook to clear up as he went along.

'Getting there,' he said, with a grin of satisfaction.

Karen wasn't sure if he was being ironic or not, so she just nodded encouragingly and collected the pile of large, white china plates, polished silver cutlery and starched linen napkins from the side. There were eleven people coming – more than enough for the small dining room – Sophie having cancelled at the last minute and huffed off to London. Things had gone from bad to worse since the day Sophie had confronted Karen. They had barely spoken and, when they did, her stepdaughter was unresponsive and cold. Karen despaired of making peace now, and just wished the girl gone. She had even, fleetingly, considered paying her money to go – and would have, if she hadn't realized that it would be a bottomless pit.

Patrick was waving towards the corner by the window. 'We're having proper *placement*. I can't bear people choosing who they sit next to, it's so safe. The list's over there, underneath my mobile.'

'Who have I got?' Karen asked.

'Well . . . me, of course, darling. And Raki's on your other side. I didn't think you'd want a challenge so soon after poor dear Harry's death.'

'Thanks, that's perfect.' She went to get the list and read the names, all ones she knew, including Maggie and Rakesh, Tom Bridges – the doctor – and his wife, the Haskells and two gay friends of Patrick and Volkan's who had just bought a weekend cottage on the other side of the village. Despite Patrick's thoughtfulness on her behalf, there was no one there she might find difficult to talk to. The only one she was nervous of, suddenly, was William. But she told herself she had imagined the look that passed between them on the path, that her present emotional turmoil was responsible.

Champagne flowed right from the start that night. Patrick was resplendent in tartan trousers, velvet slippers and a collarless white shirt with turquoise stud buttons, Volkan's dark good looks set off by a light-blue, button-down shirt, tapered black trousers and black suede Tod's loafers.

Karen hadn't needed to be smart in months, and the process of choosing what to wear was made worse because all her dresses reminded her of Harry. He'd taken a keen interest in her clothes in the past, and they'd spent many a happy hour in the foreign cities they visited, trawling the designer stores. Karen had never been that bothered about what she wore – she was self-conscious about her slightly plump figure – but Harry loved to see her in a beautiful dress, and he persuaded her to try things that if she'd been on her own she would have out-and-out rejected. Tonight, knowing Patrick loved glamour, she'd finally decided on a sleeveless, electric-blue stretch crêpe dress with a pretty flared skirt that her husband had bought her in Italy six years ago. She hadn't worn it much because she thought it showed up her bulges, but since Harry's death she'd lost quite a bit of weight, and the dress hung elegantly on her small frame.

'Wow, you look gorgeous,' Maggie said when she and Raki arrived.

'Not too gorgeous?' Karen suddenly felt brazen in the bright colour, and worried it might be considered unseemly in the light of her recent bereavement.

Maggie laughed. 'God, no. It's great to see you looking a bit happier.' Her friend gave her arm a squeeze. 'You've been so brave about it all.'

'Hasn't she just?' Patrick echoed, who knew nothing about it, but as usual was determinedly supportive. 'You're a complete trooper, darling. That Harry was a lucky man.'

William, who was also standing in the circle, smiled at her too, making her immediately ashamed, unable to blot her confessions to the vicar from her mind.

★

'Did Maggie tell you?' Raki asked her later, towards the end of the meal. 'That she's coming with me on my next trip?'

'No. To India, you mean?'

Raki nodded. He gave her a cautious glance. 'It's not till next month, but we'll be gone for at least a year.'

'A year? Oh, wow . . . that'll be so great for you both. Maggie didn't mention it.'

'No, well, she's only just decided to come too. But we're both a bit worried about leaving you in the lurch, what with Harry and . . . it's so soon . . .'

Rakesh could do the most complex surgery in the most difficult environments with the utmost skill, but he wasn't very fluent when it came to dealing with emotions. Since her husband's death he had treated her with kid gloves and taken to shooting her nervous glances, as if he thought she might suddenly collapse, or worse.

'I'm fine, Raki. Honestly. Really fine. You've both been such a support, but it was two and a half months ago now, and I'm getting back to normal.' She didn't believe she was anywhere close to normal, but it was easier to say that than try to explain the maelstrom of emotions in her heart.

'Are you?' He looked relieved. 'Well, if that's the case, it's very good to hear.'

'It's sweet of you to think of me. But please, don't worry.'

'No. Well . . . you can always talk to Maggie in India, anyway. It's not like these days we can't communicate twenty-four seven.'

'Exactly.' Karen got up. 'Just going to give Patrick a hand.'

She went through to the kitchen, where their host was putting together the cake amidst the chaos. The door was open on to the garden, bringing a welcome breath of cold night air. Outside in the darkness was a huddle of smokers, including Volkan, Tom's wife,

Nicole, and the two friends of her hosts that Karen hadn't met before.

'What can I do?' she asked, viewing the large mound of chopped fruit, the meringues, and the bowl of whipped cream that Patrick had in front of him.

He looked up with a harassed grin. 'All under control. Could you be a love and dig out the candles?' He wiped a handkerchief round his face. 'They're in an orange Sainsbury's bag over there somewhere . . . maybe under the chocolates?'

She found them and peeled the silver candles from the packet, placing them in a pile on the worktop next to him.

'Marvellous. Thanks, darling.'

She watched him work in silence for a minute.

'It's going well, don't you think?' Patrick whispered.

'Brilliantly, Volkan's absolutely loving it,' she said, just as William came into the room, carrying a pile of plates.

'Umm . . .' He looked around for somewhere to put them, but there wasn't an inch of space anywhere.

Patrick waved his hand in the direction of the sink. 'Just plonk them down, William. I'll see to it later.'

But Karen couldn't bear the chaos for one more minute. 'We can put them in the dishwasher.'

William and Karen stood side by side, the vicar scraping the food off the plates and running them under the tap, then handing them to Karen to stack in the machine. They didn't speak, but she was suddenly aware of his closeness and the quickening beat of her heart.

'Great party,' he said.

'Isn't it?'

As she filled up the machine, he leant across her suddenly to move up the edge of a baking tin, which had fallen across the racks, and their heads touched. Karen pulled back as if she'd been scalded.

'We can put this on the top,' he said, holding the tin and pulling out the upper rack, which was crammed full with soup bowls. For a moment they both surveyed the contents of the dishwasher.

'Or not,' Will said with a grin. His frank gaze, with those clear-water eyes, seemed to be taking in her face as if he were seeing it for the first time. 'I challenge Janey's stacking skills at my peril.'

'No . . . no, you're right. It won't work there either. We'll have to wash it separately,' she managed to say.

And then there was a stillness between them, when neither of them moved or spoke, just gazed at each other. It may only have lasted three seconds, but it seemed like days and Karen was power-fully aware of his every breath, the blueness of his eyes, the strand of his hair that fell over his forehead.

'Do leave that, darlings,' Patrick was saying behind them. 'The saintly Mrs J arrives at dawn tomorrow to sort it all out.'

But Karen and William just continued with their task. Her heart was racing, her cheeks probably flushed, but she didn't want to leave his side and go back to the party.

'Ta dah!' Patrick finally demanded their attention as he held both his arms out in a flourish, the beautiful meringue cake resplendent in front of him, waiting for their approval.

'William tells me you and Sophie might be up for some volunteering?'

The soup, beef Wellington, green salad, cheese, fruit and cake had all been eaten, some impromptu speeches had been made eulogizing Volkan, and a lot more wine had been drunk. The guests were now shifting seats and milling about in groups. Janey had squeezed in next to Karen, where Raki — who had just left with Maggie — had been sitting.

'Uh . . .'

'That would be brilliant. There are so many pensioners who just need someone to pop in and make a cuppa, have a bit of a chat. Or maybe you could teach somebody about emails and stuff — you used to work in an office, didn't you? The Internet is such a great connector, if only older people could manage it.'

On she went, her bright, rather bullying delivery implying a deliberate attempt at zeal rather than zeal itself. Karen zoned out, still horribly aware of Janey's husband, feet away, in an animated discussion with Volkan.

'I find it takes you out of yourself, volunteering.' Janey was still talking. 'You forget your own problems when you help other people. It's been scientifically proven.' She seemed to be persuading herself as much as Karen.

'I'm sure it has,' Karen finally summoned up the manners to reply. She had drunk too much, she knew that. When Harry had been alive, she had almost given up alcohol altogether, terrified that if she joined in it would only encourage him, although it made no difference whatsoever. 'Um . . . gosh, it's late. I'm exhausted. I think I'd better be getting home. What a great party.' She added.

The vicar's wife looked disappointed. 'Yes, we ought to get back too, I suppose. It's William's busiest day tomorrow, of course.' She got up, smoothing her black skirt over her thin hips. 'About the volunteering . . . give me a call and we can work something out. It might be just what you need right now, a focus . . .' She must have seen Karen's blank expression, because her wittering ground to a halt as she bent forward to give her cheek a peck.

When William came to say goodbye, Karen held her breath, but he merely smiled and laid a hand on her arm for a split second before moving off to Patrick.

The following morning Karen was restless. She'd been looking forward to having the place to herself for a change, without the lurking presence of a grumpy stepdaughter. But as it was, she couldn't settle to anything. Roaming from room to room, she tried to make sense of these feelings she had for William Haskell. She had a crush on him, that much was clear, but identifying that didn't seem to make things any simpler. *Does he feel the same?* she wondered. *Or were those intense stares of his merely him trying to work out what was wrong with me?* He was obviously an intense sort of person, and maybe his look last night had been quite normal for him. She was annoyed that she was even asking herself these questions. *He's the vicar, for God's sake,* she told herself, then smiled at her choice of words. *And married with a daughter to boot.* Whatever she felt for him, she knew it had to stop right there.

To distract herself, Karen thought she'd begin to check through Harry's clothes in the large walk-in cupboard off the bedroom, with a view to packing them away. She wasn't sure when she was supposed to do this. She knew that when her mother had died, her father had cleaned out the cupboards a week after the funeral, leaving anything he couldn't decide about in a black plastic bin liner in the spare room for Karen and Johnny – then twenty-two and nineteen respectively – to sift through the next time they came home. But her father had already left Gloria for tea-shop Joan by then, so perhaps that was different? Maggie said that her mother still refused to move a single item of her father's things four years after his death, despite endless encouragement.

Karen herself hadn't opened Harry's side of the wardrobe since he died, and now she did it almost absent-mindedly, her thoughts still fixed on her childish crush. But the lingering smell of her husband's aftershave, the sight of the rows of pristine shirts – Karen hated ironing, so she sent them to the dry cleaners – the tailored suits in every fabric from heavy tweed to summer linen, the racks of shoes, all polished by Harry himself, made her gasp, almost lose her breath. It was as if, suddenly, he weren't dead, as if his essence were still there, live in the wardrobe, waiting to choose an outfit for the day. She gently brushed her hand across the soft cotton of his shirts, remembered laying her cheek against them, against his broad chest, in happier times. But his shoes were the thing that made her cry. Strangely so evocative of the man she had loved, she cradled one shoe of an ancient pair of shiny brown brogues in her hand – favourites of his – and wept.

'I wanted to talk to you,' Karen said to her stepdaughter later that week, catching her as she came downstairs around ten in the morning.

Sophie seemed to have had a good time in London and was marginally more upbeat since her return. She paused on the bottom stair, her hand on the round wooden finial at the base of the banisters, eyeing her stepmother with her usual wariness.

'What about?'

'Shall I make some tea?'

This was a safer suggestion than it might have been a month ago, because the raw-food diet previously obsessing the girl had been quietly dropped, no explanation given and none requested from Karen, who was just relieved that Sophie wasn't starving herself any more.

'OK.'

When the tea was on the table, Karen went on, 'I know it's a sensitive subject, but I think it's time we began to clear out your father's things. I'd love it if you'd help me.'

'Clear out Dad's things? Now?'

'Well, not now, as in today . . . but we can't leave them forever . . . it's too weird.'

'I like his things,' came the stubborn reply, 'they remind me of him.'

Expecting this reaction, Karen was patient. 'I know, and I understand that. But he's . . . well, he's not here any more, and at some stage we'll have to sort them out . . . his clothes and stuff. I mean they could be useful to someone else. Someone who really needs them.'

Sophie's eyes widened. 'Give his clothes away? You can't do that. It's horrible thinking of some random guy walking around in Daddy's suits.'

'I know, but it seems a shame to just throw them in the bin. He had some beautiful clothes, Sophie, they deserve a good home.'

But her stepdaughter was shaking her head in that familiar gesture which implied that Karen was predictably beyond the pale.

'But it's way too early, he's only just died.'

'It's nearly three months.'

Sophie looked miserable. 'That's no time. God, I wish he was still here. It's so unfair.'

'I know,' Karen said, and was allowed to stroke the girl's hand across the table.

There was silence.

'OK . . . OK.'

'You'll help me, then?'

'Yeah, OK. But you have to let me keep things. We can't throw all his stuff away.'

Karen breathed a sigh of relief. Not just because she'd negotiated the tricky subject without a blow-up from her stepdaughter, but because she'd sensed a softening of Sophie's attitude, just slightly, in recent days.

As if she were finally growing tired of fighting with Karen.

It was almost two weeks after Patrick's party before she spoke to William again. When Karen saw his name on her phone, she almost didn't answer. He was clearly avoiding her, and she him, but she supposed at some stage they would have to speak – village life would inevitably throw them together. In the intervening days since the party, some mad part of her had run through the scenario where she asked him on another walk and then confronted him with her secret: 'The truth is, William, I've got a huge crush on you and as a result I don't think we should see each other again.'

But then she would have to stop seeing him. And while she knew that was the right thing to do, it wasn't what she wanted to do.

'Karen, hi,' his voice greeted her. 'How are you?'

'I'm alright, thanks.'

'Good, good.' Pause. 'Umm . . . I'm calling about the fête.'

'Oh, God, the fête. I'd forgotten about the fête.'

'Would we be able to meet for a discussion sometime?' His tone was businesslike. He sounded as if he were walking somewhere, his breathing fast in the background.

'Sure. When did you have in mind?'

'Well, I'm caught up in something at the moment, but I'll be back around five. Could I drop by then?'

'Yes, OK. See you then.'

As she clicked her mobile off, she realized her own breath was short in her chest. *The bloody fête.* Always held in their garden by Harry's insistence, it was a nightmare to organize and took up weeks of every summer with interminable committee meetings where people wittered on about nothing for hours on end and nothing ever got agreed. And in the end there was really nothing to agree. It was always held in the same place on the same date – the last Saturday in August – the stalls were pretty much the same from year to year, run by pretty much the same people, the small sum raised almost identical.

But that didn't prevent petty squabbles, long-standing jealousies and rivalries, snobbishness and competition getting their yearly airing in the community. And although the cause – renovation of the Norman bell tower on the church – was so far from being funded that the money was neither here nor there, the inhabitants of the village and the villages around all looked forward to the event with a curiously old-fashioned spirit. Except Karen, that is, whose lawn was chewed to ribbons, plants trampled, gravel strewn far and wide, and whose house was littered with vast tea urns, crates of tea cups and saucers, tombola prizes, waterproof fold-down canopies, second-hand books and pots of marmalade for weeks before the day – and weeks after, indeed. Even more annoyingly, Harry, who was usually a stickler for domestic order, had seemed to take an odd delight in the temporary chaos.

I don't have to do it again, she thought with a wave of relief as she waited for the vicar. And maybe he wasn't even expecting her to, now that Harry was gone. But at least it gave her an opportunity to see William again and check out if her feelings for him had just been silly imaginings.

She was in the garden when he arrived, half an hour early, clearing out the leaves and dead growth from the border beside the drive with a rake. It was a beautiful afternoon, the spring air still chilly but so clean and tangy with the scent of renewal from plants, trees and flowers just coming into bud. Spring was her favourite time of year. She stopped when she saw him, leaning on her rake, breathless from her exertions. They smiled at each other, both, she thought, revelling in the outdoors after months of winter.

'Gorgeous, isn't it?' she said, propping the rake up against the bricks of the house.

'Miraculous, spring is miraculous, don't you think?'

They stood together, gazing around them in silence for a moment.

'Every year we expect it, but there are no guarantees that Nature will do what she did last year. Then there it is again, the pale-pink apple blossom, the carpets of bluebells, that soft yellow of the primroses . . .'

Karen laughed. 'You've got it bad.'

'I know, I know. I don't care. I just love how happy it makes me feel. My grandmother used to chart each little bud, the first crocuses, the baby birds in the nests . . . it all went into these small black sketchbooks held together with elastic. And she'd do little green ink drawings alongside all the dates. I've still got them, they're beautiful . . . I'll show you one day—' He stopped and she saw him clamp his lips together, as if stopping more words from escaping, his eyes darting away from hers.

And she knew why. It was an oddly intimate moment, the desire to share something that was obviously so precious to him.

'I'll get some tea and we can sit on the bench round by the house. It'll probably be wet, but we're used to that.'

For a while, mugs of tea in hand, they said nothing. It was what they did best. Then Karen heard Will give a small sigh.

'I suppose we'd better talk about the fête.'

'Must we?'

He looked across at her, his eyes full of laughter. 'Grim, I know.'

'At least it's not in your garden.'

'No, and that's the point. I don't think anyone expects you to host the fête this year, Karen, not so soon after Harry's death. So I'm offering you a get-out-of-jail-free card.'

'Really? I can say no?'

'Of course.' Then his face took on a crafty look. 'Although it would be great if you still felt able, in Harry's name . . . perhaps as a memorial to him—' He stopped and grinned. 'That was a joke. I am assuming you'll back out. And so are all the other committee members. I just thought I'd better confirm one way or the other.'

Karen didn't have to think too hard to come to her decision. It would be a nightmare, as usual, and further down the line she would no doubt curse herself for making that choice, but it would mean she could legitimately spend the summer having regular contact with William Haskell, and that was compensation enough.

'No, I'll do it.'

His face lit up. 'You will?'

She laughed. 'Yes, I will. Why not?'

'Well, lots of reasons spring to mind, but perhaps I won't mention them just now. Are you sure? You haven't thought about it very long. I could come back tomorrow when you've had a chance to talk it over with Sophie.'

'It's got nothing to do with Sophie, she might not even be here by then. I've said, I'll do it. Harry would most certainly have wanted me to.'

'Yes, but this is your decision, Karen. Harry's not here.'

'No . . . although sometimes it seems as if he is.' She was thinking of the previous night, when she'd dreamt she'd woken to find him beside her in bed, cold and pale but still alive. But as she looked more closely, she realized it wasn't really him but a complete stranger, which was even more disconcerting. Now, in the warm spring sunshine, the image still haunted her. She told William.

'Sounds like you're making the transition from him being actually alive to him only being alive in your memory and inner life. I think it's quite normal when someone's only been dead a short while.'

She didn't understand what he was saying. 'But it wasn't actually him, it was a stranger.'

'Must have been really frightening,' Will said.

'It was. And creepy.'

'Guilt messes with your mind, Karen,' he said after a long pause. 'Maybe it's time you forgave yourself.'

'Easier said than done.'

The vicar skewed round on the bench until he was looking at her directly, laying his empty tea mug on the bench between them. She noticed he had beautiful hands – square-palmed, with long fingers – they looked strong, as they must be to pull a bow.

'Harry killed himself, Karen. Not deliberately, but through the drink. I'm not blaming him, he obviously wasn't capable of doing anything different at the time – which is so sad – but whether you went to him or not when he called is immaterial. If it wasn't that night it would probably have been another one very soon.'

Karen took a deep breath. 'It's not so much that he died – although obviously it is, of course – it's that I knew he was in real distress and I deliberately ignored it. Even if he hadn't died, that's such a horrible thing to do to anyone, let alone your husband.'

The vicar frowned as he considered what she'd said. 'OK . . . I think you're being wise after the event here. You're looking back and deciding you *did* know that his cry sounded different from usual, because a part of you had had enough and *had* stopped caring. But that's the guilt speaking. At the time you were just reacting to the way he'd been treating you.'

'Yes . . . what you say is logical, and if anyone else was telling me the story I probably wouldn't blame them. So why can't I get it out of my head?'

'It's not very long since it all happened.'

'I know that. Although it seems like a decade.'

'Well, "time heals" didn't get to be a cliché without being true first.'

She nodded, knowing he was right, but his sympathetic gaze was suddenly too much for her and tears pricked behind her eyes.

'I'm just so sick of feeling like a bad person, William. Bad for what I did to Harry, bad for not liking Sophie more, bad for doing sod all with my life.'

William began to chuckle. 'Whoa, that really is *so* bad! But hold on a minute. You're kind to animals – I'm sure Largo would back me up – and now you've agreed to have the fête here, that's got to mean a shedload of brownie points in wherever you're stashing them.'

'Don't tease.'

'I'm sorry . . .' William put his hand over hers, holding it against the warm wood of the bench.

Neither of them noticed Maggie's head popping round the side of the house.

'Yoo-hoo, Karen!' she called, coming into full view.

William and Karen shot guiltily apart, the vicar getting up and knocking his mug over in the process, then bending to retrieve it from the grass, face burning.

'Maggie . . .' Karen got up too.

'Thought I heard voices . . . the front door was open,' Maggie said, a slightly fixed grin on her face as she glanced from one to the other.

'Karen has very kindly agreed to have the fête here again this year,' William said. 'I came over to tell her she didn't have to, but she insisted.'

'Great, that'll be a big relief for everyone.'

'It certainly will be. But you talk to her. She might have just agreed out of politeness.'

'Unlikely,' Maggie replied with asperity. 'You of all people should know, Karen isn't given to being polite meaninglessly.'

She was obviously remembering the time on the Downs when Karen had been short with William, but the vicar looked bewildered.

'Umm, yes . . . I mean . . . I hadn't noticed . . .' He gave up, not looking at either woman. 'I'd better run.' Now he did address Karen. 'I won't tell the committee till the morning, in case you change your mind.'

'It's OK,' she replied. 'You can tell them now. I won't change my mind.'

When he'd gone, his footsteps safely dying away down the path towards his house, Maggie turned to her friend.

Her expression was stony. 'What were you two doing?'

Karen sat down hard on the bench. 'Nothing. We weren't doing anything. I was upset about Harry and he was comforting me.'

'Hmm . . . you don't look upset.'

'Not now, but I was.'

Maggie clearly didn't know whether to believe her or not. 'I thought you said you didn't like William and you were sick of him hanging around.'

'I was, but actually he's been great. I told you, we've had a few walks together and he's talked me through stuff about Harry . . . he's really helped.'

Maggie was still eyeing her suspiciously. 'If you say so.'

'Stop staring at me like that.'

'Well, it didn't look as if he was just "comforting" you.'

'What do you mean?'

Her friend gave her a look of mock surprise. 'You don't know?'

Karen didn't reply, just sat there, her mouth twisting with discomfort at Maggie's grilling. She did know, of course. But she found it was impossible to be with William and maintain normal barriers. They just had this instant, joyous ease with each other, which was hard to hide . . . hard because it was so unconscious.

Maggie plonked herself down next to Karen on the bench. 'OK. I'll believe it was all perfectly innocent if you look me in the eye and tell me it was.'

Which Karen couldn't do, of course.

Maggie leant forward, frowning. 'Karen?'

'He wasn't holding my hand, he just put his hand over mine as a comfort thing. Really. But you're right, I'm afraid, I do have feelings for him—'

'God, Karen!' Maggie interrupted, but Karen held her hand up.

'It's nothing, honestly. Just a stupid crush. He's been so good to me, Maggie, listening endlessly while I pour my heart out. I'm sure it's just a mad reaction to Harry's death and everything . . . I'm definitely not myself. But I promise you, Will's done absolutely nothing wrong. He certainly doesn't have the slightest interest in me, he's just doing his job.'

There was silence while Maggie digested this.

'Does he know how you feel?'

'NO, and I wouldn't dream of telling him.'

Maggie shook her head. 'Bloody hell, Karen, he's a vicar. If he was caught up in any sort of scandal it'd be curtains for his whole career, not to mention his family.'

'For heaven's sake! William's not caught up in anything. You're making a drama out of nothing. Please, can you drop it? I'll get over it soon, I'm sure. It's just been such a strange time.'

Karen saw her friend's face lighten a little. 'Please . . .'

'OK.' Maggie's tone was grudging. Then she put her arm through Karen's and gave it a squeeze. 'It's probably my fault. I've had so much to do with this Indian trip coming up and having to organize all my patients to see someone else while I'm away, I've been neglecting you.'

'Rubbish. You've been great. Everyone's been great. I'm just a bit of a crazy woman right now.'

'Your husband's just died, Kar, I think you have every right to be crazy . . . not that you are. I'm just worrying that as soon as I'm on that plane and my back is turned, you'll run off with the vicar!'

They both began to laugh.

'That's so not going to happen,' Karen assured her. And wanting to change the subject as quickly as possible, she added, 'Tell me how it's going with the trip. Have you got all your jabs and stuff? You must be so excited.'

'I am excited, but sort of nervous too. Raki's family is incredibly nice, but there are so many of them: aunts, uncles, cousins – masses of cousins – small children who seem to belong to everyone. It's quite confusing . . . and exhausting.'

'I'm sure. But you won't be in Delhi for very long, will you?'

'No, and I'm looking forward to getting that leg over with. We're only spending a week with them initially, then it's on the road, and we go back for another visit later on. It'll be fine.'

'I'll miss you,' Karen said, then regretted it because her friend looked stricken.

'Oh, and I'll miss you too. I feel so bad for leaving you like this. It's such a long time.'

'Don't be daft. By the time you get back I'll be a lot less crazy – with a bit of luck – and I'll have made some decisions about my life, maybe.'

Maggie shot her a warning glance. 'Just so long as those decisions don't include our dear reverend . . .'

CHAPTER SEVEN

They sat side by side on the bed – in harmony for once – united by a scratched and cracked leather photograph album that had been on the top shelf of Harry's cupboard, full of unnamed photos from a long time ago that neither of them could identify. Sophie pointed to a particularly stern lady in a high-necked Edwardian summer dress posed with a small boy, hair smarmed down, in a sailor suit. She grinned. It was a long time since Karen had seen Sophie amused.

'That must be Dad.' She pointed to the boy.

'Can't be, he's not that old. This must have been taken early last century . . . perhaps his father, your grandfather.'

'Didn't he ever tell you?'

'No, oddly, he didn't. In fact, I've never seen this album before today.'

Sophie frowned. 'Here's a thought. Maybe it's not Dad's album at all. Maybe it belonged to the person who lived here before. It was right at the back of the shelf.' She scrabbled through the stiff pages to the flyleaf, but there was only an inscription that read: 'Holmewood Court, 1908'.

'Doesn't help much. Harry never mentioned a house called Holmewood Court.'

Her stepdaughter was laughing. 'Hilarious. Here we are, going all gooey-eyed over some random child and assuming it's Daddy when, in fact, none of these people may be anything to do with us.'

They had been attempting to clear out Harry's things, but every time Karen picked something to put in the charity box, Sophie would drag it out and claim it was impossible to get rid of. Only Harry's clothes had made the cut so far, and even they had been subject to cherry-picking by his daughter. She'd kept three of his cashmere sweaters, his Barbour, a Ralph Lauren cotton shirt. Books were happily discarded, but his shaving bowl, his alarm clock, all his pens and pads and desk furniture, his briefcase . . . the list was long.

Karen, however, insisted that if Sophie wanted to keep things, she had to pack them up and store them in one of the spare rooms. Because she was experiencing a mounting desire to remove all physical reminders of her husband from the house, hoping that by doing so she might manage to distance herself from her guilt. And in the past weeks, her nightmares had certainly lessened, perhaps as a result of her mind being taken up, to an unhealthy extent, by William Haskell.

Jennifer Simmons' drawing-room windows were open wide, the curtains billowing in what little breeze there was. But it was an unusually hot and muggy evening for April, and Karen – wedged on the over-stuffed sofa cushions between Martha Chowney and Janet Phelps, the seventy-six-year-old organist – felt a small trickle of sweat creep down her spine.

There were six people present, five had sent apologies. Jennifer, the committee chairman, was taking notes in the absence of Bernard, the self-appointed secretary, who was in Denmark at his daughter's wedding. Karen looked across at William, perched on a wobbly ladderback chair beside the chairman, his dog collar looking very constricting and uncomfortable in the heat. Since the moment, ten days ago, when Maggie had found them *tête-à-tête* on the bench, they had stopped all contact with each other. But now the fête committee was scheduled to meet once a week over the summer, they had no choice.

For Karen, this was both something she longed for, and something she dreaded. She knew, of course, that there was absolutely no future in her relationship with Will, so she'd tried to be tough with herself, tried to move past her crush. But the vicar was everywhere in the village. It seemed that each time she went out, whether to the farm shop, walking on the hills, gardening, or a trip to town, there he was, as if some unbreakable thread bound them. And people talked about him a lot, always with a certain awe. They said he was pouring every ounce of his energy into making things better for as many people as possible.

But when they bumped into each other, they were both excruciatingly polite, nothing more. *Even if he does have feelings for me*, she told herself over and over again, *which he's certainly given no indication of beyond a couple of looks and his hand over mine that day* – and that was, she was certain in retrospect, just a comfort thing, as she'd told Maggie – *he will never be in a position to follow through. So get over it, girl*. But it wasn't proving easy. Each time she saw him, even if it was with his wife and daughter – a salutary reminder of why he would never be available – her heart raised its beat, her breath became shallow. It was thrilling and thoroughly depressing and she felt pathetic, almost helpless to do anything about it.

'If we up the admission fee, then it will exclude a whole slew of people,' Martha, a tough investment banker, was saying.

'But I'm only suggesting fifty pee more. Two pounds is hardly a lot these days. I checked out other fêtes and most of them charge at least that,' Jeffrey, a retired judge, insisted.

'Well, I did too, and the ones *I* found charged maximum one pound fifty with children free.'

'I'm not saying we charge for children,' Jeffrey objected. 'But that extra fifty pence would be pretty useful against costs.'

'These fêtes can be quite expensive once you've got past the gate,' William put in. 'Especially if you've got kids clamouring for treats and toys and stuff. It's not a cheap day out.'

'Compared to one of those theme parks, it is. Even the parking in those places practically bankrupts you,' Jennifer said.

'Yes, but we're not offering nearly such a wide range of amuse-ments,' Karen said. 'I'm with Martha. I think we should keep it at the usual one pound fifty.'

Nothing is ever quick in a committee, and it was at least twenty more minutes before it was agreed not to raise the price of admiss-ion. At one point Karen caught William's eye and they both smiled.

It was nearly nine before the group broke up. The storm that had been threatening had turned the sky to the west a deep black-berry, but there was still no sign of rain as they all headed back to their separate houses. Only Karen and Will were walking, all the others having brought cars or bikes. They were silent at first as they made their way across the village, awkward at suddenly being alone.

'I thought Jeffrey would never shut up,' Karen said.

'Yes, he's like a dog with a bone. I suppose that's what made him a good judge – rigour and attention to detail.'

'You don't know he was a good judge,' she said, making him laugh.

'I suppose not. He's good at the bells, if that counts.' He gave a small sigh. 'There seems so much to do and each committee meeting only manages to address a tiny proportion of it all.'

'It'll be alright on the night, I promise you, it always is.'

'I hope so. My grandmother sometimes used to open the one in our village when there wasn't a handy local dignitary to do the honours, and it was hell.'

'Why?'

'She made me stand up on the podium next to her and hand the committee chairman a posy of flowers. And one year, as I stepped forward, I tripped over the wire to the microphone and fell flat on my face and everyone laughed. I was only seven. It's tainted my view of fêtes.'

Karen couldn't help laughing. 'Pretty traumatic for a small boy. You should have thought of that before you became a vicar.'

'I suppose. But neither of my other posts had fêtes.'

'Listen, I've done . . . how many? Eleven? Maybe more, I've lost count. It's a nightmare, but we muddle through somehow.'

Another silence.

'So how are you, Karen?' William asked softly, making her heart contract.

She took a long breath. 'Getting there.'

'I'm . . . we haven't had a chance to talk since . . . I'm so sorry . . . if you felt I overstepped the mark . . . on the bench . . .'

'I didn't, Will. Not at all.'

'Maggie looked pretty fierce.'

'Yeah . . . she thought there was something between us, that she'd seen something. But I assured her there wasn't.'

Silence.

She thought her heart might burst out of her chest as she tried to control the urge to tell him the truth. *Don't be so selfish*, she admonished, and managed somehow to hold her tongue.

But Will had stopped and was looking intently into her face. They were in a small lane, a cut-through between two rows of houses, the hedges high on either side, the light fading fast.

She held her breath.

A dog barked in a nearby garden. It was as if the air around them were physically vibrating.

'No, please, don't say it,' he begged as she began to speak.

So she didn't. But she couldn't help reaching up and holding her hand to his warm cheek. She heard his soft intake of breath as he put his own hand over hers and kept it there for what seemed like a lifetime.

'I'm so sorry,' he said, then turned abruptly and strode off down the cut without even saying goodbye.

Karen was shaken. She stood without moving for a minute or two, before walking unsteadily towards her house.

'What's up with you?' Sophie was getting out of her cream Mini just as Karen reached the drive. 'You look as if you've seen a ghost.'

'Do I? I'm OK. It's the weather . . .'

This unsatisfactory explanation seemed enough for her step-daughter, who wasn't big on other people's problems, unless they directly involved herself.

'I'm bloody glad I'm home before the lightning starts,' Sophie muttered.

Soon after, the storm erupted. Terrifying bolts of electricity lit up the night, one after another, forked as if they were maliciously seeking a target on earth, followed immediately by deafening booms of thunder right overhead which reverberated, echoing around the skies. When the heavens finally let loose the torrential sheets of rain, it was as if someone were tipping a huge tank of water over the house.

Largo whimpered in his basket, Sophie went and shut herself in her room and hid under the duvet. But Karen welcomed it. She'd never been afraid of thunderstorms, even as a child, although Johnny certainly had been.

Tonight, though, the extreme weather felt cathartic, as if anything less would have been an inadequate backdrop to her tormented happiness.

Maggie had gone. Karen went round to see her off, watching her friend wave goodbye through the taxi's rear window en route for Gatwick. They had not spoken about William again. Karen knew Maggie would have wanted to trust her when she said there was nothing between them, but she also knew that her friend's practical, straightforward nature would mean that Maggie would believe the evidence of her own eyes. So in the days before she left, there had been a certain constraint between the two friends. On Karen's part, she was almost relieved that Maggie wouldn't be around for a while to watch.

Not that there was anything to see. She and William, although nothing had actually occurred beyond a hand pressed to a cheek, had crossed a line that night in the cut-through and she saw no way that either of them could allow there ever to be a repetition. There was too much at stake – for everyone, not just for William. Karen had no experience of what it was like to be a home wrecker – the woman people pointed at and reviled – and she was not keen to find out.

It had been bad enough dealing with Harry's ex. Because

although Theresa had decided she couldn't be married to Harry herself, she was less than keen – like her daughter, Sophie – for anyone else to have him. Whenever she saw Karen, which was mostly when she visited the office to discuss things with her husband, she would walk past Karen as if she did not see her standing there, as if she did not exist. And if she spoke to Karen on the phone, it would be with a froideur that literally made her shiver.

But if Harry, as head of his own company, had chosen to have affairs with half his workforce – and by all accounts there were a few – there would only have been the odd disapproving eyebrow raised. If there were even a whiff of William straying from his marriage, it would, as Maggie had so sternly pointed out, be over for him – not to mention the trauma for his wife and daughter. Karen liked and respected William far too much to let that happen.

But the pull of their connection was unique, like nothing she had ever experienced – even with Harry, where the balance between them had been so unequal. He had been her boss, her hero, imbued with charisma, power, money and seniority. William was her equal, her friend, the person with whom she felt completely at home.

'Come to church with me tomorrow,' Sophie asked the following evening. 'It's Easter Day. Go on, just this once. For Daddy.'

They were eating fishcakes and salad at the kitchen table. Things seemed to be improving between them. Karen wouldn't say they were exactly friends yet – they still avoided each other most of the time – but they were finding a way to live together without rancour now. Maybe, she thought, it was just weariness of hostilities on both their parts, but Karen wanted to keep it this way.

'Why do you want me to come?' she asked, curious as to her stepdaughter's eagerness.

Sophie grinned. 'S'pose I just want to see if I can make you. Dad never could.'

'At least you're honest.'

'So? Will you? Easter's fun, the kids join in. William's very good with them.'

'I'm sure he is. But I don't believe in all that stuff about resurrection and taking away the sins of the world. Even if Jesus did rise from the dead, what good did it do any of us? People still suffer in their millions despite their beliefs.'

Sophie looked alarmed. 'Whoa, don't expect me to answer any deep theological questions.'

Karen laughed. 'Sorry. I just don't get it, though.'

'So come along and see if William can shed any light. What have you got to be afraid of?'

Her stepdaughter was clearly enjoying baiting Karen, and she didn't mind.

'Wouldn't it be hypocritical to come and sit there pretending?'

'You don't have to pretend anything. No one's going to test you on your faith.' The wariness eclipsed for once, Sophie offered her a fully disarming smile.

And Karen gave in. Not, as Sophie thought, because of her powers of persuasion, but because it gave her a chance to see the Reverend Haskell doing what must mean so much to him. She had longed to watch him in action for a while now – it was a huge piece missing in the jigsaw of who this man was. The only thing that kept her away had been the possibility that William might suspect her motives and be angry.

★

The Norman church was large and light. It smelt pleasantly of cold stone. Karen had been into it a number of times, but usually to show friends around who visited at weekends. She had once been to Christmas matins with Harry when they were first married – she hadn't yet learnt how to say no – but she had not been to a service since then, except the odd funeral or christening. Now, as she and Sophie took their seats, Karen realized her dogged resistance to God had been as much to do with not being bullied by her husband as a dislike of the ritual itself. It was a beautiful, peaceful place in which to sit. The five-light, leaded-glass window behind the altar shed a soft beam across the choir stalls, and the Easter flowers positioned all around the church perfumed the air. As she waited for the service to start, she felt a welcome calm descend on her.

A calm that was destroyed as soon as she saw William in his surplice and gold-embroidered stole. He looked so happy, so completely in his element as he looked out at his unusually full congregation. At least seventy-five people, Karen reckoned, and only the odd one over ninety. It was as if she were watching him as the star of a play. She tried not to catch his eye when he stood up in the pulpit to give the sermon, which was both witty and passionate. But if he saw her, he did not react, so involved was he in delivering his Easter message.

'It's all about trying,' the vicar told them, his eyes alight with enthusiasm. 'None of us is perfect, far from it. Perfection isn't human, only God is perfect. And because being perfect is such a distant, unattainable goal, many of us think it's not worth trying to get there. But it is. We should all be striving to find a better version of ourselves, throughout our lives. I say "better", not "perfect". And we do that by being true to ourselves, by being honest and authentic in all our dealings with each other and the world. And this is where God can help. God is our conscience. If we listen to him he will always tell us when we get it right, when we stray. And he will set us on the right path if only we let him.

'Easter, with the resurrection, is a time of new life and new beginnings, a time to set new goals . . .'

As he spoke on, he became more and more animated, his words reverberating around the church in his desire to reach his congregation. Karen knew he meant what he said, and knew that his words had a deep personal relevance to himself, and to her.

The reverend stood at the door of the church after the service, shaking the hands of his parishioners as they filed out into the warm spring day. Karen would have escaped the receiving line – she could see Janey and their daughter, Rachel, up ahead and had no desire to engage with them – but Sophie was urging her towards William.

'Ah, Sophie, lovely to see you.' He patted the girl on the arm then turned his attention to Karen. 'So glad you came,' he said quietly, giving a small bow of his head rather than taking her hand.

'Don't you think I need a medal, getting Karen to pitch up?' Sophie was saying. 'Daddy would have been astonished.'

William laughed. 'Yes, wouldn't he? Lovely you both could be here.' He was already looking behind them to the next person in the queue.

'See?' Sophie said, as they walked home. 'You didn't get struck down.'

'No . . . I enjoyed it, surprisingly. Enjoyed being in the church, at least. There was a real energy in there.'

Her stepdaughter looked sideways at her. 'That's the vicar for you. Reverend Parkin's services were the worst and seemed to go on forever – I dreaded them – but with William it's kind of inspiring.'

Karen silently agreed, but her heart had contracted at his guarded welcome to her. She understood that it had to be like this from now on, but it broke her heart.

The fête committee – eight had turned up today – stood in a circle on the lawn of Karen's house. It was large and perfectly cut by Ron Daley, who had been looking after the garden for thirty years, through all the different owners of the rectory. But the last quarter of the garden sloped downwards quite steeply towards the stream that ran along behind the house to the duck pond in the centre of the village, and this always caused problems when mapping out the stalls.

Jennifer held a pink clipboard in front of her, fastened to which was a pencilled plan. She pointed to the far corner.

'We'll have the tea tent there, as usual, meaning everyone has to go past all the other stalls to get there. It's always the most popular.'

They all nodded.

'The tombola there, cakes and jams there . . .' She consulted her plan. 'Then I thought the church stall could come next, with the tea towels and mugs and information about the tower fund.'

They nodded in unison.

'The trouble is, we've got four more craft stalls this year, which is wonderful, but I don't see how we're going to fit them in, if we have the children's area taking up that side, and duck racing by the stream.'

'What about the Pimm's tent?' Jeffrey asked, only to receive an eye-roll from the chairman.

'That goes on the drive, as usual, Jeffrey. We don't want the children getting muddled up with it.'

'Muddled up?' The judge's cold eyes sensed a challenge.

'You know what I mean. This is a family day out, not an opportunity to get drunk. If I had my way I'd ban it. But they're very generous sponsors, so I keep my mouth shut.'

'We are trying to raise money here, Jennifer.' Jeffrey had a thin smile on his lips as he looked around for support from the rest of the group, getting a grudging nod from Bernard, the secretary. 'The tent's immensely popular.'

'Yes, well . . . shall we get on?'

Karen was standing beside Janet, the organist, and Will was on Janet's other side, but Karen was intensely aware of his presence. She hadn't seen him, not even out and about, for nearly two weeks now and she was desperately pleased that he had come. But he looked pale and distracted this evening and had barely greeted her when he arrived, his eyes anywhere but on her face.

Karen shivered, wrapping her arms around her body. It was a cold evening, the sky threatening rain, and she wished they could go inside. But since almost every decision Jennifer made with regard to the stall plan was challenged by someone or other – mostly Martha or Jeffrey – it looked as if it would go on all night.

She longed to talk to William, to find out what was wrong, but since the meeting was being held in her house, there would be no opportunity to walk home together.

★

'Bloody man,' Jennifer muttered when everyone but Karen, William and herself had left. 'If he wants to be chairman, he only has to say. It's not like I volunteered.'

Karen indicated the sofa. 'Sit down, I'll make a fresh pot of tea, or something stronger if you'd prefer.'

The vicar didn't move. 'I should be getting home.'

But Jennifer, sinking gratefully on to the sofa, waved her plump arm imperiously at him. She reminded Karen of Hyacinth Bucket from the nineties TV series, with her exaggerated accent and innate bossiness. But she had a good heart and worked tirelessly for the village.

'Make mine a large gin and tonic, please, dear. I've had quite enough tea for one day,' she told Karen, before turning back to William. 'Could you spare a couple of minutes, Reverend? I know you're busy, but I really need to talk to you about Gardner Moss.'

Will looked reluctant, but couldn't refuse. He sat down on the edge of the armchair.

'Can I get you a drink?' Karen asked.

'Umm . . . just water would be fine.'

'Oh, come on,' Jennifer said, 'have a glass of something stronger. Don't let me drink on my own.'

Karen saw him hesitate. 'OK, a glass of wine, if you've got a bottle open.'

She knew he preferred red, and hurried to the kitchen to unscrew a Beaujolais she had in the cupboard. The top was stiff and she had to use a tea towel to get some purchase, anxious to get back to the sitting room quickly in case William decided to leave. She poured two glasses, handing one to the vicar when she returned to her guests.

'Now,' Jennifer said, her smile one of satisfaction that she'd got her way, 'I've got a little bit of a problem.' She told them that the owner of the estate agency Gardner Moss had suggested they sponsor the fête this year. 'Everyone knows Giles Moss is my brother-in-law and I don't want people to think I'm favouring his agency over all the others in the area. I've never been quite comfortable with this commercialization of the fête, but since we've got the Pimm's tent now . . . I wanted your take, Vicar, before I put it to the committee, because I know people like Jeffrey will just say who cares, as long as we get the money.' She shook her head. 'And obviously it is for a good cause.'

William smiled. 'I honestly don't think there's any harm. It's how the world works these days.'

Jennifer nodded sadly. 'Not like the old days.'

'No, but it's not as if Gardner Moss is an arms manufacturer or a drug smuggler. Unless you know something we don't?'

'Ha! Certainly not. Giles is just as scrupulous as any estate agent ever is.' She winked at Karen, who couldn't help laughing.

They talked on for a while, the alcohol mellowing the trio, William's need to go apparently forgotten.

'Right, my dears, I must love you and leave you. Thanks so much, Karen. You've been marvellous, and in such ghastly circumstances.' Jennifer heaved herself upright, adjusted her floral cotton frock over her ample waist and said her goodbyes.

Karen thought William would go with her, but he hovered as she shut the front door.

They stood opposite each other in the dim hall. William was biting his lip, his hands clutching a scrunched-up copy of the stall plan that the chairman had given him. He looked at the floor. She felt her breath trapped in her chest like a solid lump.

William glanced up towards the stairs. 'Is Sophie home?'

'No, she's in London.'

Now he finally looked at her. 'Karen, I have to talk to you.'

She nodded and led him back into the sitting room, where he resumed his perch on the armchair, she on the sofa.

'I haven't seen you about recently,' she said.

'No . . . I've been on retreat in Norfolk. I hope to get to the abbey at least once a year.'

She clutched her hands together tightly in her lap, not replying as she tried to keep the shivering that had suddenly overtaken her body under control.

William hesitated, started to speak, then stopped. But when he looked up, there was real distress in his clear eyes.

'Listen . . . I need to apologize to you . . .' He fell silent again.

'Will—' she began.

But he held up his hand to stop her. 'No, please, let me finish.' He took a long breath. 'I've been grossly unfair to you. You came to me for help when you were at your most vulnerable and I feel I've taken advantage of you.'

Karen frowned. 'You haven't—'

'Please. My behaviour has been totally inappropriate.'

'In what way?'

He seemed surprised at her confusion. 'Karen, I know you have . . . feelings for me. I'm not blind. And recently I've allowed you to think that those feelings were reciprocated. Which is unforgivable.'

Karen swallowed hard; she felt as if she'd been slapped.

'I've let you down,' he went on. 'I put myself in a position of power over you, as a counsellor . . . spiritual advisor . . . whatever you want to call it, after Harry's death. It's my job, I do it all the time. But it's easy for that relationship to be misinterpreted.' He paused. 'I should have known better. I should have stopped it months ago.'

Karen stared at him. 'So why didn't you?'

He looked away. 'Why didn't I? I suppose I wanted to help.'

'That's all, is it?'

The vicar wouldn't meet her eye.

'I asked you, is that the only reason you didn't stop our meetings?'

'Of course.' His reply was firm, the expression in his eyes deliberately robust.

But Karen could easily detect the lie. It wasn't just that she wanted to, his eyes were like an open book, the lie shifting and sliding across the pages. She said nothing, allowing his words to hang in the air.

He got up.

'You know we can't do this,' he said, then waited, staring at her, forcing her to agree.

It was a challenge, his will against hers, his lie against her truth. But she refused to back down. Although she knew he was right in what he said, she was not going to agree about what he purported to feel. Be true to yourself, he had said in his sermon. The hardest thing.

The room was almost dark now, the air leaden with their distress. She heard a small sigh escape him as he turned on his heel and left the room without another word. Nothing, she knew, was worth saying, anyway. They were in the wrong, and no words would put that right, however much they might try to justify their actions.

PART TWO

CHAPTER EIGHT

The dawn light, not called the 'cold light of day' for nothing, laid bare Karen's stark choice. And it did seem to be her choice, not William's, to make. His chosen life path encompassed his vocation, his family, his future, all tied up into one indivisible bundle. Whereas she was a free agent. Nothing tied her now that Harry was gone. She had no allegiances, no responsibilities beyond her beloved Labrador, and no love for any person – except William, if she was allowed to call it love. So she could either stay where she was and pine, sit with him through committee meetings, bump into him on the hills, be friends with his wife, etc., all the while suppressing her real feelings for him and watching him suppress his feelings for her, or she could get out, get away from the village and try, without his constant presence in her life, to forget him.

It seemed ludicrous, however, that she could ever forget him. Karen took her jacket from the hooks by the front door and waited for Largo to go out ahead of her as she checked she had her keys in her pocket. The late spring morning seemed to her to be unfairly beautiful and she felt her heart lifting almost against her will as she took in the luminous light breaking over the hills, breathed in the cool, clear air, heard the exuberant birdsong as a backdrop to the calm, people-free silence. The pain will diminish, Karen told herself as she made for the path up on to the Downs. You can't love someone forever, not in isolation from their presence. It's a fact, love fades, history backs me up on this. Then she heard the other voice clamouring in her head. *Anything could happen*, the voice insisted. But she couldn't stay here, waste her life hoping for that thing – a thing, moreover, that was not only extremely unlikely but would inevitably bring trauma to those involved. It would not be good for her soul to wish that on others.

I've got to leave, she had decided by the time she got to the crest of the hill. *I'll take Largo and go, find a rental somewhere for the next few months, leave Sophie to keep an eye on the house. Perhaps by September I'll feel differently about William.*

But she did nothing, beyond a cursory trawl of the Internet for holiday lets – of which there were almost none at this time of year. She just carried on with her usual routine, kept bumping into William – there had been another bloody committee meeting at the house only yesterday – kept agonizing about doing so, in a futile round of heart-thumping disappointment. Until that Sunday morning, when Karen had another fight with Sophie about the mess the girl relentlessly left in her wake.

Perhaps Karen's nerves were unusually frayed, or perhaps the self-imposed inaction of two perfectly fit and capable women was finally taking its toll, but increasingly Karen was becoming more and more finicky about the house. She found herself taking all the curtains down and having them dry-cleaned, hiring a steam vacuum for the carpets, clearing out old food from the kitchen cupboards – ancient chutney, peanut butter, pickles, jams, sauces – and washing out the old jars ready for marmalade in the winter.

She was on a mission. But every time she felt she was getting on top of the work, Sophie would drag mud from her boots into the hall and up the stairs, or spill wine on the parquet floor, candle wax on the coffee table, or unearth boxes from the attic and strew their contents about the sitting room. And whereas in the past Karen might have been mildly annoyed, now it seemed almost as if her life were at stake if she couldn't control the tidiness of the rectory.

'For Christ's sake, Sophie,' she exploded, mopping up yet another spill, this time coffee pooling around the idiotic new pod machine. 'Can't you ever clear anything up, *ever*?'

Her stepdaughter, who was lounging in her dressing gown at the kitchen table, texting on her phone, looked up.

'Sorry . . . I'd have done it in a minute.'

'"In a minute", it's always in a minute, later, when you get around to it. But you never do. I'm fed up to the back teeth with your mess.'

Sophie looked genuinely startled by the onslaught. 'That's a bit unfair.'

'Is it? Is it really?' Karen couldn't seem to calm down as she ran the dishcloth under the hot tap and wrung it out. 'You've been lying about this house for months now, never lifting a finger, never contributing to the housework or the shopping. For instance, you've never once put the rubbish out or fed the dog. You just waste every goddamn minute of every day on that bloody phone. It's got to stop.'

'OK, OK, you only have to ask.'

'That's the problem. I shouldn't have to ask. You're not a fool, you can see what has to be done. Couldn't you just, for once, help out without me saying anything?'

Sophie's face had hardened into a sulk. 'God, keep your hair on, Karen. It's not that bad.'

'That's what your father used to say about his drinking, "It's not that bad." But it *was* that bad – in fact, it was a lot worse.'

The girl got up, pulling her pink towelling dressing gown around her and tightening the belt. She began to clear the table of her breakfast things, her face solid with resentment.

'What's got into you?' she muttered, not looking at Karen, who stood by the sink, her heart lurching from beat to beat, knowing she was almost deliberately picking a fight and not knowing why, because things had been quiet between them for weeks now.

'Boyfriend playing up, is he?'

Karen heard the question without understanding it. 'Boyfriend?'

Sophie slammed the door of the dishwasher shut and stood, arms crossed over her chest, eyebrows raised as she met Karen's eye.

She was waiting for Karen to speak.

'What are you talking about?'

The girl gave a small smile. 'I've seen you.'

'Seen me? Seen what?'

'You and the vicar.'

Karen's breath caught in her throat. 'Me and Reverend Haskell . . . don't be ridiculous.' And when Sophie continued staring at her with that knowing grin, she added, 'What exactly are you insinuating, Sophie?'

She gave an exaggerated shrug. 'Ooh, nothing. Just I've seen the way you look at each other . . . and then there's all those cosy walks in the hills . . . Easter Day, when you gave each other really odd looks, which I didn't understand at the time. But the clincher was yesterday . . .' She paused for effect. 'When I came past the kitchen after the fête meeting and you were holding hands –' She stopped.

'We were *not* holding hands,' Karen said quickly, remembering the moment when he'd brought through the tray of tea things and asked her if she was alright, and she'd said she was – untruthfully – and William had given her hand a quick squeeze. Karen hadn't seen Sophie at the door.

'Whatever,' said Sophie.

Karen didn't know what to do. 'William is not my boyfriend, Sophie. I told you, he's just being kind to me.' Even to herself, she was cringingly unconvincing.

Her stepdaughter turned away. 'Don't worry, Karen, I won't dob you in. Just don't take it out on me because your little affair isn't going the way you planned.' And with that she stalked out of the room, floating on the moral high ground with a heavy waft of smugness.

Karen took a long breath. It was horrible to think of Sophie watching her – watching them – all this time, clocking their every glance. And it was worrying too. The girl had said she wouldn't tell, but Sophie – although not a mean person, Karen thought – could be volatile, she'd seen it many times when Harry was alive. Quick to take offence, her stepdaughter was quite capable, if roused, of blurting something out at an inopportune moment . . . it really didn't bear thinking about.

Karen, galvanized by Sophie's revelation, hurried to the office and turned on her computer. She rarely used it except for shopping or personal email these days – there was no need since she'd stopped working – but for the next hour she was pinned to the screen, searching desperately through pages and pages of holiday rentals, finding one that might suit, only to discover there were just one or two weeks free till autumn. Most didn't allow pets, or were too big or miles away from anywhere. But she had to get away from William Haskell. And, almost more importantly, she had to remove herself from her stepdaughter and her knowing looks.

'Is that Mike Best?' By the following day Karen had found a studio flat by the sea on the Sussex coast. An individual ad, not through an agency, which gave basic details but no availability.

'That's me,' a voice eventually replied.

'I'm inquiring about the rental.'

'Right.'

He wasn't being very helpful, but she ploughed on.

'Is it still available?'

'Yeah. Interested?'

'How long could I have it for?'

'How long d'you want it for?'

'Umm . . . two, three months?'

There was silence at the other end.

'Or less, if that's too long.'

'No . . . no, s'pose that'd be OK . . . can you hold on a minute?'

Another silence, where she heard him asking someone if they wanted milk in their tea.

'Right, sorry. So you want to see the place?'

'Please.'

'It's only a bedsit . . . "studio" they call 'em these days, but it's basically a room with a bed in it and a bathroom and kitchen. Small. My daughter lived there, but she's moved away now and it's been sitting empty . . .' He paused. 'If you want to take a look, I'll be in the café across the street, The Shed. Drop in when you can and I'll give you the tour.'

'Thanks, I should be there in an hour.'

Mike Best was busy when Karen arrived. It had indeed taken her
an hour to drive there from home. A safe enough distance, by her
calculations. And a very different environment. Karen loved the
sea and stood taking a long breath of the cool salty air as soon
as she'd parked the car. There was a fresh wind today and the
faded blue awning on the café front was billowing up and down
like a sail.

She stood in the queue of people, watching the proprietor. He
was probably about Karen's age, medium height, wiry and very
muscled, his short greying hair sticking up in a chaotic fashion and
a deep tan highlighting his fierce blue eyes. He was wearing a black
round-necked T-shirt, jeans and a black apron sporting a stick-on
image of a lobster. He raised his eyebrows at Karen.

'What can I get you?'

She introduced herself.

'OK. Listen, the girl's gone on a break, but as soon as she's back
I'll take you over. Have a seat and I'll get you a coffee.'

She did as he asked, feeling a huge sense of relief at being away
from home and the village.

The café was a modern, single-storey concrete block right on
the pebble beach. It was painted sea-blue, with wall-to-wall sliding
glass doors on the beach side, leading to a wooden deck, furnished
both inside and out with pale wooden tables and stylish mustard-
yellow plastic and chrome chairs. The walls had prints of album
covers from seventies bands – Led Zeppelin, King Crimson, Jimi,
Bowie – with the serving area stretching along the back of the
café, fronted by a chill-cabinet containing little pies, quiches,
scones, white plastic containers of sandwich fillings, a bowl of

large, fresh prawns with their shells on, and a separate section for cakes. It had a bright, clean, efficient atmosphere, which boded well, Karen thought, for the flat.

'Whaddaya think?' Mike asked her, standing by the door of the living room with his arms crossed.

She looked around. It was minimally furnished and small, as Mike had warned. But it was light and fresh, painted in buttermilk, the glass doors leading to a narrow balcony overlooking the sea. The kitchen and shower room were modern, the living space had stripped pine flooring, a grey sofa bed, coffee table, small flat-screen television and oval table with two of the yellow café chairs.

Could I stay here? she asked herself, suddenly anxious. *Can I imagine myself waking up here, alone, knowing nobody close by?* And the more she imagined it, the calmer she felt, but with a small knot of excitement at the prospect. She looked at her prospective landlord, who was eyeing her with interest.

'Holiday, is it?'

She nodded, then shook her head. 'More of a break . . . not sure what my plans are at the moment.'

'OK, well, if it suits we can do a month, then see what happens. I wasn't going to rent it out, but it looks as if Kim, my daughter, won't be coming back – she's over Southsea now, moved in with her boyfriend, which has caused me a shedload of hassles because she used to work for me and the girl I've got now hasn't a brain in her head. Literally, not one single brain cell.' He stopped, let out a sigh accompanied by a wry grin. 'Anyhow, you don't want to know my life story. If you want it, it's yours.'

Driving home, Karen felt happier than she had in months – years, possibly. A crazy sense of freedom fluttered like a butterfly in her stomach, the only downside being that she could never have Largo in that tiny flat, three floors up. Mike hadn't objected, although he didn't look too keen when she'd asked, but it was far too small for a large dog used to roaming a spacious house and extensive garden. It was only for a while, she told herself, and Sophie would look after him – she clearly loved the Labrador.

'You're going away for a month or two?' Her stepdaughter, recently returned from a night in London, looked bemused. 'I don't understand.'

'I just want a break . . . to be on my own for a while.'

Sophie frowned. 'This isn't because of the other day, is it? I was just winding you up. I didn't know for sure there was anything going on with you two.'

'No . . . well, yes, partly. I . . . I just don't want to hang around bumping into him all the time.'

'That bad?' The girl's tone was sympathetic. 'Oh, dear.'

Karen, who suddenly felt sick of all the lies, nodded.

'Not a good look, a married vicar. But it seems a bit drastic, exiling yourself to the seaside. What will you do there?'

Karen smiled. 'The same as I do here, I suppose. Not a lot.'

'Won't you be lonely?'

'I might be.'

'So it'll be just me here . . .'

'And the dog. The place is too small for Largo.'

'You don't know when you'll be coming back?'

Karen had thought Sophie would jump at the chance to be shot of her, but the girl seemed unnerved at the prospect of being left to herself.

'Will you be OK?'

Her stepdaughter nodded uncertainly. 'Sure.'

'You'll have to look after the place, remember to feed Largo, take him for walks.'

'Yeah, I can do that . . .' She paused. 'You're not going so you can get away from me, are you?'

Karen shook her head, gave her a smile. 'Of course not. And for all I know, it'll be hideous and I'll be back before the week's up, tail between my legs,' she added, not really meaning it.

Sophie's face lightened. 'It's true, you might not like it.'

'But you'll be OK, won't you? I'll be on my mobile, so if you have any problems you can always phone me . . . or even if you don't have any problems. I'm only an hour away.'

They stood in silence, absorbing the change of circumstances.

'Does William know?'

'No.'

'Aren't you going to tell him?'

Karen didn't reply immediately.

'I don't want him to think I'm going because of him.'

'Even though you are. I'll tell him, if you want. Just say you've gone away for a break when he asks.'

'Thanks . . . that would be good. I'd rather not have the conversation.' A thought occurred to her. 'And maybe you could stand in for me on the fête committee? It's only every two weeks now we've got the basics organized, and I'll definitely be back for the event itself.'

Sophie was looking alarmed, and raised her hands. 'Whoa . . . hold on a minute. The *fête committee*? Totally no way.'

They both laughed.

'Well, it's in our garden, we can hardly escape.'

'You seem to be making a pretty good job of it.'

Before she and Sophie parted, Karen took the girl's arm, looking intently into her face. 'I just want to get something clear . . . about me and William. We aren't having an affair. And we both know our feelings for each other are wrong.'

Sophie nodded. 'I wasn't blaming you.'

'No, but I wanted you to know.'

Karen, as she walked away, found her head beginning to whirr with tasks she had to do before she left: people, including Jennifer on the committee, whom she must tell; things she should remind Sophie of; what stuff she would need to take to the new flat. But the most insistent thought was that she would soon be putting a distance between her and William Haskell that meant she might not see him again, at least until the church fête at the end of August, which was weeks away.

So much the better, she told herself sternly.

But her heart did not agree.

CHAPTER NINE

The weather turned very hot. Karen had been in the seaside flat for nearly two weeks now, and had sunk into an almost soporific calmness, a lull akin to convalescence, where nothing happened all day, but nothing needed to. Karen had no responsibilities now, not even to feed the dog or let him out. There was no one she knew around her, and no stepdaughter to fight with.

Although at first she was restless, pacing around the tiny space, going out, coming in, going out again, not knowing what to do with herself, gradually she had settled into a routine that involved coffee and toast at Mike's café, a long walk on the beach, a swim when it was fine, rootling amongst the second-hand bookshops along the front, buying food, another walk, an early supper at Mike's, then reading or watching television – or variations on this theme. She slept like the dead, woke to the sound of seagulls, forgot to charge her mobile, and almost managed to block out the fact that she had another life – which had been forced behind a locked door for the time being.

'So here's what I'm thinking,' Mike said one morning as she sat eating a croissant while he prepared some sandwiches for the day. There was no one else in the café this early – Gina, Mike's brainless helper, wasn't expected until nine. 'A polite, well-turned-out lady pitches up, says she wants to rent the flat for three months, or thereabouts . . . and hasn't got any plans.' He grinned at her over the counter. 'The flat's nothing more than a room, but she seems happy in it – although it's clear she's used to better. So I ask myself, what the bloody hell's she doing here?' Before Karen could answer, he rushed on, 'And I figure there's got to be a bloke involved. Some bad boy who's done a runner and broken her heart. That, or it's a bank job and she's on the run, stashed half a mil under the sofa bed.'

They both began to laugh.

'Yeah, I wish,' she said.

'So which is it?'

'Kind of Option One. Although he's not a bad boy, that's the trouble.'

Mike raised an eyebrow. 'Not bad enough? How's that a problem?' He bent his head to his task of buttering baguette chunks and filling them with ham or cheese while Karen thought about how she should reply. But before she had time, he looked up again. 'Ah, got it. He's married. Am I right? Won't leave the missus.'

She gave him a wry smile. 'You got it. I haven't asked him to but even if I did, he wouldn't. It's not like that. And it never will be. We haven't done anything.'

Mike looked puzzled at this. 'So what's the plan? You hole up here and hope he sees the light and follows you?'

'Nope. I hole up here and hope I forget him.'

'Hmm, not much of a plan, if you don't mind me saying.'

'I agree, it's a bit thin.'

Mike's expression brightened. 'But hey, could work . . .' He thought for a moment. 'Thing is, people don't leave their other halves as often as they say they will.' He turned away.

'How's it going?' Karen eventually phoned Sophie; the silence from the village had begun to unnerve her.

'Oh, you know . . .'

'Has Largo been OK?'

'Yeah, he's fine. He seemed to be searching around for you a lot in those first few days, but I've been looking after him, taking him for walks and stuff . . . I enjoy it.'

'Good, that's great.'

She wanted badly to ask about William, but she was embarrassed to do so. So she listened to her stepdaughter telling her about the tap in the kitchen seizing up and that Peggy Blake – a ninety-four-year-old in the village – had died.

'Did you go to the committee meeting?' she asked at last, unable to contain herself.

'I did,' Sophie said proudly. 'And bloody boring it was too.' She heard the girl chuckle. 'Martha and Jeffrey had a set-to, but Jennifer said afterwards that they always do.'

Karen took a deep breath. 'Was William there?'

'No, he couldn't make it . . . an archery contest or something. But I told him last week that you'd gone. I saw him with Rachel when I was out taking Largo for a walk, and we had a chat.'

'OK . . .' Karen waited, hoping Sophie would elaborate.

'He asked after you, and I said you'd gone away for a break and he just nodded.'

'Thanks for doing that.'

She felt deflated. *How did I think he would react?* she wondered. *He hasn't been in touch, no texts, no emails, so he's obviously thoroughly relieved that I'm out of his hair. Not that he'd ask too much about me in front of Rachel,* she conceded. *And I haven't texted him either.*

'How's the sea, then? Is it working out?' Sophie was asking.

'It's great . . . I've kind of switched off from everything.'

'Even the reverend?'

Not used to confiding in her stepdaughter, Karen hesitated. 'Umm, sort of,' she replied non-committally.

'Been there, done that,' Sophie said. 'Tricky thing to pull off, the forgetting thing.'

There was real feeling behind her words, and although Karen knew little about Sophie's love life – she always clammed up if ever Harry asked – she suspected it had not been a smooth ride for the girl, who always seemed to cut quite a lonely figure.

'There isn't really anything to forget.'

'Still,' said Sophie, ignoring Karen's denial.

'Listen, if you fancy a break by the sea,' Karen found herself saying, 'drive down and visit. I don't do much, and there's a nice café and a gorgeous beach.'

'Yeah, thanks.' Sophie sounded surprised by the invitation. 'I might do that one day.'

After they'd said goodbye, Karen sat with a cup of tea on the balcony of her flat. It was after nine in the evening, the sun going down to the west, lighting up the water with a shimmering path of gold. She loved sitting here in the cool sea breeze, the uninterrupted view of the ocean spread out before her, alone and at peace.

But despite what she'd intimated to Sophie, she hadn't switched off from William. It felt so much like unfinished business between them, something tantalizing but not yet real. There had to be more, didn't there? She would go home eventually, she couldn't hide out by the sea forever, and then . . . then maybe things might have changed in some way. But always, at this stage in her fantasy projection, her rational mind would interrupt. No, it told her, there was absolutely no reason whatever to expect anything to have changed. The only change that could occur would be for her, Karen, to get over her insane crush on Reverend Haskell. Everything else, the voice assured her, would remain as it was.

She had also been thinking a lot about Harry, comparing how she felt about her husband with the feelings she had for Will. It was unfair to set a new infatuation against an eighteen-year relationship, she knew that, but examining her marriage, even in this lopsided fashion, threw up truths that Karen had barely thought about before now.

Harry had always been her boss, she his PA, both in her own mind and in his. She had looked up to him, hero-worshipped him for his worldliness and charisma, his power as head of the company. And he, she felt, had never quite made the adjustment that morphed her from PA to wife. She was always his inferior, not least because she was so much younger than him, and a woman – Harry was a male chauvinist if not actually a misogynist. But whilst they were still working together they had his beloved company in common. Which they talked about night and day, year in, year out, whether at work or at home. It was their bond, their obsession, their baby . . . because Harry had refused to have an actual one, said he was too old. She took his point, but she had not been too old back then, only thirty-nine. And at the time she wasn't sure she cared that much about having a child, as she was swept up in Harry and the company. But later, when other resentments surfaced, she realized she had not been given a choice. Harry had railroaded her into agreeing with him, into not caring.

They shared almost no other interests, however. She couldn't talk to him as she talked to William, he would have laughed at her for expressing her feelings, not out of meanness but because he just couldn't comprehend what she was talking about. He wasn't interested in the wider community, although he liked to think he was, and he never listened to music – he'd banned the country music that Karen loved – or read a book. Harry was a single-focus individual who never wanted anything more from life than to sit at his desk in his engineering company and work. And when that wasn't available to him, of course, he fell apart and so did their marriage, no longer glued tightly together by Stewart Engineering.

Thinking about it now, Karen didn't feel cheated, or even sad that her marriage hadn't amounted to more. It had been enough for them both for a long time – often a lot of fun – and she was grateful for that. The thought of Harry's face now, with that tender, amused smile he kept particularly for her, brought tears to her eyes. But she knew she didn't miss her husband nearly so much as she missed Will Haskell.

'Gina, can you please get a move on and clear those outside tables?' Mike called out to his waitress in the lull following the lunchtime rush.

Gina, aged nineteen, didn't even acknowledge her boss's request, just moved towards the deck with her slow, provocative gait. She knew she was eye-catchingly beautiful with her heart-shaped face and luminous blue eyes, her dark-blonde hair, lightened in fetching streaks by the sun, floating loose down her back, the tiny shorts and vest top exposing as much as possible of her smooth, tanned limbs and perfect young body. Every man – any age – who came into the café or passed along the beach would do a double take, instantly bewitched. And maybe, thought Karen, as she watched Gina lazily collect the dirty plates from a table, she felt she didn't need to make any more effort, that her beauty alone was enough of a contribution to the world.

As she reached the counter, Gina said, 'I won't be able to come in Saturday. My gran's not well and Mum needs me to watch the kids.'

Clearly Mike didn't believe her.

'Christ, Gina, not again! You know Saturday's our busiest day. How the hell do you think I'm going to manage on my own?'

Gina shrugged. 'Sorry, can't be helped. I could give Sonia a bell, find out if she's free.'

'Yeah, do that, please.' He sighed with exasperation, hands on his hips, waiting while the waitress dug her phone out of the back pocket of her shorts and tapped the screen. But Sonia, it appeared, had plans for Saturday.

As soon as Gina had gone on her break and was safely out of ear-shot, Mike exploded.

'I'm going to kill her. I'm definitely going to kill her,' he said, to no one in particular, his back turned as he twisted the small stain-less-steel container full of ground coffee into place on the espresso machine against the back wall. The café was empty inside, apart from Karen, although all six tables on the sunny deck were occu-pied. 'My mum would've called her a floozy, but that's not it. What really gets me is she's got no bloody conscience. She never, *ever* thinks of anyone but herself.'

'She might have been telling the truth,' Karen ventured. 'About looking after the kids.'

'Ha! She might have, but it's odd how her mum only ever needs her on a Saturday, when that lout of a boyfriend comes free from the tyre shop.' He gave a frustrated sigh. 'Sure, this time she could just be telling the truth, but week after week it's the same old, same old. Sick gran, sick kids, sick dog, sick whatever – you wouldn't believe what a diseased bunch they are in that family. You can see why I don't trust the girl.'

'So what'll you do?'

He shrugged, giving her a hopeless grin. 'Sink under a tide of angry punters, I suppose. Or hope it pours with sodding rain.'

'It's not going to rain, I checked.'

'Right, well, it's the angry punters, then.'

Karen was silent for a moment. 'I could help out if you don't find someone.'

Mike looked across the room at her, surprised. 'Nah . . . thanks, but it's hell in here Saturdays at this time of year. 'Preciate the offer, though.'

'You've somehow got this idea I'm a spoilt rich girl, but I've worked all my life till recently. I won't faint at the sight of a dirty plate, you know.'

He laughed, looked embarrassed. 'No, I'm sure not. But there's no need, I'll sort something out.'

'OK, but the offer stands if you don't.'

Karen, as she walked off along the beach, was a bit disappointed that he didn't want her help.

Johnny laughed. 'So you're running away from Sulky Sophie.'

'Actually, we're getting on pretty well these days. She's not so bad, just a bit lost.'

'So why are you living in a box by the sea?'

'I've explained, I needed to get away.'

But her brother knew her better than that. 'From what, Kar? Tell me.'

She sighed. 'Oh, just someone. I don't want to go into details.'

'Mmm, I see. A man. OK . . . that was quick. But I don't blame you, you deserve some fun.'

'I'm not having fun. Not in the way you think.'

'Right. Well, if you're not going to tell me, I can't help.'

'I don't want you to help. No one can help.'

Karen could almost see her brother rolling his eyes.

'Why don't you come over here? Spend a month or so with us and clear your head. Just get on a plane, nothing's stopping you.'

'Thanks, but I want to stay here for a while.'

There was a long pause. 'If you won't come to us, I'll have to come to you,' he said.

'No, no, you can't.' She instantly regretted the panic in her voice.

'Why ever not? Karen? What's going on? Why can't I come and stay? We haven't seen each other in ages.'

'Because I'm not there. I'm not at home.'

'Yes, but you could go home if I was coming over.'

'I don't want to, not at the moment.'

Johnny's Mr Fixit mentality was finally stumped. His tone held a distinct huffiness as he said, 'OK, well, let me know when you're feeling a bit more sociable.'

'Johnny . . . please. I'm just in a weird mood at the moment.'

'Telling me.'

'Don't be upset.'

'I'm not. But it's hard to have a normal conversation with you these days, Karen. I just always end up repeating myself about Harry and his drinking, or the live-in stepdaughter. And now it's some other unspecified moron you're putting in the way of finding happiness. When are you going to take control of your life and stop being such a victim?'

Karen hated it when her brother went all pious and preachy.

There was a tense silence.

'Listen, I'll call you soon,' she said.

'Look forward to it.'

'Bye, then.'

'Bye.'

Am I such a victim? she asked herself, upset by her brother's snippiness. OK, Johnny knew her better than anyone, but he had such a different outlook on life. He never complained, never moaned about anything personal. She felt he was becoming like a wind-up toy these days, but Karen knew that didn't mean everything was rosy, it just meant he was incapable of admitting he wasn't coping. And because she did share her worries with him, he had labelled her a victim. She didn't feel like a victim. She wasn't a victim. Things had just been hard recently.

Although it was getting dark, she went through to the bathroom and took her damp swimming costume off the towel rail, struggled into it then pulled on her blue hooded towelling beach dress and pink jelly-shoes and hurried across the road, past Mike's place – closed up for the night – to the sea. It was just past high tide, the water already darkening with the fading light as she yanked off her robe and strode into the surf, the cold water making her stiffen and hold her breath for a second before she dived into the waves. Not a soul was swimming, although families and couples still crunched on the shingle and strolled down the lit-up promenade.

Karen set off out to sea, then turned right along the shore. She was a strong swimmer, legacy of the Olympic freestyle champion the school had employed as their sports director – a man dedicated to teaching his charges to swim with a proper technique, not just swim to save themselves from drowning.

Tonight the water felt cleansing, invigorating as she swam up and down, pushing herself harder in order to block out her thoughts, the only important thing the breath she gasped every third stroke, the burning of her thigh muscles as she kicked through the water, the smooth rhythm of her arms, extending forwards, pulling back, fingers pressed tightly together to get the most traction: in, out, in, out. The sea was not rough, but the wind was getting up and it was hard work keeping on course. It was only when she realized it was now quite dark that Karen dragged herself away and splashed up the beach to fetch her robe and shoes.

Shivering and breathless but exhilarated, she padded back to her flat and went straight into a warm shower. Standing there, the water pouring over her head, face, down between her breasts and across her stomach in a glistening stream that pooled at her feet, she began to cry. The tears surprised Karen, she wasn't aware of feeling distressed, and it seemed as if there was no one identifiable cause, just a terrible, overwhelming sense of emptiness. When she finally got her breath back and stepped out of the shower, wrapping herself in a large white towel, she felt almost too exhausted to put one foot in front of the other.

Worn out by the swimming and by the tears, she flopped down on the sofa in her towel and clicked the music app on her phone, selecting her current favourite, 'Blue Eyes Crying In The Rain' – a duet between Shania Twain and Willie Nelson. Harry, along with plenty of others over the years, had relentlessly mocked her love of country music, saying it was 'sentimental twaddle'. But she wasn't ashamed of her devotion to Johnny Cash and Dolly Parton, Way-lon Jennings and the like. It was a relief to be able to indulge her habit without censure.

She must have dropped off to sleep, because the next thing she knew she was waking up in exactly the same position on the sofa, still wrapped in her damp bath towel, cold and disorientated. Looking at the clock on the wall, she saw it was twelve fifteen. She had been asleep for at least two hours. What had woken her had been the ping of an incoming text, she realized, as the phone pinged again. Her limbs were stiff as she got up to retrieve the mobile from the dining table. 'Vicar' was the name she saw on the display.

She read, her heart thumping.

> *Hi Karen, hope all is well with you. We have a couple of questions about insurance for the fête. I'd be grateful if you could give me a call. Thanks, William.*

She sat on one of the mustard-yellow chairs and stared at the text, poking at the words to find anything behind the formal request on the screen that spoke of something more personal, confirmed his continued interest in her. *Is he using this as an excuse to talk to me?* she wondered, knowing it would be madness for him to send a loving text when someone – specifically Janey or Rachel – might read it by mistake. And then she told herself it would be a worse madness for her to talk to him – whatever his feelings might be – and spark off another bout of longing. OK, she hadn't made much progress in moving on from him, but talking to him would be less than no help in that department.

For what seemed like an age, her finger hovered above the phone keypad, itching to tell him that she would call tomorrow. But in the end, sense triumphed.

Hi William, best if you contact solicitor Barry Rivers,
mob 07970 655421, about insurance. Harry got him to
deal with it in the past. Karen

She sent it with a sense of having done the right thing. Anyone could read that text, there was nothing compromising. And it saved her from the agony of hearing his voice again. But ten minutes later, she fell right off the wagon, her fingers working in absolute opposition to her common sense.

Missing you x

She tapped out the words, pushing 'send' with a strange sense of relief. A relief, however, that was short-lived when William did not reply.

As the minutes ticked by without an answer, and realizing she was freezing in the skimpy towel, she pulled on her cotton pyjamas, brushed her teeth and snuggled under the duvet, still in the state of pleasurable agitation that contact with Will always engendered. Lying there, waiting for his response, however, was not pleasurable. She held her phone by her side on top of the duvet, bringing her hand up to check the screen every few minutes as if it were an oil derrick, even though any text would be announced by the usual ping.

But there was nothing, not a peep.

Maybe he's gone to sleep, she told herself, but she still waited, her heart unable to be quiet, making her own sleep impossible.

And so she lay until long past a reasonable time to expect a response from anyone, feeling angry and really stupid for having put her feelings out there, only to be rejected.

It was after three when she finally slept.

The crowd around the counter in Mike's café was already large when Karen, having slept late, arrived for her coffee. A family, which seemed to consist of three generations – five children, one in a buggy – plus another group of six older women and a single cyclist, with his helmet in his hand, were milling about waiting to be served. Mike was frantic, doing his best to take the orders, make the coffee and serve the cakes and sandwiches. But it clearly wasn't working. The queue, Karen could sense, was getting restive.

Without sitting down, she immediately went behind the counter.

'I'll help,' she said.

Mike hesitated for only a second, then let out a long sigh as if he'd been holding his breath for hours. 'If you wouldn't mind, just until this lot's been cleared.' He pointed at the hook on the door leading to the small storeroom. 'Apron's there.'

Karen took down the black apron Gina sometimes wore and wrapped it around her body, tying it at the front.

'If you could take the orders, do the sandwiches. It's the coffees that take the time.'

He gave her a cursory demonstration of the till and turned back to the machine. The man first in the queue looked relieved and gave her a broad smile as he began his order.

It was hours later when Karen and Mike came up for air. Coffee time melted into lunchtime, melted into teatime. A warm, breezy summer Saturday without a cloud in the sky had enticed everyone to a day out at the beach, it seemed, and each time Karen thought there might be a lull, another punter stepped through the glass doors. Apart from Mike's instructions, and her requests for another latte or cappuccino etc., they barely had time to speak. When five thirty came and the last couple had paid the bill and wended their way, they both grabbed a cup of tea and took it outside, sitting down heavily at a table and groaning with tiredness.

'Thanks for your help. No way I could have coped without you,' Mike said.

'It was a pleasure.' She saw his sceptical glance, but she meant every word. 'It's the first proper day's work I've done in years.'

'Yeah?' He grinned. 'Lucky you.'

'Not really . . . I used to work with my husband until he retired and sold the company. I loved it.'

'So . . . you and your hubby are . . .?'

'He died. In January.'

'Sorry 'bout that. My wife died February last year.'

'Really? I'm sorry too.'

He shook his head, a bewildered expression on his face. 'Just came home from the supermarket one day and dropped down dead on the kitchen floor. Massive heart attack.'

'Terrible.'

'Only fifty-two. No age. Ran every day, didn't smoke, wasn't fat or anything. Doctors couldn't explain it. Worst thing is, if I'd been there and called the ambulance she probably wouldn't have died.'

'Don't go there,' Karen said brusquely. 'You weren't and she did.'

Mike looked taken aback.

'Sorry, that was rude. But I'm the same. If I'd gone to

my husband when he called, he'd be alive today. I've spent the last six months feeling guilty and it hasn't changed a thing.'

A ghost of a smile crossed his face, but his expression was distant – obviously he'd retreated, as she so often did, to the day his wife died. 'Hard to live with, though.'

For a while they sat in silence with their own thoughts.

'So this man, the bad boy who isn't bad enough, he's recent, is he?'

Karen looked away. 'Just a stupid crush.'

'Losing your other half does weird things to your brain,' he said.

'You think?' Karen felt she was clutching at straws. If she were temporarily unhinged, then the William thing wouldn't be real and she would recover, stop spending sleepless nights waiting for a non-existent text.

'Yeah, listen to this. I kept seeing Margie for months . . . or thought I did. In the street, walking past the café, going upstairs in the house. Sure as I'm looking at you, she was there.' He shook his head. 'Although she wasn't, of course.'

Karen didn't know what to say as Mike, tapping his finger against his temple, went on. 'Mind playing tricks. Part of my brain refusing to accept she'd gone. Did Kim's head in.'

'You must have loved her a lot.'

Mike laughed. 'Yeah, well, I suppose. Fought like cat and dog half the time. But you kinda get used to someone being around.' He looked at her, frowned. 'Same for you, must be.'

She nodded, for a moment just allowing herself to miss Harry. No relationship is perfect, but you learn to depend on each other, even if the dependency is detrimental to you both. That had been true of her and Harry. *Was it also true of William and Janey?* she wondered. She had no idea.

Realizing she hadn't had time to check her phone – locked in the store cupboard in her bag while she worked – since the morning, she was suddenly desperate to find out if William had been in touch. Surely by now he would have replied.

'I'll help you tidy up,' she said.

'Nah, you get off, you've done enough. Thanks, I owe you.'

The text contained one single, upper case X. Nothing more. But for Karen, nothing less.

She sat on her sofa hugging her phone to her chest with delight, before plunging into her usual despair at the hopelessness of the situation. *Bloody man, bloody man, bloody, bloody man*, she ended up chanting silently to herself, renewing her vow for the umpteenth time to *move on*.

Working with Mike over the following days certainly helped to root her in a different, vicar-less reality. Any day during the week when they were particularly busy, or Gina's relatives were struck down by yet another improbable virus, Karen was happy to step in.

'You like classical music, do you?' Mike asked one Saturday morning.

'I do, but I'm not very knowledgeable about it.'

'See, Kim was given tickets for a concert tonight, but it's Beethoven or some such. Not my thing. So if you're interested . . .'

'To go with Kim?'

'No, she's off out with the thug,' as Mike termed his daughter's partner, 'but the tickets were going spare at work, so she took them and now she can't offload them. Shame to let them go to waste.'

'You might enjoy it.'

He laughed. 'Sounds like paint drying to me.' He pointed at one of the photographs on the café wall. 'Now if you're talking Bob Seger . . .'

The theatre foyer was packed when Karen arrived, even though she was early. She'd taken the tickets because she fancied a change from sitting in the flat on her own all evening, and she was glad she had come. It felt good to be out and she was looking forward to the concert. She and Russell, her boyfriend before Harry, had often gone to concerts together, usually rock or country, occasionally classical, but whatever the music, Karen always revelled in the live aspect of any performance, the fact that it was a one-off, the only time it would ever be exactly this way.

She bought a programme and decided to find her seat before the rush. But just as she was giving her ticket to the girl, she heard her name being called, the voice coming from behind her. She knew the voice instantly, turned to search for the face. He was standing in the foyer, clutching a programme and a plastic glass of water, no dog collar, just a dark-blue, open-necked shirt and black chinos. He looked well, his dark hair a bit longer, his pale skin freckled, almost tanned from the hot summer.

Karen took her ticket back and moved out of the way of the couple behind. Her heart beating like a bass drum, she walked slowly towards William Haskell.

'What are you doing here?' she asked.

His smile was amused. 'Same as you, probably.'

Flustered, she said, 'No, I know . . . but . . . well, I mean it's a coincidence.' She looked around. 'Is Janey here?'

'We've got a new puppy . . . Labrador like Largo, only black, and she didn't want to leave him.'

'Oh, OK.' She stopped, the strange feeling that she shouldn't even be speaking to him stemming her ability to make conversation.

He seemed equally hamstrung. So they stood in silence for a moment.

'This should be good,' he said.

'Yes? I know nothing about it, I was given the tickets by a friend.'

'The Fine Arts Quartet is world famous. The Haydn should be a treat.'

She nodded, not wanting to show her ignorance.

'You could sit in Janey's seat if you like. Unless you're with someone?'

'Umm . . .'

They looked at each other.

'OK,' she said softly and they walked together towards the door to the stalls, not speaking.

Sitting side by side in the large, modern and currently packed auditorium, Karen took slow, surreptitious breaths in an attempt to slow her heart rate. But his nearness was like a drug hit, catapulting her into an altogether altered state. For all she was aware, there was no one else in the theatre besides her and Will.

And the music colluded with her state of heightened awareness, gently carrying her up in a vortex of sound that seemed to soothe her chaotic emotions, forcing her to stop analysing, stop thinking and let go. Just be. When it came to an end, she felt as if she were coming round from a trance.

'Like it?' William was saying.

'Love it.'

They got up and followed the crowd out to the foyer, the evening sun pouring through the plate glass that fronted the theatre.

'Shall we go outside?' he asked, and she nodded.

They each picked up another plastic glass of water from the end of the bar and went to stand in the dying light, which bathed the adjacent park in dusty gold, the breeze delightfully cool on their cheeks after the stuffy theatre.

'You didn't say you were going away,' he said, all barriers between them washed away by Haydn's notes.

'I thought it was best for us both.'

They both knew the truth of this and he didn't speak.

'I've been trying to forget you,' she said, which brought a rueful smile to his face.

'Successfully?'

'Not yet.'

'I've stopped trying. Sometimes it's better to just accept what is.'

'Because we can't change things,' Karen said flatly, not wanting to engage in a conversation that would end the way the others had.

He bit his lip, the muscles of his jaw suddenly tensing angrily as he drained the water in his glass, crushing the plastic in his right hand.

'Come on. Let's go . . . take off to the beach.'

'The beach? Now? Miss the rest of the concert?'

'Why not? It's not yet eight thirty, and the light is so beautiful . . .'

They drove in convoy to the nearest beach. Not Karen's, but one heading east along the coast, south-east of the cathedral city. She knew the way, so she went ahead, constantly glancing in the rear-view mirror to check William was keeping up. She didn't know what to think. It was as if he had suddenly come to a decision about something as he crushed the tumbler in his hand.

The light was indeed extraordinary, the sun faintly veiled now by pinkish cloud, low on the horizon with only forty minutes or so till sunset, laying a soft shimmering silver across the sea. Karen felt her heart lift with joy as she stepped on to the shingle in the chill evening air. She searched the promenade for Will, but he was having trouble parking and it was a few minutes before she saw his figure walking towards her. *I'll just take these minutes for what they are, savour them*, she thought.

William stood beside her, gazing at the sunset, he too taking deep breaths of the sea air. Then, without a word, they crunched down towards the water until they reached the damp, firm sand – the tide on its way out . . . or in, Karen could never work it out – before turning west along the beach, into the sun. They walked in silence, but it was a buzzing, elated silence for Karen, her body alive with her proximity to him. She could have asked what the puppy was called, how William was getting on, whether the fête committee was driving him mad. He could have asked her all sorts of questions about her sojourn by the sea. But neither did.

They walked the length of the beach, stepping over the slimy wooden groins, splashing in the shallow pools left by the tide until Karen's pumps were soaked, watching the sun until it had dipped over the horizon, leaving a half-light illuminating the sand. And without a word, they turned and made their way back. It was only when they were parallel to the spot near where they had parked that they veered off the sand up the slope of pebbles to the steps leading to the promenade.

They faced each other, meeting the other's gaze.

William gave her a half-smile. 'Thank you. That was so beautiful.'

She nodded, smiled, and after a moment of hesitation he pulled her against his chest and held her close for a long while. She shut her eyes, letting out a long, slow breath, her arms folding around his body.

'Good night,' he said, when he finally pulled away.

'Night, Will.'

When she was safely back in the car she just sat there, unable to concentrate on driving for a moment. *Nothing happened*, she told herself. *We did nothing wrong. It was just a walk on the beach.*

But it wasn't to do with the doing, it was to do with the feeling.

'So how was it, the concert?' Mike asked the following morning as she stood at the counter, waiting for him to make her coffee.

'It was amazing.'

He was peering at her. 'You OK? You look kinda spaced.'

She smiled, trying to shake off the daze she had been in since leaving William.

Mike frowned. 'Like you're stoned. Didn't know that classical stuff was so powerful.'

'It wasn't just the music,' she said, lowering her voice because of the two couples sitting at tables within earshot – although neither of them were listening.

'Yeah? What, then?'

'I bumped into the guy . . . the one you call "not-bad-enough". He was at the concert.'

Mike's expression cleared. 'Ah, now I get it. Been up all night, have you?' he grinned suggestively.

'We just had a walk on the beach.'

He laughed. 'Must have been a good one.'

'It was.' She couldn't have explained to anyone that they hadn't spoken hardly a word all evening, that they hadn't made plans or anguished over the fact that they had no plans. That being together, not even touching, had been enough.

He handed her the large cappuccino, his face set. 'I hope you know what you're doing, Karen. This polisher's still married, isn't he?'

' "Polisher"?'

Mike frowned. 'Polisher, wanker, tosser . . . you get the gist.'

She nodded, recoiling from the words when associated with William, not wanting to hear what the man was saying.

'And that makes him a cheat, whichever way you cut it.'

'I told you, it was just a walk.'

'A walk that's sent you all misty-eyed.'

'I know what I'm doing. Which is nothing. We bumped into each other, it wasn't planned . . . I probably won't see him again for months.'

'Good thing too,' said Mike, and turned to a woman with a small child who was hovering, waiting to place her order.

CHAPTER TEN

It was Wednesday morning, early, when Karen received another text from William Haskell.

Meet me on the beach? 2pm?

She texted back.

My beach nearer.

She gave him the details, saying she'd meet him by the ice cream van along the front. She didn't want Mike seeing him and possibly making his opinion known. As it was, when she went for her coffee and Mike asked her what she was doing today she lied, 'Nothing much,' and changed the subject.

She texted William later, when she'd had time to think.

I'll bring a picnic.

It was another hot summer day and she dithered about what to buy for the picnic. She'd never had a meal with Will, except that dinner at Patrick's, and she had no idea what he liked . . . no idea of anything much concerning his life. Except that she felt she knew him through and through. In the end she decided to play safe and made some ham and mustard sandwiches on sourdough bread from the deli – didn't all men like ham sandwiches? She added some plain crisps, a punnet of strawberries, one cold bottle of ginger beer and one of lemonade, and some water to the plastic bag. She considered chocolate, but she knew it would melt in the heat. Then she went for a swim to pass the time and calm her nerves.

'What made you come?' she asked, when they were sitting on towels at the far end of the promenade where the shingle beach opened out into a wide sandy one as it wended its way round the coast. Karen would have thought the sandy part would be more popular with families but, in fact, the pebbles were covered with people, hardly room for a pin between them – perhaps because it was closer to the facilities along the front. The tide was right out, children splashing in the distant surf in barely a foot of water, the mid-afternoon heat fierce.

'I was in the area—' William stopped, looked ashamed of himself. 'That's a lie. I wasn't in the area, I just wanted to see you.'

'Where does Janey think you are?' Karen had vowed to just enjoy the moment, but she wasn't succeeding.

'She has a yoga class on Wednesday afternoons.' Will gave a shrug. 'I know. I know everything you're going to say about the situation is true, that we shouldn't be doing this, I know it isn't fair on anyone. But the other night . . . just being beside you in the theatre, on the beach, not even talking, it felt like it was where I ought to be.'

Karen sat there, gazing out to sea, her thoughts in chaos. 'What are you saying?'

'I don't know.' His tone was quietly desperate as he turned to her, moving round till he was cross-legged, facing her, probably baking in his trousers, dark shirt and dog collar, only his shoes and socks removed. 'Everything I want to say sounds so clichéd. And I haven't the right to say anything to you anyway . . . because I . . .'

She felt she should have been happy that he was at least being honest about his feelings, albeit in a roundabout way. But she wasn't happy. In fact, she felt like a stupid cliché herself, loving a married man who would never be free to love her back.

'These moments . . . being together on the beach . . .'

She didn't know quite what he meant.

'Say something,' he said.

'I'm not sure if I can do it,' she finally answered carefully, feeling her way around the words. 'Seeing you in this way . . . and then probably not seeing you.'

William lowered his gaze. 'No, no, I totally understand. Forget I said it, I'm just being incredibly selfish.'

They both lapsed into silence.

'But we can enjoy today. It's just a picnic,' she said, making yet another volte-face as she swung between her craving for William and the pain she knew it would cause her when he was gone. 'Paddle?'

He grinned and rolled his trousers up to the knee. They ran across the sand, splashing in the warm sea.

'I wish I could swim,' he said.

'You can't swim? Seriously?'

He laughed. 'I could if I'd brought trunks.'

Later they sat eating the sandwiches. William liked ham a lot, Karen found out. And strawberries.

'Tell me about the archery,' she said.

William considered her request for a moment. 'It's so much a part of me that I can't really see it objectively. I think I told you, my grandmother started teaching me when I was five or six and it just became something as normal to me as eating cereal for breakfast when I was growing up.' He paused, maybe remembering his grandmother. 'When you shoot you have to be totally grounded, completely still, focused . . . then the draw, the moment when you let the arrow fly . . . it's magic.'

'Jennifer says you're good.'

William laughed. 'Dear Jennifer, when she decides someone is OK, then they can do nothing wrong. I have competed a lot in the past, but mostly I just do it for pleasure and I teach when I get the time.'

'Children, Maggie said.'

'Disabled kids, yes.' His face suddenly lit up. 'It's so inspiring, seeing what pleasure they get from it, Karen. Kids in wheelchairs who have basically been written off, they find they have a real skill . . . it's just incredible to watch their confidence grow. They amaze themselves. That's the great thing about shooting, you don't have to be Superman. Even blind people can shoot.'

'Really?'

'Yeah, someone rings a bell near the target and they learn to shoot towards the sound. Just fantastic. You should come along one day, I'll give you a lesson . . .'

'I'd—' She stopped. They were talking as if they had some sort of a future together.

William must have realized it too, because they fell into a tense silence, neither daring to speak as they both lay facing each other on the sand. She had insisted he put suntan lotion on his face – which, being fair, was probably already beyond rescue – and the white cream was smeared above his right eyebrow where he hadn't rubbed it in properly. She longed to reach over and do it for him, but it seemed dangerously intimate.

'Your grandmother must have been quite a woman, to take you on like that,' she said, plucking a sentence out of the air.

'Wasn't she just? I mean she was in her sixties when I was born and she literally became my parent. Dad did his best, but he was always travelling and he didn't really know what to do with me when he did come home . . .' He paused. 'I wish you could have met her. She was a life force.'

There it was again, his almost unconscious desire to link her with his life. It made her sad.

She pulled herself into a sitting position, took a long breath. 'I thought if I put some distance between us for a few weeks, I would get some perspective. It's ridiculous. All my life I've believed in the premise that every problem has a solution if you only look hard enough. But there is no solution for us.' The words hung heavy in the still air. 'And God won't even allow you to kiss me,' she added, almost angrily.

He looked away. 'It isn't God you should be angry with . . .'

They both turned towards the sea again.

Suddenly the sexual tension between them was like a fizzing, writhing mass. Karen wished he would just go away. She got up, he followed, and without saying another word they packed away the remains of the picnic and walked back up the beach and along the promenade towards his car.

★

After she'd said a brief goodbye to him, she wandered back along the front, at a loss as to what to do. Mike was closing up the café as she drew level.

'Hi,' he said, 'I wondered where you'd got to. Fancy a drink?'

They sometimes went to the pub across the road at the end of the day, and now she nodded. She didn't want to be alone in the flat to stew.

'I'm in a mess,' she said, when they were seated at a table in a cordoned-off area on the pavement outside the pub.

'Yeah?'

'This man I like. He's a vicar.'

Mike looked incredulous and then he began to laugh. 'A bloody vicar? You're kidding me.'

She didn't see what was so funny.

'That makes him even more of a polisher. Married *and* a vicar. Blimey!'

'Anyone can fall in love, can't they?'

'Ooh, love, is it? Not just good old lust?' He sucked his teeth. 'I'm not exactly a religious man, but don't vicars get taught in vicar school how to control their feelings . . . hair shirts and suchlike?'

'Obviously not,' she said, wishing she'd never told Mike anything.

He must have seen her expression because his own struggled to become more serious. 'But hey, Karen, whether he's a vicar or not – and there's plenty who misbehave if you believe what you read in the papers – he's being unfaithful.'

'Don't start.'

'Well, he is. And you can't trust a man who cheats on his wife . . . or vice versa.'

'We haven't cheated.' Karen clung stubbornly to the only-a-picnic theory.

'What, no nooky?'

She shook her head.

'Not even a kiss?' He raised his eyebrows.

She shook her head. 'Not even one bloody kiss.'

'Sounds like it's still cheating, darlin', from the look on your face.'

Annoyed, she said, 'And you never did . . . cheat?'

He laughed. 'You didn't meet my missus. Wouldn't have dared.'

'But you wanted to?'

He thought about this a moment. 'Nope, never did. Course there were women I liked the look of over the years, but I never thought to take it further.'

'Nor me.'

Karen watched him take a long swallow of his pint.

'This wife of his, what's the story there?'

'She seems to be a very good vicar's wife.'

'I meant what's his situation with her.'

'No idea, he never talks about her to me.'

'Not even to say that she doesn't understand him?' Mike gave her an amused grin.

She wished he'd shut up. 'Can we talk about something else?'

He gave her an admonishing finger wag. 'See, that's the problem. You're in denial. Don't want to face the truth that this geezer's in a perfectly happy marriage, just can't keep his trousers zipped.'

Jaw tensed with irritation, she muttered, 'It's not like that. I told you, we aren't having sex.'

'Not yet. But that doesn't mean he's good, just means he's playing a long game.'

She wanted to smack him and bent her head to avoid his censorious glance.

Mike let out a long sigh. 'Listen, it's your life, Karen. I shouldn't judge, I hardly know you. But it won't end well. This guy'll muck you about for a while, then scuttle off back to wifey. And you'll be left with a broken heart.' In response to her glare, he held his hand up and added, 'Just saying. Wouldn't be a friend if I didn't.'

At the end of the uncomfortable drink, Karen hurried up to the flat, dying to be on her own. Her defences had been breached by Mike's well-meaning bluntness. But despite that, as she sat on the tiny balcony with another glass of white wine in her hand, she perversely allowed herself a moment to indulge the possibility that whatever Mike said, whatever Will said, whatever she pretended to believe, she and William Haskell would one day be together. Their connection was too powerful to ignore. It couldn't be right, she insisted to herself, that such a synergy wasn't meant to be. The inevitable break-up of his marriage, the ruination of his career, these setbacks were swept aside in her love-addled brain.

Love conquered all, didn't it?

Throwing practical techniques at an emotional problem, Karen spent the next day making a 'life map' – an idea she'd found when googling inspiration for those wanting to move forward out of a rut.

She picked up a drawing pad and a set of neon highlighters in yellow, green, pink and orange from the newsagents on the front. Then, starting with a circle in the middle of the paper with a naive sketch of herself, her name printed below, she drew arrows and more circles, some with factual notes of her qualifications, work experience, skills, finances, location, etc. Some with personal notes such as William, Largo, Sophie, sea, love, Haydn, beach, age. It began with her usual neatness, but quickly started to ramble, extend and criss-cross over two sheets of A4 until it looked like the disturbed doodlings of a crazy person.

It obsessed her for a whole morning. But when she finally forced herself to stop, the only positive feeling she took away was one of catharsis at the process itself.

The mishmash of neon colours on the paper in front of her just seemed to prove what a total mess her life was in. It offered no obvious way forward.

She kept it on the table and whenever she passed she took another look, hoping that a miracle might occur and a clear path would suddenly present itself. But the only relevant path – the one where she gave William up for good – must have been obscured in the undergrowth of felt tip.

'How are you?' Karen asked, when Sophie finally answered her phone after three messages left.

'OK,' was the short answer.

'What are you up to?'

Silence, then, 'Nothing much.'

Karen didn't take offence at Sophie's tone; there was something so flat and unengaged in her stepdaughter's voice that it didn't seem personal.

'How's Largo? I miss him.'

'He's good.'

'And the fête? Are things coming along OK?'

'Yeah . . . I didn't go to the last meeting. Couldn't face it.'

'You sound a bit low.'

'I'm fine.'

'Any progress on finding something to do?'

'Nope.'

Karen heard the sounds of Sophie moving around, the click of a cupboard opening, water running. She was clearly not focusing on the call.

'Umm . . . listen, Karen, I've got to go.'

'Oh. Alright. Well, let's talk another time, then.'

'Yes. Bye.'

The line went dead. Karen sat, the phone in her hand, thinking. Was there someone else there? Was that what had constrained Sophie? Or maybe the girl had just woken up, even though it was nearly midday. She hadn't sounded hostile, just very detached. Karen felt something wasn't right and decided to phone again later in the day.

But in the end she forgot, because William texted her five minutes later and said he would be in her area around five.

Might you be able to meet me, just for a very quick beach walk? X

The tone of his text implied a nervousness about her response. Quite rightly, having acknowledged last time that their situation was hopeless. But she wasn't able to be angry with him.

William did not have his dog collar on. He was wearing pale shorts and a blue T-shirt, sunglasses, trainers. There was no trace of the vicar, he looked like any other man on the beach. And there was something different about him, apart from his clothes – a sort of jauntiness, a devil-may-care aura that she hadn't seen before.

She grinned as she looked him up and down.

Will laughed. 'Too hot for the uniform.'

They set off along the beach. Karen had brought a small cool-bag with a bottle of white wine, two plastic glasses, some olives and crisps.

'I thought we agreed we wouldn't do this again,' she said as they walked.

'I know . . . I acted on impulse. I was passing—'

'Really?'

'Yes, this time I really was,' he said, earnestly. 'I had to pick up a chair Janey bought on eBay from a man who lives up the road from here. But he wasn't there and wasn't answering his phone, so I'll have to go back.'

'Today?'

'I'll swing past on my way home . . . Janey's at her parents' till Thursday.'

Karen absorbed this information, wondering if this were the reason he seemed so carefree.

'I thought you might refuse to see me,' he said.

They sat on the rug again, side by side. The tide was coming in and they moved further up, drinking wine and eating crisps, toes digging in the warm sand, the conversation sparse and general.

'Why do you think it's sandy here and pebbly there?' Karen asked.

'Umm . . . something to do with the strength of the waves, which is different depending on the geography and the type of stone. There's flint around here, so maybe it doesn't break down so easily.' He laughed. 'But don't quote me. I'm horribly ignorant of most things geophysical, but I had to help Rachel with an eco-project about sea defences for her GCSE.'

'Has she finished school now?' Karen liked Rachel, what she knew of her. She seemed like a quiet, good-natured girl. But as William seldom mentioned his family to Karen – for obvious reasons – she usually respected that.

But now his face broke into a broad smile. 'Yes! Wonderful moment when they're finally free. She turned eighteen last week. She's off to Seville to work in a hotel for the summer, improve her Spanish. She's doing modern languages at Edinburgh. Got the required three As – two of them A-star.'

'That's great.' She could hear the pride in his voice and was ashamed to feel a searing jealousy of his family life, of which she could never be a part. 'You'll miss her.'

'I will . . .' he looked off into the distance, his expression unreadable.

'Swim?' Karen said, partly to change the subject, but also because she was so overheated, so sweaty, that she thought she might die if she didn't dive into the water that very instant.

And this time Will had brought his trunks.

The sea was warmer than ever – the water coming in across sand baked for hours in the hot July sun – and very still. William was a strong swimmer, his upper torso muscled and sure. They both swam far out, enjoying the bliss of the cool salty waves closing over their heads, bringing instant relief from the heat.

Later, they lolled about on their backs, toes out of the water, arms splayed to the side, eyes skyward.

'I think there's going to be a storm,' she said, looking over to the west where a dark mass of cloud lay far off on the horizon.

'Air feels heavy enough.'

The waves lapped lazily around them and Karen never wanted this moment to end.

After they'd dried themselves – neither got out of their wet costumes, which would have involved a precarious dance with the towel they were both too shy to perform – they sat back down on the rug, hugging their knees as they finished the bottle of wine and nibbled at the olives. The beach gradually cleared of families keen to get their small children to bed, or to avoid the threatening stormcloud, moving ever closer, the sea a gun-metal grey beneath it. The breeze, now soupy with moisture, blew hundreds of tiny thunder flies across the shore.

'I think we'd better go,' she said.

They began to pack up their stuff. 'You could come up to the flat and change there,' she offered. 'Have a shower.'

Karen saw him hesitate, then shake his head.

'Thanks, but I'd better not. I should get back,' he said, no weight to his words.

But she, perhaps stoked by the wine, read a wealth of prudish censure into the sentence. *For all the world*, she thought angrily, *as if I were some prostitute luring a poor innocent off the street.* 'It's only a shower, for God's sake. What are you so afraid of?'

William raised his head from his task of pulling on his shoes, her sharpness bringing a startled look to his face.

'I—'

'You're perfectly happy to lie to Janey, spend hours on the beach with me, swim, drink wine, gaze into my eyes when it suits you. But then your conscience twinges and – oh, heavens – you'd better not go too far and actually *do* anything, be alone with me. *Anything* could happen. And then what? Maybe God will strike you dumb.'

His expression hardened. 'I told you, this has nothing to do with God.'

'No? Really? I think it has everything to do with him, or at least your slavish devotion to him.' She knew she was going too far, but she no longer cared.

'What we are doing wouldn't be right even if there were no God,' he said quietly.

'You think I don't know that? But I wasn't offering to have sex with you, William, in case you wondered. In fact, I made a decision over the weekend that I wouldn't . . . couldn't . . . even see you again.' She stood over him, hands on her hips. 'I moved to the seaside to protect you and your family from having to see me all the time . . .' She paused. 'And to protect myself, of course, which obviously didn't work so well.' Her last words were more to herself than him.

He wasn't looking at her but intently out to sea – maybe expecting the cavalry, in the shape of the on-coming storm, to rescue him.

'You pretend, with these innocent little picnics, that nothing is happening between us. I do the same, it makes me feel better. But it's a lie and we both know it.'

'What do you want me to say?' William stood up and began dusting the sand off his clothes, his tone softly apologetic.

'Shit or get off the pot, William, to use a seriously unattractive expression.' She snatched up the rug and began shaking it.

Now he faced her. 'I should never have come today. I'm sorry, it was so selfish. '

He put his hands on her arms, the rug still suspended from her hands.

'No, you shouldn't. And I shouldn't have agreed to see you. I'm struggling,' she said, looking him in the eye, her anger now replaced by misery. 'Being with you, however much I love it – and

I do – makes being apart so hard . . . not knowing when, or if, I'll see you again.'

'I know. I know exactly how you feel. I feel the same. And I wish things were different, but they're not.'

'Just accept what is, right?' she said, tears pricking behind her eyes. 'But should we do that? Should we just turn our backs on what we have? *Can* we?'

'Even asking that question seems impossible to me, Karen. Because it means giving everything else up. My family, the Church, my whole life. It's so huge. I can't do that.'

Yes, you can, were the words on the tip of her tongue. But instead she said, 'No. You can't. I know you can't.' She looked away. 'Are you in love with Janey?'

William didn't answer. He pulled her against him and she heard him let out a deep sigh. But although she wanted more than all the riches in the universe to accept his embrace and just feel the pleasure of his warm body against her own, she couldn't bear to allow another ounce of feeling for this man – who would never be hers – to leak from her heart.

She had to close the box and run.

'Sorry . . .' She pulled away, continued folding the rug, putting it neatly under her arm, emptying the dregs of wine into the sand, gathering up the cool-bag, her shorts and her towel, shaking out her flip-flops. Her movements were methodical, unhurried, perhaps her subconscious hoping, as always, for some last-minute miracle to occur.

William had dropped his hands and was standing there, dumbly.

'You'd better get back to the car before you get soaked,' she added, as the first plump drops of rain ran cool across her face.

'Karen—' he began.

But there was nothing else to say except goodbye.

The storm broke barely seconds after Karen reached her building. From her top-floor window she had a spectacular view across the bay as the sky darkened and the heavens opened. She cried along with it, her tears, abundant and unhindered, running down her cheeks just as the rain did on the glass, her sobs drowned out by the thunder and pelting rain. She hated him, she loved him; she despised him, she admired him; she trusted him with her life but she could not trust him with her heart.

She spent the next hour crying on and off, drinking more wine, listening to the saddest country songs she could find on her play-list, but mostly just clicking 'repeat' for 'Blue Eyes Crying In The Rain' over and over again, singing along with Shania when she wasn't choked with sobs. She was crying with anger at William, then at herself, then for her stupid, empty life.

The storm passed over, leaving just the rain pouring down the balcony windows.

When there was a knock on the door it was quite dark outside, but barely nine o'clock. She thought it must be Mike wanting company for a drink and went to let him in. She could do with some company too, the despair was beginning to frighten her.

William stood there. He was soaking wet and didn't look apologetic.

'May I come in?' he asked.

She hesitated, then nodded and stood back to let him pass.

He must have seen that she had been crying – her cheeks were surely scarred by runnels of tears – but he didn't comment. He just took a deep breath and pulled her into his arms. She stared at him in surprise, but he still said nothing. Instead, he pressed his mouth hard to her own.

What followed was nothing that she expected. There was no gentleness on either part – just a fury of desire, which tore at them, sent them wild as they sought to possess each other more absolutely, filling the void that months of unfulfilled desire had wrought. Their bodies seemed to be totally in sync as they fell, wordless, on to the sofa bed, scrabbling with clothes, angry and loving and desperate at the same time. His face wet with rain, hers with tears, their mouths, limbs, flesh hot and entangled till both reached their climax and fell back exhausted and in shock.

For a few minutes all that could be heard in the flat was their laboured breathing as they lay pressed naked up against each other on the cushions. William laughed; it was a joyous, exuberant sound. She joined in, her body bruised and alive. But there was no need for words. His arm was around her shoulder, her cheek nestling against his chest, but as they lay there, his hand began to caress her breast, his fingers playful as they toyed with one nipple, then the other. She turned her face up to kiss him, tasted the salt still on his lips, and once more the longing took hold and they began to make love again.

This time it was open-ended, not climax-driven. A slow, exquisite exploration, which drove them deeper and deeper into each other's soul with every touch of lips, skin, sex. No boundaries, no time, no thought, no need, only a miraculous, enveloping sensuality. The sky was beginning to lighten with the summer dawn by the time they both fell into an exhausted sleep. During the hours of love-making they had sometimes paused, drunk water, talked for a while, then, as if neither could bear to waste a single moment of that night, they had begun to kiss again.

They woke to brilliant sunlight, cramped and stiff, chilly from the inadequate throw they had drawn around them before sleep had intervened. Karen, although reluctant to lose the touch of William's skin against her own, pulled herself up, shivering. She squinted at the clock. 7.07 A.M., it read. She looked back at Will, whose responding smile was almost drugged. He blinked, running his hand over his hair, pushing the dark strands off his forehead.

She padded across the floor for her dressing gown, then came and sat back down next to Will on the sofa, which was still not pulled out into a bed. Loath to speak and break the spell, she took his hand in hers, holding it gently in her grasp, stroking her thumb across his palm.

'What's the time?' he asked, and when she told him he merely nodded.

'We could swim,' she said after a while. 'It's a stunning day.'

'It'll be cold after the storm . . . the water,' he said, pulling a face.

Which prompted her to dig him in the ribs and call him 'a wuss'.

And he was right, it was cold. Cold and still choppy, a brisk wind ruffling the surf, the reflection of the morning sun so bright it hurt their eyes. But oh how glorious to feel the water bathe their tired bodies, wash away the stiffness, send blood racing through their veins as they swam the length of the bay and back.

As they walked up the beach wrapped in their towels, Karen saw Mike pulling up the metal shutters on the café. He waved, then saw William, hesitated, turned away. She didn't care – not about him or anyone else – not this morning.

'So did you pick up the chair?' Karen asked, when they were both seated at the oval table in her flat with coffee, brown toast and marmalade. William looked scrubbed clean, his cheeks glowing, his hair damp and shiny around his face as he hungrily munched through his breakfast.

'Chair?'

'The one Janey bought on eBay? Did you get it last night.'

'No. I didn't go very far, only to the car. I was thinking.'

'You were outside all that time?'

He nodded sheepishly. 'I just couldn't make myself leave.'

Karen imagined him sitting in the car as the storm beat around him, arguing with himself, knowing by heart the two sides of the dispute and not wanting to think about them right now. She knew he was just about to go and she had to make every second count.

'Thank you for last night,' he said, after a silence. The look he gave her was steady and full of tenderness. 'Thank you so much.'

She smiled. 'Who'd have thought it?'

'Thought what?'

'That such passion lurked beneath these ordinary exteriors.'

He looked a bit bewildered for a second. 'It's not . . . for me . . .'

'Nor for me either . . . not normal at all.' The fierce, primal union with William last night was nothing like the accomplished sexual technique that Harry had offered in the early days – learnt and honed over the years with a string of women before Karen. Sex with Harry had been a lot of fun, but sex with William reached to her very soul.

When they embraced and said goodbye, they clung to each other, each knowing that as soon as he was alone and away from her, his conscience would start yelling at him again, telling him that he must behave.

She wanted to say something to override that voice, but nothing in the external world had changed since last night. Except, of course, that now there was the knowledge of an extraordinary bond between them – one that reached way beyond either of their experience.

CHAPTER ELEVEN

'The randy vicar, I take it,' Mike said, his face radiating disapproval.

Karen had gone back to bed after Will left, not waking till nearly twelve. Last night seemed unreal without his presence to confirm it. And now, as she sat at one of the café tables, she felt unable to concentrate on anything.

''Fraid so.'

'Spent the night, did he?'

'He did.'

Mike laughed. 'God, what are you like? You've sat there for days like you're listening to me. Only yesterday you're banging on about flow charts or some such bollocks that'll get you back on track. Then our friend the polisher pitches up with a cool-bag and it's all for nowt.' He saw her frown. 'I saw you last night on the beach.'

'It was my cool-bag,' she said.

'Oh, well . . . that's OK, then.'

They both started laughing.

'Good night, was it? Only you look like you're stoned again. Don't tell me the reverend trades illegal substances along with all his other vices.'

'Nothing like that. Oh, Mike, what am I going to do?'

'You could stop mooching about and help me with these sand-wiches. If you can see straight, that is.'

'Sophie, please can you call me. This is the fourth time I've tried and I'm getting worried.' Karen put the phone down.

She'd stayed in the café helping Mike out for longer than he needed her, because she felt so restless. She didn't fancy sitting alone in the flat or doing any of the other things that had kept her so contentedly occupied over the last few weeks. The come-down after last night was hard, especially as she couldn't call William to run through the experience together, couldn't plan, couldn't hope.

Why won't Sophie return my calls? she wondered. Was she annoyed with her about something? Then she decided the girl was prob-ably just on a trip to London. Jennifer had said she'd look after Largo if Sophie had to go up to town, so perhaps she should ring her and check everything was alright. But then she decided she was being stupid. Sophie was a woman of thirty, who was quite cap-able of looking after herself. Karen would be going home next week anyway, in time for the dreaded village fête. The thought of all the mayhem involved hit her suddenly – memories of previous years coming afresh to her mind. But now that dread had been partially replaced by a sense of anticipation, knowing she would be so near William again and have a legitimate reason for being together, even though it would be under the beady eyes of the village.

Sophie rang a couple of hours later. 'Sorry, yeah, phone needed charging. No need to worry.'

It sounded odd, her excuse. Sophie was wedded to her phone.

'I'm coming back on Thursday, to help with the fête.'

'Thursday?' there was a note of panic in Sophie's voice.

'Yes, there's always so much to do in the run-up. And everyone wants to know stuff and drop things off. It's not a pretty sight.'

Sophie didn't respond.

'Are you there?'

'Umm . . . what time will you be coming?'

'I'll set off after breakfast. It's only an hour, I should be home by mid-morning.'

'OK . . . OK, well, I'll see you then.'

And the girl was gone even before Karen had had time to ask about the dog, or say goodbye.

What was that panic about? she wondered, then laughed to herself. The place was a total tip, no doubt, and Sophie knew she would have to clear it up before Karen got back. But still . . .

If Maggie had been there she would have called her and asked her to drop round, but she didn't want people in the village nosing about her business, as they undoubtedly would, pressing all kinds of questions on Sophie about why Karen hadn't been at home for so long. She hoped Sophie wasn't doing anything stupid – like moving some unsuitable boyfriend in, or taking drugs – she was certainly not sounding like herself.

'Do you want to do another month in the flat?' Mike asked the next morning as they were sitting having a coffee before the crowds appeared.

'Has it really been a month?'

'Longer, five weeks . . . didn't realize myself till I checked last night.'

Karen hesitated. She would never sort herself out while she

could indulge in the distraction of Mike's café and the beach. The winters would be wearing here, she imagined. Mike shut up shop from December to March; he said there weren't enough punters to justify the costs of keeping the place open. He spent the winter doing private catering for functions, particularly around Christmas and New Year.

'I suppose I ought to go home,' she said.

He raised his eyebrows. 'Don't sound too enthusiastic.'

She laughed. 'No, well . . . back to reality.'

'And the polisher zone.'

'Don't call him that. Please.'

'I'll stop calling him that when he stops cheating on his wife and leaves you alone.'

Karen touched Mike's hand across the table. 'You're looking out for me, and I appreciate that. I don't know what I would have done without you these past weeks. But you're wasting your time. I'm a hopeless case.'

'Yeah, looks like it. I'll miss you,' he added. 'But if it doesn't work out and you need to escape again, just give me a bell. I won't get any takers for the place so late in the season.' He turned as a couple entered the café then got up, pulling his apron tighter around his narrow body. 'Anyway, I'm picky about my tenants.'

'You mean you only take hopeless cases?'

'Something like that,' he grinned as he went off to serve the customers.

Karen, now she had made the decision to go home, felt calmer than she had in a while, putting worries on hold in her mind and just enjoying these last days of freedom before the responsibility of the fête, the house, the dog, Sophie, all intervened. And she had a lot to occupy her mind. Surely the other night would have consequences, she kept thinking. Was it remotely possible to ignore the strength of their feelings for each other? Or was Will capable of putting the other night back in the box and letting the lie insidiously eat away at his soul?

The more Karen thought about it, the more it seemed inevitable that something had to give. But whenever she reached this point in her mind, where William's cover was blown, it was exactly like imagining a real explosion. The debris fell in a totally unpredictable scatter of chaos. What her part might be in the aftermath, she wasn't able to tell.

Whatever the putative position, however, the reality was that there had been complete radio silence from him since the night they'd made love. She had checked her phone every ten minutes the next day. At first she had excused him because she knew he was teaching at the archery club that morning. Then because he'd be home with Janey. Then because he was still home with Janey. But when no text was forthcoming and the excuses palled, she accepted what she had always known, that he was simply overwhelmed with guilt.

She kept hoping the silence meant that he would soon be back on her doorstep, pushing her backwards on to the sofa in an orgy of lust.

But as the days went by and there was nothing, she knew that his conscience had won this round.

Driving into the village it was as if she had never been away. She waved to Roger Standing, out with his dog, just as if she'd seen him yesterday. Up since dawn packing up and cleaning the flat, the quick coffee she'd had with Mike seemed a long time ago as the wheels of the car scrunched over the gravel of her drive. She was looking forward to something to eat and a large cup of

coffee – albeit from Sophie's annoying machine – in her own kitchen again. Immediately assailed by a barking, jumping,
tail-wagging Labrador, who rushed joyfully up to her as soon as
she was out of the car, her heart melted as she held him, hugged
him, patted his soft fur, fending off his paws on her bare legs.

'Hey, boy, hey there . . . God, I've missed you . . . yes, yes . . .
I'm back . . . glad to see you too.' She laughed with pleasure,
pushing him out of the way in order to get her bags from the
back seat.

There was no sign of Sophie.

Inside, the house was silent and appeared to be in darkness, the
curtains in all the downstairs rooms drawn closed. Karen went
round pulling them open, calling her stepdaughter, who finally
emerged from her bedroom, looming at the top of the stairs. Karen
was shocked. Sophie must have lost more than a stone in weight in
the five weeks she'd been away. She looked pale and unkempt, her
dark hair straggling in dry, bushy waves around her face, her baggy
tracksuit pants, grey T-shirt and grubby pink slipper-socks making her appear much younger than she was.

'Hi,' Sophie said, attempting a smile.

'Hi, Sophie . . .' She waited for the girl to come downstairs, but
she hovered on the landing, not moving. 'Cup of coffee?'

This seemed to galvanize her. Sophie gave a small sigh then nodded and began to descend the stairs, running her hand down the
banister as if she needed support.

Karen didn't say any more until they were both seated at the
table with cups of coffee. She felt like an intruder in her own house.
The kitchen was scrubbed to within an inch of its life, every surface gleaming, not a speck of dirt anywhere. But more puzzling
was the fact that everything that had been on the worktops – a

basket with a variety of teas, a fish-shaped trivet, a metal egg timer, coffee grinder, knife rack, drinks tray, glass biscuit barrel, salt and pepper mill, bottle of olive oil, bread bin and board – even the Lake District calendar Maggie had given Karen as a memento from when she'd gone climbing there – had vanished. It was like a holiday rental before the new tenants arrive, with only the kettle and coffee machine in sight. Karen didn't want to ask Sophie where all the stuff was just yet, she looked so frail.

'How are you?' she asked, not knowing how to express her concern.

'I'm OK,' came the laconic reply.

'If you don't mind me saying, you don't look OK.'

Without smiling, Sophie just flicked her eyebrows up and then turned her attention back to her coffee cup, which she held carefully in both hands.

'You've lost so much weight.'

'Not really.'

'You have. Haven't you been eating properly?'

Sophie didn't answer.

'Sophie, look at me,' Karen insisted. And when her stepdaughter finally raised her eyes, which looked blank and dead, not even defiant, she said, 'What's wrong? Please, tell me.'

'Nothing's wrong.'

'Are you depressed?'

'No. I said, I'm OK.' The stubborn note was warning Karen to back off.

But she was worried. 'Have you been out, you look so pale.'

Sophie gave an exasperated sigh. 'Yes, I've been out, OK? I go out every single day, twice a day, to take Largo for a walk.'

'Right . . . and what else has been happening?'

'God, I don't know. Not a lot. What do you want me to say? Can you get off my case, please?'

Karen nodded. 'Sorry . . . I'm just worried about you, that's all.'

'Well, you shouldn't be. I told you, I'm fine.' She got up, leaving her mug on the table, and walked out.

That went well, Karen thought. *I've only been home ten minutes and already I've antagonized her.*

She got up and started opening cupboards. All the things were there, neatly put away, made room for, apparently, by a drastic cull of the tins and jars that had previously taken up most of the space. The bareness felt angry and soulless, as if Sophie were deliberately trying to expunge all character from the kitchen.

She went through to the other rooms, all equally immaculate, only the bare necessities on view. It seemed strange. But maybe Sophie was just being efficient and preparing it for the fête. Because it all happened in the kitchen. The sandwiches – egg mayonnaise, ham and cucumber – were made up there, the scones spread with jam and cream, cakes and biscuits put out on plates, the teapots and milk jugs filled, crockery washed, all prior to being taken through to the tea tent. It was the place where the helpers came to rest, the hub of all activity. *So yes, it was probably a very sensible thing to clear the decks beforehand*, Karen told herself. But she was left with a nagging doubt about Sophie's real motive.

She went upstairs to unpack, her stomach suddenly knotted with the knowledge that Will was only four doors down the lane. She would surely bump into him later – or tomorrow, maybe, when the fête preparations really got under way.

Karen realized she was happy to be home. She had missed the space, her bedroom with its luxurious Heal's mattress – Harry had insisted on the best – her large kitchen, the sitting room with its deep sofa covered in cornflower-blue linen, the wide-screen television in the den, her garden, her beloved dog. The house was, by many people's standards, old-fashioned – in fact, it suddenly looked old-fashioned to Karen after her weeks in Mike's modern flat – but it was still comfortable.

Sophie slouched down for supper and sat picking at the chicken salad Karen had made. It was a warm evening, and they were eating on the table outside, overlooking the lawn at the back of the house.

'When are you going back?' Sophie asked.

'Back to the seaside? I'm not.'

'Oh.'

'You'll have to put up with me nagging you again.'

This brought a faint smile to the girl's face. 'Actually I don't like it here alone. It's weird.'

'Have you made friends with anyone in the village?' Karen asked, relieved by Sophie's response. It explained her mood. She had obviously just been lonely, nothing more sinister.

Sophie rolled her eyes. 'There isn't anyone under sixty, so no, I haven't.'

'Slight exaggeration.'

'Fifty, then.'

'There's Rachel Haskell.'

'She's in Spain.'

Karen did a mental trawl through the inhabitants of the village and realized Sophie was right, apart from the estate agent, Dominic, who couldn't be more than forty and had a wife and two small daughters.

'Anyway, I don't want friends. I've got plenty, it's just they're in London.'

'Have you been up to see them?'

'Not much,' she said.

Karen noted her shifty expression and suspected the girl hadn't budged from the house. It was pointless bullying Sophie into a circular discussion about her prospects of work and social interaction – not least because she herself was virtually in the same boat as her stepdaughter.

'At least you're over the vicar,' Sophie said.

'What do you mean?'

'Well, you went away to get over him. So if you're coming back you must have succeeded.'

'Yes . . . yes, totally. It was just a silly moment,' Karen blurted out. 'I was in a bad way after your father's death, and William was there for me.'

Sophie nodded. 'That, and probably a touch of the uniform syndrome. We've all got it.'

' "Uniform syndrome"?'

'Women love men in uniforms, you must have heard of that.'

'I thought that meant soldiers. Heroic types.'

'Yes, but priests and vicars are sort of heroic when they're all dressed up in their robes being holy. It helps us look up to them as someone special.'

Karen just nodded.

'Take William, for instance,' Sophie went on. 'He always wears black trousers, black shirt, black shoes, white dog collar. So he stands out, we respect him as a holy person. But the other morning I saw him in shorts and trainers and he looked like any ordinary Joe.' She smiled. 'And when I said hello he seemed all sheepish, as if I had caught him out in something shady. Obviously he's not cool with normal clothes.'

At that moment, the doorbell rang and Karen jumped up, relieved not to have to respond.

'Who will that be?' she asked.

'Better not be the vicar,' Sophie chuckled.

It was Jennifer Simmons.

'Karen, welcome back! I saw your car and thought I'd just drop in and touch base.'

'Hi, Jennifer. Good to see you. We're out in the garden, come through.'

'Phew!' Jennifer plumped down on one of the garden chairs, fanning her face with a sheaf of papers she was holding. 'Hello, Sophie.' She wheezed quietly for a moment. 'Can't get my breath in this heat . . . not that I'm really complaining, of course.'

'Perfect for the fête,' Karen said, handing Jennifer her own glass of water that she hadn't touched.

'Yes, now the fête . . . all seems to be going to plan on that front. The reverend has been marvellous, an absolute saint. So much better than dotty old Bob, who just got underfoot.' Jennifer said. 'Anyhoos, I won't bore you with the details now, my dears, but I wanted to warn you the men are coming tomorrow with the tent. Probably quite early. Is that alright?'

'Of course.'

'Do you want someone here to supervise? I can get Trevor to pop round.'

Trevor was the caretaker at the primary school in the next village and did Jennifer's garden in his spare time.

'Maybe get him to check they've done it right before they go. Not sure I'd know. Harry always did that.'

Even with a few whiskies inside him, Harry still functioned in areas related to their day-to-day living, such as insurance, house maintenance, the car, banking. Karen had thought she'd miss his input after he died, but in fact it felt good to be more in control, to know exactly what was what, not to be waved away as a mere woman from anything that required a form to be filled in, money to be spent. But the tent was a step too far.

'Right. Will do.' She began to haul herself upright. 'Mustn't keep you from your supper. I'll ring in the morning and we can go over a few last-minute things.'

Karen showed her to the door.

'Must say the seaside certainly agrees with you,' Jennifer commented as she said goodbye. 'You look positively radiant.' She patted Karen's arm. 'Good to get a break after what you've been through with dear Harry. Such a shame.'

Karen, as she went back outside to Sophie, felt the village closing in around her again. Which, although comforting in one way, brought with it a constant need to dissemble – or perhaps 'deceive' would be a more appropriate word.

Friday at seven thirty brought the men with the tent. There was a lot of teeth-sucking and head-shaking, despite Karen leading them to the exact same spot the tent had sat on – very successfully – for every fête in the last decade.

'Not sure that'll be big enough,' said the older man, eyeing the patch of grass, 'what with the slope an' all.'

'It is. It went there before.'

'Yeah? Same size tent, was it?'

'I imagine so.' She knew Bernard, the committee secretary and man in charge of hiring equipment, would never deviate from one of his set plans without a fair amount of torture.

Tent man was slowly shaking his head again, arms akimbo, khaki T-shirt already stained with sweat, as he scanned the grass – brown now in patches from the hot summer.

'See . . . if we put it up and it's too long, then the end'll be hanging down the slope. And a sloping tent's no good to no one.'

'Well, why don't you measure it, then?' she suggested.

The man's brow lightened. 'Yeah, that might work.' Then it fell again. 'Don't have a tape measure with us, do we, Joe?'

Joe, who was busy texting, didn't reply.

Karen sighed. 'Look, just put it up. It'll fit. And if it doesn't, I'll take the blame.'

Tent man frowned, clearly finding Karen not fit for purpose on the tent-erecting front. But he was stumped for further argument, so the pair of them slouched off, muttering, to their van.

Karen vaguely remembered a similar scenario a few years back. *Roll on Sunday*, she thought, knowing this was only the first of many such glitches she would have to address in the next forty-eight hours.

William dropped by with Jennifer after lunch. He had a clipboard in his hand and was looking every inch the helpful vicar, his hand under Jennifer's arm to steady her as they walked across the lawn to inspect the tent.

Karen could hardly look at him.

'Trevor says it's solid, though you should have heard the fuss they made doing it,' she told them, as they walked through the open side of the canvas structure.

Although providing shade from the hot sun, it wasn't exactly cool inside.

'The cream in the scones and cakes is going to melt instantly if it's hot like this. We'll have to bring them out in relays,' Jennifer said.

'We could use fans,' William suggested, not looking at Karen either.

'No electricity,' Karen reminded him, then turned to find Janey standing in the doorway of the tent. She froze.

'Hi, guys, how's it all going?' Janey's voice held its usual pitch of slightly strangled niceness. 'I was passing and I thought I'd check when was best to drop in the teapots.' She looked to Karen for a response.

But Karen was finding it hard to speak, the images from her night with William – the crumpled shorts on the floor, the sight of his fingers around her nipple – flashing like a silent film before her eyes.

'Janey, you're such a darling.' Jennifer unwittingly came to the rescue. 'How kind you are to give us your precious teapots. Tea tastes so much nicer from a pretty pot.'

'Oh, they aren't precious, Jennifer,' Janey said. 'I just collect the ones I like, but they're often just a couple of quid in a charity shop.'

'But they're your collection . . . I only hope nothing terrible happens and one gets broken.'

Karen glanced quickly at William and saw he was sweating and flushed in his black suit.

'Please don't worry about that for a single second,' Janey was saying, 'it will just give me a good excuse for buying some more.' She grinned at William. 'Which won't please my dear husband one bit.'

They were all smiling at this as they trooped outside again and stood in the middle of the lawn, Jennifer leaning on Karen this time, whilst William prepared to point out the final position of the various stalls from the diagram on his clipboard.

'Is it OK if I drop them round this evening?' Janey was at Karen's side.

'Umm . . . yes, fine. I'll be here. Thanks.'

'I'll leave you to it, then,' Janey said, and with a wave was gone.

Karen finally let out her breath, and watched William do the same.

'What a marvellous wife you have, William,' Jennifer said.

William just nodded dumbly.

Oh, how kind and dear and simply splendid, Karen muttered silently to herself as the other two droned on still more about the general marvellousness of Janey and her bloody teapot collection. *Typical that the woman would collect teapots*, she thought, although she wasn't quite sure why teapots, specifically, made her so annoyed.

When next she looked at William, the expression in his eyes was flat with resignation.

Jennifer and William said their goodbyes. In the past Karen would have wanted – and possibly engineered – some excuse for Will to stay behind and allow them a precious moment alone. But today she just wanted shot of them both and all reminders of the Reverend Haskell's incredible wife.

However, the vicar was of another mind. He walked Jennifer to her car, then came back and knocked timidly on the door. Karen was already halfway upstairs, hoping to talk to Sophie, who had appeared briefly round about midday and then shut herself up in her room again.

'Hi, did you forget something?'

'Just wanted to see how you were.'

Karen stared at him. 'We've just spent the last hour together, William.'

'I know, but . . . listen, I'm sorry about Janey coming round and stuff, but I suppose we knew this would happen.'

True, she thought, but the fact that they were aware of the problem didn't make it alright, in her opinion.

'I'm fine, William. I have no problem with Janey dropping off her teapots.' She struggled to sound genuine, not wanting him to know how much it hurt. And obviously she succeeded, because Will's face cleared and his previously hang-dog demeanour lifted, which in turn infuriated her.

'I'm so sorry . . .' he said, shifting uncomfortably on the doormat. Then added, 'This is sheer hell,' under his breath.

Her heart softened. 'Yeah, isn't it?'

'I'd better go.'

'Yes . . .'

He reached forward to lay his hand on her arm for a second, then quickly turned and hurried off across the gravel.

Janey drove into the driveway, parking behind Karen and Sophie's cars. Karen, steeling herself, went out to meet her as she began unloading the boot. Janey's greeting was friendly, Karen couldn't detect a single hint of suspicion or animosity.

'Let me help you with that,' she said, holding her hands out to take the first cardboard box.

'Thanks. There's three more to come. I wasn't sure how many pots you'd need, so I brought twenty. You don't have to use them all, of course.'

Janey had changed from the jeans she'd been wearing that

morning. She was dressed in a knee-length denim skirt, lace-trimmed flesh-pink vest top and decorated leather flip-flops that looked as if they'd been bought in a Moroccan bazaar. She looked pretty, a row of silver bracelets showing off her slim, tanned arms. Karen wondered if she and William were going out for the evening. The stabbing in her gut that accompanied this thought made her twitch violently as she took the first box from the vicar's wife.

'Wonderful. It's so kind of you. I hope none of them get damaged.' Karen conveniently parroted Jennifer as she carried the box through to the kitchen and put it on the table, Janey following close behind.

When all four boxes were unloaded, Janey hovered with her slightly unnerving book-balanced-on-the-head poise. 'So, how was your holiday?'

'Lovely, thanks. I was lucky with the weather.'

'Yes, hasn't it been gorgeous.'

'I hope it stays fine for tomorrow. I haven't checked the forecast.'

They continued in this vein – saying pretty much what you might to the newsagent or postman – while Karen waited for her to go. But Janey seemed fixed to the spot.

Does she want to say something to me? Karen wondered nervously. *Or does she want to be friends, perhaps?*

Into this awkward exchange, Sophie suddenly emerged, still in the same grubby tracksuit bottoms and old T-shirt. Karen silently prayed her stepdaughter wouldn't let her down.

'How are you doing, Sophie? Haven't seen you around much recently.' Janey gave the girl a smile of welcome.

'I'm good, thanks.'

'OK . . . well, I'd better get going.' She turned to Karen. 'Please don't worry if there are any accidents. As I said this morning, it's just a silly obsession I've had for years, and half of them aren't worth anything much.'

'We'll be careful, anyway. And thanks, it'll make a big difference to the tea.'

Karen felt an agonizing shaft of guilt as she showed the woman out. She was a genuinely good person, Janey. And one, in different circumstances, with whom Karen might have been friends.

'God, mental,' said Sophie when she went back into the kitchen. 'Bet you wish you'd stayed on the beach.'

Karen sighed, letting out a short laugh. 'It'll all be over by Sunday.'

CHAPTER TWELVE

It rained, of course. Not storms, but a glowering, persistent and chilly drizzle that started around eleven o'clock and had not let up when the fête opened at two. So instead of people taking a leisurely wander around the stalls, licking ice cream and sitting on the grass with their friends and families, they were trudging round in boots and waterproofs, buying a few pots of marmalade or a second-hand children's book, a tombola ticket, then heading for the shelter of the Pimm's or tea tent. From early on both tents were crammed to capacity with damp people, gratefully sipping hot tea from one of Janey's pretty pots or knocking back iced fruit cup.

Karen spent most of the afternoon in the kitchen, helping put out the sandwiches, whipping cream for the scones, cutting up the home-made cakes, boiling the kettle, washing the used tea things to send out again. Sophie pitched in sporadically, then just wandered off without saying where she was going. Karen was very happy to be so busy with the teas, she was deliberately staying out of the vicar's way. She'd barely seen William, except to watch him open the fête and make another one of his speeches about the importance of family and community – which was looking a bit bedraggled in the afternoon rain. Sheila, a wizard with the

193

church flowers, stalwart of the village – a woman many, including William, relied upon – had chosen to ferry the trays of food and drink to and fro from the kitchen to the tent.

'Such a shame,' she said to Karen, not for the first time, as she dumped another tray of dirty cups and plates on the draining board. Her grey-brown bob was lank with moisture, her spectacles misting up.

'No sign of it improving?'

'Nah, it's set in, this is.' She sat down heavily on one of the chairs with a tired sigh, wiping her face and then her glasses with a cotton hanky she pulled from her sleeve. 'And you mark my words, tomorrow we'll be back to blue sky and twenty-five degrees.'

'Are there many people still out there?'

'Some. Folk'll hang around as long as there's things to do. And they've not drawn the raffle or finished the duck races yet.'

'We've pretty much run out of food,' Karen said, casting an eye over the table. 'Only one chocolate cake and a few biscuits left.' She grinned at Sheila. 'Shall we have a bit of cake and a cuppa, let them fend for themselves for a while?'

Sheila nodded enthusiastically and got up to wash a couple of plates and cups. 'That cake's Mrs Chowney's, so we know she bought it somewhere posh.'

Karen and Sheila were just tucking into the cake – boozy and rich and totally unsuitable for a village fête, but delicious nonetheless – when Janey walked in. She pulled the hood of her red anorak back and shook out her dark shiny hair.

'Hi, Janey. Come and join us. Have a piece of cake,' Karen said, indicating a chair.

But the vicar's wife was biting her lip, her expression tense.

'I'll get you a cup,' Sheila said.

Janey shook her head. 'Thank you, Sheila, but I had some tea in the tent.' She fiddled with the zip on her jacket, tugging the join at the bottom until she finally managed to release it, and said, 'Umm . . . Karen . . . could I have a word, please?'

Karen felt a sickening lurch in her stomach. 'Of course.'

Sheila, her gaze flicking between the two women, must have sensed the tension, because she got up, leaving her cake half finished on the plate. 'I'll just pop over to the tent, see how they're getting on.' And she was gone.

Janey didn't make any move to sit down, just stood there like a statue, hands now pushed into the pockets of her anorak, making her look very childlike.

She's much younger than Will, Karen thought.

'This is really awkward, but it needs to be said . . .' She paused, maybe thinking out exactly how to phrase her next words. 'I know that there's something going on between you and William.'

'Janey—'

'No, hear me out.' The woman's famous steeliness now came into play, previous hesitation banished. 'There's no point in denying it. I know. But you need to know some things too.'

Karen thought she might be sick, a mouthful of chocolate cake stuck somewhere too near to her throat.

Janey moved to sit down, her eyes now on a level with Karen's opposite, her hands clasped together, white-knuckled, on the table. 'William is vulnerable. He's done this before . . .' She paused, pretending to calculate. 'You'll be the fourth. You see, he tries to make everything alright for everyone, and often his efforts are misconstrued. Then he can't resist.' Her tone was almost matter-of-fact.

The woman didn't give much away on a good day, but now

Karen marvelled at her sangfroid. She sat up straighter. 'Janey, I don't know who you've been talking to, but you've got it wrong.' She didn't see she had any choice but to call her bluff, not believing that Janey had been told anything by anyone, but rather was on a fishing trip, operating solely on a wife's instinct.

A small smile crossed Janey's face. 'Please, don't insult me. William wouldn't tell me, but someone else has.'

'Who? Who's told you what?' No one knew, no one except Sophie, and surely she would never betray her.

'It doesn't matter. And I understand that you've been going through a difficult time yourself. So I honestly don't blame you – Will's a very good listener. But he's being considered for promotion to bishop, so whatever's been happening between you has got to stop. Right now. Otherwise you will ruin his life.'

A silence descended on the room.

A bishop? Karen was shocked. Why hadn't he told her?

'You look surprised.'

'I would never ruin William's life.'

Janey's eyebrows raised a fraction. 'No . . . no, I'm sure you wouldn't, Karen. Not intentionally . . .' Another pause. 'As I say, I don't blame you.'

Karen wanted to smack her for being so smugly forgiving. *She's only fighting for her marriage*, she reminded herself. *Why wouldn't she use every tool at her disposal?* She watched Janey get to her feet.

'So we understand each other?'

Karen nodded dumbly. Out of the corner of her eye she saw Sophie drift into view in the doorway to the hall, then quickly disappear again. She wondered how much the girl had heard.

'This goes no further,' Janey was saying as she turned to go. 'And I would rather you didn't tell William we've had this conversation.'

Karen didn't reply, just got up and began to clear the tea things from the table. She had no appetite for any more cake.

As Janey got to the door, she swung round. 'I hope we can let this all blow over without any more unpleasantness. It's a small community.' Her words were accompanied by a brittle smile and she was obviously waiting for a reply, but Karen felt paralysed, unable to think straight. And Janey didn't push it as she muttered a soft goodbye and left.

The rest of the afternoon passed in a blur. Karen was shaken. How did Janey know about her and William? And how much did she know? If Will hadn't told her, and Sophie wouldn't have, it must have been someone who'd seen them together somewhere – either at the theatre or on the beach – and mentioned it to Janey.

But worse by far was the implication that William was a serial offender, that Karen was the last in a long line of dalliances. That cut Karen to the core.

It's just Janey's way of seeing me off, she told herself. She couldn't believe it of William.

The dismantling of the fête took forever, made more difficult by the continuing rain. Everyone was tired and dispirited as they bundled damp things into damp boxes. The tent would stay till Monday, but the trestle tables and canopies, the left-over merchandise and endless black bags full of rubbish were all packed up and carried away.

It was nearly nine by the time Karen was alone with Sophie. Although she had promised herself she wouldn't accuse her stepdaughter of anything before finding out what had really happened, she felt wound up, slightly mad. She couldn't banish a lurking suspicion that Sophie had had something to do with it. Karen found her curled up in her father's red leather recliner in the den with a mug of tea, watching a rerun of *Made in Chelsea*, Largo snoring peacefully at her feet. She acknowledged Karen with a brief smile as she sat herself down on the sofa. For a minute or two they both stared at the screen, where a twenty-something girl with glossed, pouting lips and lots of dark hair was delivering an indignant monologue to a louche youth slouching on a sofa.

Karen took a deep breath. 'Did you say anything to Janey about me and William?'

Sophie turned, her expression bewildered. 'What are you talking about?'

'You saw Janey in the kitchen earlier. Well, she wasn't just shooting the breeze, as I'm sure you gathered. She said "someone" had told her about us.'

'And you think I'd do that?' said Sophie, frowning. Uncurling her feet from the chair and swinging it round to face Karen, she muted the television. 'You honestly think I'd dob you in to the vicar's wife? That's a horrible thing to say.'

Seeing the hurt in her eyes, Karen was stricken. 'No . . . God, no, Sophie, of course I don't.' She sighed. 'I'm so sorry, I don't know what's come over me . . . I can't think straight.'

'It wasn't me.'

'I know it wasn't.'

The girl was watching her quietly. 'Are you still in love with him, then? I thought you said you were over it.'

'Did I?' she gave a rueful smile. 'I lied.'

With no returning smile, her face still stiff with umbrage, Sophie said, 'Do you even think of Daddy any more?'

Karen froze. Because, yes, she did think of Harry sometimes, quite a lot in fact. He had, after all, been her focus for nearly two decades. But she hadn't been able to move backwards in time and forget the period of hell when Harry was drinking, properly recapturing the fun they'd shared before the alcohol had taken over. People often said they managed this, managed to remember a person as healthy and happy, eschewing the time when they descended into a painful illness and death. But Karen's mind refused to do it, the nightmare of the last years still uncomfortably fresh in her memory.

'He's only been dead seven months,' Sophie was saying, the disdain clear in her brown eyes. She stood up, still holding the mug. 'But you never talk about him. It's like you've deleted him from your life. It's like he never existed.'

'Of course I think about him,' Karen said, truthfully. She got up too, went to her stepdaughter and, not quite daring a hug, laid her hands on Sophie's arms, gave a gentle squeeze. 'I'm so sorry. I should never have spoken about William to you, it's absolutely inappropriate. But you know I loved your father very much, don't you?'

The girl eyed her but said nothing, working her lips between her teeth.

'This thing with Will is so different. It's got nothing to do with the love I had for your dad. That will never change.'

Sophie took a deep breath, moved away from Karen's touch. 'Yeah . . .' She drifted towards the door.

'Please, Sophie. Don't just leave. Let's talk about this.'

The girl turned, her face set in the old guarded sulk that Karen hadn't seen in a while.

'Listen, it's your business what you do with the vicar. I really don't care one way or another.'

'But you think I'm being disrespectful to your father's memory.'

Sophie's eyes suddenly flashed. 'Well, face it, Karen, you are. Dad was hardly buried before you started drooling around after Reverend Haskell. What am I supposed to think?' She crossed her arms tightly across her chest, the mug dangling from the fingers of her right hand.

Karen didn't know what to say. It was a fair comment. But she was surprised at the girl's reaction. When the subject had come up before, Sophie had seemed quite sympathetic. She was annoyed with herself for not being more sensitive to her feelings.

'And the whole village obviously knows about it now. Everyone must be laughing at Dad behind his back. It's humiliating.'

'No . . . no, I'm sure they aren't. No one knows anything.'

Sophie raised an eyebrow. 'Well, that's not true, is it? Someone does – the person who told Janey whatever they told her – and this village is like a tinderbox when it comes to gossip. One spark and the whole place goes up.'

'Maybe someone saw us together and said something vague. She can't know anything else if William didn't tell her.'

'So there is something else to know?'

Karen looked away.

'Right,' Sophie muttered. 'You realize this will end badly for everyone?'

'Yes, I do realize that.'

'So what are you going to do?'

'Nothing. Janey said William's up for a bishop. She made it totally clear that I would ruin his life if I didn't leave him alone.'

'And will you?'

'I don't have any choice.'

Sophie continued to stare, clearly not believing her intentions.

'I don't,' Karen insisted, hating Janey's implication that William was the spineless victim of his own ego and she the pathetic love-struck widow.

'So will you go back to the coast?'

'I don't know what I'll do.'

The girl lowered her head at this. 'At least if the vicar makes bishop he'll leave. You won't have to keep bumping into them all the time.'

'True,' Karen said, although the prospect didn't hold much joy for her at that precise moment.

Sophie's phone rang, and she pulled it out of her tracksuit pocket, checking the screen.

'Daisy . . . I'd better get this,' she said, telling her friend to hold on as she hurried towards the door and upstairs.

Karen sat down on the sofa again. She hoped she hadn't ruined her relationship with her stepdaughter, just when it seemed to be getting on a more even keel. She wanted so badly in that moment to have a friend to confide in. *If only Maggie were here*, she thought, then remembered that her friend would probably be as unsym-pathetic as Sophie – and with reason. Maggie sent emails about every two weeks or so, but they were mainly telling Karen of all the incredible things she was doing and seeing in India. And when Karen replied she kept it short, filling her friend in on the most general items of village gossip. She didn't feel able to confide in Maggie in an email, when she couldn't properly explain her position.

Doing what she was doing, falling in love with a married man, was a very lonely business.

★

The following morning as she took herself through the village towards her favourite walk on to the Downs, Largo bouncing along at her side, she found herself fervently hoping to bump into Will, and also dreading it. It was as if her brain and her heart were running along parallel lines. She was equally balanced on both, like a train carriage on tracks, and both, although diametrically opposed, were vital and made total sense.

End it? her mind would ask. Yes, obviously the right thing to do.

Continue to love him? her heart countered. Well, of course, why wouldn't she?

And as she rounded the bend at the top of the hill, she saw a figure slumped in the dawn shadows on the bench she and Will had chosen in the past. Largo rushed up, nuzzled his hand, tail wagging, barking a welcome. But Karen, as she came close, was shocked at the vicar's appearance. He was very pale, unshaven, dark hair sticking up at all angles, dressed in jeans and a lumpy grey sweatshirt, his eyes red and blinking up at her.

She sat down next to him. 'What happened?'

He shot a quick glance at her, looked away again. Talking to the hills, he spoke in a low, strained voice. 'I've failed. I've failed everyone. Janey, Rachel, you . . . everyone who believed in me. And God. I've failed God. I've been so selfish.' He fell silent for a moment. 'I knew, from the first time I saw you, there was something . . . that day Harry asked me and Janey round when we first arrived. Small thing . . . I noticed the way your hair curled up on the back of your neck as you poured the tea . . . so beguiling. I should have ignored it. I told myself to ignore it. And I did try. But that's not good enough, is it? I didn't try hard enough because . . . because it's heaven being with you and I was too weak to give you up.' He stopped his diatribe and turned to her. 'Please forgive me, Karen. I have done the worst thing to you.'

She didn't know what to say. The sun was just coming up over the hill, fingers of light spreading across the last green of summer. The air was cool and she thought how heartbreakingly beautiful it was up there.

He grabbed her hand, held it tightly in his own cold, clammy one, gazing at the sun. She was aware of the callous on his index finger, just below the first joint. A legacy of his bow-string, he fiddled with the hard skin often.

'How did Janey know?' she asked.

'Does it matter?'

'It does to me. I need to know who knows about us.'

He sighed. 'It was Felicity Hill. I'm sure she didn't mean any trouble by it, just mentioned to Janey in passing that she'd seen us sitting together at the concert. And because I hadn't told Janey about bumping into you, she smelt a rat. That's all. So Felicity doesn't really know anything.'

'What does Janey think has gone on between us?'

'She thinks I'm in love with you.'

Shocked, Karen asked, 'Did you say you were?'

'No, but I didn't have to. She knows me too well.'

There was silence, just the early-morning birdsong, the drone of a distant tractor engine.

'She said you'd done this before . . . had a thing for one of your parishioners, not that I'm exactly one of your parishioners. I'm the fourth, apparently.'

William's expression barely changed. 'That's not true.'

But he didn't say any more, didn't seem interested in defending the accusation, although whether from innocence or guilt, Karen couldn't tell.

'She also said they're considering you for bishop. Why didn't you tell me?'

'Because it'll never happen, Karen.'

'Do you want it to happen?'

He just shook his head wearily. 'None of this is what I want.' He straightened up, held his hand to his back as if he were in pain.

'What will happen with Janey?'

William began to say something, then hesitated, cleared his throat instead. 'Janey's tough.'

'Meaning?'

'Meaning she'll ignore it like she ignores everything else personal between us.'

It was the first time he'd ever made any comment about his marriage, his matter-of-fact tone suggesting this was not a new observation.

Neither spoke for a long while. They both sat side by side on the rickety wooden bench, linked by this indefinable connection, yet lost in their own thoughts.

'I can't bear to lose you,' Karen whispered, almost to herself.

'I can't bear it either.'

'You could run away with me. Leave all this, just take off and we'll find a new life together.' She was only partly serious, but although she spoke with bravado, the tears ran down her face.

William pulled her into his side, his arm around her shoulder. 'I'm not worth it, Karen.'

'You are to me.'

'No . . . honestly, I'm not. You deserve better.'

She sat upright, turned to face him. 'So that's it, is it?'

But he wouldn't look at her.

'How can it be, Will? How can what we had go for nothing?' A desperate anger welled in her chest. 'Why did you hunt me out, make love to me? Why didn't you just leave me alone? I could have coped before, but now . . . now it's so much harder.' She stood up, tugging her jacket around her body. It wasn't cold but she felt freezing.

He stood too, grabbed her arms. 'Look at me, Karen,' he said. 'Just look at me. I'm a wreck, a weak, indulgent wreck posturing as a man of God. Why would you want to be with me?'

She thought this was a pretty stupid question. 'Because I love you.'

William shook his head again. 'No, you don't. You love who you think I am.'

'Don't tell me what I feel.'

At that moment, Jeffrey crested the hill, followed by his cocker spaniel, Daisy. Karen and William sprang apart.

'Morning, morning,' the judge said, waving his hand at them. 'Glorious day.'

'Isn't it beautiful?' Karen said, when William said nothing.

Jeffrey seemed not to notice anything was wrong. 'Did pretty well yesterday, I thought, Vicar, despite the bloody rain. Let me know the take, will you?'

'Of course,' Will muttered, his expression dull and exhausted.

The judge whistled up his dog and stomped off with a backward wave. They stood, looking after him, not speaking.

'I'd better get back,' William said. 'I've got matins.'

'Right.'

'Bye, Karen.'

Karen stood watching his retreating figure, hardly believing he had gone. It felt as if he were taking her heart with him as he tramped away, yanking it by the strand that bound them so that all she was left with was a scraped-out cavity, raw, burning, throbbing, so painful she wanted to scream.

Don't go, she yelled silently. *Please, please don't leave me.*

Slumping back on to the bench, she closed her eyes. Her body, held rigid with despair, seemed to block her breath.

What did you think he was going to do? The chant in her head was whispering but unequivocal. *He's taken, he doesn't belong to you, never has. He belongs to Janey and Rachel and God. He's done it before, done it before, done it before.*

Karen couldn't even cry, she just felt cleaned out, empty, as she plodded slowly along the path towards home.

When she got to the rectory, Sophie was in the kitchen, despite the early hour.

'What's the matter?' she asked, eyeing Karen with a frown.

'Nothing.'

'You look awful.'

Karen just shrugged and sat down, her jacket still on.

'I'll do you some coffee.'

'Thanks.'

The radio was on, an annoyingly upbeat male voice insisting they send him texts 'right now' telling him how they were feeling and what they were doing this sunny Sunday morning.

You don't want to know, thought Karen as she slowly sipped her warm coffee.

'Why are you up so early?' she asked Sophie, suddenly jolted out of her misery to register the girl's pale, too-thin face opposite.

'Couldn't sleep.'

'Was it our discussion last night that freaked you?'

'No . . . I always wake early these days.'

'Really?'

Sophie seldom surfaced from her room till nearly midday.

'I don't get up usually, but I'm not asleep.'

'Is there any reason? Are you worried about something?'

The girl pulled a face, didn't answer.

'Stupid question,' Karen conceded.

'So are you leaving again?' Sophie asked after a silence, during which they both listened to a song Karen found vaguely familiar with a chorus that repeated 'You-oo . . . are, you-oo . . . are, you-oo . . . are' over again.

'I haven't made any plans to.' Karen wasn't sure if her stepdaughter wanted the answer to be yes or no.

Sophie nodded slowly.

'Why, are you dying to get rid of me so as you can move your boyfriend back in?' It was a poor attempt a lightening the mood and Karen instantly regretted it when she saw the flash of despair on her stepdaughter's face before she dropped her eyes. 'Sophie, are you OK?'

'Yeah, fine,' the girl mumbled.

'You seem so thin and pale . . . and the not sleeping . . . maybe you should go off somewhere, get a break before winter.'

Sophie raised her eyebrows. 'Like I can afford that.'

'I'll help out.'

But the girl shook her head. 'I don't feel like going anywhere, not even London right now.'

Karen frowned. 'I'm worried about you.'

'Don't be.'

'Why don't you ask Daisy down for a weekend?'

'Nothing for her to do down here, is there?'

'Have you talked to your mum?'

'She's in Greece. Nanu's not well . . . Mum's been there all summer.'

Karen felt bad she didn't know this, and realized how self-absorbed she'd been, leaving Sophie alone for such a long time without any thought for the girl's well-being.

'Maybe you should go out there, get some sun, lie on the beach for a bit.'

'Nanu lives in the centre of Athens in a tiny flat. And anyway, like I said, I'm fine here.'

'OK . . .'

She was trying to think of a tactful way to suggest that Sophie make an appointment to see Tom, the doctor – she seemed so depressed – when her stepdaughter abruptly got up from the table, took her mug to the sink, flicked off the radio and left the room without another word. Karen watched her go, wondering what she could do to help.

The noise of her phone interrupted her thoughts.

'Morning, Mike.'

'Hi, Karen. How's it going?'

'Been better. You?'

'Yeah, you know . . . busy.'

Karen waited for him to state his business; Mike wasn't one to ring for a chat.

'OK, I'll get to the point, you don't fancy a few more days at the seaside by any chance?'

'Why?'

'Just bloody Gina's taken off to Fuengirola with the lout. Not the family come down with Ebola for a change, which I suppose is a blessing, but she gave me zero notice and there's an arts festival in town Thursday. Plus the weather's going to be scorching and I've no sodding help. I've asked everyone and his dog, but no joy. Don't know how you're fixed, but if things aren't so great, you could take your mind off real life and come and pull some coffees for me. Chance of a lifetime, no? I'd pay you, of course.'

Karen laughed. 'This week?'

'Thursday to Sunday.'

She didn't have to think for long. Sophie wouldn't mind being left alone for a long weekend. In fact, she probably liked it better when Karen wasn't there, although it was hard to know. She said it was weird being alone, but she didn't seem to take advantage of having Karen around. Nothing else was keeping her in the village except her unreasonable expectations.

'Sure, I'll come.'

She heard Mike let out a huge sigh of relief. 'God, Karen, that's outstanding. I properly owe you for this.'

'You know me, the eternal runaway. I'll be there Wednesday around seven.'

Karen felt every nerve in her body begin to calm down as she drove out of the village late on Wednesday afternoon.

The last two days had been horrible. She had been obliged to spend Monday afternoon with William and the rest of the fête committee. They had met in the dusty, drafty church hall, sitting around the table on plastic chairs while Bernard droned on about 'housekeeping', as he called it, which meant a detailed inventory of who needed to be paid, who needed to be thanked, who had behaved well, who badly – only the ice cream vendor came in for some stick because she hadn't stuck to the allotted patch for her stand and as a result had upset the ladies selling marmalade.

Karen placed herself as far away from William as possible – but that wasn't far, as there were only six people present. And it seemed every time she looked up, he would be staring at her. His eyes told her nothing, however. They just looked tired and distant. At the end of the meeting, she made an excuse to Jennifer and hurried off before Will could speak to her alone, although he'd made no move to do so.

And then, on Tuesday, Janey had come round to pick up the teapots. Karen had made the arrangement, then asked Sophie to deal with the vicar's wife, making sure she herself was out. Better for both of us, she thought. She'd spent the afternoon in town, wandering aimlessly from shop to shop, with no desire to buy anything. But when she got back the boxes were still there – Janey had rung to say she couldn't make it till the evening.

'I can't face her.'

'She'll know you're here, the car's outside,' Sophie had said. 'Just give her the boxes, you don't have to ask her in. But you can't hide, it looks bad.'

The girl was right, of course, and Karen answered the door to Janey Haskell with her best smile. Ushering her in, she said, 'None broken, thank goodness,' as she went to pick up one of the boxes stacked in the hall.

Janey looked tired and uneasy as she hovered, her eyes flicking towards Sophie and back to Karen, perhaps wondering how much Sophie had been told. Karen felt sorry for her. It must be the worst form of hell to be in a marriage with a man who was being unfaithful – even if she didn't know the full extent of his betrayal – and to have to confront the 'other woman'. She wanted to tell

Janey that she needn't worry any more, that she wouldn't be seeing William again, that she had him totally to herself again. She wanted to say sorry.

Instead she said, 'Thanks again for lending them. They really made a difference.'

Perhaps Janey heard the unsaid apology in Karen's voice, because she gave her a soft smile. 'I'm glad it worked out.'

When she had gone, Sophie gave her stepmother an amused look. 'Thought at one point you were going to fall on your sword and 'fess up.'

'She looked so sad. None of this is her fault.'

'I'm sure they'll sort it out.'

'Yes, I'm sure they will.'

And she believed what she said, despite William's morose mutterings up on the hill the other morning.

The third incident, and the most defining one, had happened only this morning. Karen had taken Largo out early, as usual. It was raining, but she hadn't slept again and was sick of lying there hoping she might. As soon as she was out of the house, she was checking around for William, but warily this time, not sure if she really wanted to confront him again.

As she crested the hill and spotted his square shoulders in the black anorak up ahead, striding purposefully away, head bent, she quickly turned tail and started back down the path, much to the distress of the Labrador. On the point of calling to him, she had stopped, realizing she couldn't bear to hear – even one last time – what he would inevitably say to her.

'There's nothing I can do. I've let you down. I'm sorry.'

However true it was for him, it was, in fact, not true. He did have a choice, like everyone else in the world, and his choice wasn't her. *I don't blame him — he has too much to lose*, she told herself.

But he should have been brave enough to say that.

Now the sharpness of the early-autumn air seemed to contain a strange recklessness as she got out of her car and stood gazing at the sun going down over the sea before walking along the pebbles to Mike's café.

CHAPTER THIRTEEN

'You've saved my bloody life, you have,' Mike told her when they were ensconced in the pub having a drink that night.

'You've probably saved mine too,' she said.

'Escaping the randy vicar again?'

She hated Mike's contempt for William, but right now it was probably good for her to hear, she thought, not rising to his jibe.

'He's going to be a bishop.'

He pulled a face. 'That's reassuring.'

She didn't reply for a moment.

'You can't think worse of William than he thinks of himself.'

Mike made a disparaging sound in his throat. 'God, those are the worst sort, the ones who feel bad but do it anyway. If he really had a conscience he'd have kept it in his trousers.'

'Yeah, I know. I know it all. I know it was stupid and I know it was wrong and I know I never stood a chance with him. So tell me something I don't know . . . how the hell do I forget him?'

He gave her a wry grin. 'Ah, now that's a whole other thing. The truth? You won't. You just have to wait and wait till time chips tiny bits off. Then one day you'll wake up realizing it's too small to be significant and you haven't thought about him in days.'

'And how long does that take?'

'That's the bad news. Too long. But it's a tried and tested formula. Not that anyone in your current state ever believes it.'

Karen smiled at Mike's wisdom. 'Thanks. Thanks for not saying I should do this or do that, pull myself together, get a life, move on.'

'I was getting to that part.'

She punched him on the arm as they both began to laugh.

The next couple of days, as predicted, were completely manic in the café. The crowd this week was a very different one from the usual seaside clientele. This was a trendy, earnest, opinionated bunch, dressed for the city, not the beach, impatient and demanding high-quality service as if they were in a Central London café. Karen preferred the shuffling holidaymakers with too many children who couldn't make up their minds.

'That lot have been there since three with one sodding coffee each,' Mike complained on Saturday afternoon. 'And now I want to close up and they're still sat there gabbing.'

A group of four men and one girl were lounging on the terrace in the dying sun, all talking loudly at once and laughing a lot. As Mike said, they had each ordered a coffee about two hours ago and nothing since, but when Karen went and asked if they wanted anything else, they'd barely stopped long enough to wave her away.

'Bet they earn six times as much as me for doing bloody nothing all day except making stuff up.'

Karen laughed. 'Says Mr Meldrew.'

'Well, don't you think they're annoying?'

'Sort of, but you'll probably find they have very high-stress, insecure jobs and are shouting to keep their courage up.'

'They'd do better ordering a ham sandwich to keep their protein up. None of them look as if they've had a square meal in decades. And those ridiculous clothes . . .'

Karen frowned at him. 'What's up, Mike? You're not your usual chilled self, and it can't just be those skinny media types winding you up.'

He sighed. 'It's Margie's birthday today.'

'Oh . . . I'm sorry. You should have said. That's really hard.'

'I miss her so much. Promising you the other day that time'd sort your obsession was only wishful thinking. I haven't hardly got to first base with Margie.' He took up the dishcloth and began scrubbing an already pristine sink.

Karen laid a gentle hand on his back. 'I'll tell that lot we're closing and then get you a coffee and some cake.'

Later they sat together at the table recently vacated by the festival mob. There was a soft breeze from the water, which was up to the high-tide mark.

'What did you used to do on her birthday?'

Mike gave a slow smile. 'Worked. We were always working. And it was bloody exhausting most of the time, but at least we had each other. That's what I miss, having someone around to moan at in the early mornings, to joke around with, share stuff about the punters, like we did today. Gina really is just a pretty face.'

'Have you been out with anyone since?'

He shook his head. 'Nah. Not because I wouldn't like to – and Margie would wallop me for being such a wuss – but I don't know . . . seems kinda weird . . . I'd have to feel strongly . . .' He cleared his throat. 'I envy you the vicar. I know it's not working out so well, but it's probably got you over the hump of losing your old man.'

MEET ME ON THE BEACH

Karen didn't know how to answer this. Her feelings for Harry were clearly so different from Mike's for his wife Margie. She wasn't over losing Harry, not really, although she'd convinced herself that she was. She still felt his shadow sometimes, heard his voice or his booming laugh. But her mourning for Harry had been masked, overridden by her feelings for William Haskell.

'You can borrow him if you like, I'm over it,' she said. 'He's perfect. And so reliable. He'll bugger off back to his wife as soon as things threaten to get serious.'

Mike looked more horrified than amused. 'Might give that one a miss.'

'Very wise.'

'Think we deserve a drink.'

'Think we do.'

They finished up, pulled down the shutters, locked the door and made their way over to the pub.

Mike stuck to his beer, Karen ordered a bottle of white. She quickly got drunk. It didn't seem to matter any more what she did. She was free as a bird to behave as she liked, no one would care.

'You know, I've noticed, you don't have a very high opinion of men,' she said, later on in the evening. 'Polisher, thug, lout . . . what's that about?'

Mike looked puzzled. 'Yeah, hadn't thought about it . . .' He paused. 'But now I do, it's a no-brainer.'

She waited for him to go on, but he just stared into his beer.

'Grew up with a compulsive gambler for a father who gambled the milk money, the rent, the shirts off our backs. Begged for forgiveness then did it all again the next night. Led Ma a proper dance.

Reckon I'm waiting for any bloke to behave in the same way. And let's face it, I'm not often disappointed.'

'Is he still alive?'

'No, stupid old bugger. It was the sorrys that drove us all nuts. He was always sorry, so charmingly bloody sorry. But he just couldn't stop himself.'

'I had a good dad, it's not always men who are to blame. I know some good men . . . great men . . .' Karen wasn't sure who she was talking about, or even if she was making sense. She hadn't eaten all day and suddenly she was beginning to feel really out of it, her head spinning, having trouble focusing on her words.

'If this is the warm-up act for letting your vicar off the hook, it won't wash.'

'He's not my vicar, he's Janey's vicar . . . and God's vicar . . . and whoever's sodding vicar. And they can bloody well keep him. I said, you can keep him . . . just not . . . me.'

She saw Mike frowning at her. 'Do you think we ought to call it a day?'

'Now? No, no, we can't go to bed, it's waay too early.' She blinked as she grabbed her glass and brought it to her lips only to realize it was empty as she sucked on the dribbles. 'Need some more wine.'

But Mike pulled the bottle out of her reach. It only had an inch left. She'd drunk the whole bottle single-handed.

'No, listen, you've had enough. Come on, I'll get you home.'

Karen pulled her arm away as he tried to get her to her feet.

'Stop it. I don't want to go home. It isn't my home anyway, my home is empty except for . . . Soph. She's there but she doesn't do anything, nor do I. Nothing, nada, niente . . . I really need another drink.'

Mike finally succeeded in hauling her to her feet and had to practically carry her out of the pub. The chilly autumn air hit her and she staggered even more. She was sure she was just about to vomit, so she bent over the gutter, but she wasn't sick, just dizzy and clammy as she brought her head up again. Mike had to drag her up the three floors to the flat, where he made her drink a large glass of water while he put the kettle on for some tea. After a while, head still spinning if she moved too quickly, she began to feel less nauseous.

She was sitting on the sofa bed, Mike perched on the mustard-yellow chair next to the table.

'I'm so sorry,' she said, when they'd both finished their mugs of tea. 'I can't believe I did that. I haven't been sick-drunk for literally decades.'

He grinned. 'Not a pretty sight.'

She groaned. 'God, I daren't lie down, my head will spin off.'

'Still, you'd better get to bed. I'll help you pull it out.'

She stood to the side while Mike took the cushions off, yanked the metal bar to raise the mattress out of the frame, padded the gap at the head with the cushions. He looked around for the bed linen.

'I put them in the cupboard.' Karen walked carefully over and opened the door, grabbing the folded duvet, sheets and pillows from the bottom shelf. She buried her face in the softness of the pillows and wanted just to fall asleep right there, upright, without moving another step.

Mike rescued her bundle and set to work making up the bed.

'There, you can do the rest, can you?'

She nodded.

'I'll get home, then,' he said, still looking at her as if he wasn't sure she could manage even to get undressed and into bed.

She nodded again. 'Listen, thanks, Mike . . . thanks so much. I've been a total pain tonight.'

He shrugged off her apology and picked up his jacket from the back of the chair. 'Night, then.'

But suddenly she didn't want him to go. She couldn't face being alone. She found she was crying, awful drunk-woman tears of self-pity that she couldn't control. And after a moment's hesitation, Mike put his coat down and took her in his arms and hugged her.

'Hey, come on, love. It's not that bad.'

It felt worse than bad, however, and she clung to him, desperately trying to avoid being alone with herself, her head buried determinedly in his T-shirt as he tried to push her gently away. And as she looked up at him, his fierce blue eyes seemed so discomfited that she wanted to laugh.

Instead she reached up and kissed him, planting her lips firmly on his own and drawing her body back into his embrace. She felt his body stiffen. For a second his mouth responded, slowly returning the kiss, his arms tightening around her.

Then he pulled sharply away.

'Karen . . .'

She came to her senses with a terrible feeling of shame.

'God, Mike . . . God, I'm so sorry. What am I like? I honestly didn't mean to do that . . . it just sort of happened.' She buried her head in her hands.

Mike looked slightly stunned, then shook his head, a slow smile spreading across his face. 'Didn't expect that.'

'No, well . . .' Karen went and sat on the edge of the bed. 'Bloody embarrassing.'

'Hey, don't be embarrassed, it wasn't so bad.'

She shot him a rueful glance. 'Don't tease, I'm not up to it.'

'Best we forget it ever happened. Get to bed and I'll see you in the morning, if you can stand up straight, that is.' He checked his pocket for his keys and went towards the door. 'Sleep well.'

She could still hear the amused note in his voice and cringed, longing for the door to shut behind him so she could be mortified all by herself.

She didn't sleep very well – just a few hours of oblivion – before her dry mouth, throbbing head and embarrassment woke her. She drank pints of water, took two paracetamol and went for a long swim.

By the time she heard the clatter of the shutters going up on Mike's café, she was feeling relatively perky, aware of the uneasy energy that comes from overtiredness. Dreading confronting Mike, but knowing that leaving it would only make things worse, she clattered down the stairs and across the road to meet him.

Far from being self-conscious about seeing Karen, Mike beamed at her, the amusement from last night still clear in his eyes. 'How are you feeling?'

'Physically, not good. Mentally, awful. I—'

He held up his hand, interrupting her flow. 'Stop right there. You got drunk. We kissed. It wasn't meant. End of.'

She stared at him. 'I can't believe I did it.'

He laughed. 'No, well, we all do daft things. Just have to suck it up.'

Karen tried to feel as sanguine as he did. 'Alright for you. You didn't make a total fool of yourself.'

'Let's get Brenda up and running. I need a coffee and I reckon you do too.' Mike had christened his unpredictable coffee machine after a fickle girlfriend from his youth. 'Those media types won't be in for hours, it's Sunday.'

'By the way, have you got my phone?' Karen asked, when they'd finished their drinks and were getting going on the sandwiches. 'I couldn't find it this morning.'

Mike shook his head. 'Nope. You probably left it in the pub.'

'I'll go over in a minute. Not that anyone'll have called.'

'Poor old Norman-no-mates.'

'Shut up, will you? I said I was OK, but I'm not that OK.'

The next couple of hours passed fast and painfully. She took a quick break during a lull in customers to nip over the road and ask about her phone. The landlord, almost before she'd said a word, retrieved it from behind the bar and held it up with a question on his face.

She nodded gratefully.

'I saw you leave it, but you didn't answer when I shouted. And I was too busy to run after you.'

'Not my finest hour.' She took the phone.

'You should see some people,' he said.

The phone was switched off and she pressed the on-button as she walked back to the café, waiting for it to power up. Glancing at the screen in the bright light, she could see there were a number of calls, but not who they were from. As soon as she was through the door, she looked again. The screen was packed with a list of missed calls, all from Patrick Gascoigne, her next-door neighbour.

Puzzled and alarmed, she listened to her voicemail.

'Karen,' Patrick's voice sounded frantic, 'call me as soon as you can. It's urgent.'

The second message was shorter. 'Darling, please call. It's Sophie.'

Karen didn't listen to the other ones. Heart in her mouth, she pressed call-back.

Patrick answered on the second ring.

'Karen? God, darling, where have you *been*? I've been calling you since eleven o'clock last night.'

'Sorry . . . what's happened? Tell me.'

'It's Sophie. She's OK now, well, she's sort of . . . anyway, there's no nice way to say this . . . She tried to kill herself last night.'

Karen went cold. 'Tried to kill herself? Sophie? Oh my God!'

'She's in hospital, they pumped her stomach. I saw her a couple of minutes ago, I'm just outside her room, and she's awake and talking, so I imagine she's going to be OK, but the doctors are waiting to see if there was any damage from the pills.'

She sat down heavily on a café chair.

Mike, seeing something was wrong, was by her side. 'What is it?' he mouthed.

But she just looked at him, unable to explain.

'I'll come now,' she said. 'I'll be there in an hour.'

'Do you want to speak to her?' Patrick asked.

'Please, yes . . .'

Her hand was sweating so much, the phone felt sticky in her palm, but she clung on to it, waiting with a pounding heart for Patrick to go back into Sophie's room and give her the phone.

'Hi,' Sophie said, eventually.

'Sophie, are you alright?'

'Not really.'

Then Karen heard her burst into tears.

'Oh, Sophie . . . listen, I'm on my way. I'm so, so sorry I wasn't there. My phone was switched off, I've only just got Patrick's messages.'

'It's OK,' the girl said flatly.

'I'll be there as soon as I can.'

'OK,' she said again.

'Will you pass me back to Patrick, please?'

'He's gone to get a coffee.'

'Right. Well, see you in an hour, darling.'

Sophie hung up.

Karen told Mike what had happened. 'Sorry to leave you in the lurch, but I've got to go.'

'Of course. Are you sure you're OK to drive?'

She shrugged. 'I'll have to be.'

'I can close up and take you if you like.'

'God, no. Thanks, you're very kind, but I'll be fine.' She hugged Mike tightly. 'Talk later.'

All the way to the hospital in the car, Karen's head was spinning. Not with the after-effects of the white wine, but with the horrible certainty that she could have stopped Sophie harming herself. It was so clear that the girl was depressed, but Karen had chosen to ignore it, or at least do nothing about it, too wrapped up as she was in her own pointless love affair.

How could she have been so selfish? How could she have left Sophie yet again, when it was clear as day the girl was so thin, fragile, lost? By the time she was fumbling with the coins for the exorbitant hospital car park ticket machine, she was close to tears.

Patrick met her at the door to the ward. Without a word, he immediately wrapped her in his strong arms.

'Am I glad to see you,' he said.

He looked anxious and exhausted, unshaven – obviously he'd been up all night with Sophie.

'How is she?'

'She seems to be coping. She's been asleep most of time since they pumped her out. The psych woman can't come and assess her till tomorrow, but they say she'll have to stay in tonight, anyway. Something about potential liver damage not showing up for the first twenty-four hours. I didn't get it all, you'll have to ask the doctor.'

'Poor Sophie . . . this is my fault, I should never have left her on her own. I knew she was depressed. It would never have happened if I'd stayed at home instead of swanning off to the beach again.' The self-blame poured out of her in a desperate torrent.

'Darling, stop beating yourself up. No one ever knows, that's the point.' He gently took her arm and drew her along the shiny corridor. 'Come on, I'll get you a coffee and you can tidy yourself up before you see her. We don't want her to feel guilty for upsetting you on top of all the rest.'

For ten minutes they sat by the coffee machine at the end of the corridor. The coffee was strong and hot and surprisingly palatable. Karen cradled the paper cup, glad of the warmth between her hands. She was cold as ice, although the hospital air was hot and stuffy with the abiding smell of disinfectant.

'How did you find her?'

'Well, I wouldn't have if it hadn't been for Largo. I was on my own in the cottage – Volkan didn't come down this weekend, he was working – and I heard the dog barking. It was gone ten, and I thought it was just Sophie putting him out for his last wee before bed and he'd seen a fox or something. But then I realized he was inside, not outside, and he was barking his head off, really frantic . . .'

Patrick took a breath. 'So I went round and banged on the door, called out to Sophie, but of course she didn't answer. When the dog heard me he came racing to the front door and was scrabbling at it, still barking. I didn't know what to do, both doors were locked, but I found a window at the back – into the den – which wasn't fastened properly, and I crawled in.' He shook his head, smiling. 'You can imagine, with this bulk that wasn't easy. And as soon as I was inside, Largo jumped up at me, then raced off upstairs. She was in her bedroom, just lying there unconscious, white as a sheet. I honestly thought she was dead.'

'God . . .'

'To be frank, I nearly had a heart attack myself. But you learn bits and bobs hanging around film sets all your life. After I'd called 999 I put her in the recovery position, made sure her airway was clear – she'd been sick at some stage – kept her warm and waited. It was agony, darling, I'm telling you. The ambulance only took about fifteen minutes, but it seemed like five years.'

'You literally saved her life, Patrick. Suppose you hadn't been down, or hadn't noticed the barking . . .'

He shrugged modestly. 'It's Largo who gets the medal,' he said.

'Do you know what she took?'

'A possible combination of blood pressure pills, paracetamol and Night Nurse, apparently.'

'Blood pressure pills?'

'Yes, beta blockers. Harry's, judging by the label. There were some missing from the blister pack, but that could have been Harry. We don't know if she took any, or whether she just had them there.'

'If she did, you'd think a cocktail like that would have killed her instantly.'

'Sophie hasn't told anyone how many she swallowed of everything – she probably doesn't know herself – but it must have

been a fair old number of something, she seemed pretty ill . . .'
He paused. 'The doc said that if we hadn't found her when we did,
she might well have died.'

'She must have really meant it.'

Patrick's look was full of sympathy. 'So you think she was
depressed?'

Karen nodded. 'I'm sure she was. I should have done something.
I knew she wasn't right. But she'd been the same for months. And
Sophie's never the most communicative girl . . . not with me,
anyway.'

'Harry's death must have hit her very hard. She always was his
princess.'

They sat in silence, Karen barely able to contemplate the horri-
fying implications if Sophie had succeeded. She would never have
forgiven herself.

'I just don't know how to thank you, Patrick. You're amazing,
knowing what to do, coping with it all. I'm so sorry I wasn't here.'

'Shush, darling. Come on, drink up, let's go and check on
Sophie. You'll feel better when you see she's alright.'

Her stepdaughter, however, looked quite dreadful. White as a
sheet, eyes sunken in their sockets, hair scraped back into a low
ponytail that revealed the painful thinness of her face. She had her
eyes shut as Karen and Patrick tiptoed up to the curtained bed, but
they flew open as soon as she heard them.

Karen bent and laid her cheek against Sophie's, gave her a kiss as
she squeezed her shoulders. 'Oh, Sophie, I'm so sorry.'

The girl did not resist Karen's embrace. She seemed drugged
still, her movements slow as she tried to hoist herself up on her
pillows.

Patrick took the chair on the opposite side. Karen sat on the bed itself, took Sophie's hand.

'What happened?' she asked gently.

Sophie gave a huge sigh. 'I don't know . . .'

'I wish you'd told me how you were feeling.'

The girl didn't answer.

'Maybe I could have helped.'

'I . . . I didn't want to worry you.'

'And I was so pathetically caught up in my own life.'

'It's not your fault. I just . . . I just . . . it all seemed so pointless. I'm useless. I don't have a job or a relationship, I can't get my life together . . . and . . . I don't know . . . seems I can't even kill myself properly . . .' She trailed off.

No one spoke. Karen felt her heart break for the fragile girl. She looked across the bed at Patrick, his kind face also pained by Sophie's distress.

'I know something about what you're going through. I've felt like that myself at various times in my life,' Patrick said quietly.

This surprised Karen, and clearly Sophie too, because she frowned, bewildered.

'You? You've felt like there was nothing to live for?'

The actor nodded emphatically. 'Oh, yes. It's quite awful at the time. Everything's grey, there's nothing to look forward to, nothing gives you an ounce of pleasure. And not being able to cope creates so much guilt, but you still can't make yourself cope. All I wanted to do was hide under the duvet all day and cry.'

Sophie's face lightened a little. 'You felt like that?'

'Absolutely, darling. As I say, on more than one occasion. I'm not always this jolly soul you see before you now. I never actually got around to trying to kill myself, but I certainly thought about it and lined up the pills. I didn't know what else to do.'

'That's how I feel,' Sophie murmured, tears forming in her dark eyes.

Patrick patted the hand that Karen wasn't holding. 'Well, I'm extremely glad you didn't succeed. Now you need to get some proper help. Meds and a spot of therapy should do the trick. I know a great person I'll put you in touch with if Tom doesn't have one up his sleeve. You won't believe me now, darling, but *this will pass*. It may take a bit of time, but I promise you, in a few months you'll feel like a new woman.'

Sophie gave a faint smile. 'New would be good.'

A nurse put her head round the curtain. 'Do you want anything to eat, Sophie?'

The girl shook her head.

'You couldn't eat that muck, anyway,' Patrick whispered. 'I saw the trolley on my way in. Smelt like old socks. I'll bring you in something tasty later on.'

'Thanks, but I'm not hungry.'

Patrick looked horrified. 'You've got to eat if you want to get well, dear girl. I don't want to hear any of this silly starving nonsense. Anyway, my chicken broth is to die for. And,' he put his head on one side, considering, 'maybe a little cheese straw on the side, some panna cotta for pudding – nothing too heavy.'

'Sounds delicious,' Karen said as Patrick got up, clearly on a mission.

He bent to kiss Sophie on the forehead. 'Listen, sweet pea. All the best people feel this way sometimes. It's part of being human. But you won't be like it forever, do remember that.'

After he'd gone the atmosphere within the shady, womb-like curtains felt very flat. Karen didn't know what to say.

'How do you feel?'

'Very tired. And stupid.' Sophie met her eye. 'I don't think I really wanted to die.' She looked away briefly. 'I don't know, maybe part of me did . . . Daddy would be so horrified if he knew.' Tears fell silently down her cheeks.

Karen handed her a tissue from the box on the bedside cabinet. 'I've really let you down. I knew you were depressed, but I didn't do a thing to help.'

'What could you have done if I didn't tell you how I felt?'

'I could have made it easier for you to tell me, instead of winding you up even more by dumping my confessions on you like that. I'm so sorry.' Suddenly she had a thought. 'Have you told your mum?'

The girl's eyes flew wide open. 'No. No, I can't tell her, she can't ever know. Please, Karen, don't tell her.'

'Of course I won't tell her, you're over eighteen, it's your call. But this was very serious, Soph, you were this close to dying.' Karen held her thumb and forefinger a centimetre apart. 'Don't you think she should know? She is your mother.'

'She'll freak if she finds out. She'll want to rush back from Greece, but she won't be able to because Nanu's dying. Telling her would just wind her up.' The girl was looking beseechingly at Karen. 'And I'm fine now. There's no point in upsetting her now I'm OK, is there?'

'Up to you, but I would want to know if my daughter tried to commit suicide.' Karen saw Sophie wince at the word 'suicide'.

'I'll tell her sometime, just not now.'

'Well, if you want me to talk to her, I will.'

'Thanks . . .'

They both fell silent. Karen watched her stepdaughter, her head turned away on the pillow, pale-blue hospital gown up to her neck, drip in her left forearm. She felt very sad for her. There was no easy answer to the problems of her life, and she seemed ill-equipped to galvanize herself. As she watched, Sophie's eyes began to close and the pressure of her hand in Karen's slackened. Karen eased herself off the bed, tucked the girl's arm beneath the sheet and smoothed a hand gently across her forehead.

'I'll be here,' she said.

But Sophie was already asleep.

CHAPTER FOURTEEN

Karen sought out the doctor, but he wasn't around. She finally got to speak to the ward sister.

'It seems she was found not too long after she took the pills,' she said. 'So the doctors think it's unlikely she has sustained any liver damage. Obviously we've carried out full blood tests, and we'll monitor her over the next twenty-four hours for liver function, but it's likely she's going to be fine.'

'Do you know how many she took?'

'She's vague about it, they often are. The bottle of Night Nurse was three-quarters empty – there's paracetamol in it – and the paramedics found an empty sixteen pack of Panadol and another sixteen pack with five missing. But we don't know how many of either pack had been consumed at a different time. Luckily she didn't add alcohol to the mix.'

'What about the beta blockers?'

The nurse shook her head. 'She says she didn't take any, and there's no evidence that she did, thank goodness.' She gave Karen a resigned look. 'She's a lucky girl, but she's going to need a lot of monitoring for a while. We don't want her trying it again.'

Karen went to the cafeteria to get some tea with a heavy heart. She had no idea what she should do with Sophie. Getting her a therapist would be a start, and antidepressants, but how was she going to inject meaning into the girl's life? She wanted desperately to talk to William because she was sure he would know what to say in this situation, comforting words for Sophie as much as for herself. She toyed with the idea of phoning him. Should Sophie be denied his wisdom just because she, Karen, had vowed to avoid him? Was that fair? But then she realized the vicar was probably the last person her stepdaughter wanted to see right now. She was sure Sophie blamed William as much as she blamed Karen herself for cuckolding her father – beyond the grave – in the eyes of the village.

After a cup of tea and a dried-up fruit scone, Karen made her way back to Sophie's ward. She was awake, plugged into her iPhone, which Patrick had picked up for her along with some toiletries and magazines.

She pulled out the earphones when she saw Karen. 'Hi.'

'Did you sleep?'

'A bit.'

Karen sat in the chair Patrick had vacated earlier.

'You don't need to stay, you know,' Sophie said. 'I'm fine.'

'I thought I might go home, pick up some pyjamas for you. Those gowns are grim.'

'I haven't got any pyjamas. I always wear tracky-bums and a T-shirt.' She gave Karen a half-smile. 'The room's a tip, you'll never find anything.'

'I'm sure I'll manage.'

'But there's no point if I can go home tomorrow. I will be able to, won't I? No one will give me a straight answer here.'

'Probably because they don't know for certain. But if your liver's OK . . . and you've seen the shrink.'

Sophie pulled a face. 'What's the point? She'll just ask me why I did it, and I don't really know. I'm not mad or anything . . .'

'She has to check you out. Make sure you're not going to do it again.' Karen's tone was light. She didn't want to get into anything serious with Sophie while she was still in such a fragile state, but she couldn't decide whether the girl wanted to talk about it or not. She was always so hard to read.

'If I was serious about doing it again I would hardly tell her, would I? I'd say everything was fine and it was just a stupid mistake, then go home and get on with it.'

'Right . . . but you wouldn't do it again, would you? You're glad you were rescued?'

Sophie sighed. 'Yeah, I suppose I am . . . although my life's still shit. Nothing's changed.'

'Nothing's changed, I agree, but the pills and therapy might help you look at life differently. Less gloomily.'

'It won't get me a boyfriend or a job, though, will it?'

'No, but when you perk up you'll probably be able to do that for yourself.'

Sophie just raised her eyebrows at Karen, as if what she said was derisory, and Karen knew it was pointless to try and persuade her otherwise. It was the depression talking. Sophie used to be feisty and engaged with life before her father died – an apparently sociable girl with lots of friends. Yes, she was spoilt and indulged and had never needed to fend for herself, but Karen was sure she was fundamentally capable, given the chance.

The curtain tweaked and Patrick's round face peered in.

'Permission to come aboard,' he said, before delivering a small

233

wicker picnic basket to the end of the bed with a triumphant grin. 'Hope I'm not interrupting anything?'

They both shook their heads vigorously, because the truth was they were both very pleased to see him and end their awkward exchange.

The picnic was a small miracle in that drab, functional environment. There were pristine linen napkins, silver cutlery, blue pottery bowls and a single, pale-pink rose in a glass vase, placed on Sophie's bedside locker. Patrick poured clear chicken broth – delicate and aromatic – from a wide-necked Thermos. Flaky, crisp, cheesy twists, tied decoratively together with a red ribbon as if it were Christmas, accompanied the soup. For pudding there were brown earthenware ramekins filled with smooth, cool panna cotta, which he served with a bowl of blueberries. Then mint tea, brewed with hot water from another Thermos and fresh leaves in a Japanese teapot, accompanied by tiny, square chocolate thins.

'You're a real miracle worker,' Karen told him, as she noticed Sophie eating every tiny delicious morsel she was offered. 'Not only do you rescue damsels in distress but you feed them up, back to health and strength, too.'

The meal had indeed brought colour to her stepdaughter's pinched features, and a look of pleasure – almost contentment – that Karen hadn't seen for a long time.

'Picnics for me are ham sandwiches and a punnet of strawberries in a cool-bag,' she said, remembering the beach and William's bare feet in the sand. The memory stabbed her like a lance and she pushed it firmly away. 'Although they used to be chicken and ham paste baps and tomato soup when I was a child.'

Patrick chuckled. 'You're lucky you had picnics. We didn't. Everything I ate as a child was out of a tin: potatoes, peas, corned beef, pork luncheon meat, peaches with Carnation milk as a special treat on Sundays. A gastronomic desert. When I left home I vowed never to eat anything tinned ever again.'

'What's Carnation milk?' Sophie asked.

Patrick laughed. 'Ooh, it was *marvellous*. Evaporated milk, it was like an alternative to cream back when we didn't all have fridges. Went splendidly with peaches.'

'Daddy loved corned beef,' Sophie said, tears suddenly welling in her eyes. 'He used to have it with sliced tomato and bread for his lunch.'

'Dear Harry,' Patrick murmured. 'He loved you so much, you know.'

Sophie's tears slid silently down her cheeks as she lay back on the pillows, head turned to the side. Karen knew she should say something, *anything* decent about her husband. He had been a loving father, as Patrick said. But the degree to which he had spoilt his daughter had also ruined her life, helped drive her to this drastic point. Now, she felt tongue-tied in the awkward lull.

'Maybe you'd better get some sleep, Sophie,' she said, eventually.

'Yeah . . . probably.' Sophie sniffed and reached for a tissue.

Patrick packed the picnic things back into the wicker basket with great precision. 'I'll be back in the morning to see how you are, dear heart,' he said as he dropped a light kiss on her forehead.

She smiled tiredly, thanked him again for the beautiful meal. 'I hope I'll be home tomorrow.' Sophie looked anxiously at them both for confirmation.

'I imagine so,' Karen agreed.

She said goodbye too and followed Patrick down the corridor and out to the car park.

'I'll go on thanking you for this until the day I die,' she said, giving him a long hug and bringing a blush to his ageing cheek.

The house felt eerie with the atmosphere of near-death when Karen got home, especially as Largo was still with Jennifer. She couldn't help herself picturing Sophie, alone and in terrible distress, coming to the tipping point, deciding how many pills she would take, pressing them out of the blister pack, drinking the cold medicine, waiting, waiting for something to happen. She must have been so scared, and in such total despair. Did she have a moment when she regretted her actions, but it was too late to do anything about it?

'How am I going to cope with a suicidal stepdaughter?' she asked Mike, who had phoned to see how Sophie was.

'Awkward, you guys not being that close and all. Be easier if you knew her better.'

'Yeah, she barely spoke a civil word to me when Harry was alive. And although it's got a lot better recently, I still don't feel I really understand her.'

'All that sitting around does nobody any good. I'd want to shoot myself if I had nothing to do all day. Send her to me, I'll work her so hard she won't have time to breathe, let alone feel suicidal.'

Karen laughed. 'Wish I could. It'd be the best tonic in the world.'

'She'd have to be better than Gina . . .' He paused. 'Are you OK?'

'You mean apart from feeling guilty about Sophie, cringing with embarrassment at kissing you, totally exhausted and gutted to have lost William?'

'Yeah.'

'Oh, you know . . . just dandy.'

She heard Mike chuckle. 'That's my girl! Listen, come and visit if you get the chance. Things'll calm down here from now on, so we'll have a bit more time.'

'Thanks, I'll do that.'

She sat with Patrick in his garden, wrapped in her coat, sipping a large frothy coffee and nibbling a croissant around ten the following morning. It was brilliant sunshine, the autumn air was so clear and inviting they neither of them could bear to stay inside.

'It's a shame Sophie can't avail herself of our dear vicar's wisdom,' Patrick said as he helped himself to more home-made blackcurrant jam.

'Why can't she? I think it would really do her good to talk to him. He was so brilliant with me after Harry died. And I'm sure he wouldn't be judgemental about the suicide thing. He's not like that,' Karen said.

'Judgemental or not, darling, if he's not here he can't help her.'

'Not here?'

Patrick's eyes widened. 'Don't tell me you haven't heard?'

'Heard what?'

'Ooh!' Patrick was relishing his power to surprise. 'The news has got the village by its ears . . .' He paused for effect. 'Reverend Haskell has done a bunk.'

'William? What do you mean?' The words sounded so forced, her cheeks instantly draining of colour. She hadn't told Patrick about her relationship with Will. Although she would have liked to confide in the actor, he loved to gossip too much and she knew he would never have been able to keep her secret.

'I'm amazed you haven't heard. No, he just upped sticks on Thursday and ran out on poor Janey without so much as a by-your-leave. Didn't tell her where he was going or why. And quit the Church, if rumour's to be believed. Mrs J had the low-down when she came in on Friday. Apparently, he might have been a naughty boy, bit of a ding-dong with some woman in the parish. I'd love to know who.'

Karen was having trouble breathing.

'She said Janey was in a right old state, which is to be expected, of course, poor dear. But no one's seen her since Friday either. Seems she packed her bags and went to stay with her mum, or at least that's what Jennifer said when I took Largo over. But gossip can never be relied upon, can it?' He frowned. 'Karen? What's the matter? You look desperately pale all of a sudden.' The delight at a juicy tale so clear on Patrick's face a moment ago had been replaced by concern.

She brushed her hand over her sweaty forehead. 'I'm OK. Too much caffeine, I expect.'

Her mind was in turmoil. Here it was – the moment she'd been secretly waiting for, the moment when things did actually change. But William was gone.

'Someone must know where he is,' she managed to say.

'Haskell? I don't think anyone much cares, do they? Such a dreadful thing to do, just walking out like that. Poor Janey, who really is the perfect wife. So humiliating. And what about us, his parishioners? He obviously doesn't give a tinker's cuss for his responsibilities. You really would expect better from a man of God. Jennifer is incandescent about it all.'

'Maybe he had a breakdown . . . you don't know what goes on in people's heads, as we've discovered with Sophie.'

'True, but William always seemed so sane, so dedicated. All those wonderful things he did for the old people and those disabled kids over at the archery club. And there's no question he loved his wife. Couldn't he have done the decent thing and had a breakdown at home?'

'He's probably only gone for a day or so . . . to clear his head. He's bound to be back.'

'You'd have thought. But Mrs J says that Sheila says that he told Janey the whole thing was over and to forget him. As if she could! Very peculiar indeed, don't you think?'

Peculiar, thought Karen, *is an understatement.*

But it did sound like William in his current mood of despair. That time she had bumped into him on the hill he'd been almost catatonic with guilt and self-blame. Maybe he really had just given it all up.

Patrick held his hands up in a theatrical shrug. 'Nowt so queer as folk, as my old mum used to say.'

Karen tried to smile. 'I suppose I'd better get off to the hospital. Sophie texted me to say the shrink was coming at eleven. She's hoping to get out after that.'

'Are you worried about having her home?'

'Yes. I'm worried as hell, worried that if I turn my back she'll try again.'

Patrick thought about this for a moment. 'I have a feeling she won't. She seemed pretty relieved she was alive – which, if you were truly intent on ending it all, you wouldn't be, you'd be furious that you'd failed.'

'Maybe . . . but how will I know?'

Patrick pulled her into one of his famous bear hugs, strength, comfort and kindness radiating from him like a physical heat. Karen didn't fight it.

'You know I'm here, dearest, even if I'm not. Always on the other end of the phone if you need me.'

'She would be dead if it weren't for you,' Karen whispered, the full, tragic enormity of what had just happened to Sophie hitting her yet again.

'Yes, yes, well, she's not. And you mythering about whether she is or not, or whether she might be or not, isn't going to help the girl. Just give her lots of love and chicken soup and she'll come round, you'll see.'

Karen laughed. 'Thanks, Patrick, I couldn't—'

'Don't! You've thanked me far too much for doing what anyone would have done in similar circumstances. Now, go!'

The first thing Karen did as she sat in the car about to drive to the hospital to pick up Sophie was to phone William. His mobile went straight to voicemail, as if he were on the line, and she left a message: 'Will, it's me. Ring me.'

She was sure that he would be in touch. Although a man who could walk out on so much must be in a pretty deranged state. And she felt partially responsible, of course. Because what had seemed like something so private and contained, just between the two of them, had slowly burgeoned into a nightmare that affected everyone. Although she had always known what they were doing had an explosive potential, she had not foreseen this outcome.

Surely he would come home. Where would he go otherwise?

Karen realized she knew very little about his extended family. His father was dead – and his grandmother, of course – and he didn't have any siblings. She was worried for him. As Patrick said, it was so out of character. What if he were really ill, suicidal even? She dismissed the thought quickly – it was too painful to contemplate – and started the car.

I don't have time to think about this now, she told herself. *I have to concentrate on Sophie.*

Sophie was quiet on the way home. She wanted to go straight to her room, which Karen had cleared up as best she could the night before. Sophie had been right to say it was a mess. Aside from the unmade bed and stale vomit on the sheets, there were piles of clothes draped over every surface – even hanging from the window and the edge of the cupboard – plates, glasses, mugs with festering remains of coffee or tea, magazines torn and squashed open, piles of computer printouts, a bulging wastepaper basket, numerous make-up items scattered here and there, creams, perfume, wipes, jewellery, scarves, shoes . . . It was like a teenager's room, not that of a woman of thirty.

Nervously, Karen waited for Sophie's reaction to her efforts. But the girl just sank down on the bed, sat there, her hands in her lap, and looked around.

'I thought I'd better get it straight,' Karen said.

Sophie smiled. 'Thanks, you didn't have to.'

'Shall I bring up some lunch?'

The girl didn't reply, but Karen went downstairs and heated up some soup, made some toast and butter. She had to eat. It wasn't quite Patrick Gascoigne's standard, but she knew Sophie liked tomato soup.

Setting the tray down on the now-cleared desk in the bedroom, Karen was about to leave Sophie to it, when she said, 'Don't go.'

Karen hesitated, then perched on the armchair, feeling slightly self-conscious. Her stepdaughter got up and sat at the desk, brushing her chaotic hair back from her face and into a ponytail holder she pulled from her wrist, then began to take cautious sips without moving the bowl from the tray.

After a few moments, she turned to Karen. 'You don't have to feel responsible for me, you know,' she said. 'I foisted myself on you, but that doesn't mean you have to look after me. I'm a grown woman.'

It seemed to be a speech she had rehearsed. Karen didn't know how to respond. She did feel responsible for her now, after what Sophie had done, but she didn't want to say as much.

'I've been a total pain, I know it,' Sophie went on, laying the spoon down on the tray, soup barely touched, and lifting her socked feet on to the bar of the desk chair, wedging her hands under her thighs in a childlike gesture. 'You didn't want me living here, and I can understand that. But it was only supposed to be for a few months, I thought I'd get something together sooner and move back to London. And then . . . it didn't happen . . .' She bent her head and fell silent.

'It's not been an easy time for you.'

'Nor you, either. And it can't have helped having me hanging around being so bratty all the time.'

'It wasn't that bad.'

Sophie raised her eyebrows. 'Really? I wouldn't have wanted me around being like that.'

Karen smiled. 'OK, well, it wasn't great. But then my behaviour hasn't been exactly brilliant either.'

The girl nodded. 'Well, what I'm saying is, I'm sorry. And I'll try to do better in the future.'

'I'm sorry too, Sophie. Really sorry. OK, I'm not technically responsible for you, but I could have been a lot more sensitive.'

There was an awkward silence.

'Hey, what are we like? Bring on the hair shirts,' Sophie said, then added, 'but seriously, I'm really going to make an effort to get myself sorted.' She paused. 'That scared me . . . what I did.'

'Good, but don't pile more pressure on yourself. It'll take a while before you feel properly better.'

Karen left Sophie to sleep and took the tray downstairs, where she stacked the lunch things in the dishwasher.

She checked her mobile again. Still nothing from William.

Dying to find out more details about his disappearance, she wondered who might know the truth, not the gossip. Sheila might, or Jennifer, she thought. But she didn't know what Janey had said to them. She baulked at asking either woman the details, only to read in their faces that they knew about her involvement already. It was pretty unlikely, surely, that Janey, in the throes of her husband's defection, wouldn't at some stage have blurted out Karen's name as the cause of all her misery.

Her instinct was to lie low and wait for someone to say something, so that she could see how the land lay. But the village gossip machine, if Janey had fingered her, would be in full swing by now, anyway. She couldn't hide. She would know immediately she went out and bumped into a local whether she had become persona non grata in the community.

She was desperate to talk to Will. But if he were determined not to speak to her, there was little she could do. Presumably the church email wouldn't work if he had left his post. How would she find him? Should she even be thinking of finding him? It was a low thing to do, leaving Janey like that. Running away. Childish. But she wasn't convinced he was in his right mind. *Be careful what you wish for*, she thought. *I wanted him to be free and now he is. Free of me as well as everything else.*

In the end she decided she would tackle Sheila before she went to pick up Largo from Jennifer. She was always in the church on a Monday evening, clearing up the flowers from the weekend. A kind, uncomplicated woman, Karen would just have to take it on the chin if she blamed her.

The church door was open. At first Karen couldn't see Sheila. It was raining heavily outside and the nave was unusually gloomy.

'Sheila?'

There was no reply, then the door to the vestry swung open and Sheila, wearing a padded maroon gilet over a pale-blue sweater and jeans, came into the chancel carrying two tall glass vases. She jumped when she saw Karen.

'Oh, Karen . . . didn't hear you come in.'

'Hi, Sheila. How's it going?'

Sheila kept walking, taking the vases to the back of the church where she bent down, resting them carefully on the stone floor by the door.

'Not so bad. Need to give these a good wash and it's impossible in that piddly sink.' As she stood up, she raised her eyebrows at Karen in a question. 'Did you want something, dear?'

Karen, suddenly wishing herself a million miles away, found it hard to frame her question, even though Sheila's tone held no hint that she knew anything bad about Karen.

'Umm . . . I was passing and I wondered if you'd heard any more about Reverend Haskell.'

Sheila let out a long sigh. 'Well, wasn't that a turn-up for the books? I couldn't believe my ears when Janey told me.' She sat down in the open pew near the door, at the end of which were stacked neat piles of prayer books. 'I don't know what on earth went on. There must have been trouble in his head he wasn't sharing with anyone, not even his poor wife.'

'Patrick told me William didn't even say where he was going.'

'That's right. It was after breakfast on Thursday, apparently. He hadn't dressed in his black shirt and dog collar, which was unusual, Janey said, and he was dead quiet at breakfast. But he often was quiet, apparently, when he was thinking out a sermon or whatever. Then he suddenly asked her to sit down and jumped straight in, she said, told her he was leaving that minute and that she was to forget she'd ever known him.'

'God . . . what did Janey do?'

Sheila shrugged. 'Not much she could do, poor soul. She said she just stood there in shock. She asked where he was going, tried to reason with him, but it seems the reverend had made up his mind, wouldn't be budged.' She got to her feet. 'No rhyme or reason to what folks'll get up to. There's a man who had everything. Loving family, dedicated to his work, part of a proper community . . . and he turns his back on the lot. Just can't make head nor tail of it, I can't.'

Karen nodded. She wondered where Mrs Jason, Patrick's cleaning lady, had got the gossip about the supposed affair. But since Sheila hadn't mentioned it, and seemed to be utterly baffled as to the cause of the vicar's defection, she felt she couldn't ask.

'Poor dear Rachel will be in bits, is my guess. She idolized her dad, she did,' Sheila was saying as she picked up the glass vases again. 'Ah, well. Better get a move on, these vases won't wash themselves. I suppose that dim-witted rector from Ashleigh will be standing in till the Church sorts out a replacement. What a mess.'

Karen, finally hearing the details of the drama, couldn't help but feel desperate for William, as well as having sympathy for his family. She knew he must be in despair to have behaved in such a way.

She followed Sheila out of the church and walked slowly across the village to Jennifer's house to pick up Largo. She was dreading seeing her friend. If Sheila – kind-hearted and charitable by nature – had not picked up on the full gossip, Jennifer, beadier by far and considerably more moralistic, certainly would have. Which was born out as soon as she answered Karen's ring. No smile, no welcoming Karen inside as she usually would have, just a tight-lipped nod in response to her hello.

For a moment Jennifer stood there, breathing hard, hand on the front door, bulk solidly filling the space as if she were guarding her home against invasion, then she gave a small harrumph and stood aside.

'I suppose you'd better come in.'

Karen could feel her stomach tighten with dread. So this was it.

Largo ran through from the kitchen at the sound of her voice and jumped up joyfully to be patted.

'Come through,' Jennifer commanded, going ahead of Karen to the sitting room, her hands seeking support from the corridor walls, then from the back of the sofa before slowly lowering herself into her wing-backed chair by the fireplace and placing her right foot – the one that was still giving her trouble from a bad sprain the previous winter – on to the tapestried footstool. She waved Karen imperiously towards the sofa, as if she were a servant come for a job interview.

Karen sat on the edge of the cushion, instinctively wanting a quick escape if necessary.

There was a chilly silence in the room, broken only by the heavy tick-tock of the antique French ormolu clock on the mantelpiece. Jennifer had her hands clasped across her girth, her mouth working in distaste.

'Jennifer—'

Jennifer held her hand up to silence her. 'I don't want to know, Karen. I have no details and I want none. Suffice it to say I am truly shocked by Reverend Haskell's behaviour. And although I loathe rumour and gossip, it hasn't escaped my notice that you are somehow involved in all this too.'

Karen hung her head. She couldn't think of anything to say except 'sorry', and she didn't feel she owed Jennifer Simmons an apology.

'But as far as you're concerned, I can see you might have been vulnerable . . . after poor Harry's death. I know you turned to William and, fair enough, you couldn't have imagined he would take advantage of you in this way.'

'It wasn't like that.' Karen's tone was fiercer than she intended. 'He didn't "take advantage", as you put it.'

Jennifer's eyebrows shot up. She said nothing, her faded blue eyes steely as she waited for Karen to go on.

'He . . . we . . . didn't mean anything to happen. We knew it was very wrong . . .' It sounded pathetic, even to her own ears.

Jennifer's pursed lips made it clear she too was unimpressed. 'So where is he now?' she asked.

Karen shook her head. 'We aren't together. We'd ended it . . . whatever "it" was. I didn't know he was going to walk out on Janey like this—'

'*And* the Church. He's resigned his ministry, given up his whole life. I got Bernard to call the diocese and check, after Janey told me what William had said. I simply didn't believe it.'

'I know you think this is because of me but, honestly, I don't think it is, Jennifer. He never said he would leave Janey – in fact, he said completely the opposite. I had no expectations . . . I knew how much his work and his family meant to him.'

Jennifer was clearly suspicious as to whether Karen was telling the truth. 'So you're saying you don't know where he went?'

'No, I've no idea. It wasn't till Patrick told me that I knew he had gone. I tried to call him, but he wasn't answering.'

'Hardly surprising. I would be hanging my head in shame if I were him.' She absently reached down to stroke Largo's head.

'This isn't like him. I'm worried he's having a breakdown,' Karen said softly.

But Jennifer ignored her remark. 'I'm livid. Such a cruel, heartless thing to do. The man's clearly lost his senses. All that talk about family and community, and then he does this? And he seemed such a good chap, so caring. But if he thinks he can come back, tail between his legs, and carry on as before, he's got another think coming . . .'

Jennifer rumbled on, her ire gradually subsiding in mere grunts of disapproval. Karen got up. There was no mileage in going over it all again.

'Thanks so much for looking after Largo.'

'It's been a pleasure . . .' She paused. 'Oh, heavens, I haven't asked about Sophie. How is the poor girl?'

'She's OK, I think. Exhausted and very low, but she seems happy she's alive.'

'Well, that's the main thing, I suppose.' Jennifer closed her eyes briefly, her face looking worn and tired. 'I don't know what's happening to everyone at the moment. So much trouble, wherever you look.'

CHAPTER FIFTEEN

It was four weeks since Sophie's suicide attempt and nearly the beginning of October. The time had passed for Karen like the steady drip of a tap: measured, relentless, without purpose. Sophie was slowly improving. The antidepressants took a while to kick in, Karen knew, and the girl had only had a couple of sessions with the therapist Patrick recommended, but she seemed less withdrawn, more willing to engage with Karen. And she was eating better, taking Largo out each morning.

Karen found herself watching Sophie like a hawk, hurrying back if she went out – which she tried not to do too often or for too long – always with a faint sense of dread as to what she might find at home. But as the days and weeks went past, that dread lessened as she realized she was beginning to trust the girl to stay alive.

Over all her daily tasks, however – every breath, thought, walk, meal, drive – hung an unbearable ache for William Haskell. But it seemed no one had heard from him, or if they had, they weren't broadcasting the information. Janey had not returned to the village either, just a van, pulling up very early one morning to take away all the family's belongings, supervised by a woman around Janey's age, whom none of the neighbours had seen before.

So over the weeks the Haskells gradually slipped from the top spot on the gossip chart. Not least because a new vicar, Sarah Attwater, had been appointed, creating a fresh drama, this time from the grumbling traditionalists about the suitability of women to disseminate the word of God. But Reverend Attwater was a plump, energetic, middle-aged woman with a warm smile who appeared completely undeterred by the dissenting voices in the parish. So unlike the troubled Reverend Haskell, the word went out.

'He must have told someone where he was going,' Sophie said one Sunday evening, as they sat in the den, each with a baked potato, chilli, sour cream and salad on a plate on their laps. It was still fifteen minutes before *Homeland* began and the screen in front of them was switched off.

William Haskell seemed to have piqued Sophie's curiosity again, triggered, perhaps, by going to church for the first time in weeks that morning and seeing Reverend Attwater in action. Karen, remembering her stepdaughter's quite reasonable ambivalence on the subject in the past, had initially tried to steer the chat away from Will, but Sophie was clearly intrigued by the situation, as if she were suddenly hearing about it for the first time. Karen decided that anything that kept the girl interested, when currently not much did, couldn't do any harm.

'I don't know . . . who would he have told, if he were looking to make a clean break?'

'You, I suppose.'

'Yes, well, I wish he had. It's driving me mad, knowing he's out there, probably in distress and with no one to talk to, no one to comfort him in the way he's always tried to comfort others. Doesn't seem fair.'

'Don't you think he's behaved badly?' Sophie asked.

'Of course I do, if all the gossip is true. But I think he must be having some sort of breakdown. He never had any intention of leaving Janey . . . I'm sure about that.'

Sophie looked sideways at her, swinging the red chair back and forth as she thought about this.

'Why don't you look for him, then?'

Karen stared at her. 'Look for him?'

She knew she sounded surprised, but the thought was not a new one. It was, however, the first time she'd had the idea validated. Till now, Karen had felt it was just a feeble limb of her ongoing obsession with a man who was obviously not obsessed with her.

'Yes. Track him down, find out what happened. Have the conversation.'

'How?'

The girl shrugged. 'Well, I don't know. Social media? Was he on Facebook . . . Twitter?'

'No.'

'No, suppose he wasn't really the sort. Although he could have sent God tweets, sort of inspiring stuff to lift the souls of the faithless masses.'

They both smiled at the thought, then fell silent as they pondered the problem.

'This is where I say, "You were close to him, where would he be most likely to go?" like the detectives in *Without a Trace*,' Sophie said.

'Yeah, and I'd think for a while and not be able to come up with a single idea, then after the ad break someone would say something handy to trigger a memory and we'd all leap in our cars and drive off and find him,' Karen sighed. 'Shame this is real life.'

Sophie was quiet as she ate her food.

'Still, there must be something you can do . . . put an ad in a Church paper . . .' Her voice trailed off, then her face lit up. 'I know, I could check out Rachel's Facebook page, that might have some clues . . . maybe she's going to meet him somewhere and we can spot it.'

'Don't you have to be Facebook friends to find out what's going on in people's lives?'

'I am friends with Rachel. We sort of bonded a few times before she went away. I've hardly been on it recently, so I haven't looked at her page, but I could.'

'Wouldn't she have de-friended you when she heard about me?'

Sophie shrugged. 'She might have, but then on the other hand she might not have heard about you. Her dad won't be rushing to tell her, that's for sure.'

'But Rachel's not going to be proclaiming her father's where-abouts, is she? Not if he's told her he wants to be left alone.'

'I'll look in a sec,' Sophie said, munching the last of her potato skin.

Rachel Haskell hadn't removed Sophie from her friend list, but there was no inkling of the painful family drama in the postings on her page, only weeks old fun snaps of her in Spain with darkly handsome boys and girls posed in front of landmarks in the hot summer sun, gurning happily for the camera.

'Hmm, not much help . . .' Sophie put down her iPad. 'But I can keep an eye on her page. There might be something.'

'I suppose the Church would be no use.' Karen had thought about phoning the diocese and asking for a forwarding address, then realized it was stupid.

'They probably don't know any more than we do. God, they must have got a shock when he told them. Their golden boy, up for bish . . . quite funny really—' Sophie must have caught sight of Karen's expression, because she added quickly, 'Not funny for him, of course, but I'd have liked to have seen their faces.'

'Maybe they knew it was coming. Maybe he'd already said he wasn't happy . . . maybe we were just the last to know.'

Sophie got up and took Karen's plate, piled it on her own, glancing down at her. 'The archery club?'

'Tried that. They said he left because of family problems but they didn't know anything else. I felt weird asking because everyone these days has mobiles and email, they can't have thought I knew him that well if I didn't have his contact details.'

'You could always hire a PI. They'd find him in no time.'

Karen thought how horrified Will would be to be followed and spied upon by a private detective. She shook her head firmly and saw Sophie nod.

'Yeah, maybe not . . .' The girl paused. 'So if you did find him, what would you say?'

The answers to Sophie's question, played out in Karen's head over the previous month of long wakeful nights, were various and predictable. From 'I love you' to 'You bastard' and all permutations in between.

She thought perhaps they'd say nothing much.

'I'd be furious with him, if it were me,' Sophie was saying.

Karen spent the next few days on the Internet, searching options for finding someone who had gone missing. But the individuals the missing person sites were talking about were nothing like William. Many seemed to be either too young to have left home, had mental health problems – their families feared for their safety in the big bad world – or were running away from financial

meltdown. It did seem extraordinary to Karen that so many people – a quarter of a million reported missing each year in the UK
alone, apparently – could just slip away without being found by the
various agencies on their case. Especially with CCTV on virtually
every corner and each click of a mouse telling the world what we eat,
whom we meet, how much cash we have, where we go on holiday.

The truth was that William was not missing. No doubt Janey
and Rachel, his extended family and friends knew exactly where
he was. No doubt his bank knew. He wouldn't have changed his
name or cancelled his debit cards, dyed his hair blond or taken to
wearing glasses and a moustache. William could only be considered
missing to herself, Karen. Knowing that he had deliberately walked
away from her, she had tried to be tough with herself in her internal
dialogue, tried to talk herself down, close the door on her feelings
for him.

But she had not succeeded.

And unless he suddenly turned up on her doorstep, texted her
his whereabouts, or bumped into her in some random place, she
might never see him again. That was not acceptable to her. Even if
he finally rejected her, she needed to hear it from his own lips, not
just by default. They had unfinished business and William at least
owed her a proper explanation.

I won't give up, she told herself. *I'll work it out. I'll find him sooner or
later. I'll have that conversation with him. Then at least I'll know for
certain.*

Whatever she was doing these days, Karen was aware of a constant pick, pick in her head as she trawled through her conversations
with William, searching desperately for a clue to some place or
person that held a particular significance for him. A link that might
draw him back when he was in distress.

But she realized William had been a listener, not a talker.

The village prided itself on the annual Guy Fawkes bonfire and fireworks night. People came from all over the area to enjoy it and from September onwards, brushwood was being collected to make the pyre even bigger and better than the previous year.

'Come with me?' Karen asked Sophie, as she got ready to leave for the village hall meeting to discuss arrangements for the night.

The girl shook her head, then paused, narrowed her eyes as if considering the proposition.

'Hmm . . . maybe I will.'

Sophie, although she went out for walks with the dog and had once attended matins at the church, avoided contact with the village as much as possible. And whereas Karen sympathized, and for different reasons felt very much the same herself, she knew it wasn't good for Sophie to hide away any longer. The more you hid, the harder it became not to, she knew that.

'It'll be boring as hell and the usual suspects will take charge and bully the rest of us, but Patrick promised to bring goodies, which are never to be missed.'

'I know I should get out more,' Sophie said, more to herself than to her stepmother.

Karen didn't reply, not wanting to nag the girl into something she didn't feel ready to do. She couldn't help treating her with kid gloves, constantly monitoring her own speech for anything that might be misconstrued or cause offence.

Sophie took a deep breath. 'I'll come, but I'm worried they'll all stare at me and think I'm a terrible person for doing what I did.'

'I wouldn't worry. This is the village, remember – yesterday's gossip is for wrapping the fish and chips. They're currently gripped by the new vicar and Peggy Blake disinheriting her two sons.'

The old lady, who had died in the summer, had left all her money to a cousin who had cared for her in the last decade of her life – unlike her lumpish, mostly absent offspring.

'OK. You're probably right. It's being on my own too much that makes me think everyone'll be focusing on me. Stupid, really.'

'Not stupid. Now go and get ready before you change your mind.'

The meeting was as dreary as Karen had predicted. But Patrick's tiny, flaky, spicy, warm-from-the-oven sausage rolls, stuffed cheese and bacon baby potato skins and crisp toffee apple slices on sticks went a long way towards alleviating the pain. Sophie, despite her fears, had been welcomed with open arms by Jennifer and Sheila and the others who knew her.

'I heard from Janey yesterday,' Sheila told the group around her, her voice dropping, as they nibbled on the snacks at the end of the hour-long meeting, fingers sticky, red paper napkins pressed to their lips.

'How is she coping?' Patrick asked.

Karen held her breath.

'Well . . . better than I expected, in fact. She's moving back to London. Oh, it all came out. Never took to village life, she said. Never took to being a vicar's wife either, it seems. Although you wouldn't have guessed it. So maybe all this is for the best.'

'Did she mention William?' Sophie asked, flicking a surreptitious glance at Karen.

'I asked if she'd seen him, and she said yes, they'd met up, then she went all peculiar and sort of clammed up. I said "Did you have a go at him?" and she said, "It's a lot more complicated than you think, Sheila," but she obviously didn't want to talk about it, whatever it was, and I let her be.'

'So is he sorry?' Patrick asked.

'She didn't say one way or the other. But she wasn't as cross as I'd have expected her to be, given what he's done to her.'

'Hmm . . .' Patrick said.

'So where's he gone?' Sophie asked.

'Seems he's camping out with this man from his distant past,' Janey said. Sort of mentor character, if I've got that right. She was none too complimentary about him, either.'

'Why, what's the fellow done?' Patrick asked.

'Not sure, she wouldn't say. Just said he was "extremely shady". But then she also said he's a do-gooder, works with down and outs on the coast somewhere . . . can't remember exactly where.'

'Intriguing,' Patrick said, his eyes alight with the mystery.

Sheila shrugged. 'She seemed annoyed that William had turned to this man when he knew full well she didn't approve of him. More bothered about that than anything else.'

The group was silent. Karen was silent. A million questions hovered on her lips, but she didn't ask any of them. How could she justify wanting to know where this man lived and what his name was?

'Anyways,' Sheila shook her head sadly, 'from the way Janey was talking, there didn't seem much prospect of them patching things up.'

'People always say things in the heat of the moment,' Patrick suggested. 'But then they mellow later on, realize they really love each other.'

'Maybe. But she didn't sound angry . . . can't put my finger on it, but there seemed to be something else going on that she wasn't telling me about.' Sheila shrugged again. 'Sad, really . . .'

'Did you know about this guy, this mentor?' Sophie asked, as she and Karen walked home from the village hall.

'He mentioned a man a couple of times – a vicar in Putney, where they used to live – who had been part of the reason he went into the Church in the first place. Maybe it's the same person.'

'No wonder Janey doesn't like him, if she never wanted to be a vicar's wife and this guy persuaded William to quit his trendy advertising job.'

'I wish I could remember his name . . . although I'm not sure Will ever told me.'

'Did he imply he was dodgy in any way?'

Karen wracked her brains to recall the conversation. But it had been around the time when she was in turmoil over Harry's death and she hadn't really been listening. 'No . . . I know he said his church burnt down.'

Sophie's eyes widened. 'Wow, you think this guy's an arsonist?'

Karen laughed. 'Seems a bit unlikely that you'd burn down your own church. You might burn someone else's, but your own? That'd be perverse.'

'OK . . . well, what else would make him "shady"?'

'Money? Sex?'

Her stepdaughter was nodding. 'Probably ran off with the candlesticks.'

They walked in silence for a time.

'If he's working with homeless people then he's obviously not a vicar any more. Maybe he got defrocked, or whatever you do to bad vicars.'

'Maybe he isn't bad, it's just Janey doesn't like him,' Karen sighed. 'Whatever, it doesn't help much with finding William.'

'If we google "church burning down in Putney" it's bound to mention the vicar's name. He'll have said something at the time, like how devastated he is, which'll be quoted.'

'OK, but if it was a long time ago . . .'

'It's quite a big thing, a London church burning down. I'm sure we'll find it. If the vicar was implicated in the fire, the papers are bound to suggest that, don't you think? And if he wasn't, then we can check the sex offenders register.'

'Can you do that? Just put in a name and find out where someone is?'

'Not sure . . . I think you can. Didn't they change stuff because of Sarah's Law?'

A small piece in the *Wandsworth Guardian* in August 2001 read:

> *Police have arrested a local man, aged 32, in connection with the blaze that gutted the historic church of St Barnabas, Delling Road, late on Saturday evening. Rev. Alistair Fisher, the vicar of St Barnabas, who sustained minor burns to his face and hands when he tried, unsuccessfully, to rescue the 17th century altar tapestry, refused to comment on the arrest, but it is thought the man is known to the church community.*

Sophie looked up from her laptop in triumph. 'See? That must be him, Reverend Alistair Fisher.'

Karen nodded. 'If it's the right church, and the right vicar.'

'It's the only church fire I can find in the last fifteen years in Putney. And how often do you hear of a church being gutted? It's got to be him.'

'True . . . and obviously he's not the one who did it. Seems like no one was too surprised by the arrest of the thirty-two-year-old man.'

'So shall we try the sex offenders register next?'

Part of Karen just wanted to leave it, to have nothing more to do with finding out some grim truth about Will's friend. Was she really going to chase after a convicted paedophile and question him about the whereabouts of a man who didn't want anything to do with her?

'OK,' she said, finally, unable to contain her curiosity. 'Give it a go.'

For a while the girl clicked and typed and waited for the various sites to respond.

Karen sat on the bed, waiting.

'Seems like you can't just type in a name on the register. You have to go to the police and ask them to check their database if you think someone in your neighbourhood is a sex offender,' Sophie said after a while.

'Which we aren't going to do.'

The girl glanced round at Karen. 'Shall I keep looking?'

Karen sighed. 'No, no point. Listen, thanks for trying, but William doesn't want to be found, so it's pretty dumb of me to try. Even if we did track him down, he'd probably refuse to speak to me.'

But Sophie wasn't listening, just intently typing away on the keyboard. After a few minutes, she stopped, pointing to the screen. 'Look at this . . .'

Karen peered over her shoulder.

' "Homelessness as a New Addiction", by Alistair Fisher . . . he's written an article in *Pavement* . . . it's a homeless mag. Look, there's a photo of him next to his byline.' The small head shot showed a man in his sixties perhaps, thin and balding, his expression quite stern.

They both glanced through the text, which was decrying the fact that many rough sleepers became so habitualized to being on the street, that they weren't able to adjust to normal life, even with help. He gave Hastings as his example.

'So maybe he lives there,' Sophie suggested.

'Big place, Hastings. But Sheila said he was working in a home for down and outs, didn't she? Can't be that many of them.'

'You wouldn't think so.'

Sophie sat back, turned to look at Karen, who was still standing behind her chair, bent forward to see the laptop screen. 'Seems like a good sort, caring about homeless people. Wonder what it was Janey didn't like about him?'

'His influence over William?'

'Maybe. So shall I google "homeless hostels, Hastings"?'

Karen shook her head quickly. 'I need to think about this. Anyway, they won't have lists of people who work there.'

'Might do. Staff lists. Can't hurt to pin down his location, in case you decide to check him out . . . wouldn't take a sec.'

But Sophie drew a blank. If Alistair Fisher worked with the homeless in Hastings, there was no mention of him – although there were quite a number of centres for homeless people and drug-addiction clinics in the town.

Karen felt dispirited all of a sudden. *Just forget the man*, said a loud, insistent voice in her head.

'You'd probably have to go there, sniff around some of the shelters and drop-in centres.'

'I'm not going to do that.'

Sophie shrugged. 'Why not? William might be working with

him for all you know. It'd be right up his street. You might bump into each other.'

'Yeah, and how do I explain to William what I'm doing there?'

'You tell him straight. Actions have consequences. He has to face up to how he's treated you, Karen.'

'He never promised me anything.'

Sophie just shook her head.

CHAPTER SIXTEEN

Karen heard Mike harrumph at the other end of the phone. It was a couple of days since she and Sophie had traced the possible location of William's putative mentor and she'd done nothing more about it, except think about it obsessively. Now she was lying on her bed, unable to sleep.

'And you want to see William why?'

Karen groaned. 'Yeah, yeah, spare me another lecture. You know why. OK, he never said he'd love me forever and run off into the sunset with me, but we had something. Really we did. I need to know where that went.' She could almost see Mike rolling his eyes.

'Can you really see a future with someone who's just walked out on you like that, without a word. Pretty mean, no?'

'I'm not planning a future with him, I just want to have the conversation where he explains what's gone on.'

'Right. And what's he going to say in this conversation, eh? I'll tell you exactly what. He'll clutch his brow and his eyes will fill with crocodile tears, then he'll say, "I'm so, so sorry, Karen. I let you down. I wasn't thinking straight. I couldn't cope with life. I'm such a terrible failure. You want nothing to do with me."'

Karen couldn't help laughing at Mike's melodramatic delivery.

'So now you don't have to find him. You've heard what the pillock's got to say. Put the whole bloody thing behind you and get on with your life.'

'Ha. Wish I could.'

An exasperated sigh was Mike's response. 'OK, well, if you're dead set on it, then get on and do it. Go to Hastings, hang out with some druggies, talk to the dodgy mentor, find the tosser. But DO IT, Karen, NOW. Stop fucking around.'

She was taken aback, he was almost shouting at her.

'OK. Just get on with it. I hear you.'

'Good. Tomorrow, do it tomorrow.'

Tomorrow? Her stomach flipped at the thought.

'There'll never be a better time.'

She began to say that she couldn't go tomorrow. She was already inventing a reason – Sophie – why it would be difficult. But Mike's insistence refused the lie.

'Tomorrow it is.'

Mike laughed. 'Don't believe you, darlin', but at least you're sounding like you're thinking about it, which is progress of a sort. Sorry to be such a bloody nag, but I've seen you over the last few months, mooching around after a guy who's clearly not got your best interests at heart. And it's doing my head in.'

'Doing mine in too.'

'So sort it. Won't be easy, but it's got to be easier than wasting your life wondering. Ring me when you get back from Hastings.'

'Will do. And thanks, Mike.'

She woke Sophie at eight with a cup of tea.

'What's up?' was the girl's sleepy response.

Karen hovered by the door. 'I'm going to Hastings this morning.'

Sophie pulled herself up in bed. 'Whoa. OK. What made you decide?'

'I talked to Mike last night. He said I was wasting my life. He said I had to find William, get it over with.'

'I said that too,' Sophie pointed out.

'Yeah, I know. And I did listen. But you're both right.'

'Will you be back tonight?'

'Absolutely. It's about a couple of hours' drive. I'll try to be back around six thirty, but I'll text you when I'm leaving.'

Sophie nodded. 'And text me if you find him.'

'I don't suppose I'll find anyone.'

'Worth a try.'

'You'll sort Largo out?'

'Course. Good luck.'

As Karen set off she was aware of a fluttering, churning excitement in her gut. She kept telling herself the facts: she didn't even know if Alistair Fisher *was* William's friend; she didn't know where to find him; she didn't know if he had seen William; she didn't know if he'd tell her where William was, even if he had.

This is a wild goose chase.

But it made no difference to her anticipation. And at least, as Mike said, she would be doing something, not just thinking, thinking, thinking, dreaming, dreaming, dreaming.

Hastings, on a wet October morning, was dismal, like all seaside towns out of season. The painted houses on the sandstone cliffs to the north looked precarious in the wind, the sea wild, the pebble beach almost deserted, the front blowy and cold, full of huddled, head-down anorak-clad figures, mobility scooters, dog walkers,

giant seagulls with mean yellow eyes. After driving up and down
the steep roads for a bit, she settled on an underground car park
between the beach and the town centre. Then she found a seafront
café and had a cup of coffee. The whole place reminded her of
Mike – although the café wasn't a patch on his – and she wished he
were here with her right now, holding her hand as she set about
her strange, probably hopeless task.

Karen, organized as usual, had printed out a map of the town
and pinpointed the various centres and hostels for drug addicts and
homeless people, which were mostly in the New Town, west of
the older part. There were seven that looked promising. She hoped
someone had at least heard of Fisher, even if he didn't work with
them.

The first one was a hostel. The group of men hanging about the
steps, smoking, eyed her with faint curiosity, then turned away.
The man in the office – young, scruffy, bearded – looked harassed
as he dragged his gaze unwillingly from the computer and waited
for her to speak. When she asked about Alistair Fisher he shook his
head quickly, then fired a couple of questions at her.

'Never heard of him. Is he a relative? Does he stay here?'

'No, neither. I'm . . . just looking for him. I thought he might
work here.'

'Nope. Sorry. Can't help.' He turned back to the screen.

Karen waited for a second, not sure if he was going to say any
more, but when he didn't she drifted slowly back out on to the
street. *What did I expect?* she wondered. The cosy world of her
middle-class village seemed miles away from these men's lives.
Why should the hostel guy be interested in her inquiry if it didn't
relate to one of his clients?

She checked her map for the next option, a drug-rehab centre and needle exchange a few streets away. But she was met with the same response – although this time a less abrupt one, as the woman in the grey wool cardigan thought hard about whether she'd heard of Fisher before telling Karen no, and smiling kindly. Clearly everyone she asked assumed she was searching for a long-lost relative.

The next three were pretty much the same. Karen reckoned she spent, at the most, five minutes in each. They were places that obviously provided a vital service, but the buildings themselves were worn and functional, the staff either businesslike or determinedly upbeat, doing what must be a difficult job at times.

In the last, another homeless hostel, a youngish man, a rough sleeper from the look of his filthy clothes and tattered trainers, was kicking off, hitting out at the two workers – a man and a woman – who were trying to reason with him. When he turned towards Karen, she saw his pale eyes, bloodshot and full of rage, his skin taut and weather-beaten on his sinewy frame. He waved his arm at her, then his gaze suddenly softened as if he recognized her. For a moment their eyes met and he seemed to calm down. She held her breath as he mumbled something into his scraggy ginger beard.

'Come on, mate, come and sit down . . .' The male hostel worker took advantage of the lull and began coaxing him towards the open door of the office.

And despite shaking his head, the man finally complied, stumbling as he went.

'Can't help, sorry,' the woman said, obviously remembering Karen's query before turning away.

Karen, thoroughly depressed by her fruitless morning, went back to the seafront and found a fish and chip shop. She sat at one of the beige Formica tables set with a round plastic tomato ketchup container and vinegar bottle, and phoned Sophie.

'It's pointless. There are so many places he could be, if he's here at all. These hostels are grim. The whole thing's grim.'

'Hmm . . . there must be a better way . . . have you thought of the churches? I mean, even if Fisher isn't a vicar any more, he's probably still religious. There's going to be a church he goes to, right?'

'Right. But there are millions here. And unless he happens to be going in or out when I'm passing, it's not going to help.'

'I wasn't thinking of waiting for him, but you could ask someone there if they know him.'

'I suppose . . . I'll give it a go if I see one. But I think I'll have to come back another time. If I bother. I feel so stupid wandering around looking for someone who might not even be here, in order to find someone else who might not even be here either . . . and if he is, might not want to see me.'

Sophie laughed. 'Yeah, does sound a bit dumb if you put it like that. But don't give up yet. I'm sure you'll find him.'

'William or Fisher?'

'Both.'

'I hope you're right. I'm getting some fish and chips to boost my strength for another bit of Philip Marlowe re-enactment.'

'Ha, hope you don't get into the sort of trouble he did. See you later, then.'

The fish was not the freshest, the batter greasy and soggy inside, but the huge mound of chips were hot and sharp with salt and vinegar. With the café so warm and steamy, the mug of tea strong enough to stand her spoon up in, she wanted to stay there forever and forget her mission.

It was weeks now since she'd seen William. Was she fantasizing about how much she had loved him? It had been a moment for them both, but now it had passed. If she saw him again, would her heart beat faster or would she just wonder what all the fuss had been about?

That's what I've got to find out, she told herself, suddenly full of motivation again.

On her way into the next centre, Karen, on impulse, spoke to a dark-haired girl in her early twenties, dressed in jeans and a black Puffa jacket, who was leaning against the railings by the entrance, smoking. She shook her head, uninterested, when Karen asked about Fisher.

'He used to be a priest,' Karen said. 'He's in his sixties, thin, balding, works with homeless people.'

'Oh, him. Yeah, he's the guy helps out at the soup kitchen. Is that his name?'

'I don't know.'

The girl looked puzzled.

'I mean, I don't know if it's the same person.'

'He's OK, like,' the girl said, 'if it's him.'

'Could you tell me where the soup kitchen is?'

The girl pulled herself up off the railings, stubbed out her cigarette with the toe of her tan faux-sheepskin boot and pointed east along the road. 'It's in the church on the square. Go down the corner and turn left, up the lane, can't miss it. But it won't be open yet.' She paused. 'What's the day . . . Thursday? Yeah, I think they do today and Saturdays.'

'What sort of time?'

She shrugged. 'S'pose about six?'

'Thanks. Have you met Fisher, then?'

'Nah, but my boyfriend has. He works here,' she indicated the drop-in centre behind her with a flick of her head, 'that's who I'm waiting for. He's told me about your friend . . . if it's him. The dossers listen to him, Rob says.' She grinned suddenly, the smile lighting up her pale, pinched face. 'Rob even listens to him, which is a fuckin' miracle, I'll tell you.'

It was now after three thirty and beginning to get dark, but Karen thought she'd go and find the church, see if there was anyone about she could talk to. If they were opening the soup kitchen in the evening, as the girl suggested, they'd need to be getting on with making the soup.

Karen twisted the cold iron ring in the church door, but it was firmly locked. The lights were on in the prefab annex adjoining the building, however, and she heard the sound of voices and a radio playing a Cliff Richard song. The door was slightly ajar, but she knocked anyway and waited. No one came, even after a second knock, so she pushed the door open, calling 'Hello?' as she went in.

The annex was little more than a large box of a room with seven mostly bare plywood trestle tables. Only the one at the far end, presumably the serving table, had a red and yellow striped oilcloth covering it. The chairs were moulded blue plastic, the lino speckled beige. The only other ornament was a noticeboard with various flyers and cards pinned up. The kitchen led off at the back, from whence all the noise was coming.

'Hello?' Karen called again.

The chat stopped at the sound of her voice.

'Oh, hi there.' A middle-aged woman, her grey hair in a bun

and wearing a large butcher's apron, appeared in the doorway to the kitchen. 'Can I help?' She had a chopping knife in her right hand, and with her left she pushed her rimless glasses back up her nose.

'Sorry to interrupt. I'm looking for someone. A man called Alistair Fisher. I was told he sometimes works here.'

The woman's face broke into a warm smile. 'Alistair, yes. He doesn't work here exactly but I expect he'll be in later.' Then her face clouded. 'What's it about?'

'Umm . . .' Karen hesitated, unsure how she would explain herself. 'He's a friend of a friend, and I'm trying to track down this other friend. I thought Mr Fisher might be able to help.'

It sounded garbled, but the woman just nodded.

'Do you want to leave a message, then?'

'Would it be alright if I come back later and talk to him?'

The woman shrugged. 'Up to you. He's normally in about six thirty.'

'I think I'll do that, then. Thank you.'

'Can I tell him a name?'

She shook her head. 'He doesn't know me. But my name is Karen Stewart.'

'Karen Stewart. Righty-ho, I'll let him know.'

As she left the building and walked across the square in the direction of the sea she was aware of her raised heartbeat.

What would she say to this man?

Alistair Fisher in the flesh was nothing like his photograph on the *Pavement* website. It was clearly the same man, but he was no longer as thin, nor as stern-looking as the photo had managed to imply. This person was tall, medium build, with a residual seaside tan, dressed in an over-large navy pullover – the collar of a denim shirt poking out at the neck – brown cords and old, much-polished brogues. He was sitting at the end of one of the tables when Karen arrived, deep in conversation with a jittery youth opposite, both of them nursing a cup of tea.

All the tables were now covered in oilcloths but were otherwise bare, with the exception of a small plastic salt and pepper pot on each. No one else was inside, just these two – apart from the woman Karen had spoken to earlier, who was organizing the serving table by the kitchen, still swathed in her apron. The visitors, all men, were hovering about outside, talking in groups, inevitably smoking. They had looked self-conscious, slightly shifty as Karen passed, as if they were embarrassed to be there, which perhaps they were.

She noticed the soup had not yet been brought out of the kitchen, although the sliced white bread was piled high on the serving table, beside a giant-sized tub of margarine, open and pierced by a knife sticking upright. There were also three towers of unmatched bowls, a metal cutlery tray full of plastic spoons and knives, a stack of white napkins and one of small paper plates, clear plastic beakers lying in a snake along the back.

The woman who had spoken to Karen before saw her at once and waved her over. Fisher did not appear to notice her as she walked behind him.

'Hello again.' She pulled Karen towards the kitchen. 'I told Alistair about you and he's quite happy to chat, but he's having a session with someone at the moment. Would you mind waiting till he's finished? Shouldn't be too long.'

'Of course.'

'I'm Sue, by the way. There's a brew just made if you fancy a cuppa while you wait.' She indicated a battered white teapot and mugs on the table.

But Karen was awash with tea and she declined the offer, perching anxiously on a stool beside the sink as Sue went on with her task of heating up the contents of two vast stainless-steel pans, stirring the soup continuously – first one pan, then the other – with a wooden paddle.

'Trouble with parsnips and potatoes is the starch,' the woman said. 'It catches so easily and this gas hob doesn't go low enough.'

Karen nodded, smiled.

'But the boys like a bit of substance in their soup,' she went on, 'can't just feed them carrots and the like.'

'Must be hard to ring the changes.'

Sue shrugged. 'Veggies arrive on the table and I just have to cook 'em up.'

Karen was just about to ask where they came from, when Fisher appeared in the doorway. His eyes went directly to her, his gaze questioning.

Karen jumped up from the stool. 'Alistair Fisher?'

He nodded. Karen saw Sue glance round curiously from her task, then look swiftly away.

'Could I have a quick word, please?'

He nodded again. 'We can sit at one of the tables, there's no one in yet.' He turned without waiting for her to agree.

She followed him, both of them sitting where he had recently talked to the man he was counselling. He folded his hands together on the table and waited for her to speak.

'Umm . . . this is an odd request.'

A faint smile lit up his brown eyes, which seemed to imply that he found nothing that odd any more.

'I'm a friend of William Haskell.' She took a long breath. 'And I'm looking for him and thought maybe you would know where he is.'

Fisher's face gave nothing away, but he nodded. 'I see. Why did you think I might know?'

Karen was embarrassed enough at being there, without having to explain all the trouble she'd gone to in order to track him down. But his expression seemed to brook no evasions, and she plunged in.

'Gossip. I was talking to someone who'd spoken to William's wife, and she said he'd run off to an old mentor, someone working with down and outs on the coast.'

He didn't say anything, so she ploughed on.

'Will had mentioned you to me. I remembered he'd said your church had burnt down, so I looked you up—' She stopped, knowing she was gabbling unnecessary information, wishing she had kept her mouth shut, hoping this would be enough, wanting to avoid telling him that Janey had said he was a bad lot, that she and Sophie had thought he was an arsonist or a thief, or worse.

But he was ahead of her. 'And found out I was a convicted rapist.'

Shocked, Karen just stared at him. She thought she might have misheard.

'Oh, I see you didn't find that bit out.' Alistair shook his head, gave a rueful smile. 'Sorry . . . so you've come to ask about William.' He made no attempt to address the issue of the conviction.

'Yes.'

'Why?'

'I . . . I'm very fond of him.' The words, spoken softly, brought tears to her eyes.

Alistair's gaze was steady. 'Ah, yes.'

'So is he here?' She was suddenly hopeful, desperate to see Will again.

For a moment the man looked down at his hands.

'I can't tell you where he is, Karen. He has asked me not to.'

'Not to tell me?'

'No, not you specifically. Anyone.'

She nodded dumbly. 'Is he alright? I'm so worried about him.' She swallowed hard, but couldn't help the tear that trickled down her cheek.

Alistair got up and took a napkin from the pile on the serving table and handed it to her.

'I'm in a difficult position because he's spoken to me in confidence. I'm sure you'll understand, I can't talk about him or how he is, it wouldn't be fair.'

They sat in silence, neither looking at the other. Sue was hauling one of the large soup pans out from the kitchen to put on the serving table.

Hearing the consideration this man was affording Will, something cracked inside Karen.

Cheeks blazing, her voice raised and harsh with distress, she said, 'Fair? What's that got to do with anything? It isn't fair that William just walked out on us all without a single, sodding word. It isn't fair that he hasn't been in touch with me when he said he loved me. It isn't even fair that he loved me in the first place. Nothing's bloody fair. Never is, never has been. And you, of all people, should know that.'

She wasn't sure why she added the last sentence, as if she knew somehow that Alistair Fisher had been the victim of unfairness at some juncture. Or maybe just hoped.

Fisher did not seem surprised by her outburst, but his focused expression told her he was really listening, completely involved with what she was saying. It was as if he were mentally holding her until she was finished. It was a technique William must have learnt from him.

'I think we all need a safe place to talk.'

Karen wasn't about to debate the point. 'Yes, well . . . I don't even know why I'm bothering to try and find the bloody man.' She pushed out her chair, which squealed wildly on the linoleum floor. 'He's made his position crystal clear.'

'It's never that simple . . . but I'm really sorry I can't help.'

She eyed him. 'Are you? Seems to me you're colluding with him, letting him off the hook. He's hiding behind you instead of facing up to his responsibilities. I mean, how pathetic is this secret squirrel rubbish? Does he think that if we find out where he is, the village will grab their pitchforks and descend on him en masse?'

Fisher didn't reply.

'At the very least, William owes me an explanation.'

Karen watched him take a deep breath, and waited, hoping he was on the brink of deciding to come clean.

But the silence lengthened.

'Will you tell him you've seen me?'

'Yes, I'll tell him.'

'Not that it matters.'

'It does matter.'

She stood up, not bothering to respond to his comment, picking up her coat from the chair adjacent to her own and slinging it over her arm.

'Thanks for meeting me,' she said, holding out her hand, which he took as he got to his feet. Shaking it briefly and muttering a curt goodbye, she turned to go, pushing past the throng of shabby men filing into the hall for supper.

Alistair Fisher's smug silence infuriated her. How dare he shield William like this. Nobody had the right to do that.

She marched off down the pavement, across the lighted town, back to the car park, holding herself together until she was safely in the car, when she burst into tears again. She was a fool. Fisher probably felt sorry for her, no doubt saw her as some middle-aged, lovesick parishioner who'd got the wrong end of the stick with his friend. While he'd seemed to know about her, he hadn't said in what context.

It's quite conceivable that Will hasn't told Fisher the whole truth about our relationship, she thought. *He's probably left out the part where he said he loved me, just represented it as a mad fling he wants to forget.*

Then her mental gymnastics were stopped in their tracks as she realized William had never actually said he loved her. She had said she loved him, but he had never said the words back.

OK, he didn't say it, she told herself, but she couldn't help remembering William's face as he made love to her. *He did love me, he really did,* she told herself. *So why is he being such a coward? Why doesn't he just ring me and tell me it's over, let me off the hook?*

Then another voice interrupted her thoughts. He *had* told her it was over. Wasn't a month of silence enough? How much clearer did he need to make it?

Sophie had made Karen supper, although it was after nine when she got home. She sat down at the kitchen table with relief.

'You're a star, thanks so much,' she said, as Sophie spooned macaroni cheese on to her plate, pushed an earthenware dish of tomato salad towards her, filled her glass with red wine.

'So? Spill,' the girl said as they began to eat.

When Karen had finished telling her about her meeting with Alistair Fisher, Sophie shook her head.

'A rapist? Wow.'

'He seemed OK . . . although I know that's a stupid thing to say. But I suppose we shouldn't judge until we know the circumstances. He was annoying, but I didn't get the vibe that he was violent or cruel.'

'Whatever he's done, it's a result. If Fisher tells William about you visiting, William is bound to get in touch with you.'

'Frankly I don't care if he does or not.'

'You don't believe Fisher'll tell William?'

Karen thought about this. 'No, I think he'll tell him. It's William's reaction I doubt.'

'OK. So you're saying you don't give a toss about speaking to William?' It was clear from Sophie's expression that she didn't buy this.

'Exactly that. Seeing Fisher was good, not because he might lead me to William – which he wasn't going to do, anyway – but because it's finally opened my eyes to how much I'm humiliating myself, chasing after him.'

Sophie chewed her bottom lip, said nothing.

'Blindingly obvious, I know.'

'If he's ill, though, perhaps had a breakdown . . .'

'I just made that up to make myself feel better. There's no evidence for it. And Fisher certainly didn't imply he was ill.'

'No, but you said he didn't imply anything because it wasn't fair. So you don't know.'

Karen took a large gulp of wine. 'Whose side are you on, anyway?'

Sophie laughed. 'Oh, always the side of true love.'

'Well, in that case you should be trying to persuade me that William has two heads.'

The girl was silent for a moment, holding the stem of her glass and turning it slowly in the candlelight, eyes fixed on the reflection. 'I thought he was a good guy,' she said, not looking up. 'You thought he was a good guy too, Karen. We all did. He *was* one in lots of ways.'

'I know . . .' Karen sighed.

'I'm not saying you should bother with him any more if you don't want to, I'm just saying it's not like Reverend Haskell to deliberately cause so much grief.'

And Karen had to agree.

Sophie's mobile rang.

She glanced at the screen and pulled a face. 'Mum. Better get it, she never rings this late.' She answered the call as she got up, speaking in the strange mixture of Greek and English they always used as she walked slowly out of the kitchen.

Karen's thoughts returned to Will. Finding Fisher had been a sort of diversion, she realized, a way to put off facing the truth. William wasn't ill and in despair, and even if he were, it was still possible to send a text telling her so. She must stop pretending otherwise, or go stark raving mad. Maybe she really was just a sad, middle-aged obsessive who had got the whole thing totally wrong.

Her stepdaughter came back into the kitchen, her face fallen. 'Nanu died this evening.'

'Oh, Sophie, I'm so sorry.' Karen got up and went to embrace the girl.

Sophie allowed Karen to hold her for a moment, then pulled

back, her dark eyes wide and bewildered. 'Mum said it was peaceful in the end. Nanu's hardly been awake this past week, so I suppose it's a mercy she didn't linger any longer.'

'Your poor mum.'

Sophie sat down at the table and let out a long breath. 'Yeah, she sounded really tired. It's been pretty full-on. Nanu's not the easiest of people on a good day.'

'Weren't they close?'

'Oh, nobody was that close to Nanu. She made it her business to fall out with people for no apparent reason. I think she enjoyed the drama.'

'Even you?'

'No, she was good to me. But I didn't see her enough. We usually went out in the summer, but I haven't been for a couple of years now . . . I should have, but it was always such a nightmare because there were only two bedrooms and one was filled with junk. So me and Mum had to sleep on sort of camp bed things in the living room. And Mum and Nanu bickered about everything, all day long. She was scary, Nanu . . .'

'Still, it's sad.'

'I'm sad for Mum, really. Sad she didn't have a better relationship with her.' She took a sip of her wine. 'I'll have to go out there tomorrow, help Mum with the funeral and everything.'

'Are you OK with that?' Karen knew Sophie hadn't been outside the village for months.

'I guess I'll have to be,' she said, with a wry grin.

'I'll come with you if you like,' Karen offered.

Sophie's eyes welled up at Karen's offer. 'Thanks . . . thanks so much . . . I'll be fine.'

'Well, at least I can take you to the airport.'

'You don't need to. I can leave the car in the long-term car park. I won't be there more than a week, I hope.'

'Sophie! Of course I'll drive you. Don't be ridiculous.'

And the girl slowly nodded her agreement.

Bonfire night came and went without incident. November dragged on, down into the darkness.

Johnny rang to harangue Karen about coming to Canada for Christmas and called her 'stubborn' when she refused.

Sophie stayed on in Athens. 'It's complicated,' she whispered to Karen when she called to check how things were going. Clearly Theresa was close by.

Meanwhile Karen felt as if she were existing in a sort of suspended state. She didn't feel sad or lonely or anxious, but neither did she feel any sort of optimism for the future. She was merely plodding from day to day, waiting. And if anyone had asked her what she was waiting for, she would have been quite clear: William. It wasn't even remotely rational, but that didn't matter to her.

It was the waiting that sustained her and stopped her from plummeting into despair.

'I've got some incredible news,' Sophie told Karen three weeks later, when they were on their way back from the airport. 'Nanu left me everything. Her apartment, her money, the lot.'

Karen gave a quick glance round at her stepdaughter. The girl looked exhausted but there was a look of hope in her eyes that Karen hadn't seen before. 'That's brilliant.'

'Mum thinks the apartment could be worth as much as a hundred and fifty thousand euro, although the market's flat at the moment with the economy still in such a mess. And then there's some cash as well.'

'Was your mum upset not to get any?'

'I think she was. It's a sort of psychological thing rather than a financial thing, I think – Mum's got money. Like Nanu not loving her enough. I offered to give her some of my share, but she won't hear of it. Anyway, we've cleared the worst of the stuff, it would only need a bit of tarting up to make it nice. Then I can rent it out or sell it.'

'That's such good news, Sophie.'

'Yeah, isn't it? But it's been really hard on Mum.'

They were silent for a while.

'Maybe I'll take a course with the money, learn how to do something profitable. Mum's always pooh-poohed education, said college was just an excuse to doss for three years. Which is a joke considering I've been virtually dossing for ten years at least.'

'Good idea. What would you like to do?'

'Don't know, but something I can really get involved in.'

Karen felt a sudden lightness of spirit hearing Sophie talk on about her future as they drove home.

The dark pall of the girl's despair over recent months had hung over the house and over Karen, allied to a constant nagging worry about her stepdaughter's state of mind, her actual safety. But now there seemed to be a tentative sea change in Sophie's psyche.

PART THREE

CHAPTER SEVENTEEN

Christmas again. Decorations went up in the windows of the village houses. The fairy lights on the huge spruce, situated on the village green by the duck pond, twinkled reassuringly in the darkened evenings.

'I wish I didn't have to go,' Sophie said as she stood in the hall, a small wheelie case beside her, grey parka on, a red scarf hanging loose around her neck.

'It'll be good to see your mum.' Karen tried to encourage her.

Sophie pulled a face. 'I've only just seen her. And there's sod-all to do up there, it's right bang in the middle of nowhere. No pub, no shop even. Worse, no mobile signal to speak of. And if this weather keeps up it'll be knackeringly cold.' Her eyes widened. 'Oh, God, I hope I don't get snowed in . . .'

'It's only for a few days.' Karen laughed, reaching to kiss the girl goodbye.

'Will you be OK on your own?'

'Of course. I've had three invitations to Christmas lunch already, and I'm sure that's just the tip of the iceberg.' Karen didn't add that she had no intention of going to any of them. She liked Christmas normally, and Harry had always thrown himself into the festivities with an almost childlike zeal. But Harry wasn't here now. The thought brought a pang of nostalgia for her husband, for the companionship, the friends, most of whom had faded away over the year as Karen made no effort to engage with them.

Sophie laughed. 'Yeah, that's the upside of village life, you're never alone . . . and the downside, of course.'

'Listen, you'd better get off.'

They said goodbye, Karen and Largo watching from the door as Sophie drove off into the wet morning mist.

'Just you and me now,' Karen told the dog, ruffling the hair behind his ears.

Christmas morning dawned. Karen had, as she'd intended, excused herself from all the invitations to lunch. If Patrick had asked her, she might have felt more enthusiastic – she could be herself with the old actor – but he and Volkan had taken off to Mauritius 'till after the new year.

It's just another day, she told herself, deciding to read and walk and watch bad TV, avoid any people in the village, go to bed early, pretend she was not so alone. She texted Sophie Christmas wishes, with little hope that the girl would get them, given the lack of mobile signal in the Cumbrian hills. Then she texted Mike, who was spending the day with his daughter and the 'thug'. She would call Johnny later.

But as she lay there, summoning the energy to get up and get dressed, suddenly there was a burning imperative to do something quite different with the day. And before she had time to consider it more carefully, she had showered, dressed, eaten a slice of toast and marmalade, gulped a cup of black coffee and jumped into the car – with the dog – setting the satnav for Hastings. Instinct told her that William would be there today, at the soup kitchen, making Christmas lunch for the homeless people, along with Sue and his friend Alistair. She was as certain as she'd ever been about anything in her whole life.

The roads were empty this early in the day. Later, no doubt, there would be scores of families setting off to visit relatives, but now there was an almost eerie absence of cars and people as she passed through the grey, windswept Sussex towns, the strung lights and trees bright in the dull winter morning. She felt like some lone adventurer off on a quest. And she was as excited and nervous as if it were a real quest.

This was what she had been waiting for. *Today I will see him*, she kept telling herself. *Today I will talk to him, find out once and for all*.

Find out what, she wasn't sure, but she was sure that things would be instantly clarified as soon as she looked into his eyes again. There was no part of her that worried William wouldn't be where he was supposed to be.

Parking the car near the church, she arrived just after eleven. Light was spilling through the stained-glass windows and she could hear the rumble of the organ, the sound of raised voices singing 'O Come, All Ye Faithful'. Suddenly nervous, she sat in the car for a while, not knowing how she would explain her presence to Sue, not least if Alistair wasn't expected today. For all she knew he had gone to Mauritius too, taking William with him.

Pull yourself together, she told herself firmly. *You've come all this way, don't fall at the last fence*. Steeling herself, she got out of the car and knocked on the door to the annex before she lost her nerve.

Another woman answered the door. Very thin and very tall, she wore a jumper with a reindeer on the front and a red Christmas hat with a white trim and bobble over her short grey hair.

'Happy Christmas,' she said, before Karen had time to speak. 'We aren't open for another hour or so. If you could come back after twelve thirty.' Her smile was slightly forced, her accent with a hint of something European, Karen thought.

'Umm . . . I haven't come for the lunch,' Karen said, amused she was being taken for a homeless person.

'Sorry, I just assumed . . .' The woman looked embarrassed.

'I was hoping to see Alistair Fisher . . . are you expecting him later?'

'Alistair? Yes, he'll be round after the service,' the woman said, stepping back from the doorway. 'Come in and wait if you like.'

Karen thanked her and went to fetch Largo from the car. She left him pottering about in the main room, which contained a large tree in the corner with multi-coloured lights, the six tables laid with red paper cloths and decorated with baby gold and silver tinsel trees, a pyramid of crackers at each end. The kitchen was hot and steamy, fragrant with mouth-watering smells of roasting bird, the central island covered with three large baking trays of potatoes and various smaller ones containing ranks of chipolatas and extra stuffing waiting to go in the oven.

The radio was playing 'Deck The Halls', volume high, and Sue was singing along in a croaky voice as she chopped a vast pile of carrots on the draining board. She turned as Karen came in. 'Oh, hello,' she said, knife poised. 'Karen, isn't it?'

'Well remembered.' Karen felt the eyes of the two women on her and knew she had to offer an explanation.

'Happy Christmas,' Sue said, coughing. 'Sorry, got a bit of a chesty thing going on.'

'And to you. I . . . er, I thought maybe Alistair would be here today . . . and your friend said he was coming later . . . I could help while I wait.'

Sue grinned. 'That would be marvellous. This is Ursula, by the way.'

Neither woman queried Karen's presence. But then they were used to dealing with a transient community and perhaps didn't think it particularly odd that she should turn up out of the blue, on Christmas morning, to see someone whom Sue, at least, was aware Karen barely knew.

Karen was delegated to take over the carrot-chopping, while Sue got on with the bread sauce, Ursula taking the enormous turkey out of the oven to baste, and clucking as the steam misted up her glasses. For a while all was quiet, just the radio belting out Christmas favourites as the women worked.

'The service should be over in a minute,' Sue said, looking at her watch. 'We'll need to get those sausages in soon.'

'I have nowhere to put them until I take the turkey out,' Ursula said.

'Is it nearly ready?'

'Another twenty-two minutes.'

Sue laughed, blowing out her cheeks, which were bright red from the heat. 'Very precise, Ursula. Thank God for the microwave, otherwise we'd have six puddings steaming on the stove and nowhere to put anything else. Don't know how we'd have coped.'

Karen was relieved to be in the stuffy, congested kitchen redolent of so many past Christmas lunches, with people she didn't know, the radio making conversation unnecessary. It stopped her thinking too much about William. But every few seconds she would glance towards the door, waiting, her nerves jangling with anticipation. With her back to the room, however, as she mixed a ton of custard powder with milk to a smooth, yellow paste in a Pyrex bowl, she did not hear William's mentor arrive. She was only aware that he was in the kitchen when she heard Sue greet him enthusiastically. She turned just as Alistair Fisher noticed her.

His expression was almost shocked. 'Karen . . .'

'She's been helping us out,' Sue said. 'It's been a godsend, having an extra pair of hands.'

'Good,' Alistair said, taking off his brown tweed overcoat and hanging it on one of the hooks behind the door with the other coats. 'Glad you could be here, Karen,' he added, as if he had been expecting her all along.

She didn't know what to say, so she just smiled and got on with the custard.

There would be no time to talk privately to him in the hectic run-up to lunch, and anyway, it wasn't Fisher she had come to see. Where was William? Had she got it wrong after all? She was aching to ask the man, but instead she worked alongside him and the two women, putting the finishing touches to the turkey meal.

Later, when both she and Alistair were in the main room, carrying through the trays of roast potatoes, she began to speak, to ask him where William was.

But he interrupted her. 'It's wonderful that the Church can give everyone a proper celebration at Christmas,' he said, turning away, back to the kitchen.

Karen counted nineteen men and two women around the tables. Plates piled high, they were tucking into the dinner with gusto, many of them with a paper hat perched on their heads, not talking much, just listening to the radio. Largo was a big hit, making his way around the tables to be patted and made a fuss of, accepting tidbits from anyone offering.

Sue, Ursula, Alistair and Karen sat together at one end of the table by the kitchen. All of them were hot and exhausted, but so happy to have pulled it off and be able to relax for a minute with their own lunch, before the next stage of the meal had to be dealt with.

'I think we did pretty well,' Sue said, her gold cone hat skewed on the back of her head, the string digging into her double chin.

'You did brilliantly,' Karen agreed, glancing over at Alistair, still waiting for him to make some comment on her being there, which he seemed determined not to do.

Would he warn William not to come? She hadn't seen him making a call since he'd arrived, but he could have done. Her previous conviction about William was slowly waning as the hours ticked by. It was only just after two thirty, but if he were intending to help with the lunch he would have been here hours ago.

The first chance Karen had to talk to Fisher without being overheard was when Sue delegated them to organize the tea. Alistair was piling mugs on to a tray as Karen waited for the two kettles to boil, the large white teapot and an equally large brown one standing by. She was furious with him. He must know she wasn't here on some philanthropic mission; he could have taken her aside hours ago and told her what she needed to know.

'So is William coming today?'

Fisher stopped what he was doing and looked at her. He didn't reply at once, just seemed to be turning things over in his mind.

'This is awkward for me, Karen—' he said, then stopped.

'Oh, for goodness' sake! I just want to know if he'll be here today. I'm not asking you to betray your country, Alistair, just tell me if I can expect William to walk through that door. Or am I wasting my time?'

'I honestly don't know if he'll come or not.'

'But he said he might?'

Fisher nodded reluctantly.

She let out an exasperated sigh. 'See? That wasn't so hard. What do you think I'm going to do, exactly? Come at him with a meat cleaver? Anyway, it's none of your business, you aren't the guardian of William's soul. Or mine.' She turned back to the kettles.

Her heart was thumping with indignation, her breath short in her throat. The man was infuriating with his smugly protective attitude towards William. *It's as if he's an anxious parent*, she thought, her hand quivering as she picked up one of the kettles.

There was silence behind her.

Then Fisher said, 'You make me sound like some Svengali. I'm not, as you seem to think, controlling William in any way. He's perfectly capable of making his own mind up about what goes on in his life.'

'So are you worried he'll think this is a set-up? That you told me he'd be here and he'll feel betrayed?'

She hadn't realized she was raising her voice, but Ursula, who was just coming into the kitchen, looked quickly from her to Fisher.

'Everything OK in here?'

'Fine, tea's nearly ready,' Karen said briskly, pouring the boiling water in a steady stream on to the tea bags in the bottom of the pots.

A few minutes later she and Fisher were alone in the kitchen once more.

'Listen, Karen. We seem to have got off on the wrong foot, you and me. But we're both on the same side. We both care a great deal about Will . . .' He paused, smiled at her. 'Can we be friends?'

Karen pursed her lips. 'I'm too annoyed with you at the moment, but I'll think about it.'

Which made Alistair laugh, his face lighting up with real delight. Karen could see his charm suddenly and held out her hand.

The afternoon wore on, seamlessly morphing from turkey to pud to tea and Christmas cake – courtesy of Ursula – to cracker-pulling and more tea. The men were in no hurry to leave, the wild wind and rain that had sprung up during the day no incentive for someone with only a dismal hostel to go to.

Karen helped with the washing-up – not as bad as it might have been because of the paper plates and plastic cutlery and glasses – then sat amongst the men and listened to their stories. They were of all ages: some obviously had mental health or substance abuse problems, their twitchy anxiety and inability to relate painful to watch; some seemed bewildered as to how they had got themselves into this state; others were almost comfortable with who they were. But there was a good deal of humour and very little whingeing about their lot.

She had long since given up on William Haskell when he finally walked through the door of the church annex. And for a second she wondered if it was really him. He had lost weight, his dark hair was longer and wild from the wind outside, and he was dressed in jeans, heavy black work boots and a grey cable jumper. He looked younger. It was as if he had literally stripped off his old life to reveal a different human being beneath.

He didn't notice her at first as he greeted some of the men at the tables – they clearly knew him and were pleased to see him. Fisher got up, his face tight with concern, and began to make his way across the room. But before he had reached his friend, William's gaze, scanning the hall, lighted on Karen.

She held her breath.

He looked stunned, did a double take, a small frown appearing as he bit his lip, turned to listen to what Fisher was telling him. Karen couldn't hear what he was saying, couldn't hear anything any more, in fact. The hum of chat, the scraping of chairs, the laughter, the wind rattling the flimsy roof covering had faded to zero. It was just her and William in this cocoon of silence. The room could have been empty for all she was aware. Then he was making his way towards her.

She got up slowly. 'Hi, William.'

He took a deep breath. 'Karen . . .'

William's expression was unreadable, but the softness in his eyes as he looked at her was enough.

'I suppose you thought you'd escaped me,' she said, smiling up at him.

He smiled too now. 'I suppose I did,' he said, but was prevented from saying any more as Sue came up to give him a hug and wish him Happy Christmas.

They were shutting the hall at seven and the men slowly shuffled out into the night. The storm had passed and it had stopped raining. Small groups still lingered outside the hall, smoking and chatting, reluctant to move on. The kitchen was back to its pristine state, pots and pans stacked on the shelves, the meagre remains of the meal packed into foil parcels and handed out to the men for later.

Karen didn't know what to do. There had been no chance to speak to William as various people claimed him in the hour before the hall closed. She wasn't even sure if William would want to talk to her. Perhaps he would just go off into the night, disappear again – guarded by his friend, Alistair, of course – and refuse to communicate with her.

But as she said goodbye to the two women, got into her coat, extracted Largo from the clutches of a burly, bearded man with a Polish accent who had become the dog's new best friend, William was suddenly at her side.

'Are you going home now?' he asked.

Karen looked at him. 'I was, but I'm pretty tired. I might stay here tonight, go back in the morning.'

She saw him hesitate. 'Well, if . . . if you have time and want to talk . . .'

'Of course I want to talk,' she said softly.

'Alistair . . .'

'I don't want to talk with him there,' she said.

Will nodded. 'No, I understand . . . but there isn't really any-where to go on Christmas Day except a noisy pub.'

'It's stopped raining. We could just walk down to the beach.'

His face cleared. 'The beach, good idea. There's bound to be at least one café open along the front.'

Alistair came up, eyebrows raised as he looked from one to the other. 'Is there a plan?'

'We're going for a walk,' William said. 'I'll see you later.'

Fisher nodded and smiled at Karen, held his hand out as he said goodbye. 'I hope I'm forgiven,' he said.

'Almost,' she said.

The promenade was dim, except for the swaying strings of col-oured Christmas lights hanging between the lamp posts, with the arcade and most of the cafés closed up. There were few people about on such a rough night, most of them probably comatose in front of *The Sound of Music*. The wind was still buffeting the shore, the black sea roiling over the beach in high, foamy lines.

For a while they stood in silence together, watching. They hadn't said a word on their walk down to the seafront. The café they found was badly lit and empty except for a group of five teenagers – two boys and three girls – at the back, cans of Coke and Fanta and two white polystyrene containers of chips open on the table. The girl behind the counter, earphones in, cheap Santa hat pulled down over her pasty face, took their order for tea. They sat in the steamed-up window. Karen would almost have preferred the silence to continue. She decided to let him speak first.

'It's good to see you,' was all he said, only glancing briefly up at her.

She nodded and silence fell again, only interrupted by the girl bringing two white mugs of tea and setting them down on the pale laminated table.

'I suppose you want some answers,' he said when she had gone. She nodded, waited.

'Where to start . . .' He took a deep breath, looking down at his mug as he began to talk in a hesitant voice. 'I suppose it was like the perfect storm. You, Rachel leaving home, the possibility of being promoted, Janey finding out. I haven't been happy for a long time now, as I'm sure you realized.' He paused, cleared his throat. 'Not just my marriage, but my work too. I'm not cut out to be a vicar, Karen—' He stopped again. 'I passionately believe in God – I hope that will never change – but I can't be the one to persuade other people to stick to the Anglican doctrine.'

'I didn't know you were unhappy in your marriage.'

William shrugged. 'No . . . well, we tried our best to make it work. Janey's a good person, but she wasn't cut out to be a vicar's wife any more than I was to be a vicar. She hated it from the start, never understood why I'd made the change from a good career in advertising. And I admit, it is quite a burden on a wife – she has to be part of the whole Church package, like it or not.' He paused. 'In the light of what's happened, maybe she knew me better than I knew myself.'

'She put up a good show of liking it.'

'Yeah, in public. But at home she was miserable. Rachel was just about the only thing that kept us together.'

'When she confronted me about you, she seemed so keen on the bishop thing. As if she really wanted you to be one. Said I'd ruin your life if I messed that up.'

'I think she thought that any change would be better than staying a vicar's wife. At least bishops have status, bishops' wives don't have to do all the community stuff. But even the thought of being a bishop helped to focus my mind, made me realize what I didn't want.'

There was silence between them as they both contemplated the ruins of William's marriage and career.

'She told Sheila you hadn't warned her you were leaving till the morning you did. Then you just walked out. She said she didn't even know where you were going. Everyone in the village thinks you're a monster for doing that.'

William's face tightened. 'It wasn't like that. Things . . . I didn't deal with it well . . . but we both knew the writing was on the wall as far as our marriage was concerned.' He looked down. 'I didn't know what else to do.'

Karen was puzzled. 'Why was Janey so upset about me, then? She was acting like someone who wanted to save her marriage, not someone who had accepted it was all over. She did everything in her power to put me off, including saying you were serially unfaithful.'

'That was before——' He stopped. 'Before things got really bad.'

Karen frowned. She believed what he was saying, but he seemed to be holding something back.

'But I assure you there were never any other women before you. A couple of women maybe were keener on me, as their vicar, than they should have been. But there was nothing more to it, I promise.'

William leant back in his chair, his hands around his mug of tea, which he had hardly touched.

'And that's the thing, Karen. What we had . . . I'm not sure it was real.'

She felt her stomach tighten. 'Wasn't real?'

'I wasn't me . . . I was playing the vicar. Well, not playing it exactly. I meant it, or at least tried to mean it, but I was struggling every second of every day. I told you before, that day on the hill, but you didn't believe me, that you were in love with the person you thought I was. A man of integrity, a good man, a man of God . . .' He paused. 'I'm not that person.'

'You think I'm so shallow I'd fall for just an image?'

'Not an "image", but a package. You fell in love with a vicar, Karen.'

'Stop saying that. I get it. But I didn't, you're wrong. I fell in love with you, William. I didn't give a toss if you were a vicar or a beach bum. It was you I loved.'

She spoke about her love in the past tense, she realized. And she asked herself now if there was any truth in what William was saying. She had met him at a vulnerable time in her life, he had saved her from guilt and despair. Was it, in fact, the counsellor, the priest whom she had loved?

Neither of them spoke for a moment. Karen's mind was boiling up like the sea outside, the whole fabric of her dreams suddenly threatened.

'So you're saying you were never in love with me.' She didn't make it a question.

There was a long moment of silence, stretching out her words until they reached breaking point.

'I was always in love with you,' he said, finally, his voice hardly above a whisper. The depth of his sincerity brought tears to her eyes. 'From the first minute I set eyes on you.'

'Will . . .'

He shook his head vigorously. 'But that isn't the point. I lied to you, I led you up the garden path. The fact is, you have no idea who I am, Karen, who William Haskell is. You can't, because I myself have no idea who I am right now either.'

She could see the tears in his eyes too.

'And anyway, all that's in the past,' he went on. 'Things have changed so much.'

'So you're saying that although you loved me, you don't love me any more, now that you're someone else?' She almost wanted to laugh, what he was saying was so tortuous, so ridiculous.

Her heart had contracted to the smallest, hardest stone when he insisted their love was a mirage, but then, seconds later, had soared like a bird escaping a cage as he admitted the exact opposite. And it was his confession of love that she heard, the rest just flimflam, stupid, so much white noise.

'I'm not talking about my feelings, I'm talking about yours,' he said.

'That isn't for you to decide.'

He sighed, as if the discussion were too much for him. As it was becoming for her too. Did he have to make it so complicated?

'Listen, all I'm saying is that my life is chaos. Everything that I had has gone. I have no career, no home, no family, no money, no . . .' He let out a long sigh. 'I literally don't know which way is up at the moment. If it weren't for Alistair . . .'

Silence.

'You remember that night at the beach, don't you?' she said.

He nodded. 'Of course I do.'

'That was as real to me as anything I've experienced in my whole life.'

Another silence.

'But it was a different time. It's not now, Karen,' he said.

His lack of acknowledgement about their time together made Karen begin to doubt whether it had meant anything to him or not. Nor did she understand what he was getting at, this stubborn insistence that he was another person. It didn't make sense.

'So this new life of yours . . . it obviously doesn't include me.'

It seemed like an age before he replied, 'It's not that simple.'

And there was something in the way he spoke that stopped her from asking William what he meant.

'I'd better go . . . I have to find somewhere to stay.' She got up, her heart thumping furiously. 'I feel as if we've been here before. I say I love you and you say I don't. I could have saved us both the trouble of repeating ourselves.'

William got up too, put his hands on her arms. 'Karen, please. Don't be angry with me. I have nothing to offer you . . . really, nothing, you have to believe me.'

'You could have just told me so, months ago. You could have sent a "Dear John" text telling me it was over. It would have been the decent thing to do.'

He looked into her eyes as they stood there, and she could see a desperate pain.

'I should have done that,' he said quietly as she wrenched herself free and slammed her way out of the café, running along the front like a demented woman, her heart bleeding and in tatters as if she had been stabbed.

CHAPTER EIGHTEEN

Karen sat in the car outside the church for a long time. She wasn't crying, barely even thinking, but she didn't have the strength to drive anywhere. She knew she ought to get on and find somewhere to stay, but pulling out her mobile to look online she couldn't get a signal. After sitting there for a while longer, Largo snoring peacefully on the back seat, she started the engine and drove back down to the seafront, knowing there would be a plethora of hotels there.

The first one she picked, a discreet building in the middle of a Georgian terrace, had rooms, but said they were very sorry but they could not, under the terms of their insurance, accommodate the dog. They sent her off to another, further down Grand Parade at White Rock. It was modern, clean and dog-friendly, a raucous din emanating from the dining room where a Christmas party was obviously in full swing. Karen didn't mind, she just wanted somewhere to lay her head for a few hours until she felt strong enough for the drive home. Shivering from the time in the chilly car, she had a hot shower and then watched television for a while, knowing she would not sleep yet, if at all.

Her thoughts of William were so jumbled, so incoherent, that she couldn't focus and she was too tired to make sense of the millions of fragmented, unanswered questions that seeing him had raised. Was it true that his life was such a mess that he had no space for her? Or was that just an excuse for the fact that he had never really loved her, just used her to medicate himself at a time when everything else was going wrong? Was his addiction to doing the 'far, far better thing' getting in the way of him making a rational decision? She'd definitely seen the light in his eyes when he said he had loved her – that wasn't her imagination. But he was different now, that also was true. If she were assessing Will clearly, she'd say he seemed happier, more himself than he had in his vicar incarnation. He did not appear dragged down by chaos and uncertainty as he kept insisting. Yet . . . there was something darker there, something he wasn't telling her.

And Alistair Fisher.

William was obviously staying with him, because he'd said, 'I'll see you later.' The ex-priest had behaved, now she thought about it, like someone who was not only extremely fond of William, but possessive too. He had done everything in his power to keep Karen away from him both at their first meeting and at the one today. It was only when he realized Karen wasn't going anywhere without seeing William that he had finally given way. And he obviously had a strong hold over Will. No wonder Janey was suspicious of him.

Karen did sleep. It was as if her mind had suddenly had enough and the fuse had blown. She fell into a dreamless slumber and didn't wake till her phone went off. Looking blearily at the clock as she reached for the mobile, she saw it was six thirty in the morning, still pitch dark outside. The mobile number meant nothing to her, but she answered it nonetheless.

'Karen?' William spoke in a low voice and she imagined Fisher within hearing distance.

'Hi.'

'Where are you?'

'In a hotel somewhere on the front. Can't remember the name of it.'

'So you stayed. I'm glad I caught you.'

She waited.

'Will you meet me before you go?'

'Why?'

He didn't reply at once. 'I need to tell you something.'

His tone was emphatic.

'Do I need to hear it?'

'No, no, I suppose you don't. It's your choice. But I feel I owe you an explanation.'

She hesitated. Maybe she should just run while she had the chance, jump in the car and begin the process of forgetting the man. But she knew herself too well. If she didn't find out what he had to say, she would spend the next two years speculating and driving herself – and everyone else, for that matter – mad with it.

'OK.'

'If you tell me where you are, I can come to your hotel. They probably do breakfast.'

Karen knew they did, because the girl at the desk had told her it would be later than usual, it being Boxing Day.

'They don't start serving till eight thirty.'

'Well, shall I see you then?'

'Alright. I'll text you the name in a minute.'

As she clicked off her phone and fell back on the pillow, she knew that part of her did not want to see William again. There was too much mess, too much pain, she was tired of it all. The other part, masochistic to the last, could barely contain herself.

William looked worn, as she herself must do. His dark tartan-pattern shirt was creased and buttoned up wrong, making one collar higher than the other. His hair was brushed but still windswept, his face pink from the cold morning air. And her heart went out to him, she couldn't help it, seeing him sitting on one of the orange, foam-cushioned chairs in the hotel reception, just staring into space, waiting.

They went through to the dining room, which was about half full, human noise subdued this morning, with just the overall chink of cutlery and china. A breakfast buffet was laid out on a long table against the far wall.

The waiter seated them looking out on to the winter sea and the blowy, deserted seafront. They both ordered coffee, then looked nervously at each other.

'Did you sleep?' William asked.

She nodded. 'Surprisingly, I did.'

He smiled. 'I didn't.'

'So what did you need to explain?' She didn't want to be drawn in by his charm.

'OK . . .' He paused. 'Last night . . . it was horrible seeing you go and knowing you were thinking that I didn't care for you. Of course I did.'

She noted the past tense again and steeled herself for this meeting to be over.

'I didn't want to tell you. In fact, I was determined not to. But Alistair has persuaded me that I must.' He paused again, his hands clasped tightly in his lap, a slight frown on his face. 'I'm ill.'

'Ill?' So she'd been right. 'You've had a breakdown?'

He shook his head. 'I wish it were that simple . . . not simple, I'm not implying depression is simple. But no, I've got cancer.'

Karen held her breath.

'Something called Multiple Myeloma. I'd never heard of it, but apparently it's a sort of bone marrow cancer that affects the white blood cells.'

'Cancer? Oh, my God . . . is it serious?'

'Well, yes. It's incurable, but they can do a lot to keep it under control. And they've caught mine reasonably early . . . which is lucky because there aren't many symptoms at the beginning. All I had was backache.'

'When you say "incurable", what do you mean?' She realized she was trembling, stone cold from shock.

William shrugged. 'Statistics are notoriously unreliable, as I'm sure you know, but around a third of people diagnosed live for five years, and more than fifteen per cent for at least ten.'

'*Five years?*'

'I'm fit and reasonably young, I've got a good chance.'

'Oh, Will . . .' she was speechless.

'Please, don't look at me like that, Karen. That's what I hate, that terrible pity. I'm not dead yet.' His laugh held a tight, angry note.

'You can't tell me something like that and expect me to cheer.'

'No, sorry. I'm sorry. I've been trying to come to terms with this for a few months now, and mostly I'm fine with it. Alistair's helped with that. But sometimes the unfairness just gets me. Like now, with you.'

'Are you having chemo?'

'Not yet. But I will, and there's the possibility of a stem cell transplant in the future, if I don't respond to the drugs. It's not such a bleak outlook, really.'

'And you didn't tell me . . . why?'

William gave a long sigh. 'I didn't think it was fair. You don't want to be saddled with a dying man. And what I said yesterday is still true. We were different people when you loved me. I'm not that person today. I couldn't bear it if you only loved me because I was ill.'

She shook her head in disbelief. 'You think I'd do that? Honestly? You think I'd pretend to love you just because you've got cancer?'

'No . . . not pretend, I didn't mean that. But you might pity me, confuse that with love. It does such weird things to people.'

'When did you find out?' The build-up of sorrow and anger in Karen's heart was making her feel light-headed.

'A week before I left Janey. I had some blood tests because I was feeling so tired and I had this chronic back pain, and they came back with this.'

'But why did you leave so suddenly?'

'I was quite deranged, I think. As I said, we had been discussing splitting up ever since Rachel left home. Things were pretty bad between us. But when I told her about the Multiple Myeloma, Janey was brilliant, said she'd stand by me, look after me, all the things you'd want someone to say. And at first I was relieved. I was so scared. But I knew she was only saying it because it was the right thing to do, not because she wanted to spend the next five or ten years looking after a man she no longer wanted to be with.'

'This was after the fête, that you found out?' Karen was trying to sort out the sequence of events. 'After Janey tried to persuade me to back off?'

'Yes.'

'So she was still trying to fix your marriage then. Why are you so sure she doesn't want to be with you now?'

'She wasn't really trying to fix our marriage. She was just furious with me . . . quite rightly . . . because she knew I was in love with you. Her pride was hurt. But she'd made it perfectly clear for months that she no longer loved or respected me.' William met Karen's gaze, his eyes full of sadness. 'It was a nightmare. We were both very cruel to each other, especially when the filter of Rachel being at home had gone.'

'So all that she told Sheila about you walking out suddenly after breakfast and not telling her where you were going wasn't true?'

'In parts it was. We'd had a terrible row the night before. I told her I wanted to leave, despite the cancer, for reasons I told you earlier. I thought we both deserved better.'

'Why did that make her so angry?'

'She thought I was being melodramatic and selfish. And she was offended that I was rejecting her offer of help.' He shook his head. 'I think the truth was she wanted to see me differently. The cancer made me seem more heroic – and her more heroic for looking after me – but cancer isn't heroic, it's just cruel and random and hellish.'

'So you told her you were going to stay with Alistair.'

'No, I didn't tell her that. She's always hated Alistair, and my association with him. So it's true, she didn't know where I was going. I only told her afterwards, coward that I am.'

'I see Janey's point about Alistair, if he really is a convicted rapist.'

William didn't reply immediately.

'Did he? Rape someone?'

He looked resigned at having to answer the question. 'Alistair didn't see it as rape, he and this young guy had been having a relationship for weeks before the accusation. But he blames himself totally because the boy was vulnerable and he knew it. He should never have gone there. It was only when the boy's brother found out about the sex that the boy cried rape. But Alistair didn't defend himself then or now. He feels it was a gross abuse of trust and he deserved to go to jail.'

'Abuse of trust . . . what you accused yourself of with me.'

'Yes, and it was, Karen. I took advantage of you, you must see that.'

'So if I'd cried rape after that night at the beach, you'd have felt I was justified?'

William frowned. 'No . . . no, that was different. It wasn't just sex . . . for me . . . I don't know . . .'

Karen felt almost too tired to respond. Her head was spinning with all that William had told her. Dying. William was dying. Not now, not today, but his lifespan had been cut short. Part of her felt as Janey had felt – insulted that William had chosen Fisher, not her, to stand by him in his hour of need.

'Anyway,' William sighed. 'That's why I said I have nothing to offer you, Karen.'

'What might you have offered me if you hadn't been diagnosed with this myeloma thing?' She asked almost forensically, to find out the answer rather than having any expectations.

William looked away. When he turned back, his eyes were brimming with tears. 'We never had a chance, Karen.'

She didn't answer. This man had inhabited her heart for so long, had appeared to take her into his own, yet he seemed so fearful of her, as if he must hold her at arm's length at all cost.

'I'm sorry,' he said, brushing the tears from his eyes with an impatient gesture.

'I'm sorry too, Will. Sorry that you're ill . . . and . . .' But she couldn't finish. She stood up. 'I've got to go . . . I can't . . .' Her breath was caught in her throat, her eyes were burning. She just had to get away. He didn't love her, that was all she knew for certain.

William got up too, ran after her as she pushed her way through a crowd of people coming in for breakfast. He caught her arm as she reached the stairs.

'Karen . . . please.'

But she kept on going, wrenching her arm away from his.

Karen drove at a reckless speed away from the shuttered town, as if the Devil were on her tail. She had no idea where she was going, she just drove, finding herself, a couple of hours later, outside Mike's café. She pulled up on the promenade and sat in her car. The café would be closed, she knew that, and Mike probably still with his daughter. But she couldn't go home yet. The empty house, the thought of everyone celebrating in the surrounding village, felt daunting to Karen. She knew she would sink. *I'll have a walk, sit with a cup of coffee somewhere*, she thought.

It was raining, a damp, biting wind stinging her face as it came in off the sea. She pulled her hood over her head, hunched her shoulders, took off along the beach. But as she drew level with Mike's place, the shutters were up. Peering in, she saw Mike in the process of taking the album prints off the walls.

'Hey, Karen!' He waved her in. It was almost as cold inside as it was outside; Mike still had on his leather jacket and scarf. 'What the hell are you doing here?'

Karen looked around, not answering. 'Are you decorating?'

He grinned. 'Nope. Big news, I've sold the bugger. That's why it's so bleeding cold in here, the boiler's on the blink. But hey, it's someone else's problem now.'

'Sold?' Their breath was like smoke on the air. 'When did that happen?'

'Bloke came along and made an offer I couldn't refuse.'

'I didn't know you were even thinking of selling.'

She began to help him with the prints, folding them in sheets of bubble wrap while he layered them into the cardboard box sitting on one of the café tables, sealing it with silver duct tape when it was full. She blew on her icy fingers.

'The truth is I'm bloody knackered by the place. When I closed up for the year and had time to think, I realized I was already dreading another season. It's not been the same since Margie died. We were such a team, we made it work, but slogging on by myself is just that, a slog. It isn't any fun. So when this bloke came along on spec, I thought why not? Get rid of it and start somewhere new. Somewhere I'm not always haunted by what it was like when Margie was alive.'

'Hope you got a good price.'

'Yeah, not bad, not bad at all.' Mike grinned. 'Bloody brilliant, actually. He obviously wanted it and I wasn't in a hurry, so . . .'

'Will you start another one, then?'

'A caff? No chance. Too much bloody trouble. Listen, let's finish up here and go over the pub, get warm. Then I can tell you my plans and you can tell me what the hell you're doing pitching up out of the blue on Boxing Day.'

They settled in the blissfully warm pub, Mike with a pint, Karen with a hot chocolate.

'You go first,' he said.

Karen sighed. 'Oh, just more of the same old dreary saga.'

'Our friend the polisher?'

'None other.'

'Go on.'

'He's got cancer. Multiple Myeloma.'

'You're kidding. Seriously? Is it like, a bad cancer?'

'Yeah, pretty bad. It affects the blood cells. He was talking about survival statistics of five years, ten years . . . I didn't really take it all in. He says it's incurable but they can keep it under control.'

'Whoa, that's pretty rough.' He eyed her cautiously. 'How are you feeling about it?'

'I don't know, Mike. I'm gutted, obviously. I can't really believe it yet. But what upsets me, selfishly, is that he's cut me out of the whole thing. He's living with Fisher, this mentor person, and he wouldn't even have told me if Fisher hadn't persuaded him to. So he was just going to die without a single word of explanation, without ever seeing me again.' She burst into tears.

'Hey . . . hey, love, come here . . .' Mike pulled her towards him along the wooden pub bench and wrapped his arm around her shoulder.

For a while she couldn't speak, she just sobbed quietly into his jumper.

'So he doesn't want to see you again?' Mike asked, when she'd stopped crying and was sitting upright again, clutching her coat around her cold body, although the room itself was warm.

'Apparently not. He thinks what we had wasn't real. I fell in love with a vicar, not with him, he claims.'

Mike frowned. 'I don't get it. What's that got to do with cancer?'

'Oh, nothing. None of what he said made much sense. Basically, he doesn't think I loved *him*, I loved him because he was a vicar. That's number one. Then I suppose he doesn't trust me to love him now because he thinks if I said I loved him it would only be because he was dying. Whatever, he's freezing me out, clearly doesn't want anything more to do with me.' She closed her eyes briefly.

'Sounds like he might be reacting to the illness. It must be a bloody shock to be told you're in the checkout lounge.'

'If he loved me, though—'

'Yeah, but I sort of get it, the thing of not wanting the pity, not wanting to feel people are just being kind.'

'What's wrong with people being kind, for God's sake?'

Mike shrugged. 'Did you still feel the same about him, seeing him again?'

'Yes . . . no . . . he didn't give me the opportunity to really find out—' She stopped. 'But I saw it in his eyes, Mike. He still has feelings for me, I know he does.'

Mike frowned.

'Don't look so sceptical. He does, I saw it.'

'OK, I'm just saying he's got a funny way of showing it.'

'You think he doesn't love me?'

'Who am I to pass judgement? But maybe he doesn't, Karen. You have to face the possibility.'

Karen didn't reply. She remembered the deep, companionable silences on their beach walks, the electricity when they caught each other's eye, the explosive desire that had existed between them when they had finally allowed it full rein. She had never felt so deeply about anyone before, and it defied reason. How could he not feel the same way?

'He said we never had a chance,' she muttered.

They sat in silence for a long time. Karen's chocolate had gone cold on the table in front of her. Her stomach felt as if it were screwed as tight and small as a marble, she couldn't even contemplate the drink.

'You really love him, don't you?' Mike said softly.

'Yeah, well, it's over now, so whether I do or not isn't exactly relevant, is it?'

'Over, over? You won't try to see him again? Even though he's ill?'

'Nope. It's over, over. End of. Kaput.' She looked up. 'I'm worn out by him, Mike. He's taken up a whole year of my life, for nothing. The cancer is horrible, but what can I do? You can't ever make somebody love you if they're determined not to.'

'True,' he said.

And they didn't say any more for a while.

'So tell me about this plan of yours.' Karen firmly changed the subject.

'Sure you want to hear?'

'Of course. As long as it's something that'll cheer me up.'

'OK,' Mike began, on further prompting from Karen, taking a deep breath. 'I'm going into cupcakes.'

'Right. Cupcakes as in a cupcake shop?'

'Yup.

'Go on.'

'A place came up, at the far end of the front . . .' Mike pointed right. 'Small, used to be a pasty shop, but the bloke died – probably from eating too many of his rubbish pasties – and his son was gagging to offload it. I reckon it'd be perfect for cupcakes. There's a small kitchen in the back, and cupcakes are still trendy, they haven't peaked yet. I'm thinking those families who came into the caff

314

could pick up a cupcake and a cold drink to take on the beach instead. And you can charge a mint for them.'

Karen thought about this. 'Yeah, I can see that working. Would you cook them yourself?'

'Could do, to start with. Get someone to help out in the kitchen. Haven't thought it through properly yet. But it'll be way cheaper to run than the other place, and less knackering. I'll have nine to five hours, and I'm up for an online business. People ordering stuff for kids' parties, weddings, anniversaries and the like. No one can afford those huge posh cakes these days. I reckon it's a winner.' He raised his eyebrows at her. 'In fact, I was thinking of asking you if you'd be interested in coming in with me, doing the online side of the business . . . but I reckon it's not the right time. You've got enough on your plate. Probably not your thing, anyway.'

Karen was taken aback. She thought for a moment. Cupcakes. The idea appealed to her.

'How would it work?'

Mike's face brightened. 'Not sure, haven't really nailed the details yet. I don't need your money, if that's what you're thinking.'

'I wasn't.'

'No, well, I was sort of hoping not to have to do this all on my own. I'm good at some things – like customer service – and I'm prepared to work all hours, as you know, but me and computers don't get on, and I'm crap at marketing. The caff marketed itself. It was a monopoly, the only caff on the beach, so we never had to sell ourselves.'

'You'd be the only cupcake shop on the front,' Karen pointed out.

'True, but the shop won't bring in enough on its own. And if the website's going to be profitable, that'll involve all sorts of marketing I know nothing about.'

'Not sure I do, either . . . but I'm kind of interested, Mike. I think I could find out what I need to know. Selling was my forte when I worked with my husband. And I was OK at it, although I say so myself.'

He laughed, suddenly visibly animated. 'Wow . . . this could be good. But maybe you should go away and think about it, Karen. Give me a ring in a couple of days. I don't want to rush you into anything.'

'OK, I'll do that. But the more I think about it, the more I like the idea. I could do a lot of the work from home. I'm not keen on leaving Sophie alone too much, after what happened last time I took my eye off the ball.'

'I was planning to refit the new place this winter, open up around April, when the punters begin to come back. But it would be a year-round business, with the emphasis on website orders over the winter months when there's less footfall on the seafront.'

Karen found her heart lifting. 'Could be exciting, Mike. We'd be partners . . . as long as I promise not to hit on you again.'

Mike chuckled. 'Yeah, kisses not part of the deal,' he said, getting up to order another pint.

Karen got home by late afternoon. She felt a manic, exhausted energy, her mind buzzing with ideas for Mike's cupcake business.

She refused to think about Will. Each time he crept into her consciousness, she batted him away. She had told Mike it was over, and it had to be. She couldn't afford any more heartache. He loved her deeply, in his own way – she was certain of that, despite Mike's doubts – but his love was so compromised by his fear of being vulnerable that he would never allow her to get close. Janey had found that out, to her cost. There had been the odd moments when the strength of feeling between her and Will had broken through his fear, but he was determined enough to put those memories – and Karen – back in the box.

And now the cancer, she felt, had given him the perfect excuse not to commit.

Ever.

It broke her heart.

Sophie came home from Christmas a day early.

'It was not good,' she said, as they sat by the fire with a glass of wine her first evening back. 'Mum was exhausted and feeling sorry for herself, which given the whole Nanu business was totally understandable. And I was really sympathetic. But she kept narking at me all the time as if she blamed me for something. I couldn't do a thing right.'

'Maybe the money thing?'

'Yeah, I'm sure it is, whatever she says.'

'It must be pretty galling to do all the work and then be cut out of the spoils.'

'I agree.' The girl sighed. 'Anyway, I couldn't wait to leave, but of course that was the wrong thing to do too.'

'Oh, well. You and half the country must be sighing with relief that it's all over for another year.'

'So tell me what you did?'

Karen laughed. 'In a nutshell? I saw William. I was dumped by him. I'm planning a cupcake business with Mike.'

Sophie's jaw dropped. 'In four days?'

'Yup. Shows it's not safe to leave me alone for a second.'

She told Sophie the details of William's illness.

'Poor William,' Sophie said.

'Yes, it must be awful.'

'Not the cancer,' Sophie said, 'although that's real crap. I meant him not being able to share his life with you. It's so sad he can't be true to himself.'

CHAPTER NINETEEN

Spring was a long time coming. It rained relentlessly throughout February, the ground sodden, rivers tipping their banks, everyone on permanent flood alert. The anniversary of Harry's death had come and gone, Karen and Sophie marking it with a trip to his grave, where Sophie gave a loving and heartfelt eulogy. It was something of a relief for Karen to have passed the year marker. And as Sophie spoke the words, standing on the damp grass facing her father's headstone, Karen realized she was beginning to appreciate the loving sentiments spoken by her stepdaughter and to forgive Harry's excesses – to remember him more as he had been before the drink took hold.

And although Karen, like everyone else, found the dark winter months difficult, this year – despite William, despite the foul weather – she was full of inspiration, her single-minded focus being Mike's cupcakes.

She had canvassed everyone she knew for a good website designer, whom Volkan finally came up with. She spent days with Mike discussing the layout and design of the website, the shop, the cupcakes themselves and talking to Barry Rivers about contracts. Mike had done most of the renovations by the third week in March and they both thought the shop looked perfect.

They had opted for a simple interior for the narrow space, with a reclaimed wood (painted sky blue) and glass counter, brown cardboard boxes with a matching blue logo for the cakes, bright seascapes on the white walls and an art deco multi-coloured glass ceiling light.

All that was needed now were the cupcakes.

'Look at this lot,' Karen was saying as they hovered over her laptop. 'Spiced banana, peanut and caramel, Earl Grey, carrot and parmesan . . . they all sound so yucky.'

'Yeah, but someone must like them. They'll have tried them out before they put them on the website, surely.' He sighed. 'How are we going to know what varieties to choose?'

'I think this lot are missing a trick. People with small kids want something simple. We should combine simple with exotic. I mean, who would walk in here and order an Earl Grey cupcake? Tea *with* cake, but tea *in* cake?'

'Here's a gooseberry one. Sounds good. But no one eats gooseberries these days, do they? Half of our customers wouldn't recognize one if they fell over it.'

'We've got time to experiment. We can spend the next two weeks making ourselves sick trying out different combos.'

'They've got to look really good as well as taste good. Most of these have more icing than cake, that must be a sugar hit to send you into outer space.'

'That's the plan. Get them all addicted.'

Mike laughed. 'Scary, isn't it, now it's so close to being real? I sort of started this on a whim, but now I really want it to work.'

'Me too.' Karen stretched her arms above her head, yawning. 'Easter's a good time to open, so long as the bloody weather perks up.'

'No worries there. Easter weekend's always busy on the coast, even if it's pissing down. Can't be sitting indoors all day with a houseful of kids and two bank holidays.'

Karen and Mike had both decided to be in the shop the first week, although Karen would mostly be working from home drumming up orders on the website in future, leaving Mike to sell the cakes in the shop and Darren – a friend of Kim's – to make the cakes in the kitchen behind the shop.

'Will you miss the café?'

'No way. It's the first summer I've looked forward to since Margie died.'

Karen didn't reply. She realized with a shock that it was the first of any of the seasons for a very long time when she'd felt a glimmer of hope about her life. But even now, when she was so involved in the new business, the shadow of William still hung over her.

Mike had noted her expression. 'Were you thinking of him?'

'No . . . well, yes. I can't help it. How do you think he is? You don't think he's . . .?'

It was a thought that haunted many a dark night. And then the agony of not being with him – not being able to say that she loved him one final time – would drag her down, threaten to overwhelm her.

'Dead?' Mike said. 'No. I'm sure you'd have heard. And they can do miracles these days, doctors.'

'Yeah . . . OK, well, let's not dwell on it. Because all this is so good, Mike. Your cupcakes have saved my sanity.'

'I always said, cupcakes lift the soul.'

She laughed, remembering a similar conversation on the hill above her house with William, right at the beginning of this whole saga, when she'd replied with some clever riposte about blood sugar.

'You're not tempted to go and see him again, are you?'

She shook her head.

This wasn't true. She was tempted, sorely and often, to the point where she was seconds away from getting into the car and heading for Hastings. What stopped her was the knowledge of the pain she would feel when she saw William and was reminded that he didn't want her in his life.

'The one that got away,' Mike said sadly.

When, three days after opening, William Haskell walked into Best Cupcakes, holding the hand of a small child, it was hard to know who was most surprised: Karen, William or Mike. The shop had done a brisk trade all morning, the sun shining for all it was worth outside, the Bank Holiday Monday drawing record crowds to the seaside after such a dismal winter.

Mike was joshing Karen about her sky-blue apron, which was way too long and made her look like a Victorian grocer. She was bending over, trying to fold the waist to make it shorter and didn't see William until Mike nudged her, by which time he had drawn level with the counter.

'Oh . . .' William's fair skin blushed scarlet at the sight of Karen.

He was dressed in jeans and a dark jacket, trainers on his feet. He looked thin, his hair beginning to grey around the sides, but not ill. The child, a girl, could have been no more than three or four, her blonde hair a pudding basin over solemn blue eyes. As she clutched William's hand she was gazing at the glass on the cabinet, where the coloured light from the ceiling shade was reflected in rainbow prisms as it swung in the breeze from the door.

Karen didn't say a word. She couldn't.

'What can I get you?' Mike asked, when he had finished serving the previous customer.

'Umm . . .' Panic clear in William's eyes, it looked as if he were about to turn tail and flee.

But the child pointed to the cupcakes. 'Chocolate,' she said without hesitation.

And he was trapped.

'Yeah, OK . . . I'll have one . . .' he peered at the labels beneath a row of cakes, 'one Chocolate Dream . . . two Lemon Freddies . . . one Minty Choc Chip.'

The cupcake names, spoken by William in his careful diction, sounded infantile to Karen, who stood fixed and silent by the till.

'This is Molly,' he said, suddenly addressing Karen.

'Hi, Molly,' she said, her mouth dry.

'She's Alistair's great-niece.' When Karen didn't reply, he added, 'I like the shop.'

'Glad you do,' Mike said. 'We opened three days ago.'

Karen saw the 'we' registering with William, making him cast a quick glance between her and Mike.

'Right.' He took the box of cupcakes and proffered his money to Karen. 'It's good to see you,' he said, the blush once more flaming his cheeks.

'Yes,' she said. 'How are you?'

'I'm not bad—' he began.

But Molly was tugging at his hand. 'Can I have mine now?' she asked.

'Better wait till we find Mummy, don't you think?' He glanced at Karen. 'I should get back . . .'

She nodded.

He was almost at the door when he turned. A crowd of girls had just come into the shop and were checking out the cakes, giggling in anticipation. William had to peer over their heads. She was watching him, and Mike was watching her watching him. When William looked back, searching for Karen, their eyes met.

There. The same. It was the same.

For an eternal moment they stared at each other. Then the child must have pulled him away again, because he looked down at Molly, turned towards the door and was gone.

'Aw . . . he likes the shop and he's kind to little kiddies. I think I'm warming to the fella,' Mike said, a mischievous grin on his face.

Karen knew her own face must be burning like Will's and she quickly involved herself with the girls, packing up their choices in the brown cardboard boxes, taking their money, ignoring Mike.

'Bit of a coincidence,' he went on, when the shop was clear again. 'Unless he knew you were here, of course?' He was waiting, eyebrows raised, for her explanation.

'If you're implying *I* told him, you're wrong. I haven't heard a peep out of him since last year,' she said crossly.

'OK, keep your wig on.' He grinned. 'Of all the gin joints in all the towns . . . I reckon he must have been tipped off, no?'

Karen thought about this. 'By whom? Who would have told him?'

Mike shrugged. 'You'd know that better than me. Sophie? Someone in the village?'

'I doubt it. He burnt his bridges there.'

'Must be that old six-degrees-of-separation thingy, then,' Mike said, giving her a wink.

'Must be.'

'Still, now he knows you're here—'

'Shut up, will you?' Karen growled under her breath as another family came through the door.

But she spent the rest of the afternoon hoping William would come back, wondering if he had, in fact, known she would be there. Was the blush on his face one of surprise, or one of embarrassment? She had no idea. But as the afternoon wore on and he didn't appear, she began the painful task of closing down her heart again. If he had been with Fisher and his family, he would have gone back to Hastings by now, she was sure of that.

It was when she and Mike were having a drink in the pub after work that her mobile, lying on the table between them, pinged with a text. The number was unknown, but as she reached for her phone she knew it was from William.

The text read:

Is there any chance you might meet me sometime? Will x

'What did I say?' Mike's look was triumphant. 'Now he knows where you are . . .'

Karen put her phone down without answering William.

'Aren't you going to reply?' Mike asked. 'The man's dying, Karen. Have a heart.'

She dug him in the ribs. 'Shut up, it's not funny.'

But she did have a heart. And it was pumping nineteen to the dozen with excitement.

'Go on, you know you want to.'

'Yeah, yeah.'

'Seems like a nice guy,' he encouraged, when she showed no sign of texting William back.

'Well, you've certainly changed your tune. Hope it's not cancer sympathy talking. He'd hate that.'

Mike laughed. 'Maybe. But I saw that blush, Karen. That wasn't a guy who was just popping in to buy a cupcake. He was on a mission. Trust me, I'm a bloke, I know these things.'

But Karen couldn't go there.

Later, when she was home and alone, she texted William.

We could meet on the beach one evening.

And a reply came almost immediately.

Tomorrow? 5.30?

His sudden eagerness made her laugh.

William looked decidedly nervous when she found him waiting outside the shop at five thirty. The weather had changed for the worse, a cold wind bruising the sea. But at least it wasn't raining. Karen called goodnight to Mike, who was staying to lock up, and she and William crossed the road and walked down on to the beach, turning away from the small scattering of families huddled on the shingle.

Neither spoke. They walked by the water, the sand soft, giving way beneath their feet. Karen had on canvas beach shoes, William the trainers from the day before. He wore a navy cotton T-shirt, navy sweater and black jeans, the dark colours reminiscent of his Church clothes. But otherwise he seemed very different from the vicar she had picnicked with an age ago on these same sands. If he had changed, however, so had she. And maybe both of them, back then, had loved people who were not their real selves.

When he finally broke the silence, he said, 'It was such a shock, seeing you in the shop yesterday.'

'Mike thought you must have known I'd be there. He thought it was too much of a coincidence, you pitching up like that.'

William turned to look at her. 'Mike was right. I did know.'

Stunned, she stopped, stared at him. 'Who told you?'

'Patrick Gascoigne.'

'Patrick? How come?'

He gave a brief smile. 'Odd how these things happen. I've become friends with a guy at the archery club, Gavin – I'm teaching there two days a week now, and I hope to get back into competition in the autumn. Anyway, Gavin had a fiftieth drinks party and asked me, and there was Patrick and Volkan. I have no idea how they're friends of Gavin . . .'

Karen wasn't paying attention to William's narrative. It didn't really matter. Patrick hadn't mentioned it to her, but then he didn't know the significance William had for her, as she had never told him.

'And I asked him how you were and he told me about the cupcake shop. So when Alistair's sister, Shona, who lives a mile away from here, asked us to come over for Bank Holiday, I thought—'

'So why was it such a shock to see me?' Karen found her heart had slipped the leash, come out of the box and was yammering away in her chest.

It wasn't chance, as Mike had somehow known. William had come in search of her.

They were not walking any more but standing on the shore, looking out to sea, watching the veiled pink of the sunset bathing the sea.

'Because . . . because I wasn't sure you'd really be there, I suppose.'

'Why did you want to see me?'

Now he turned to her. 'Why? Because I've been a total idiot, Karen. I thought I was doing you a favour in walking away . . . and I probably was.' He stopped, lips pursed, as if gearing himself up for the rest of his speech. 'I was in such a mess . . . then the cancer. I didn't want your pity.'

She started to speak but he held up his hand to stop her.

'Let me finish, please, Karen. I've been rehearsing this for weeks and if you stop me I shall get flustered and forget what I need to say.' He took a deep breath. 'I have been in denial about my feelings for you ever since we first met. I just couldn't go there. And then I lost sight of myself . . .'

'It's understandable.'

'No, it's not understandable, treating you the way I did. I was so stubborn. I should have told you, I should have been more honest.'

'Yes, you bloody well should have.' She glanced up at him, then turned away. It was safer not to look at him.

Tears brought on by the sheer tension of their meeting were building behind her eyes, but she was definitely not going to cry. They stood like two statues at the water's edge.

'And now?' he asked.

'Now?' She finally turned to face him.

His expression seemed to freeze in disappointment when she didn't go on. But she didn't know what to say. She didn't dare to understand what he was saying. Or feeling.

'So much has happened. I suppose you're right, we can't say we know each other now,' she said, when the silence had stretched awkwardly between them.

And he nodded, resigned. Then suddenly he shook his head vehemently, took a step towards her.

'Wait . . . no. *No*, Karen. That's wrong. I think we think too much, you and me. Because I *do* know you. I know you and I love you.'

Both of them seemed to freeze at his words.

Then his face took on a look of determination and he went on, his tone softer. 'As I said last time we met, I have loved you since the first moment I set eyes on you. Loved you with all my heart and only a tenth of my dumb brain.' He paused and she could see he was shaking slightly. 'You can think what you like, but it won't alter the truth. Not for me.'

His face was bright with passion, his blue eyes sparking as he grabbed her hands in his, brought them to his lips, turned them and kissed her fervently on her palms, his mouth warm and soft against her cold skin.

The sun was sinking now, only half of the golden sphere visible above the pink cloud layered on the horizon. *In a moment it will be gone*, she thought.

She gently wrested her hands from William. 'Hold me,' she said, the tears welling in her eyes so that his face became blurred. 'Just hold me, William.'

'Oh, my God,' Sophie said. 'You and the vicar? Hallelujah!'

'Hold on a minute,' Karen said, laughter bubbling through her with an effervescent joy.

She was still floating on air, but she hadn't had a chance to tell her stepdaughter till now, as Sophie had been up in London staying with her friend Daisy. They were out in the garden, Karen having got up very early and gone out into the sunny spring morning to strip away the ivy under the hazels.

'I've only seen him once, nothing's been decided about anything—'

'What about the cancer?' Sophie interrupted her. She was perching on the arm of the wooden bench, coffee mug in hand, watching Karen work.

'He's OK at the moment. He's had a shedload of treatment and it seems to be working so far. Although obviously it could come back at any time.'

'And you're cool with that? Having to look after him. It could be grim.'

'We'll cross that bridge when we come to it.'

'Ah, true love,' Sophie said, grinning. 'What made him finally see sense?'

Sophie was well again, off the antidepressants and more like her old self, but a more grounded self, Karen thought. Her grandmother's legacy seemed to have given her purpose rather than an excuse to laze about being spoilt. She was planning a summer in Athens to spruce up and sell the apartment, then she was signed up for an online course in architecture and design – she intended to use the money from the Greek sale to buy a property in England and renovate it, sell it on. Sophie had no plans at the moment to move out of the rectory, which pleased Karen. The last year hadn't been entirely wasted, she told herself, if she had finally forged a proper relationship with the girl. Harry would have been proud.

'Sense is not something William is particularly blessed with,' Karen replied with a smile.

When Sophie had gone back inside and Karen was alone in the garden, she stopped what she was doing and just leant on her rake, gazing off towards the hills, where the sun was casting a purplish haze, her thoughts replaying every second of her time with William.

They had left the beach after their walk, gone to the pub to get warm. Being with him, Karen found it hard to believe that he was ill, that he wasn't a vicar, that he wasn't married.

'Karen,' William began, when they had collected a pot of tea from the bar, 'listen, coming to find you . . . it was purely selfish. You know I have this condition, this myeloma, and I don't know what will happen with it, or when, but it will happen, there's no getting away from it. And when it does it won't be a pretty sight, not by all accounts. It's a huge thing, being with a sick person, having to deal with stuff that no one should have to cope with—'

'Stop, Will. Yeah, I get it. It won't be fun. And I'm as pissed off as you about the bloody thing. But would I rather be with you and the myeloma, or not be with you at all? It's you and the myeloma every time. And don't tell me to go away and think about it. I've thought about it almost daily for months now. Not that you gave me the slightest hint that being with you might be an option.'

He smiled. 'Right.'

'So why did you finally decide to find me?'

'Alistair again. He got sick of me mooning around and finally he lost it and ordered me to ring you. He told me it was up to you whether you wanted to be with someone with cancer. He said that he thought you were a woman who knew her own mind. And was I really going to give up on the chance of happiness without even asking? But I couldn't do it. I thought about the burden I'd be putting on you and I . . . well, I didn't have the nerve. You were so angry with me last time we said goodbye.'

She waited for him to go on. But she found she didn't care what he said any more — she didn't care if he spoke or didn't speak, laughed or cried — she was just revelling in every single precious moment of being in his company.

'Then we bumped into Patrick. And he told me about the cupcake shop and Mike. And I thought you were with him . . . you know, like *with* him . . . an item. Anyway, Alistair insisted I at least go and take a look — he wouldn't let me off the hook where you were concerned.'

Karen laughed. 'I did try and kiss Mike once, when I was drunk and miserable because of you, but he wasn't having any.'

William frowned. 'You don't have feelings for him, do you? When I saw you together in the shop . . . you looked very close.'

'Were you jealous?'

William blew his cheeks out. 'Oh, not jealous, exactly, more completely catatonic. Terrified that I'd left it too late and you'd moved on. It made me feel physically sick.'

'God, if you knew how hard I've tried to move on from you, William Haskell. And you know what? I finally had.'

'Sorry I went and ruined it.'

'Ha! So you should be.'

He laughed, then his face grew solemn. 'So Mike and you . . .'

'Are friends, and now business partners. That's all.'

His expression relaxed. 'It would have served me right, if I'd lost you.'

They fell into silence as they drank their tea, but he kept glancing at her, and she at him, unable to keep from smiling.

'How is Rachel taking it all?' she asked.

'She's been amazing. Two shocks at the same time. I wish I could have spared her that. And it was hard for us all, her being in Scotland at college. She's been back a couple of times, and obviously she's pretty upset about the cancer. I think the separation was a shock for her, but not much of a surprise. She'd had to listen to all the sniping and angry silences for years.'

'And Janey?'

'We're OK, just about. She's got a new man. He's a journalist, works for the *Economist* – much more up her street than a dreary, country vicar.'

'More stupid than dreary, I'd say . . . pushing me away like that, inventing all sorts of rubbish about why I didn't love you, why we couldn't be together.'

They were leaning against each other now, delighting in the closeness, the warmth of their bodies, holding hands lightly, her fair head touching his dark one.

'Maybe,' William replied, 'but to be fair I'm not completely dim. I love you and there's nothing stupid about that. In fact, it's the most sensible thing I've ever done.'

'I don't think sense has got anything to do with it,' Karen said softly.

CHAPTER TWENTY

Four years later

It was two weeks after William died before Karen finally plucked up the courage to watch the video selfie. His last days had thankfully been peaceful, ending a cruel and painful interlude that he had endured with extraordinary stoicism – perhaps helped by his faith in God, which never wavered. Rachel had been by his side, and Alistair. And herself, of course. It had been a slow draining away of life, almost silent, William bowing out long before they would accept that he had. But his gentle decline did serve at least to prepare them in some measure. Not to prepare them for the agony of losing him – nothing could do that – but for the certainty of it.

And then the funeral: Rachel and Janey; Sophie with dear Danny, her new husband; Mike and his daughter, Kim; Sheila, Patrick, Alistair and his sister. So unlike the crowds at Harry's service.

Karen had existed through it. No more.

Will had shot the video a couple of months ago, then made her promise she wouldn't look at it until he was gone. And she'd had no wish to cheat. His death, back then, had not seemed possible. It didn't seem possible even now.

She and William had made a vow when they first got together. They would not give oxygen to his cancer, not waste the time they had in talking about it, worrying and being angry. They would just try and deal with each manifestation as best they could. And they had mostly stuck to that promise.

She had got on with the cupcake business, and he had begun to train hard at the archery club, hoping to take part in competitions. Which he did, although his practice was often sabotaged by ill health or the after-effects of treatment. Karen would go to watch him at the shoots. To her he looked so heroic as he slowly drew back the string of his recurve bow, his back straight, bow arm aligned with his cheek, eyes focused as the arrow was let loose to fly to its target. He was in his element, an echo of his formidable grandmother apparent in every muscle.

'You know, we're lucky in a way,' William had said one night, as they ate a supper of fresh grilled fish and salad. 'The cancer has stopped us living too far in the future. I reckon we savour every minute in a way most people never do, who think they'll live forever.'

Karen had laughed. 'Strange sort of luck, but I know what you mean.'

Because their time together was intense, they snatched each moment as if it were the last. Every time they made love or ate a meal or went for a swim or just walked on the beach or in the hills, it was imbued with a singularity. Even the very ordinariness felt like a gift. And sometimes this tired Karen out. She would have welcomed the luxury of normal time, without the sword of Damocles hanging over their heads. But mostly she just lived as much in the present as she was able.

Mike echoed Will's sentiment. 'Margie died without any bloody warning,' he said. 'I had no idea we'd have such a short time together. And it was hell knowing we'd wasted so much of it working . . . and winding each other up, for that matter. If I'd known, I'd have had a bit more fun.'

But they both understood it wasn't that simple.

Karen settled herself in the deep, cosy armchair – it had been Will's almost permanent home in the last few weeks – in the sitting room of the flat where they had been living for over three years. It was a few doors down from the cupcake shop and looked out on the sea, like Mike's studio had, but it was more solid, more spacious. She and Sophie had sold the rectory, neither woman wanting to live there any more – too many memories for both of them. Sophie, with her builder husband, had used her share of the money to construct their own house along the coast, only five miles from Karen and Will.

Now Karen slowly pulled open her laptop, steeling herself before clicking on the file entitled 'Will'. Seeing him breathing and alive . . . how would she be able to bear it?

But as his face appeared, she found herself smiling.

'Hi, Karen,' he said, his mouth screwed up in an awkward grin. 'This is at least the tenth try, so let's hope it works. I never thought it would be so hard to get right.'

His smile relaxed as he leant forward, the computer obviously on the coffee table. She wondered where she had been while he was doing it. Elbows on the arms of the chair, hands clasped, Will paused. He was still reasonably well back then, although his hair, short from a previous bout of chemo, was mostly grey, his eyes very large and luminous in his thin face.

'OK . . . so if you're watching this, I will be dead.' He chuckled. 'I've always wanted to say that. Uh . . . that sounds awful, but you know what I mean.' He swallowed, cleared his throat. 'Right, start again. This is supposed to be a celebration, Karen. A celebration of our amazing love.' He looked down briefly, then up. 'You are an incredible woman, you know that? You have given me some of the happiest years of my life. Loved me in a way I didn't deserve. Understood me. Coped brilliantly with our friend Myelo—' The tears welled in his eyes. 'Basically, you have filled my heart with love. God, I love you so much.'

She saw him pause, swallow.

'I love you now . . . and I want you to know that I will love you forever and eternity. Even when I'm no longer here to tell you so.' He quickly wiped his tears away with the back of his hand. 'Sorry. But the truth is, however brave I want to be, I hate the thought of leaving you.' He took a deep breath. 'So here's my promise. Wherever you are, I will still be there, by your side. When you choose a cupcake or drink a glass of wine or curl up in bed at night, whatever you are doing, I will be with you. I will never leave you, Karen. Never.'

Tears streamed down her face as she waited for William to finish. But for a while he said nothing, just gave her this intense look, a look which held all the love he had to give. It was as if he believed she was already there, in front of the screen, waiting to receive it.

'OK, well, this is it, then,' he said. 'I've banged on long enough, shed enough tears.' He took a deep breath. 'So goodbye, dear heart of my life, goodbye. But walk by the sea at sunset and know that I am there beside you. Always.' William stared into the camera for a moment longer, then gave a small, self-conscious wave.

And it was over.

Karen sat there, gazing through her tears at the frozen face of the man she had adored.

Then she played it again . . . again and again. She sat there for a long time, just watching him over and over, unable truly to believe that he wasn't about to walk through the door and laugh with her at his dodgy video performance.

Crying was so tiring, it bled from the eyes, contorted the face, but it wracked the whole body too. Karen had cried so much in recent days. But gradually the repetition of his words of love began to soothe her, providing a healing balm to her soul, even while they broke her heart into a thousand agonizing pieces and made each breath rasp painfully in her chest.

Coming round from a sort of exhausted half-sleep, she realized it was late and the sun would be setting soon. She got to her feet and found her shoes, took her jacket from the peg by the door. For a moment she looked around for Largo, but he had died of old age over six months before. It was a hard habit to break. She hurried down the two flights of stairs to the street. Hardly anyone was about on the chilly May evening. Karen set off to the west, as she and William had done almost every night in past years, even in the rain and cold, until he could no longer walk easily.

Tonight cloud covered the sinking sun, but she walked on into the grey dusk, her body so stiff with grief that she felt like an old woman. Then as she turned at the furthest groyne, just as she would with Will, the cloud shifted and suddenly a deep golden radiance spread across the sea and sand, washing the water with shafts of shimmering light, shadowing the curved sand patterns made by the outgoing tide a dark purple.

It was unbearably beautiful.

Karen stood alone on the near-empty beach, watching as the light slowly faded across the sky.

'Will?' she called softly into the evening. 'Will, are you there?' She closed her eyes and waited, her body so still she was hardly breathing.

And a moment later she knew he was there, right beside her, just as he had promised he would be. She thought she heard him sigh as she reached for his hand.

Then they walked back along the beach in the dying light, together . . . always.

ACKNOWLEDGEMENTS

Huge thanks, as always, to my brilliant editor, Jane Wood and all the Quercus team. And to Laura Morris, Rosie and Jessica Buckman, my husband, Don, who has been crucial and patient in plot discussions, Clare Boyd for her trusted editorial eye, all my unfailingly supportive friends and family and the beach, of course.